Daily, Before Your Eyes

To have the vision of death before one's eyes, daily

—St. Benedict, *RB* 4:47

Daily, Before Your Eyes

Margaret-Love Denman

Michigan State University Press
East Lansing

∞ The paper used in this publication meets the minimum requirements of
ANSI/NISO Z39.48–1992 (R 1997) (Permanence of Paper).

Michigan State University Press
East Lansing, Michigan 48823–5245

Printed and bound in the United States of America.
10 09 08 07 06 05 1 2 3 4 5 6 7 8 9 10

Library of Congress Cataloging-in-Publication Data

Denman, Margaret-Love.
Daily, before your eyes / Margaret-Love Denman.— 1st ed.
    p. cm.
ISBN 0-87013-743-3 (alk. paper)
1. Death row inmates—Fiction. 2. Middle class women—Fiction. 3. Female
friendship—Fiction. 4. Loss (Psychology)—Fiction. 5. Women
murderers—Fiction. 6. Women prisoners—Fiction. 7.
Ex-prostitutes—Fiction. 8. Widows—Fiction. I. Title.
PS3554.E5336D35 2005
813'.54—dc22
2005004078

Michigan State University Press is a member of the Green Press Initiative and is
committed to developing and encouraging ecologically responsible publishing
practices. For more information about the Green Press Initiative and the use of
recycled paper in book publishing, please visit www.greenpressinitiative.org.

Cover design by Heather Truelove Aiston
Book design by Bookcomp, Inc.

Visit Michigan State University Press on the World Wide Web at:
www.msupress.msu.edu

This one's for my children:

Pepper
Laura
John
Stanton
Hunter

Acknowledgments

❧

There are many who have made this book a possibility. So to faithful, honest readers like Barbara Shoup and Deborah Navas, to Alex Hoole who runs the best B&B in Chapel Hill, to the assistant attorneys general in Mississippi and North Carolina who gave me interviews, to Diann Coleman who checked my history and my legal facts, to the members of the bar who represent Death Row inmates, *pro bono* and who regularly have their hearts broken, to those who work at the jails and prisons I visited, to the University of New Hampshire for granting me time and financial support to write, to Martha Bates for her belief in the book and her keen editorial eye, and most of all, to the young woman living in the hell that is Parchman Prison, who made such an impact on my young self, I offer my thanks and gratitude.

Daily, Before Your Eyes

Chapter 1

Tory Gardiner was a woman who had never heard the word "fuck" said aloud. Except once in her own voice, years before, when she had seen it, scrawled in black paint on the side of a train trestle, on the road to Memphis, somewhere near Byhalia. She asked her mama what it meant.

"Heavens, Mary Victoria, don't ever let me hear you say that again!" her mother said. But Mary Victoria didn't think that was much of an answer. After they crossed the Tennessee state line, her mother repeated the warning: "Don't you *ever* let me hear you say that word again." Later, she said that people who have to use bad words are "limited." "They lack imagination," she announced, her lips pulled together like a purse.

Mary Victoria and her mother went to Memphis regularly the year she was ten. They went to shop. At Lowenstein's and Goldsmith's. Her mother wore a hat, white gloves, and high heels. Mary Victoria sat hunched down in the back seat with a Nancy Drew mystery while her mother drove the big gray Packard with its flying bird on the hood up Highway 78, slinging around the curves to Holly Springs, then to Byhalia, and finally into the city. Once Mary Victoria rode all the way on a volleyball, rolling back and forth on the deep blue seat covers from window to window. Her mother said it made her nervous.

"I don't see why you put up such a fuss, Mary Victoria; most of the girls your age would love to have a chance to shop," her mother said.

Trying them on was the worst.

"Do you have something that is a little plainer?" Mary Victoria's mama would say to salesgirls who called her names like "precious" or "darling."

"You know it's hard to find clothes for this age that are really classic." That's what her mother said, but she meant that it's hard to find clothes for a fat girl. Once, a wonderful navy blue dress with a black-watch plaid ruffle around the bottom almost fit. But the zipper wouldn't quite close. She gathered the extra skin—the roll of "baby fat," as her mother called it—in one hand, held her breath, but it still wouldn't close. The sting of tears made her wince as she lifted the wide skirt over her head. Underneath the canopy of navy, with the strong smell of sizing, she wiped her eyes, and emerged to see her mother watching her with careful eyes, the smallest hint of a frown playing across her forehead, and then just a bit of a sigh and a shake of her head.

"I would have liked that one," Mary Victoria said.

Later that same day, they went to the Helen Shop, where her mother looked at clothes that were classic and expensive and just the right size— an eight. There, Mary Victoria sat on a cushioned bench, swinging her feet, and watched as her mother tried on elegant outfits, sliding the watery pastels over her silk slip and fastening them with ease, wondering aloud to the salesgirl if the color were right, if the waist could be taken in just slightly or if that would ruin the lines, and finally, if the price would make her husband blanch. The clerk assured her that once he saw her in this outfit, he would have no arguments. In the car on the way home, on that very day, Mary Victoria determined to be slender and beautiful like her mother. Retracing their path out of Tennessee, curving back toward Clayton City, Mary Victoria placed the volleyball on the floor, beneath her feet, and vowed that her life would follow the script that she would write, although she did not yet know the words. It would include happiness, comfort, and being loved. Her life would resemble her mother's, her friends' mothers, and all the women who played bridge in the afternoons, sipping coffee from translucent cups, eating small sandwiches that had no crusts, always leaving at least two bites on the plate. It would, in short, mean being a wife and perhaps a mother, loved, supported, and cared for by a good man.

ॐ

This morning's *Times Picayune* is full of advertisements for those same dresses, sketched in fluid black lines, draped across slender women with long necks and faces found from the blending of several races. The lead story, complete with a grainy photograph, recounts the latest eruption in a gang war in the Jefferson projects. A wasted city playground—grass pushing up through broken concrete, a heavy chain-link fence sagging between the poles—stands empty in front of a red brick government-issue apartment building. The windows, covered with large sheets of plywood, announce earlier warfare. FUCK THE WOLVERINES is written on the backboard of the basketball goal. Two Wolverines are dead, the paper says. Three members of the Black Knights in custody. The rest of the front page is reserved for rapes, murders, robberies, and how the state of Louisiana is flat broke. Tory sighs and turns to the "Lifestyle" section. The feature story is a review—negative—of the art exhibit that she has come to New Orleans to see, borrowing her friend's apartment for the weekend. She rattles the paper against the warm April air, folds it in upon itself.

Inside, a story appears about a man from Michigan who moved to Florida to open a vacuum-cleaner repair shop, complete with a photograph of a seven-foot alligator. It broke into his shop and ate an electrical cord. Came in for water, so the ranger from the Everglades said.

"Drought must have caused it."

"At first, I thought it was one of those blow-up balloons. You see them at Disneyland, you know," the man from Michigan said. "I thought to myself, now what son-of-a-bitch went to all this trouble to scare me?" he went on. "Some retired somebody with not much else to do, I figured."

Tory smiles as she reads, takes a sip of the strong coffee and chicory that's sending a string of steam into the warm humid air, and turns slightly to watch the morning. The runners making their way around Audubon Park in the quiet of an early spring morning don't know about the Wolverines and the Black Knights or this man from Michigan yet. Tory watches them strain on April-tanned legs and push their way around the road circling the park, sweat shining on their bodies in the morning light. Paul threatened just last week to take up jogging. Tory smiles, thinking of his still-young body, feels warm at the memory of his stepping naked from the shower the morning she left.

The phone, inside the bedroom, rings three short rings. Tory jumps at the sudden sound and spills her coffee on the edge of the wicker sofa. "Shoot!" she whispers. Brushing the drops away with her hand, she smears the brown stain into the creamy background of the floral chintz. It'll be Paul, offering more names for the dinner party this coming Saturday night. He will tell her that she can do wonders with a table, chide her about her nervousness when she entertains. "You're the best," he'll say. She will laugh and rearrange the seating in her mind.

Another insistent ring breaks into the morning. The screen door sticks just a bit as she pulls against it. Humidity taking its toll. Another ring. Tory hurries, the heels of her bedroom slippers tapping against the waxed parquet.

"Hello," she answers.

"Mrs. Gardiner?"

"Yes."

"Mrs. Paul Gardiner?" It's not Paul, or his secretary.

"Yes, this is Mrs. Paul Gardiner." Tory tries to place the voice, to identify the sounds behind it.

"This is Montfort-Jones Memorial Hospital in Kosciusko, Mississippi." The sounds are sirens.

"Yes?"

"Well, there's been an accident."

"Yes?" she hears herself answer again.

"There's been an accident. Your husband's involved. He's been hurt. You'll want to get here as soon as you can." There's a silence. Then, "Can you get here soon?"

"An accident? What kind? Is he hurt?" Tory reaches for the phone's tangled cord, tries to pull the kinks apart so that the voice on the other end will come to her clear and distinct.

"Well, really, I think it's best if you just come to the hospital and talk with the doctors. They told me to get in touch with the next of kin and ask you to come." The voice pauses for a second, and Tory notices the morning sounds of New Orleans: the grind of heavy diesel trucks and the lighter sound of morning commuters on Magazine, the distant ping of trolley bells on St. Charles. She pulls at the telephone's cord again.

"Can you come, Mrs. Gardiner? Can you get here soon?"

"Yes," Tory answers.

Tory holds the receiver to her ear long after the woman's voice fades into the morning. Dappled light eases its way into the apartment, dances on the floor, swings in time with the breeze, flickers like some misplaced candle. The buzz of the dial tone hums against the room's alien city sounds. She carefully replaces the phone, straightens the fat New Orleans directory so that the corners fall in line with the table's edge. The long flag of a siren flutters across Audubon Park. Tory watches the phone, lying in its black cradle, intently. She traces the conversation in her mind again. Paul, hurt—what did the nurse say? An accident—did she say wreck? She offered no particulars.

Tory forces herself to move, throws her bag on the bed; it flops open. Quickly she slings blouses, skirts, shoes, underwear inside. Rushing to the bathroom, she makes her face, brushes through her short, frosted hair. Picks out something that won't wrinkle, a peach-colored cotton knit. It looks good with her skin. Gives her cheeks color, she decides.

Tory makes a quick check around the room, zips the suitcase, checks again for forgotten stuff, and pulls the door closed behind her. She drops the key in the long white planter filled with new impatiens, their buds still tight, waiting for the summer sun. She throws the suitcase in the back seat, dumps her makeup kit on top, and slams the door. Inside her sensible Volvo, complete with dual air bags, moisture steams against the windows, and the humid New Orleans morning wraps around her, tightening the band around her chest.

Early morning traffic moves slowly along St. Charles Avenue. The trolley bell rings a warning as a slick New Orleans—trained driver scoots across the track. Tory waits her turn, giving the trolley its due. She moves stop-and-go through the traffic. K&B on the corner, the Dominican convent across the street. Eager morning joggers run along here as well—not as well dressed as the Audubon Park ones. A black teenager, ear phones plugged in, jumps the curb on a chartreuse skateboard. He pivots, switches directions, singing, drumming the air in time with his music. He wears a black and fluorescent green jacket, bearing the words "The Wolverines" across the back.

The light changes, and the car behind her honks impatiently. A little foreign car similar to Paul's, bright red and low to the ground, pulls into her lane. Tory hits the brakes; her car pulls sharply to one side. She hits the horn, and a hand appears out of the red car's window, hoisting a tanned middle finger at her.

Traffic pushes around her. The cars all have their windows rolled up. The long light at the intersection of Carrollton and Benjamin gives Tory a chance to roll her window down, breathe the last fecund smells of the city before she eases into the right lane toward the interstate and finally to the Causeway.

At the toll booth, on the New Orleans side, she hands the man a dollar. It's been a dollar to cross Lake Pontchartrain since she was a little girl.

"Ma'am? Ma'am?" he says to her. "It's just a dollar. You're ready to go." The toll-booth attendant flings his hand out towards Mandeville, showing Tory that she has the whole bridge to herself. Lake Pontchartrain spreads out on either side of her like a pewter dinner plate, evenly arched by the thin white line of the bridge.

"Oh, yes, and thank you." Tory nods to the man in the booth, his circling arm still waving, a dagger-through-a-heart tattoo moving in time with the sad country song on his radio.

The mile markers and the steady click of the bridge expansion joints keep time for the twenty-four miles or so. More wrecks here than any other section of road between Memphis and New Orleans, Tory remembers. Easy to get hypnotized, Paul once told her.

What could have happened? Tory wonders. How could he have had a wreck? He's an excellent driver, good quick reflexes left over from his days as a pilot in Korea. The short leather flight jacket cinched tightly around his waist in the photograph that she keeps on the secretary in the library outlines his slim pilot's frame. He's smiling in the picture, leaning against his plane with his flight helmet balanced on the wing, his eyes hidden behind aviator glasses that catch the sun's reflection. Able Baker Charlie Paul, he called the photo. The wreck must have been caused by someone else, Tory decides. Not Paul—he's too quick, too good in a crisis to have a wreck, always lands on his feet no matter what. Lucky, was what his crew members told him. They liked to fly with him, they said. Felt like they'd always make it back.

The Causeway ends, and Mandeville and Covington feed their early-morning traffic into the city—lake dwellers heading for New Orleans for the working day. Sealed inside their BMWs, Saabs, and Volvos, people don't want to know about the Wolverines and the Black Knights. No alligators in their back rooms, not in Covington. Tory makes a flight check—she feels a catch in her throat, remembering Paul's phrase: ten o'clock, the gas gauge three-quarters full. The flat, sandy roadside eases into small hills and farms dotted with Jim Walter homes.

A roadside stand has put out a sign announcing that Louisiana strawberries will be ready next week. She'll get some for Paul as soon as he feels like eating, Tory decides, and makes plans against what she may learn from the doctors in Kosciusko. Mamie can make him a pound cake to go with them. She'll bring it down to him, if he's still in the hospital, feed him carefully, help him get his strength back. He'll be fine; he always bounces back. It'll be a good thing, caring for him again. She'll find books to read aloud, maybe a murder mystery or two, or something funny, something to keep his mind off the wreck, off what's happened. When he had his appendix out, in high school, he read *No Time for Sergeants*, but said he'd have to put it down to keep from laughing and making the stitches grab. He told her that right after the Andy Griffith Show started on TV. Said it always made him laugh just to look at that man. Maybe she'll find some of the reruns of the show, put them on video, and bring the VCR to the hospital. Make him laugh.

The exit for the Natchez Trace veers off to the right. Tory shifts down to make the turn, brakes slightly at the "Yield" sign, and pulls onto the rebuilt ancient way. The manicured edges of the Trace slide back about twenty feet before the woods begin. There, pines and dogwoods thrive, the undergrowth carefully trimmed beneath them. The speed limit is fifty—radar enforced, a sign warns her. Tory watches the speedometer move up to sixty. They won't stop her for just ten miles over the speed limit, surely, Tory reasons—especially since it's an emergency; she won't get a ticket. Up ahead, a pickup truck pulling a fishing boat eases out of a rest area. Tory slows to let him in. A lank, tow-headed boy of about sixteen sits in the back of the truck, squinting in the wind and sun. He leans out into the wind and motions Tory around. She nods a thank-you to him as she pulls out, following the deep curve that circles the west side of the Ross Barnett Reservoir. Kosciusko should be only about twenty more miles, she figures.

Tory pulls in at the rest area at River Bend and freshens her makeup. Pulling a damp sponge under her eyes to remove the traces of mascara, she stares at her own image in the mirror, wondering what Paul will see when she arrives to pick him up. He'll probably flash her his old why-were-you-worried smile and admonish her for her anxiety. Telling her again how she exaggerates everything. She can just hear him, half-teasing, half-scolding her as though she's still a girl, foolish and slightly hysterical. There's no way that he can be seriously hurt. No way in heaven.

Near Bethsaida, the dogwood trees are in full bloom, arching their silk-soft whiteness against the angular green of the pines—all reaching for the edges of the road. Now there's texture, contrast for you, Mr. *Times Picayune* art critic. Just come up the Trace a-ways. Tory knows she should never have gone to that show. She should have gone to Jackson with Paul, encouraged him to get a little more rest before he started the drive home. Told him to be careful, not to push his luck. She should have been with him.

7

Kosciusko, there's the sign. A big white H on a blue background beneath the town's announcement indicates that the hospital is off the main road, to the right. The town square, untouched by "Whiskey" Smith's raids during the war, has a Greek Revival courthouse. Paul used to come all the way down here to check titles when he first started his law practice. Loan closings were important then. Good easy money, always got paid—the bank saw to that. They celebrated each one with a bottle of wine. "One with a cork!" Paul would notice and laugh, then toast the new homeowners, his voice only slightly mocking.

These days, his practice is limited to wrongful death and personal injury. Sometimes one settlement equals what one year's income used to be when Tory was his secretary and office assistant. The stoplight is at the top of a steep hill; Tory rides the clutch and the brake to keep from rolling back down into the grill of the pickup truck behind her. The glare from the black macadam road pushes up like a heavy wave. The blue hospital sign has a white arrow for a left-hand turn. Tory glances behind, puts on the turn indicator, catches the eye of the driver behind her; he nods permission for her to change lanes and she gives him a little wave. Turning, looking for the emergency room entrance, she slows down, makes a final right turn, and pulls the car to a stop. She switches on the hazard lights as the security officer heaves himself out of the chair and walks toward the curb.

"Yes, ma'am?" he asks, his voice creamy against the morning heat.

"I'm Mrs. Paul Gardiner. I got a call earlier this morning that my husband had been in an accident and that the ambulance had brought him here."

"Wreck down on the Trace?"

"Yes, well, I suppose so. The operator didn't say, just said that he'd been brought here." The security guard doesn't move, just keeps watching Tory's face. "Where can I park?"

"Well, suppose you just leave the car here and I'll park it for you. Head on in and I'll bring the keys to you." He opens the door for her and offers his hand.

"Why, thank you," Tory answers, stepping out, straightening her skirt as she moves into the morning sun. The tar on the parking lot oozes black drops. The heel of her sandals suck against the soft wet surface.

"You want to get anything out of the car before you go in?" he asks.

"No, I'll come back for my things after I see my husband. Thank you." Tory reaches for her purse, slings it over her shoulder, and starts toward the emergency room doors. "You don't know anything about the wreck, do you?" she asks the guard.

He shakes his head. "I only came on at seven. I think the wreck was somewhere in the night—'bout two o'clock or so."

Warnings against smoking because of oxygen, bright red signs about exiting ambulances are posted on either side of the doors. As Tory steps on the grey outdoor carpeting with the initials M-J-H painted in black, the doors swing inward with a pneumatic whoosh. The air inside is clean, sterile, air-conditioned. It rushes toward her face, chilly and impersonal. A young nurse sits behind a desk, just inside the door. "Information," the sign announces. She looks at Tory expectantly.

"Yes?" she asks. "Can I help you?"

"Well, I hope so," Tory begins. "I'm Mrs. Paul Gardiner. I got a call from someone here early this morning, about my husband, that he'd been in a wreck. I've driven from New Orleans, I don't know anything about him, just that he's here." Tory's voice wavers a bit toward the last, sounds strange, unfamiliar to her—impersonal, like the air that settles around her.

The nurse looks down at the list in front of her. "Let's see, Adams, Babson, Coatsworth . . ." She drags a finely-sharpened pencil down the list of admissions. Her nametag says Teri Young. "Oh, yes, here it is. Paul Gardiner and . . . I can't make out the writing . . . says here that he's still in the OR. Let me call and see how they're doing."

"Still in the OR?" Tory repeats. "Does that mean that they're operating on him here? In Kosciusko? Shouldn't we transfer him to Jackson or to New Orleans or something? I mean if he has to have something big done, maybe we should go ahead and call somebody in Jackson. I have several friends from college who are married to surgeons in Jackson. I know several people I could call." Tory fumbles in her purse, looking for her address book. To prove to the nurse that she knows people, other places where she can get help.

The nurse smiles, nods, and waits for Tory to finish. "Well, you see, Mrs. Gardiner, we'll just do what we can here and see how he gets along. Then maybe you'll want to move him as soon as he's able. I wasn't on duty when they brought them in, so I don't know exactly the extent of his injuries, but I'll find somebody who can tell you more."

"Well, really I just want to see him first and then talk to the doctors, see about moving him to Jackson as soon as possible. Not that I don't think that you've done a marvelous job here, it's just that if there's much to be done, I think Jackson might be a better place. You know what I mean. More facilities, more specialists, that sort of thing."

The nurse smiles again, picks up the phone, punches a few numbers, and waits. "This is the information desk. Mrs. Paul Gardiner has arrived. Can you give me an update on her husband?" She covers the mouthpiece with her left hand; it sports an engagement ring with a single tiny stone set in white gold. "It'll take a minute for her to get the report." She wiggles her fingers to move the stone to the center of her finger, then she stretches her hand slightly and examines the ring. "Okay, I'll send her up. Thanks." She replaces the phone with her left hand, and the stone catches a bit of the morning light and spreads a prism on the surface of the desk.

"Yes?" Tory leans over the desk, trying not to sound impatient.

"Well, he's been moved out of surgery for the time being and relocated in the ICU. You can go up and see him for a few minutes. The nurse there will give you instructions."

"Yes, thank you."

Tory turns and heads down the hall, listening to the hospital sounds all around her. A couple, young and fragile, stand in front of the elevators, holding hands, watching the numbers above the elevator flash in descending order. The woman, in blue jeans and a white T-shirt which bears the blue Nike swish and the words "Just Do It," runs the back of her hand under her nose. She sniffs as the elevator doors slide open. They wait for Tory to enter. She nods a thank-you. Inside, she pushes the button for the third floor. They watch, and the man steps forward in heavy work boots and pushes it again.

"ICU, too?" Tory asks.

"Uh-huh," the woman says, "our baby," and she sniffs again.

"My husband," Tory says, and the three of them risk a quick look at each other.

The elevator moves up slowly, passes the second floor, and slides to a stop at three.

A red arrow painted on the wall across from the elevator door points to the ICU, to the right. Tory follows its direction, obedient. Ahead of her, a nurse on crepe-soled shoes squeaks down the corridor. At the end of the hall, the ICU desk is covered with small television monitors, alive with green lines and dots, shifting and moving. A heavyset bleached-blond woman watches them, moving from one to another, charting what she reads on an aluminum clipboard.

Tory clears her throat. The nurse keeps working on her charts.

"Pardon me," Tory tries again. The nurse twists a dial on the monitor in front of her, frowns slightly, flips the top paper aside, and traces the edge of the paper with her fingernail. She turns back to the front page, checks the monitor again, and writes down what she sees.

"Excuse me," Tory says, louder this time—wonders if this woman is deaf.

"Yes?" the nurse answers but doesn't look up.

"Yes, I've come to check on my husband, Paul Gardiner. He was in a wreck sometime early this morning—on the Natchez Trace, I believe. I got a call from somebody at the hospital." Maybe it was this nurse who called. Tory knows that she will recognize her voice when she speaks. She can still hear it—Mrs. Gardiner, Mrs. Paul Gardiner? This is the Montfort-Jones Hospital. In Kosciusko. Tory can hear it all over again. "I was in New Orleans. I don't know how they found me, but I didn't hear until just a little bit ago. Can you help me?" Tory waits for a second, and the nurse puts the chart down and finally looks at her.

"Yes?"

"My husband? Paul Gardiner? A wreck this morning on the Natchez Trace? I've come to see him."

"Yes?" the nurse answers. It is not the same voice.

"Can you tell me how he is? Can I see him?" Surely she knows what I want, Tory thinks. Surely she doesn't have to be told every single little thing.

The nurse picks up another chart, glances over it, purses her lips while she runs her finger along the side of the page.

"Well, Mrs. Gardiner, your husband has been taken from the OR into ICU."

"Yes, that's what the lady downstairs told me. But how is he? Do we need to move him to Jackson?"

"Well, he's really not in any position to be moved right now. Perhaps I can page the doctor and you can talk with him. He can give you a better idea about what the situation is than I can."

"But can I see him? Now? While I wait for the doctor?"

The nurse checks the chart once more. "Let me see what I can do." She flips the chart shut, calls to an orderly leaning against the smooth white countertop. "Emmett, check on the status of Paul Gardiner and see if Dr. Perkins is still in the hospital."

"Sure," he answers, turns and heads for the set of double doors at the end of the hall, marked "ICU: Authorized Personnel Only."

"You can have a seat in the family waiting room across the hall, if you'd like," the nurse says. She wears a badge that rests right above her breast. L. Grisham, ICU Nurse, it says.

"Can you tell me anything, while I wait? I really don't know a thing. Just that he was coming back from Jackson. He'd gone down to take a deposition for a case he'll try later. That's all I know. I was in New Orleans. What happened?" Tory's words tumble out, and she can hear the frustration, anxiety in them.

Mrs. Grisham shakes her head slowly, and her blond hair doesn't move a bit. "I really don't know. He was already here when I came on at seven."

"I'll just wait"—Tory turns and points—"over here, until you can get somebody for me to talk to."

"Yes," says Mrs. Grisham, "that'll be the best thing. It shouldn't be too long."

The family waiting room is painted a soft green, tending toward yellow in the morning sun. When Tory was a Pink Lady, the director of volunteers explained that green is soothing, puts people at ease, makes them feel good about where they are. It's not helping, she thinks. She sits, picks up a two-month-old *U. S. News and World Report*, thumbs through it, sees nothing. The young couple from the elevator pass by the open door, still holding hands, leaning into each other, watching their feet as they walk. Tory looks around the room; a slim young woman sits on the far end of a grey couch, her arm and leg bandaged, her eyes puffy with crying. She looks up at Tory, and Tory stares back at her magazine, uncomfortable with any kind of shared grief.

"Mrs. Gardiner?" A crisp nurse, all white and angled, stands in the doorway. The young woman on the couch looks up, startled, stares at the nurse, then at Tory.

"Yes."

"Dr. Perkins can see you now." Tory replaces the magazine on the table, careful to place it squarely on top of the other, and then manages a weak smile as she crosses the room to follow the nurse.

In the hall, a man about Tory's age, clad in surgical green, is reading a chart. He looks up as Tory and the nurse approach.

"Mrs. Gardiner?" he asks.

"Yes."

"I'm Dr. Perkins, the attending surgeon. I was on call when they brought your husband in." He closes the aluminum chart and holds it by his side.

"Yes?" Tory asks.

"His injuries are pretty severe. We've got him stable for the moment, waiting to see what we need to do next."

"Yes?" Tory asks again.

"Well, we've attended to the most pressing things. Stopped the bleeding, tried to assess which injuries are the most critical. Wasn't wearing his seat belt, so he took the brunt of the impact mid-torso." He pulls the chart up to his chest and pats it. "His spleen was crushed, so we removed it. There was some damage to both lungs; broken ribs punctured one"—he glances back at the chart—"the left one, and there was some impact damage, bruising, to the heart as well." He keeps on reading, looking for more things wrong.

"How is he?" Tory finally manages.

"Well"—Dr. Perkins looks up from his reading—"the next few hours are critical. If his blood pressure stabilizes and he starts breathing on his own, I think his chances are pretty good. We'll just have to wait and see." He offers Tory a little smile. "Dr. Jacobs will be on duty for the rest of the day, and he can reach me on my beeper, if he needs to." Dr. Perkins smiles again, a little wider this time, turns to the nurse, and hands her the chart. "Mrs. Gardiner can go in for a few minutes, I think." Without looking at Tory again, he starts down the hall, peeling the green skullcap off as he walks.

"Mrs. Gardiner?" The nurse taps her fingernails on the aluminum clipboard—the tap, tap, tapping right in time with the doctor's gait.

"Yes."

"You can go in for about five minutes every hour, for as long as he's in ICU. He isn't conscious, but you can talk to him. Sometimes people feel better if they can talk." She spreads her arm toward the large double doors at the end of the hall. "He's in the second bed, on the left." She turns, taps the front of the clipboard once more, puts it on the desk, and begins to watch the monitors.

"Thank you," Tory tells her.

Her footsteps echo hollow in the hallway. The click of her sandal heels tapping, bouncing against the still, white walls. As she pushes against the double doors, the crisp angular nurse calls to her, "Remember, only five minutes this time."

13

Tory nods and steps into the ICU. The room is filled with beeps and swishes, bright light, and labored breathing. Curtains hang from metal frames, separate the beds. Several nurses move in and out between the cubicles. A hush, suspended everywhere, is nearly visible. Second bed on the left, Tory thinks. She takes a deep breath and tiptoes over. From behind the curtain she hears a quiet blip-blip, a rush of air, and crying. She puts her hand against the curtain. Her nails look pink and shiny against the stiff hospital white. She pulls, and the metal grommets make a slight squeak against the curtain rod. Paul lies centered in the bed, a white bandage angled across his face; his legs are elevated, held by pulleys; a tube runs into his nose and disappears. A mask hides his mouth. His nose, the flesh around his eyes are swollen. So much so that Tory wonders if she is in the right room. A small white square rests on his throat. A trach tube, she remembers from her Pink Lady days. His chest has wide, thick strips of cotton draped across it. Another tube sticks out of his side. A plastic bag, hanging on the end of the bed, slowly fills with urine—bright yellow and healthy, she's sure of it. Sitting in a chair beside the bed, the young woman from the couch in the waiting room rests her head against the sheets.

"Paul?" Tory asks.

The young woman lifts her head. Her eyes, still puffy, are wet now, and she wipes her face with the edge of the sheet.

"Mrs. Gardiner?" she asks.

"Yes?" Tory answers.

"I'm Debbi McCaslin. Mr. Gardiner's court reporter."

"Oh," Tory says.

"I went to Jackson with him to take the deposition. We had a wreck. Paul—that is, Mr. Gardiner—wasn't wearing his seat belt."

"I know, they told me." Tory glances back at Paul. "When was the wreck?"

"Sometime after midnight, I guess. I went to sleep soon after we left Jackson."

"Was the wreck on the Trace?"

"Yeah, just above River Bend. I guess he fell asleep, too. We hit a tree."

"Oh." Tory watches the mask over Paul's face move in and out with the bellows on the machine pulled up close to the bed on the other side. Tory straightens her shoulders. "They told me that only one person could be in here at a time." A thin metal pole holds a bag of plasma and one with a clear solution. A y-tube from them is attached to Paul's hand. A bruise covers his left cheek.

"Yeah, I know," the young woman answers, and grimaces as she stands. "I just slipped in for a minute." She leans over, reaches for Paul's hand, and touches it just slightly with a pat. Tory watches. "I'll be back," she promises, and doesn't look at Tory as she leaves. The stiff white curtains swing slightly as she slips through, limping. Tory turns back to Paul; the respirator thumps air into his chest, keeping time with the dripping of the IV bags.

"Paul?" Tory asks.

Nothing.

Tory moves around the foot of the bed, towards the chair where Debbi was sitting. She hesitates, then turns to go to the other side. The skin around the IV needle puckers, the flesh lifted into a discolored little heap. Tory pushes the IV pole toward the wall, smoothes the sheet around Paul's hand, and looks for a place to sit down. He groans just slightly, and a little frown wrinkles its way across his forehead.

"It's all right, Paul. I'm here now. It's going to be all right. I saw signs for Louisiana strawberries just south of here. Mamie will make you a pound cake. We can read and laugh, and you'll be fine. I promise." Tory's voice falls in line with the pressed air of the respirator. She reaches over to pat his leg, feels the bulk of a bandage beneath the sheet.

"Time's up, Mrs. Gardiner." The nurse with all the starch and angles appears at the opening in the curtain. "You can come in again in an hour or so." She pulls the curtain to one side and ushers Tory out. The sounds of the ICU follow them through the aluminum double doors. The nurse stops at the desk, picks up the chart and a manila envelope. "Perhaps you could give us some information now"—she looks up at Tory—"while you wait."

"Yes, of course," Tory answers.

"Insurance?" asks the nurse.

"Yes."

"You do have insurance?" asks the nurse again.

"Yes," Tory tells her.

"Who's it with?"

"Blue Cross. There may be a card in his wallet."

"Here are the things we took from his clothing—personal effects and such." The nurse—Miss Stimson, her name tag announces—holds the envelope out to Tory. Personal effects: Paul Gardner, ICU, is written on the front. "You might want to look through them, see whether the card is there or not." She pushes the package towards Tory; it bends slightly on one end.

Tory holds it to her chest, not looking down. "Thank you," she answers.

Miss Stimson starts back to her monitors. "I'll be here if you need me." She looks at her watch, makes a note on one of the charts. Tory waits. "You can go back in around 12:30. There's coffee in the family waiting room, if you want some. And the cafeteria's downstairs, other end of the hall."

Back in the cool green of the waiting room, Tory fumbles to open the envelope. Someone has sealed it, signed it across the flap. She makes a ragged tear at the top, destroying the name, and slides the contents out into her lap. Paul's wallet, slick brown leather, small and neat, slides out; his Ray-Bans, so like the aviator's glasses from Korea, fall on top of it. Tory holds the envelope upside down, gives it a shake. Paul's wedding ring, narrow and gold, falls into the peachy folds of her skirt. She lifts it, notes the inscription: "Tory to Paul, November 26, 1958. With all my love." She slips it on her middle finger so that it fits next to her own wide band and the diamond that was Paul's grandmother's.

"Paul's wallet," she says aloud, then checks around the room to see if anyone has heard her. But the room is empty. She flips the wallet open. Inside, in the carefully cut pockets, credit cards peep out. VISA gold, MasterCard, American Express, Gulf and Texaco. The colors plastic and permanent against the brown leather. Inside the pocket, she searches for the insurance card. A card for the Mississippi Bar Association notes that Paul has been a member since 1960. Another that he is a blood donor, another that he has membership privileges at the Jackson Country Club. His driver's license, due to expire in 1992, records that he is five feet eleven inches tall, weighs 175 pounds, has brown hair and eyes. Really his hair is auburn—touched with grey now. He's handsome, even in the driver's license picture. Blessed with good strong features. Mary Vic looked like him, only a smaller, feminine version. She would have been a pretty young woman by now, twenty-three, maybe married with a child of her own, if things had turned out differently.

She checks in the compartment where the bills are. Three twenties, a ten, a five, and some ones. Folded at the back are two receipts. One is from the Hilton. Room tax in Jackson is eleven percent now. The room, a double, rented from Thursday night until Sunday, was one hundred and ten dollars a night. Paul paid for it with his American Express card. He must have gone to Jackson soon after she left for New Orleans. Funny, he'd called her on Friday night, didn't say anything about being in Jackson. Not that she ever expected him to tell her everything.

She examines the bill again. Yes, Thursday the eighteenth through Sunday the twenty-first. The deposition was on Monday, the twenty-second. The wreck, this morning. Tuesday, 2:30 a.m. He was heading home. He and Debbi. Tory checks the bill again. Double occupancy, it says. A tourniquet of anger, hotter than her fear, tightens across her chest; it feels very different from the terror of the morning.

She holds the Hilton's bill in her hand, just above her lap. The paper wavers, as though a breeze has somehow risen in the greenery of the waiting room.

࠙

"Mrs. Gardiner?" Miss Stimson asks, waiting in the doorway. "The man from Jack's garage towed the car in last night. It's on the lot there—downtown. There may be some things in it that you'd like to get out." She waits, watching Tory.

"Yes, that's right," Tory answers. "I'll do that." She looks directly at Miss Stimson, waiting for her to leave so that she can reorder Paul's wallet. Miss Stimson turns on her heel, military fashion, and crosses the hall back to the desk and her monitors.

Tory opens the other receipt. It's from the Sundancer, Paul's favorite restaurant in Jackson. A meal, on Sunday night. Two hundred twenty-eight dollars, including the tip. Bar charges make up nearly one hundred twenty-five of that. Tory refolds this one and adds it to the Hilton receipt, tucks them both back into the wallet, behind the bills. They will not be there when she hands the wallet back to Paul. She'll absorb them and what she knows for now. She slides it all back into the envelope, drops in the sunglasses, and wonders what she should do with the ring.

࠙

The weight of the air in the family room hangs suspended on the later-morning light. Tory feels as though she's floating away, grabs the edge of the chair to steady herself. She closes her eyes, sighs, and tries to relax.

17

Downstairs, the cafeteria is empty except for two orderlies, lingering over thick white mugs. Their conversation is subdued, almost whispers. Tory picks up the Styrofoam tray, looks at the menu posted above the steam tables, and decides on coffee and an English muffin.

"Toasted, no butter," she tells the girl behind the counter. She pours a cup of coffee and the steam rises slowly, in a lazy curl, just like it did on the porch of Martha's apartment, before the phone rang. Just exactly the same way, as if nothing had intervened, nothing had shattered the morning quiet on the edge of Audubon Park. The natural world keeps its own rules: steam rises, the sun chases away night shadows, a car smashes into a tree in the darkness, destroys itself, people, lives, even the cared-for lives of the lucky.

"Ma'am?" she hears the girl ask. "Ma'am, that'll be $1.25."

"Oh," Tory answers. "Yes, $1.25." She fumbles for her coin purse, hands the girl a bill, some coins, and starts to a vacant table by the window.

"Ma'am?" the girl asks again. "Your change."

"Oh"—Tory stops, puts out her hand—"yes, my change," and stuffs it in a wad into her purse.

The table by the window looks out onto a small concrete patio. Late-morning sun hasn't reached it yet, and the shadows from the edge of the building fall in precise, rectangular shapes. Tory sips the coffee slowly, feeling only slightly the weight of the liquid in her mouth, the heat. She tries the English muffin, finds it remarkable that it surely tastes very much like the Styrofoam tray on which it sits. The minute-hand on the clock on the wall behind the cash register jerks intermittently around the face: 11:46. Forty-four minutes before she can return to the ICU. Tory pushes the tray away from her and watches the shadows on the patio being slowly eaten away by the sun's rays.

Upstairs again, she calls Paul's office. The crisp, efficient voice of Mattie, the receptionist, announces that she's reached the law offices of Gardiner, Tolliver, and Bench. Tory quickly tells her all she knows about the wreck, nothing about the receipts.

Mattie begins her little clucking sounds of sorrow almost as soon as Tory begins. "Oh, Mrs. Gardiner, I'm so sorry. What can I do to help?"

"Well, just keep your fingers crossed and pray."

"You can be sure I'll do both," Mattie assures her.

"And tell Sam and John for me, will you? I'll call back as soon as there's something to report," Tory promises.

"Well, call us as soon as you know something definite, Mrs. Gardiner, or if there's anything else you need."

Tory agrees and the line goes dead. She holds on to the receiver for a long minute, unwilling to let go of Mattie's good wishes. The lightheadedness returns, and she wonders if she'll faint.

It's 12:06 when she calls the wrecker company, arranges for the contents of the car to be sent to her at the hospital, and for them to send the bill to her at home. The man she talks to tells her that the car's totaled.

"Totaled?" she asks.

"Yeah, not even good for parts," he explains. "Squashed like a bug. Miracle they made it out alive," he goes on in the gravelly voice of a long-time smoker.

At 12:28, Tory enters the ICU. Not bothering to look at Miss Stimson for permission, she taps the broad metal plate that opens the doors electronically, slips in, and takes her place beside the bed. The respirator still wheezes air into his lungs; he moves slightly, frowns as he does, and his features reflect what must be pain. His face, contorted this way, still and swollen, is the face of a stranger.

When Mary Vic was ill, he kept up a kind of fierce bravado, unwilling to believe that anything could be wrong with a child of his, that there was any bad luck or ill fortune in his future. So brave, all their friends had said—such a rock for Tory during that time. So hard and unwilling to mourn with her—that had been Tory's reality.

She watches him carefully, pinned and stationary against the white of the hospital sheets. Each movement of the respirator forces his chest to lift, keeping time with the steady drip of the IVs. Tory relaxes just a bit, sits on the edge of Debbi's chair, and leans toward Paul's face.

"It'll be all right, I promise," she tells him again. "We can work all this out when you're better." She eases her hands to his face, strokes it, feels the stubble of his heavy beard coarse against her palms. Paul flinches, moves his head, and groans. Tory jerks her hands away, folds them quickly in her lap. Paul moves again, with greater force this time, and the groan is louder. Maybe he is regaining consciousness. What will I say to him? she wonders. How can I comfort him now, knowing all that I know? His movements become more agitated; he struggles against the restraints on his arms, and a low guttural sound, almost a growl, rattles below the trach hole.

"What is it, Paul? Can I get you something?" Tory tries to whisper in his ear, tries to reassure him. But he pulls away, moves as much as he can, and the monitor on the bed, just above his head, records the ferocity of his movements. The little green line pulses up and down, a crazy, jagged wave. Tory strokes his arm, careful of the IV lines, murmurs his name, over and over. Her touch, her voice don't calm him; he throws his head from side to side.

"Paul, I love you," she whispers, wonders if he knows, wonders if she does. He pushes his head deep into the pillow, arches his back into the air, thrashes from side to side. The monitors jump crazily and Paul fights the air around him. The line on the monitor hits the top of the screen, then the bottom. Tory sits frozen by the sounds. She should do something. Get help.

Paul quiets for a moment, seems as though he might speak. His eyelids flutter and Tory catches a glimpse of iris, then a wild rolling—like a deer they once saw on the highway, newly struck by a car. She puts her ear close to his mouth, hoping to catch what he's trying to say. He struggles to whisper, still frantically searching for focus, perhaps for some familiar form.

He whispers a word that sounds like damn or daddy, or is it Debbi? Tory can't make it out.

"What is it, Paul?"

He tries again, flailing against the sheets, the restraints, the machinery—seems to focus on her face, catch her in his glance. He frees his arm, slings it into the air, and the bandage pops hard against the side of Tory's face. She falls back into the chair, her ear ringing with the blow. Paul's face, wild in agitation, stretches into a grotesque mask.

"You hit me," Tory cries, jerks her head out of his way. "You hit me," she tells him again. Paul drops his head back into the pillow and the monitors steady. A deep sigh hisses out of the trach tube; he settles, wearied from his struggle.

Silence covers the space inside the curtained cubicle. Tory touches her ear; it feels stung, as if it's growing large and swollen, matching his face and mocking her. She pulls at the curls on the side of her face, willing them into enough length to cover her ear. Paul lies still now, beside the shallow indentations in the sheets left from his struggle.

She turns her face away from Paul's bed, listening to the respirator, breathing in time with it, even as Paul's chest moves up and down. Her time is almost up. She can see the minute hand on the clock above the double doors, inching its way along toward 12:35.

Paul groans, louder than before, more anguished. A pitiful gurgling sound. Tory finds that she cannot look at him, she cannot move to comfort him. She stares above the bed frame, watching the monitor—the band of anger tightening once more around her chest. The jagged movements arc higher and higher, and a red light flashes on the bottom of the screen. The green line bounces wildly from top to bottom. She must look at him, must make him know that she is there, dutiful and loving. But she cannot.

The beeper on the respirator starts offering little metallic clicks into the early-afternoon air. And a warning light beeps on. A second red light—now another—on the monitor. The nurse, she must call the nurse. Something is terribly wrong.

But she waits, watches Paul's face register what must be excruciating pain. The nurse at the station should know these lights are going off. She must know. It's not Tory's job to tell her. A warning bell begins to ring, cracking the silence.

Tory sits back, touches her ear once again to see if it has outgrown the side of her head, wonders if the blow is visible, if the nurses will be able to tell what has happened. She watches the monitor, the red dot flashing a new warning on the bottom of the screen. The pulse of the green line on the screen slows and then quiets into a steady descent, eventually forming an even string of green. Tory feels the color drain from her face, move then up her neck, into the side of her head. She pulls at her earlobe in time with the flashing of the red light. She feels the weight of Paul's hand wrapped in plaster and tape against her head. Slowly, she shakes her head to ward off the blow, but it comes again, stronger in memory, hitting her with new force. He hit me, she thinks.

Two men pushing a gurney fling back the curtain. They look at Paul, then the monitors. Quickly they slide him onto the slick metal slab, jerking the IV pole into place, sliding a pillow under his head. With sharp, deft motions, they release the traction from the sling and wheel him away. The intercom is calling Dr. Perkins, calling Dr. Perkins.

Tory feels pinned to the chair, unable to move. She crosses her ankles, feels the silkiness of her stockings slide against her calves. She folds her hands in her lap and listens to the throbbing in her ear. Her breath is shallow, hesitant; without the rhythm of the respirator, she is uncertain how to breathe.

"Mrs. Gardiner?" Nurse Stimson's voice breaks into the morning. She peers around the curtain, angling her head into Tory's vision. "Mrs. Gardiner?"

"Yes."

"Perhaps you'll want to wait in the family room. It's more comfortable in there."

"What does all this mean?" Tory asks.

"We'll have to wait and see, won't we," Nurse Stimson says. "Now, let's go into the other room, where you'll be more comfortable. Isn't there someone you'd like to call to wait with you—some family or friends?"

Tory shakes her head and follows her through the curtains, through the doors, and into the green space of the family waiting room.

Debbi sits in the corner of the couch, huddled against a pillow, her arm propped up at an angle, severe and white against the green of the walls. Awkwardly, she holds a large white handkerchief to her face. She watches Tory cross the room and settle herself in one of the overstuffed chairs.

"Mrs. Gardiner?" Her voice hardly a whisper, she fans the handkerchief out into the space in front of her nose. Tory thinks she sees a monogram on it. "What's happening?"

"Nothing that's any of your business. I want you out of here." The voice is remarkable, not at all one that Tory recognizes. Stern, impolite, demanding.

"I want to stay, to see how he gets along." Debbi's voice is stronger now, telling Tory what she wants as well.

"No, that's out of the question." Tory shifts in her seat, watching Debbi pat her eyes, her nose, waving the handkerchief like a banner in the afternoon stillness. Tory doesn't turn away. Debbi snuffles, then drops her eyes and turns away from Tory.

"I'll get your things from Paul's car and send them to you when I get home. I'm certain that his secretary knows how to get in touch with you. Now, you should call someone in your family to come pick you up. This is no place for you."

Debbi pushes herself up from the couch and limps across the room. She does not look at Tory, and her shoulders move in silent sobs as she disappears down the hall. The room falls quiet, and Tory feels the silence, palpable and alien.

ॐ

She touches her ear, finds it warm, certain that it's swollen. She removes her diamond stud earrings, the ones Paul gave her for an anniversary, fifteen years ago. Laughing, he had said they might not make it to their sixtieth—the traditional one for giving diamonds—so he was doing it early, just in case. He had laughed, made some joke about what good would it do him to please her later with diamonds when he was so old. He had caressed her neck when she put them on. He told her she was beautiful.

When had she lost him? While she nursed her mother through the ordeal with cancer? Or earlier, when Mary Vic was still alive? During the long months when she was consumed with doctors, hospitals, clinics, looking for cures for what was hopeless? When had he begun to look elsewhere? How had she let this happen, let him slip away from her when her only plan for her life had been to be with him?

Tory watches the clock, willing time to stop, to rescind its pace, to retreat to New Orleans, to last week, last month, last year. To a time when things made sense, when the shape of her life had definition and meaning. Was that just this morning? Sitting on a porch overlooking Audubon Park? The minute hand jerks on around the face of the waiting-room clock, slowly counting out the minutes of her wait. Every minute that passes is good, though, she tells herself. They're doing something for Paul, fixing whatever it was that made all those beepers go off, all those crazy lines appear on the monitors. They *are* fixing it; she knows that now. The doctors have had plenty of time. She won't tell Paul that he hit her. She won't bring that up, not when he's struggling to get well. Maybe later, when he's himself again, maybe then she'll tell him and they'll laugh. Laugh because it was just a muscle reflex, just a fluke, just because he was angry over all the restraints. And he'll touch her ear and say how sorry he is, how he never meant for any of this to happen. Tory settles back against the chair, relaxes just a bit, closes her eyes, and thinks that she just might rest for a moment. She must maintain her strength for what's ahead; she must be able to be there for Paul when he needs her. The fatigue of the morning overcomes her with a kind of severe mercy, and she wills her breathing into a long, slow rhythm.

༝

"Mrs. Gardiner?" A small dark man, thick-set with dark circles under his eyes, calls to Tory from the door of the waiting room. He tells Tory his name, but she cannot hear him. He slides the green skullcap off as he enters the room.

"Mrs. Gardiner," he asks, again.

"Yes."

"Dr. Perkins will be along in a minute."

"Oh," is all Tory can say. Then, "How is Paul?"

"Well, that's what he wants to talk to you about. He won't be long."

"Oh," Tory says again.

The faraway beeps of the monitors, the soft squish of the crepe soles of nurses' shoes, the mechanical click of the clock jerking the second-hand, and the weight of the small doctor's presence hover around Tory. He watches her carefully, as if he fears that she will ask him some hard question. She doesn't. The nap has made her groggy, and she stifles a yawn. She looks toward the door, willing Dr. Perkins into sight. The sounds continue and Tory wonders what she should do. Then the small man to her side suggests, "Maybe you'd like to call some of your family, some friends?"

Tory shakes her head. Who could come to be with her? Her parents are dead, Paul's mother in a nursing home; there are no children. Without Paul, she is utterly alone, the sole survivor of a shipwreck.

"Perhaps you have a minister, back home, who could come?" the little man asks.

"No, no, I wouldn't want to bother him—not now, not yet," Tory says. The man, he must be Indian, twists his skullcap around his hand—his face creased with worry lines. Tory tries to read his name, but it blurs out of focus. "You mustn't worry about me, I'll be fine," she tells him. "I'll just wait here for Dr. Perkins. I'm sure he'll be along in a minute."

The Indian doctor seems relieved, glad to be given permission to leave. He offers her a weak smile and turns to disappear through the door and down the hall. The hospital's sterile quiet is broken by his footsteps and the sounds of life-support systems.

The pillows on the couch remain stacked as Debbi left them. A *People* magazine is open on the coffee table; a bit of cotton fluff from the inside of her cast proves that she was here, that she was with Paul when he had the wreck. Tory thinks that she can still smell her, the last remnants of her cheap perfume.

"Mrs. Gardiner?" Dr. Perkins stands in the doorway.

"Yes?"

His face is drawn; Tory thinks that he has been too long without sleep. "I'm afraid I have bad news for you." He starts to speak as he crosses the room, sits in the chair next to Tory. "One of the clots caused by the impact worked its way loose and lodged in the aorta. We tried to remove it surgically, but the damage was already done. I'm sorry." He looks at Tory for an instant, as though he has given her the answer to a difficult puzzle. Then he examines his hands.

"Damage?" Tory asks.

"Yes, it stopped the blood flow to the heart. Then the arrhythmia—that's what set off all the monitors—destabilized the heart function, cut off blood supply to the brain, even though we shocked the heart numerous times. Then, after we got to the clot, the heart didn't respond." Dr. Perkins gives Tory another glance, longer this time, seems to find comfort in all the medical language.

"Didn't respond?" Tory asks.

"Yes, the heart muscle, which as I told you this morning was terribly bruised from the impact, just didn't respond. That happens sometimes." Dr. Perkins glances out the window, then back at his hands, finally at Tory. "Occasionally, we are able to massage the muscle, and if the impact damage isn't too great, the heart will start again, even slightly, and we can use a stimulant to provide help until the heart takes over on its own. But that wasn't the case this time. I'm sorry."

"Paul didn't make it?"

"No, Mrs. Gardiner, I'm afraid not. I am sorry."

Tory is silent. She doesn't know how to ask the next question, or the next, or the next. Dr. Perkins leans forward as if he might be waiting to catch her should she slide out of the chair. His face is close to hers and she can see the slight indentation of the surgical mask's clamp on his nose.

"Is there someone you can call, someone who can help you with the arrangements?" he asks.

"No, that is, yes, I'm sure there is, but I'll have to wait a minute until I get hold of myself. You're telling me that Paul is dead, aren't you?" Tory finds the words, and they hang before her face, right in front of Dr. Perkins, like so many shirts on a line, but there is no wind to move them away. Nothing but hospital silence.

"Yes, ma'am, I am. And I'm sorry to have to be the one to bear this news. We did everything we could, but his injuries were just too great. He took a huge impact at the time of the crash; that alone would have killed a lesser man."

"A lesser man, yes," Tory answers.

"I've called the hospital chaplain. He should be here in just a few minutes." Dr. Perkins looks toward the door in anticipation. "Dr. Babcock from the First Baptist Church. He will be here soon, and I know you will want to call someone to be with you." He stands, rubs his eyes, looks away, then quickly back at Tory. Embarrassed, he says, "There are some forms to fill out and arrangements for the . . ."

"Body," Tory finishes for him.

"Yes, for the body, and the death certificate which you will have to give to the funeral director. We'll provide you with copies for the probate court, all that sort of thing." He speaks more quickly now that the conversation has moved away from grief and failure. Tory doesn't answer him. He moves in a sideways gesture toward the door.

"Please don't feel as though you have to stay, Dr. Perkins. I'll be fine, really I will. I just need a moment or two to get myself together. There are some calls I have to make, and I'll be ready to sign the paperwork in a bit. I must call his law partners, the funeral home, his mother. There are things I need to do." Tory stands in order to allow the doctor to leave. He mustn't feel that she's holding him here.

He gives her a short nod, extends his hand, and repeats that he is sorry.

"Yes, so am I," Tory answers. As he reaches the doorway, she calls, "Dr. Perkins, don't send me a Baptist. I can do fine until I get home to my own priest." He nods quickly and is gone.

The duties in the hospital take only an hour or so; her calls made and the contents of Paul's car loaded into her trunk, Tory begins her ride up the Trace, home. Who will be there waiting for her? Friends from a thirty-year marriage; others from grade school, high school, university days; people who touch her life only tangentially, those who make polite chatter at weddings, funerals, baptisms, garden-club luncheons. Who will be there that she can talk to? She has made her life's work caring for Paul, being there when he left and there when he came home. She is bereft of companionship, the sole survivor.

Chapter 2

꒰

The Trace, Highway 9, the little farm towns of central Mississippi rush past Tory as she focuses on the white line in the center of the road. This morning's sense of the world as a watercolor wash has faded; now there's only a black-and-white movie, badly made, to fill her vision. On the outskirts of Clayton City, she turns into the Golden Years Nursing Home. She must be the one to tell Paul's mother. She gave the office strict instructions that no one was to call her. At the front desk, she nods to the receptionist and hurries down the corridor, a familiar sterile place, disinfectant overriding the acrid smell of urine and old age. She comes every day to see his mother, calls to check in when she is out of town, takes the laundry home, washes the lingerie by hand, preserves the lace and ribbons. Those were the conditions under which Paul would allow her to be moved from her home on North Lamar. The possibility of her living with them, a reasonable choice for Paul, was unthinkable to Tory. So she had promised to see her every day, to make certain that she was cared for, agreed readily to the list of chores. Was that where the breach had occurred? Did he resent her refusal to take on Mother Gardiner?

The hallway, empty and cool, reminds her of the hospital, and Tory steels herself for this terrible visit. She ducks into the bathroom, pulls down her blouse, straightens her skirt, fluffs her hair, and dabs a bit of powder on her nose. Paul's mother puts a great deal of stock in grooming, in presenting a beautiful face. Straightening her shoulders, sucking in her stomach, she stands before the door of her mother-in-law's room. A bright yellow chick, covered in down, popping out of a heliotrope egg decorated with rickrack, holds the calling card of Anne Bondurant Gardiner, engraved and in a florid script.

"Mother Gardiner?" Tory asks, with a faint tap on the door.

"Yes, come in."

Tory pushes the door open just enough to allow herself entrance. Paul's mother sits propped against three pillows in satin pillowcases, working the crossword puzzle in the Memphis *Commercial Appeal*. Her rose-colored bed jacket—ashes of roses, she calls the color—is overlaid in ecru lace, her hair combed, her face powdered.

"Why, Tory, what a surprise! I thought you were still in New Orleans. At some art show. Nice to see you." Her voice is still strong and clear, like a flute. She was a marvelous soprano in her day. Sang all the solos in the *Messiah* at the First Presbyterian Church. "Sit here, my dear." She sweeps the paper to the floor and pats the side of her bed. "Paul still in Jackson?" Finished with her greetings, she finally looks at Tory. "Heavens, what's wrong?" she asks, and pulls her hands to her face.

"It's Paul, Mother Gardiner; he was in a terrible wreck down on the Trace last night." Tory finds that her words don't have any of the weight they need to tell this frail little woman of the death of her only son, the sun for her solar system, the sole reason that she has doggedly held on to her life in the face of crippling arthritis and fading strength.

"Is he all right?"

"He was terribly injured, Mother G., and I got there in time to be with him for a little while. He never was really conscious, I don't think, but some kind of blood clot broke loose . . . and his heart didn't respond." Tory echoes Dr. Perkins's words of quiet failure. "The doctor said they did all they could, but the impact damage was too great." Tory waits, shakes her head slowly, then chances a look at her mother-in-law. Mother Gardiner's back is straight, no longer nestled against the satin pillowcases that she brought from her home. Her face is set with the same fierce intensity that Tory recognizes from thirty years of dealing with her. The ferocity of a mother's love sweeping away anything and everything that would stand in the way of her son's happiness.

"No, no, no," she cries. Her voice soaring into the upper register so that it becomes shrill and quavery. Tory moves to console her, but she pushes her away, refuses to be touched. "No," she cries again, "not Paul." And she breaks into weeping, her little body shaking, the ruffles of her bed jacket trembling with each sob. "Not Paul," she repeats. "A mother is not supposed to outlive her son, never, never, never. It's not right, it's not natural. Oh, God!"

The door to the room opens and a nurse steps in. "Mrs. Gardiner? Are you all right?"

"My son, my son," she cries, and Tory watches, outside her mother-in-law's grief, watches her keen and wail, hears her grant a high, terrible voice to the events of the morning.

The nurse scurries to the bedside, puts her arm around Mrs. Gardiner, and begins to rock her. Slowly, Mrs. Gardiner's sobs grow even and measured. She clutches the nurse's arm and says, "Dear God, whatever will I do?"

Tory shakes her head, unknowing.

Tory eases off the edge of Mother Gardiner's bed, smoothes the wrinkles away, nods to the nurse. "I'll come back later this evening. Maybe you could give her something to help her rest." The last glimpse Tory has is of the nurse, soothing, caressing Mother G., clucking softly, telling her that it will be all right.

Outside, under the hard brilliance of an April sky, Tory drives home, wondering what she must do next. Her hand shakes as she pushes the key into the lock, and when she forces it, she hears the tumblers fall and the door swings open. The house is dark and cool, and the smell of years of living greets her. Eucalyptus leaves from the urn on the foyer table, the forced sweet smell of paper whites, a slight whiff of cologne. The light on the answering machine in the kitchen is blinking. There will be calls of condolences, and later, visits from well-meaning friends, associates. Much to tend to. Much to arrange before she can afford the luxury of grief. She wonders if the sedative has taken effect on Mother Gardiner yet.

Tory ignores the blinks of the answering machine, walks through each open door, inspects each room of their home, her house, looking for traces of her life with Paul, hints, clues of them together. The carefully selected furnishings; the collections of paperweights, sealing in the beauty of butterflies, pansies, bits of amber; pottery from local galleries; a watercolor of Mary Vic when she was two, only her lovely face, no sign of the leg braces, the horribly contorted little body—all tell her that she has poured herself, her energy into this place.

Mary Vic's portrait smiles on Tory now. In the short space of her life, she offered much; her death brought a kind of wrenching grief that Tory had not known existed. Losing her drained the world into a dull gray, all color and texture vanished. After Mary Vic's death, Tory discovered more and more excuses to stay at home, reasons not to go to bar conventions, to country-club dinners. Condolences were just too hard to bear. She spent her time in the garden, reading self-help books, trying on various kinds of spiritualism, therapy, activities. None seemed to help, and now, with new grief in hand, she looks at the painting with the same sense that someone has thrown a leaden x-ray cape over her heart.

Her own face in the mirror reveals the toll on Tory. But Paul, smiling, strong, went on with his life, built his law practice, took in two partners, played golf with bankers, doctors, and architects on the weekends, leaving church and his mother to Tory's keeping.

In the master bath, the space on the vanity top is neatly divided. A tall jar of Jean Naté Shower Splash, yellow as egg yolks. A porcelain dish of little lemon soaps, shaped like shells, offers a quiet citrus smell to the afternoon air. A tiny African violet with one solitary white blossom, planted in a teacup that had been her grandmother's, marks her portion of the vanity.

Paul's military brushes sit stacked, bristles locked into each other, the tortoiseshell backs straddled by brown leather loops. Tory pulls the brushes apart, slides her hands into the handles, feels the slick cool of the shell beneath her palm. Thirty years of daily brushing has conformed the leather to the shape of Paul's hand. Tory's cannot fill the spaces. His father's razor strop and straight-edged razor hang on the wall beside the medicine cabinet. All Paul's toiletries will be in the Dopp Kit in the trunk of her car.

Tory kneels and opens the door under the sink, checking. There, on top of his shoeshine kit, sits Paul's pillbox. Inside will be the pills that regulated his blood pressure, fought the indigestion that plagued him. Never, never did he leave it out so that she might see it. Never would he admit to feeling less than vital, healthy, confident, to being less than able to handle any situation that came his way. And he had left it behind when he went to Jackson, careful that Debbi would not know. That she would only see the strong, self-confident man, sure, easy, and lucky.

Tory slides to the floor, her back against the cool of the tile, and flips open the tabs for Monday, Tuesday, Wednesday—all empty. Thursday's pills, the day he went to Jackson, are all still there. She feels the bump of her shoulders against the tile, as though they belonged to someone else. The grief that overtakes her knocks her again and again into the wall. The wailing resounds against the tight tiled walls, and she allows the sounds to overtake her.

The pallbearers are his partners, his golf cronies, the few men from his squadron who have called and asked to help. Mother Gardiner, awash in a black silk, follows the coffin in her wheelchair, pushed by the same nurse who offered her consolation. She carries a single white rose and speaks in whispers to those on either side of the aisle. Tory follows her. There are no others to fall in behind as family. The service is straight 1928 Prayer Book, no eulogy, a short homily, hymns of resurrection and joy. Tory doesn't hear a word of it. She carries a yellow rose and finds it impossible to sing the hymns.

At the graveside, in the older section of St. Peter's, Tory stands beside her mother-in-law, pushes her chair forward so that she can lay the rose on the coffin. She steps back, then up again to add her rose to the casket blanket. There are no tears from Tory and Mother Gardiner. Each of the pallbearers adds his boutonniere; the funeral director hands Tory a clod of dirt to throw into the grave, as Father Duncan reminds everyone that we are "ashes to ashes, dust to dust." Mother Gardiner refuses her bit of dirt with a stern shake of her head.

At the last words of consolation, Father Duncan invites all to join him in the Lord's Prayer. Looking down, eyes open, Tory realizes that the stretch of green Astroturf stretched under the tent, under the wooden funeral-parlor chairs, under the feet of Paul's friends and associates, covers the grave of Mary Vic. She stood just there where Paul's grave has been dug when they buried their daughter—Paul holding his mother's arm, whispering quietly to her, offering words of strength, just slightly on an angle, in his mother's ear. Tory's mother, frail and stricken, was her burden through that service. But they had wept together, and Tory had marveled at the weight and the power of grief.

Someone tells her later that Paul was a blessed man to have two good, strong women always at his side. Tory smiles and greets the next mourner.

Holding Mother Gardiner's hand while the nurse navigates the uneven ground, Tory catches a glimpse of Debbi. She is on the far rim of the crowd, her arm still in a sling; she is hatless and wears dark glasses. She disappears quickly across the manicured green of the graves.

"Ma'am?" Tory asks.

"I thought it was a beautiful service, didn't you?" Mother Gardiner says.

"I suppose. You know, Paul used to joke about how St. Peter's would have been a great putting green."

"Tory!" Mother Gardiner says. "What a thing to say!"

"Well, he did." Tory feels her heels sink into the soft turf. "I guess Paul never figured that he'd ever be here."

↳

A respectful two weeks after the funeral, Paul's partners call on Tory. In the meantime, she has greeted the stream of those who came with casseroles, flowers, words of comfort, suggestions of how she might handle her grief. Many bearing stories of victory and meaningful lives after the loss of a loved one. Tory hears them only distantly, wishing they would go and leave her to wander through the house once again, looking for whatever it is she cannot find. Most marvel at how well she's holding up, remind her of her blessings: she had a good number of years with Paul; he left her well-fixed, they assume. Tory doesn't answer. She knows that they wonder at her calm, chalk it up to strength of character, wish she were more forthcoming about her state of mind. But she shuts them all away; thanks them for the food, the flowers, the concern; and wishes them good-day. She never mentions the wreck, the fact that she tried to sleep with Paul's tweed jacket for a night or two after the funeral, but that the smell of it turned her stomach sour and gave her terrible dreams. But today, Paul's partners call on Tory. Formally, in suits and ties, with a briefcase apiece, to see if they can help and to talk business. Only they both say "bidness," like Paul's family. They explain the kind of partnership they had. Limited, Paul the managing partner—the first among equals, one of them jokes. Then quickly, ducking his head, covering his forehead with his hand, reminds Tory, that no one, really no one was *ever* Paul's equal. A little bit of silence, formal and careful, follows. Then the younger man, the newest to the firm, draws out several documents.

"After Paul's will is probated . . . of course, we'll take care of that. I believe that John, here"—he points to the other man—"is the executor, or myself if John's not able to serve." He brings his hand against his chest. Theatrical motions, Tory thinks. Orchestrated to help the grieving widow. Wonder how many times they have to do this to get the proper intonation, the motions, the careful combination of sorrow-but-we-must-get-on-with-life phrases? Paul would have had it down perfectly. Could have done it in his sleep, she bets.

"Part of the will discusses the care of his mother, sets up a management account, with John or myself"—again, the extended palm to John, then the hand against the chest—"as trustee, and the remainder to you. A few charities were remembered, small bequests, but indicative of Paul's concern for community . . ." His voice trails off, waiting for Tory's murmur of approval, she guesses. She gives none.

"Well," Sam Bench continues, "there's stock, some bonds, some wise investing that will make both you and the elder Mrs. Gardiner quite comfortable." He smiles, seems pleased with himself, as though he has some responsibility for this good news.

"Good," Tory finally answers. "That's nice to know."

John, the elder partner now, takes up the script. He leans forward just slightly, inclining himself toward some kind of intimacy. "Tory, Sam and I want to buy the practice. Keep Paul's name on the letterhead, of course, but we'd like to get the firm appraised and establish a plan to buy out Paul's interest. I doubt that you have any reason to wish otherwise?" He forms it as a question, but Tory knows that it is not, is merely a statement of fact, but he allows her to agree. A kind of perfunctory graciousness. The kind of tone one might use with a child, a servant, one not quite up to understanding the intricacies of business.

"I'll have to think about it," Tory says, slowly, so that neither man will ask her to repeat it.

"Think about it?" John asks, a slight tilt of his head, a little sign of bewilderment.

"Yes. I'll come in the office on Monday, clean out his office, and decide what I'll do." Tory stands, extends her hand, wishes them good-morning, and leads them to the door. She watches them down the front walkway, briefcases swinging, conversation animated. They drive away, and the sounds of their voices linger in the living room. Monday. On Monday, she'll decide.

After John and Sam leave, Tory wonders what she would do with one-third of a law practice. She has no training, no skill, nothing to offer the firm. Of course she'll sell. What else can she do?

When Mary Vic died, she ordered daffodil and tulip bulbs from Holland, two hundred and fifty of them. And a bulb planter from Smith and Hawken. She and Phil, the yard man, planted and mulched, watered and fertilized until the entire hillside behind her house was covered with blossoms every spring. It seemed a redemptive act, lively and important. No such project comes to mind to ease the loss of Paul. Perhaps when she sees the charities he favored, perhaps in his office there will be something that will guide her to similar kindnesses. But so much more than his death must be reclaimed, set right. When she allows herself to think about it, her sense of outrage threatens to cut off her breathing.

His closet offers her no solace: the straight line of starched shirts, crisply creased trousers, a rack of good silk ties, suits (dark worsted for winter, khaki and poplin for summer), his court suits, then slacks and sport jackets, a belt hanger—black, brown alligator belts, 34, same size as he'd been in college, in the air force. At the back, his golf clothes, with the spiked golf shoes, brown and white saddle oxfords, sitting underneath them. She picks up the shoes, knocks off a little tuft of soil and grass—picked up as he settled in to make a putt. She stacks the clothes neatly in a pile on the bed, the shoes in boxes and brown paper grocery bags. The lingering smell of cedar fills the room. Tory wonders how she will face the empty space. Should she divide her clothes, winter and summer, fill both closets with her things, with a modest separation between each one? Make an effort to fill the void?

Tory glances at the piles of Paul's things stacked around the room. All she sees speaks to the present, the surface of Paul's life; there are no clues as to what went on inside him.

On Saturday, Nita Beeler from the Church of the Redeemer Clothes Closet comes with the church sexton to load all Paul's clothes into the church van. She marvels over the quality, the quantity, the generosity of the gift.

"We can give you a contribution estimate. Help you with the taxes," she tells Tory.

"Fine, that'll be fine," Tory answers as she hands a box of freshly laundered shirts to Simon, sweating inside the van's close interior. "I don't know what they're worth. Probably a good bit, but I haven't any idea how to price them."

"Oh, that's all right; we'll do it for you," Nita answers. "Somebody is gonna be mighty well-dressed with these things. You might see these clothes in church on Sunday, good as they are."

The thought of church on Sunday makes Tory shiver. Sitting under the watchful eyes of the parish is not something she can do, not just yet. She wonders if she should tell Nita. But she and Simon are rearranging boxes, stacks of coat hangers, sacks of shoes, trying to get it all in one trip. The last of the plastic bags, filled with pajamas, socks, and handkerchiefs, are wedged into the few open spaces, and Nita and Simon close the doors, remove the keys, and prepare to leave, taking so much of Paul with them. Taking away his smell from the closet in their bedroom, removing his traces in one simple trip. Tory feels the loss rise in her throat, wonders if she will cry in front of them. Now, with the last of Paul shoved into the church van.

"Could you wait just one minute? I have another box in the attic that I want you to take. I think it'll just fit on the top. It won't take but a minute," Tory asks.

"Sure, if it's not too big," Nita agrees.

Tory hurries into the house, quickly climbs the stairs into the attic. There in the corner, a box from Levy's, bound and sealed, holds her wedding dress. She had kept it for Mary Vic to wear. White peau de soie overlaid in lace and pearls, a cathedral train, wide leg-of-mutton sleeves—she has no use for it, now or ever. Mary Vic will never wear it, and Tory will not have it cluttering up the attic or her life anymore. She should have given it away years ago. She brushes the dust off the lid with the sleeve of her blouse, notices the address, says her married name aloud.

"Mrs. Paul Bondourant Gardiner."

The name doesn't belong to her anymore. It started drifting away from her in the hospital in Kosciusko; try as she might to reclaim it, she cannot. Like trying to save the fragrance from yesterday's flowers, or a sand castle as the tide washes in. Tory tucks the box under her arm and carries it outside. Nita and Simon are leaning against the van, with the doors open again.

"Here," Tory says with a shove. "That's everything."

Inside again, Tory thinks that she should feel something, something more than just namelessness, emptiness, like a scooped-out summer melon, but she cannot for the life of her muster any feelings. All she can wonder is if Debbi kept Paul's handkerchief, the one she was using at the hospital.

༄

The light from a crescent moon and a slight spring breeze turn the back garden into ghostly waves. Tory walks among the daffodils, pinching off dead blossoms. "White Princess," an early bloomer with a fluted trumpet, moves just slightly in the wind—its heavy head bowed down, curtsying to the earth, a self-conscious debutante. Tory bought this variety for Mary Vic, set it in the earth so that something would remain, remind her of the promise of resurrection. Seventy-five bulbs set in a line across the hillside—just at eye level for Tory standing at the kitchen window. Just below, a row of delicate blossoms—the palest yellow, a ruffled trumpet edged in coral—her most exotic bloomer, called "Mrs. Backhouse." Paul nicknamed these "Mrs. Outhouse." Thought it odd for flowers to have names, pedigrees, to cost so much, but he had humored her—in the same way the partners had: a sense of toleration for someone not quite bright, someone who has to be pacified, like a colicky baby, a petulant teenager.

The evening's dark surrounds Tory, still standing in the garden; the bells from the clock on the courthouse chime eight, which means it's at least eight-thirty—it hasn't kept good time since "Whisky" Smith marched through, torched the square, and headed south to Vicksburg.

"Damn," Tory mutters; she's missed her visit with Mother Gardiner today. A first for her. How can she explain that she was ridding her house of Paul's clothes, her wedding dress, the tangible evidence of his very presence in her life? Losing her very name. How can she admit this to a woman who kept every report card, every athletic letter sweater, every newspaper clipping from a life that was full of public commendations? And how can she even admit that still she feels nothing, only numb and empty? Scooped out and used up? Perhaps the office will offer her the feelings that she is searching for. Perhaps on Monday.

Tory spends most of Sunday in bed, reading every line of the *Commercial Appeal*, surprised by the want ads, the personal ones that advertise divorced white male, 47, desires single/divorced WF, 25–35, for dining, dancing, cuddling. Another one declares that the writer is 53, drug-free, HIV-negative, and "looking for Lolita."

"Oh, for goodness' sakes." Tory speaks into the silence of her bedroom and slams the paper down.

In the late afternoon, she makes her visit to Mother Gardiner, complete with apologies about yesterday, rambling on about how the time got away from her, how she was trying to put her house back in order after the past few weeks. Mother Gardiner nods, allowing space for Tory's repentance. "Paul's partners came by on Friday, to talk about business," Tory explains, relieved to mention something concrete. "They explained about Paul's will, how he set up a trust to take care of you—and me, too, really." Their voices blend in Tory's mind, falling one upon the other, speaking the phrases of will, probate, trust management, buyouts. "I really didn't get it all, but they said that they'd take care of everything."

"Yes, I thought they would." Mother Gardiner nods, straightens the bow on her bed jacket, flutters her hands against the sheet's folds. "I'm sure that Paul's affairs were much in order; he wasn't one to take his duties lightly. Responsible, *that* he always was." She looks past Tory at the photograph of Paul on her bedside table and sighs—a deep, body-shaking sigh. Her eyes fill with tears.

Tory looks away and doesn't answer her, wonders what she can say to relieve the moment. Responsible in some ways, in public ways, but absent when the care of souls was at stake.

"Father Duncan came by yesterday, Tory. Said the church was receiving lots of gifts in Paul's memory. He wondered how we would want them spent. Something silver for the altar, maybe? A paten, a second chalice? What do you think?"

"Oh, I don't know. I'll have to ask the Altar Guild what they need. Seems to me we've got more silver than we can keep polished as it is. And fair linens filling every drawer in the vestry." Service day is always in early summer, and the smell of silver polish, starch, and brass cleaner fills the tiny, dark sacristy beside the apse for days. The grainy cleansers turning Tory's fingernails a pale grayish hue, like some workaday stigmata.

"Tory?"

"Yes, ma'am?"

"I said, what are you going to do?"

"Do?"

"Yes, with your self, with your life?"

"Ma'am?"

"With your life, what are you going to do?" Mother Gardiner's question points directly at Tory, pushes its way into her lungs, presses out all the air, and pins her to her chair.

"I have no idea, Mother G., none at all. After Mary Vic died, I could see a little way into the future, just barely, like following the headlights in a car at night; I could follow, just on low beam, a little at a time, but now the road is completely dark." Tory holds her hands out, palms up, as empty of life as she is. "I never really had a life outside of Paul, so now that he's gone, I have absolutely no idea what I'm to do."

"Well, I think you need to put that question to yourself every morning until you discover an answer. That's what I did when Paul Senior died. There's lot of work to be done—charity, community service. You mustn't just lock yourself in your house and mourn." She pauses, watching Tory, sending out some kind of below-the-surface signal, Tory feels. "Get out among people, do something." Mother Gardiner waits another long minute. Tory doesn't say a word, hardly allows herself to breathe. Then, with a deep intake, Mother G. continues: "Now, Tory, I don't want to be hard on you. But you mustn't hibernate like you did after Mary Vic's death." That's it—the unspoken articulated; Tory hears the criticism. "Maybe you could work at the art museum. You've always had a penchant for art. Use it now." She stacks her hands, one on top of the other, on the carefully folded sheet. Finished, she releases Tory from her gaze.

"Yes, well, thank you, Mother G. I'll think about it."

On the way home, Tory stops for strawberries, milk, a loaf of bread— the first groceries she's bought since the funeral, choosing instead to heat the casseroles, brought in by neighbors and friends, again and again in the microwave. She signs the check, notices that both her name and Paul's appear on it. Mr. or Mrs. Paul B. Gardiner, JTWRS. She had asked him what it meant. "Joint tenants with right of survivorship," he'd told her. Something legal, something to do with being able to get money should one of them die or be incapacitated. He'd put that on after Mary Vic had died and he thought Tory was losing her mind.

Mother Gardiner thought so as well. Thought she shut herself up on purpose, shut herself away from Paul; thought Tory was abdicating some kind of wifely duty. She as much as said so today. Chiding her to get out, get busy, get over her loss. Yet the nurses tell her that Mother Gardiner spends the days going through her scrapbooks, reading and rereading the articles about Paul's flying days, his high school football heroics, his legal successes. They mention that they find her lost in the scrapbooks, that she hasn't eaten well since his death, that she is simply wasting away.

After Mary Vic's death, Mother G. asked Tory—quietly one rainy afternoon, nearly a year later—if she wouldn't like to have more children. Tory felt stricken, as if she'd been uncovered, found wanting in some shameful way.

"I've thought about it, wondered if I can ever love another child, give myself over to mothering again."

"Of course, you can," had been Mother Gardiner's reply. "Of course, you can. It would get your mind on something else, too—give you and Paul a new center for life. You could manage, Tory, I'm sure of it." She hesitates. Then, "And this time, it just might be a boy."

Tory remembered nodding in agreement, withholding her shame from Mother Gardiner. Taking the blame for no more children, for not producing a son, refusing to admit that it was Paul who had said, "No, no more children. The next one might be handicapped"—that was his word, handicapped—"just like Mary Vic," and he would not take the chance. Would not entertain such notions. He moved out of their bedroom, and they had not slept together for months after that. He removed himself to the golf course, to his office, to his community work, abandoned Tory in every way. He smiled to the rest of the world and treated her with surface good manners, as though she were a house guest, a distant cousin who had fallen on hard times, come for an extended visit. The cause for some deep family shame, the reason that Mary Vic had been born crippled and unfinished. The medical journals she read on spina bifida indicated that perhaps it could be genetic, inherited, passed on unknowingly by a "deficient partner." Tory offered to take the test, to see if she were the guilty one, the one responsible for visiting this terrible fate upon her child. If so, she said, perhaps they could adopt.

Paul had refused absolutely, said that he would not allow anyone to poke around on him, would not be party to some kind of medical witch hunt—and never would he entertain the idea of raising another man's child. Tory could not bring herself to tell Mother Gardiner of his refusal, his cruelty, for somehow she felt diminished by his attitudes. The shame of it all made her flimsy, flat, like a paper doll.

Perhaps it was then that she determined to turn to house, garden, and her art for solace, to look to solid, concrete, built things that could not slip away so easily. She sought the reality of daffodils, oriental rugs, of paint, canvas, brushes, jars of turpentine, a solid oak easel reaching the ceiling, filling the entire corner of Mary Vic's old bedroom. A palette knife that built the colors, strong and solid, on the white surface. Things to touch, to stand alone, that stated themselves in vivid strokes. She painted late into the nights, even with poor light, until her shoulders ached and her mind was numbed by the profusion of color, the swirl and movement on the canvas. Only then could she fall asleep, exhausted, atoned.

Later, when Paul returned to her bed, it was only slightly, only physically, only for a moment, leaving her before dawn so that he never woke there. Their love-making always awkward, tentative, and seldom.

Monday arrives with the dark threat of a spring storm. The daffodils bend low in the wind, and the chimes outside the kitchen window bang against the porch columns. The gurgle of the coffee pot, the pop of the toaster, a tiny drip in the bathroom lavatory magnify, echo through the empty house. Tory has been awake since the storm began, early, long before daylight, wondering if she can survive the day's chore: looking for Paul again in the furnishings of his office.

Tory shakes her umbrella fiercely, noting the little brass marker that announces Gardiner, Tolliver, and Bench, Attorneys at Law, PA on the heavy oak door. She slips in, stows her umbrella in the porcelain stand decorated with a fierce Chinese dragon, hangs her coat in the closet, and bids Mattie good-morning. The local public radio station plays quietly in the reception room; Mattie offers Tory a cup of coffee and some boxes for packing.

She stands before the door to Paul's office—Paul Bondourant Gardiner, LL.B., J.D. blazoned in gold on the upper crossbar. Armed with a fresh cup of coffee, she enters through the smallest space possible, quickly closes the door behind her, and drinks in the smells and sights before her. In here, in this place, perhaps she might find her husband.

His desk, a Williamsburg reproduction of a planter's desk, feels smooth as a gardenia leaf beneath her fingers, highly polished to a deep mahogany red. The brass lamps, the leather accessories, the silver mono-grammed letter opener all speak of maleness, Paul's world outside of Tory. He had brought the office-furnishings catalogs home, pored over them at night when he moved his office to the refurbished old Carr mansion on the end of North Lamar. She had asked to help, but he had declined. Said he wanted to try his hand at decorating this office himself. Tory had outfitted his first one when she was working for him. Chosen the drapes, the furniture, the line drawings, caricatures of the magistrates at Lincoln's Inn in London. But this office was entirely Paul's.

"Mrs. Gardiner"—Mattie sticks her head in the door—"John and Sam are both in court this morning. They should be back by afternoon and asked if you would mind saving some time to talk to them."

"That should be fine, Mattie. I guess I'll be through by then."

Mattie turns, closes the door, and Tory hears the beep of a computer, the incessant click of the copy machine, and the low, intimate voice of an NPR announcer explaining the background of a Mendelssohn piece.

Tory drags a large packing carton to the small bathroom next to Paul's office. Toiletries, an extra tie, pair of socks, a towel from the country club fit neatly into the bottom. A print of the Kitty Hawk hangs above the towel rack. She leaves it in place and pulls the box beside the desk. The middle drawer, cluttered with paper clips, a nail brush, various pens from various places, a rubber band or two, and an open package of breath mints, could belong to anybody. Doctor, lawyer, Indian chief. Anybody.

A leather address book, with slots for business cards, lies in the right-hand drawer. Tory thumbs through it, sees most of the same names that appear on her Christmas-card list, at home on her desk. Lawyers, judges, clients, former clients, business associates, a few couples from their days at the University. A smattering of distant relatives. A second cousin or two. An old fraternity brother—Tory believes that he has died. In a small plane crash, some years ago. She stops flipping the pages at the "Mc" tab. Holding her breath, Tory looks, sees written, in black, in Paul's careful print, Debbi McCaslin—Court Reporter. Her card is tucked in the pocket beside her name. Then, in another pen, blue this time, her home phone number. And another notation, a series of dates, including one that Tory cannot decipher.

She leans back in Paul's chair, rests her head against the soft red leather. A sigh shudders through her. The morning news from the speaker behind Paul's desk hums through the office, and Tory finds that she cannot understand the words. They fall in patterns she cannot untangle, use syllables that she does not understand. Debbi's name, address, and home phone number are patently clear, highlighted in Tory's mind in neon colors, brash and bold.

The other drawers offer her no insights. Business letterheads, envelopes, copies of the *Bar Journal*, a court calendar, an advertisement from West & Company—publishers of the *Southern Reporter*—the *Mississippi Code*, a brochure announcing this year's bar convention in Vicksburg.

A folder of American Express bills, corporate gold card, lies underneath the blotter on the desk's surface. Hotel receipts, cellular phone charges, restaurant tabs, mileage, a time sheet with portions of hours engaged—all followed by case names and numbers—noted in Paul's even print, all in capitals. Tory reconstructs the trips, wonders who was with him, who ate those meals, called home on the cellular phone to check on her family, who slept in his bed. She pushes the folder to one side, rests her head on the slick, cool surface of the desk, like a schoolchild.

A light tap on the door, Mattie's voice offering another cup of coffee, a doughnut perhaps?

"No, no, thank you," Tory calls, straightens her back, moves into the bathroom to repair her face. Dabbing cold water on her eyes, she feels the puffiness beneath them, longs for some astringent. She grabs the towel from the packing crate, pats it against her eyes, glances in the mirror at the long streaks of mascara smudging her face and the towel, just above the Winchester Country Club logo.

The bottom of the packing crate is hardly covered, so little of Paul remains anywhere. She'll sell the furniture to the partners, complete with the paintings on the wall, the letter opener, the flame bargello drapes. The photographs of Paul—skiing in Aspen, sailing off St. Thomas, spelunking near Sewanee—those she will give to his mother. The baby picture of Mary Vic and her sorority photograph, along with the wedding announcement one, she will keep. Perhaps between those she can pick up the script where she left off living.

Heavy wooden legal files, disguised to look like fine old bureaus, line the walls of the office. Absently, Tory looks through them, back through the closed files from the years that she worked as Paul's secretary. Some of the names are familiar—Babcock, Woodson, FHA home loans for some of the county's poor. In the far back of the bottom drawer, a "pending" file hangs. Tory pulls it out, sits, and opens it into her lap. The memory of that time floods over her as she leafs through the file, stuffed with papers, court documents, letters handwritten on lined notebook paper. The People versus Theresa Marie Magnarelli. Newspaper clippings, yellow and faded; a photograph of a dark young woman dressed in prison garb—a haunted, desperate look in her eyes. The file, opened in 1976, bears Tory's writing on one of the pink "while-you-were-out" slips.

Paul,

The DA called from the coast, said the judge wanted to change the venue on this case. Wants you to represent her. Call him as soon as you get in. [601] 783–7070.

Love,
Tory

Mary Vic had been very ill by then, and soon after, Tory left the office to take care of her full-time. She died on Christmas Eve that year, a day or so after the trial ended. Carefully, Tory rearranges all the correspondence, court documents, letters, clippings in chronological order. Some of the appeals are recent. And the last entry is a letter, dated on March 29, 1989, from the defendant, begging Paul for help. It's from the Women's Prison, in Meridian. The envelope stapled to the letter bears an inmate number. "Dear Mr. Gardner," it begins:

You probobly already no this, but they are due to move me to MSU at Parchman soon as they've set my date. I guess from what I hear all the courts have said no, so time is running out. There's one more try, the supreme one, I think. I no its been a long time since you've heard from me, but somebody in here told me that you would be the one to get things started since you were the lawyer for the first trial. Is that true?

If so, you better get something started soon, since I hear they don't give you much time from the last appeal and the real date. The people in Jackson have been in touch from time to time, but if it's true that you have to do it. I thought I'd better get in touch.

I've been doing pretty good down here at the womens prison, but I dred going to Parchmen, people say it is rough. But there's no death row here, so they have to move me soon. Also once I get moved, I cant have any visitors and I've been trying to get in touch with my boyfriend, Tiffany's dad, hoping that maybe, if things go bad, he might bring her down here to see me. I don't want to die and not see my little girl grow up. Well, I don't want to die period, but I haven't seen her since the sheriff tok her away from me 13 yrs ago. She'll be a teen-ager now. Can you help me?

Sincerely yours,
Tracy Magnarelli

Tory slides the photograph out again, looks at Theresa Marie Magnarelli, feels her heart tighten for the writer of this desperate letter. Someone else who pinned her hopes on Paul. Someone else left comfortless, defenseless.

"Mrs. Gardiner?" It's Mattie again.

"Yes?" Tory answers.

"John and Sam are back. They'd like to talk to you, in the library, when you finish up here."

"I'm just about through. Tell them I'll be there in a minute."

"I'm about to order them a late lunch. Would you like some?" Mattie continues her kindness to Tory.

"No, I'm not hungry. Not now, not yet." Mattie closes the door, and Tory stuffs the two photographs and the thick file into her handbag. The top won't close even after she rearranges the contents several ways.

"Shoot," she whispers, makes an attempt to fix her face in the bathroom, now as empty of her husband as her house. She closes the file drawers, pulls the chair up behind the desk into the kneehole, even and straight, glances around the room once more, and walks down the hall to the firm's library.

John and Sam stand when she enters. Each fortified with a briefcase, a Diet Coke, and a legal pad and pencil.

"Hello, Tory. How are you?" they say, almost in unison.

"Hope the job wasn't too bad," John remarks as he sits. Sam nods.

"No, no," Tory answers. "Not too bad at all. There are very few personal items in his—Paul's—office, at all." She sits in the armchair at the head of the table. Situates her purse in her lap, counterpoint to their briefcases.

John begins by showing her the appraisal of the firm's assets, drawn up by a consultant in New Orleans, balanced against the accounts outstanding, cases in progress, overhead, salaries, debt against the building. The numbers blur before her eyes. She digs about briefly in her purse for the reading glasses that she has just bought at the drug store, but they offer little clarity to the puzzle spread before her.

"The bank has agreed to restructure the debt against the building, take Paul's name off the note, if the sale is completed within six months. We have reason to believe that everything can be accomplished within that time." John doesn't look at Tory as he talks. Using his finely sharpened pencil, he checks off the debts, the bank's numbers, the interest rates. Then sits back in his chair, smiles, and nods to Tory. "The offer to buy must be drawn up, of course—presented to them—and upon their approval, they will release Paul's estate from any liability there. All that will be necessary is for you to quit-claim any of your marital interest to the remaining partners."

"My marital interest?"

"Yes, whatever interest you might have had in the practice as Paul's wife," John explains.

"Oh," Tory answers, thinking it odd, almost amusing somehow, that after death she still has a marital interest in Paul, that now she is offered some legal stake in his life.

"We would like to buy out Paul's portion over five years. For the amount here." John points to a figure; Tory cannot make it out. "Interest only for the first four years, then a balloon payment for the rest of the amount at the end of that time."

"Oh," Tory says again.

"Actually, you probably won't need the money. Paul's income from other investments, social security, retirement fund should keep you very comfortable." Sam finally interjects something into the conversation. "The five years will allow us to offer you the full amount of the practice's worth, help us and you, I should think." Sam seems pleased that he has figured out how to best serve them all.

"That seems fine to me," Tory says. "I'll need a little time to think. I'll call you on Wednesday." Why Wednesday? Why not tomorrow, why not right now? Tory doesn't know.

"Sure," both John and Sam agree quickly—too eager, Tory thinks— but their questions hang unspoken.

They say their good-byes, make promises to keep in touch, get her to agree that she will call if she needs anything, and finally, both men vow to get the paperwork on the sale completed in due time. Tory shakes hands with each of them—the first time she's touched a man, except in grief, since patting Paul's leg in the ICU. Their hands are warm, soft, impersonal, manicured and lotioned, familiar. Like Paul's.

Tory makes a quick stop at Golden Years to visit Mother Gardiner, then hurries home, eager to warm herself with a cup of tea, to close the doors against the April chill and read the file of the People vs. Theresa Marie Magnarelli.

She clears the dining-room table of the stacks of sympathy cards, lists of who sent what casseroles, which dishes are to be returned to whom, and the little boxes of folded notes engraved with "The Family of Paul Bondourant Gardiner appreciates your kind expression of sympathy."

Carefully, she spreads all the documents from the file before her. Stacks the maze of legal sheets in chronological order. Then she arranges the newspaper clippings in their own pile, by city and date. The letters from lawyers, Paul's answers to them, she intersperses with the ones on notebook paper, written in flowery girlish script, the i's dotted with small circles. Tory takes out the photograph again, examines it, finds it difficult to balance the image of that hardened young woman with the writer of the letter, a young mother who only wants to see her daughter grow up.

First, she reads the newspaper accounts. The *Sun Herald,* in Biloxi, has the earliest date: August 3, 1976. The headline simply "Motel Murder." Then an account by the local coroner, the police chief, and the owner of the local motel where the body was found. He mentioned that this kind of stuff is not good for business.

The deceased, Dwayne Dewey, allegedly the owner of a local call-girl agency, was reported to have ties to the Dixie Mafia. The police chief couldn't comment on that, he said. The accused killer, Theresa Marie Magnarelli, was picked up only hours after the body was discovered. She was at a local McDonald's, having coffee and feeding her two-year-old daughter, Tiffany, a sausage biscuit. There was blood on her clothes, on the child, and under Magnarelli's fingernails, so the story read. The police chief says that the clothing has been sent to a serologist in Jackson, along with samples of Dewey's blood. Tory had called a specialist there sometime during that same summer asking about a new treatment. He'd said that Mary Vic's case was probably too advanced to be benefited by such measures.

The arraignment was front-page headlines on August eighth, and the judge reconvened the grand jury that same day. The foreman, Brazil Newton Jr., read the findings to a packed courtroom. The county coroner testified that Dewey had nineteen stab wounds. "When the throat was cut, the carotid artery was severed; both the internal and external jugular veins and the esophageal airway were severed." Tory shudders when she reads this part. The coroner said the crime scene was "a bloody mess." The district attorney, the same one who called Paul that summer when Mary Vic was so ill—Hewett Gaston Sr., she remembers the name now that she reads it in the *Harrison County Daily Herald*—reminds the folks that in his district "the swift system of justice" represented by this case is typical of his tenure as DA. He noted in his statement reported in both papers that "within fifteen days of the alleged crime, the suspect had been apprehended, assigned an attorney, given a preliminary hearing, indicted, arraigned, and had the trial dates set." A few pages inside the paper, there is an ad for Gaston's reelection, listing his strong law-and-order stance, urging the voters to reelect him in November.

Later, in the *Biloxi Sun,* a statement from the judge stated that the "sensational and lurid publicity surrounding this case" had been the reason for his decision to grant a change of venue for the trial. Hewett Gaston was quoted as saying that "unfair trials haven't been something troubling Harrison County while I've been the DA. Seems to me that wherever this one is tried, it'll be big news. But the judge has spoken, and the trial will be moved." It was then that Paul and Clayton County were chosen.

For Tory, the events are blurred after that. She spent much of her time, the fall of 1976, in the Children's Hospital in Memphis. Sleeping on a cot beside Mary Vic, listening deep into the night to the sounds of her labored breathing. Standing at the edge of the hospital's little roof garden, a blanket wrapped around her, trying to decipher the whereabouts of the river, hoping that by establishing its course she might discover where her own life was going without Mary Vic. The doctors had told her by then that there was nothing more they could do. She simply could not live much longer. Some sort of septicemia would eventually set in, followed by what they called "good pasture syndrome." The myelomeningocele had about run its course. Mary Vic's lungs were weakened by the numerous bouts with pneumonia; renal failure was a definite threat from the constant kidney infections, caused by the very catheter that kept her alive. They were simply running out of options. One thing or another would eventually prove too much for her, make one last assault which she and they could not counter. The doctors gathered outside Mary Vic's door, explained these things—heads bowed, voices lowered—then were off to see the healthy children in their clinics who needed a measles shot, a throat culture, a physical for camp. Leaving Tory to sift and weigh their words against the morning.

"After all, Mrs. Gardiner," one young pediatric specialist had told her, "she has already lived much beyond the expected life span of most children with this disease. Ten years is a long time for a child with this much . . . with these many difficulties to survive." He offered that to Tory, one morning after a long, busy night of high fever and sweats, as though it were some sort of bouquet, some gift he brought with daylight. "I think you should know the truth; you need to be prepared for the eventuality of all this," he'd said. "I don't want to offer you any false hope."

"False hope is not what I'm looking for," Tory had told him, surprised at the calm in her voice. "Real hope is what I want. Hope coupled with action. That's what I came for." Then Tory had turned on her heel, opened the door, and ushered him out. He had not returned before Mary Vic died.

Each morning, after she bathed her daughter, she called Paul from the pay phone in the lobby while the nurses irrigated the catheter and the physical therapist worked with Mary Vic's poor spent body. She told him of the night's sleeplessness, the latest signs of their daughter's weakening, the cards and flowers from friends, of a new doll that she bought at Gold-smith's which brought a smile to Mary Vic's drawn and aging face. Paul offered little hums and un-huhs when she talked. Said little of what he was doing, only mentioned obliquely the trial and the publicity. Said it would make or break his practice. He came to Memphis on the weekend twice, seemed distracted, and left early Sunday morning to go back to work. He had told Tory that things were going all right, but he would be glad when the trial was over. Too much time in the spotlight, he said, and he was bound to make a slip, say something in haste that he would regret. But he seemed to thrive during that fall and winter. There, Tory sees it—a little crack, a space that would grow wide enough to include Debbi, the Hilton, the Sundancer, eventually.

Growing more sure and confident that fall, more ready to face the cam-eras and the reporters, Tory saw him being interviewed on Channel 5 in Memphis, and she realized that he was a celebrity. She was sitting in the family lounge, outside the ICU. Mary Vic had been rushed in that after-noon when her blood pressure had fallen disastrously low and her breath-ing almost stopped. Tory sat there as her daughter's life diminished and her husband's expanded, feeling trapped between the two.

Mother Gardiner phoned every evening to see how the days had been spent. Tory listed each visit from the doctors, the nurses, the chaplain, the Pink Ladies, the physical therapists. She shielded her mother-in-law from the verdict the doctors had given her. In return, Mother Gardiner read her long passages from the *Clayton County Eagle* about the trial, but Tory did not hear them; she would not be distracted. Mother G. had offered, once, to come to stay with Mary Vic, but then recanted in the very next sentence, reminding Tory that Paul was staying with her these days, eating his meals with her and studying late into the night for this most dif-ficult and sensational trial. She read the parts about the brilliant defense that local attorney Paul Gardiner was offering. Asking Tory, wasn't she proud? Tory remembers nodding her head, then having Mother G. ask her again. She had worked to find the words to satisfy Mother Gardiner, and then lied that Mary Vic was calling her and she really must hang up. After the trial, Paul came to Memphis, rented a room at the Peabody Hotel for several days, came by the hospital in the mornings, and told Mary Vic about the ducks in the lobby.

He pranced across the hospital room, filled with stuffed animals, flow-ers, books, and IV poles, showing Mary Vic how the concierge led the waddling mallards, their heads iridescent in the afternoon sun, down from the roof, across a red carpet, and into the fountain in the hotel lobby. He folded a wash cloth at his neck, tucked a towel in his belt to mimic the concierge in his white tie and tails. "And all behind him, Mary Vic"—with this he waved the towel behind his back—"a string of waddling little ducks, quacking to beat the band." He laughed at the image, glancing in the lavatory mirror to catch sight of himself, never looking at his daughter. She had smiled, worn and fragile from the effort of staying alive.

As soon as she was asleep, Paul would leave, asking Tory to go with him. She always refused, reminding him that Mary Vic might wake and need her. It had seemed the right thing to do.

Once they argued in tight whispers in the hallway outside Mary Vic's door. Paul's voice fierce and insistent that Tory come with him, just for brunch. They could leave a number and the nurse could call them if Mary Vic waked. Tory shook her head. Wondering how he could think of such a thing, how he could not understand what she—no, what they were facing. He seemed still to be playing a role, in front of some jury that Tory could not see.

Paul left for Clayton City without returning to the hospital. News of his daughter came to him through his mother during the last few days. He came back to Memphis only when the doctors said that Mary Vic would probably not live until morning. He spoke to doctors, nurses, the chaplain, asking careful questions of them. Was she in pain? Would she have any idea of what was happening? Did she hear them, know that they were there? All posed and framed with the precision of the defense attorney that he had become while Tory wasn't looking. The doctors answered him with caution, covering facts that Tory had heard before. Paul's face reflected the gravity of their answers. Tory wondered if that, too, was practiced—a performance entitled "The Caring Father." He spoke for some time with the young specialist whom Tory had dismissed, outside in the hallway. He left to call his mother, to tell her the news around midnight. But never, during that long night, did he speak to Tory, offer her any part of himself. When others were present, he spoke *at* her, about her—in some way including her in his feelings, never dreaming that she might have some of her own.

The next morning, he made all the arrangements and drove home by himself. Tory rode in the hearse with Mary Vic's body, marveling at the Christmas lights as they circled the town square.

Chapter 3

⁓

Tory finishes going through the file long after midnight, makes a few notes on the back of a sympathy card, and wonders if she will be able to sleep. The storm has passed, and quiet has settled around the house. Paul's favorite time to fly was after such a storm. "I can see for miles, and the air is so calm that it's like riding in a Cadillac," he'd tell her as he packed a little flight bag, headed for the airport in Ackerman. The single-engine Cessna was his most cherished possession, and he found excuses—daily, sometimes—to take it up and "hotdog" over the county. The local paper did a feature story on him, called him the "barnstorming attorney," compared him to a circuit-riding preacher, taking his expertise to clients all over the state. He said that story would convince the IRS that the plane was a business expense. Tory knew better and refused to fly with him, said it made her sick, when in reality the unnecessary risks seemed foolish, immature to her, almost a character flaw, some leftover from adolescence. The same kind of mindset that played practical jokes. She'd remind him that they had a child, someone to care for and to be careful for. Once, when she'd been angry—strident really—about his flying, he'd laughed and thrown his hands up, palms toward her, and backed out the door, aviator sunglasses perched on top of his head. Looking more like a handsome boy than a man with a wife and child. Tory wonders if Debbi had flown with him, delighted in the rolls and loops that he did over the flat, open fields of the Delta, laughed with him, marveled at his skill, saw him as he saw himself—reckless, daring, some kind of hero, lucky and charmed.

In the guest room, the sheets are clean and fresh and smell of sunshine. Tory slides her hand along the side of the bed where Paul most often slept, thinking she might be able to feel some kind of indentation, some remnant from the times he slept there. She buries her nose in what had been his pillow once, hoping to catch some scent of him, persistent and strong, against the overlay of detergent and bleach; but there is nothing. She's startled to discover that there's not even grief. She can't for the life of her figure out what it is that she has missed.

⌇

On Wednesday, Tory calls the office, wishes Mattie a good morning, and asks for a time to meet with John and Sam. Mattie puts her on hold, and Tory listens to canned office music for several minutes. Mattie offers a time, later in the day. Tory agrees to be there.

The shadows of late afternoon angle into the conference room. Tory is early, positions the folder in front of her, flips through the clippings once again, sees Theresa's face, the lined notebook paper, the stacks of pleadings, the death sentence signed in a big John Hancock hand by Judge Frizzell. And once again, she is struck by how those few weeks in 1976 defined her life as much as they defined Theresa Marie Magnarelli's. Both of them lost their daughters that year; both had hoped that Paul could help. Both, trapped by their choices, later abandoned.

John and Sam bustle in a few minutes late, making apologies. Both sit, lean back, and are silent for a moment. Tory clears her throat, begins. "I think the details of the buyout look fine." Both men nod, maintain serious faces. Tory waits a moment. Then, "But I just have one thing to ask."

"Anything," they say in unison. Then Sam, laughing slightly, mentions, "All those numbers can be a little overwhelming, I know."

"It's not the numbers at all," Tory answers, feeling his condescension.

"Of course not, but sometimes things can get real *legal* and confusing." Sam covers his tracks.

Tory nods, continues. "Well, in going through Paul's things, I found a file, left over from when I worked for him." Now it's the partners' turn to nod. Tory taps the file with her nails, wishes she had one of their finely sharpened pencils. "It was a murder case; he was court-appointed—a public defender, I think they call it." The men nod again. "The trial was moved up here from the coast. A young woman killed her..." Tory hesitates, stumbles. "Her pimp." A look of knowing crosses both men's faces. "I want you to help me try to get her some help. Paul got a letter from her just a few days before he died, asking him to help. I want to do that, for him, for her. Perhaps you could finish the case for him."

"Now, are you absolutely certain that you want to open this can of worms, Tory? This whole thing was pretty grim, really unsavory. Not the kind of thing that I think you'd be very interested in—certainly not involved in." John sounds hearty, avuncular.

"Paul did the best he could, considering the facts, Tory," John says. "She confessed, after all. Even told them how she planned it." He leans back in his chair as though there was absolution in those last two sentences. "It was premeditated, murder one, any way you slice it."

"Well," Tory says, "I still want to try. Maybe I could go visit her at Parchman. She's been moved up there, from the Women's Prison." The last postmark announced that. Parchman, twenty thousand acres in the Delta. No place to run, no place to hide, just camp after camp, overseen by trusties and men on horseback, all the prisoners under the gun, home of Black Annie and the electric chair. "A hell hole, if I ever saw one," Paul had said once. Had he been down there to see her? Tory couldn't remember.

"Whoa! Just a minute, Tory. I don't think you have any idea what you are asking for." John leans forward on his elbows, reaches a hand toward Tory, shaking his head and smiling. Sam nods in agreement.

"Maybe not," Tory says, "but last night, when I read her letter, it just broke my heart." Now it is her turn to nod. "I know what it's like to lose a daughter—not in the same way she did, but she lost her nonetheless."

Both men lean back, cross their arms, look doubtful.

"So, will you help me with this? It's the only thing I can think of that I would want to do with my third of the practice." Now it is Tory's turn to lean back, cross her hands over her purse.

"Well, I'll make some calls and see what I can work out," Sam volunteers. "I can't promise anything, but sometimes they'll give permission for a visit when there's mitigating cause. Can't think of one right now, but I'll come up with something." He offers Tory a little smile and a slight shake of his head. "You know, Tory, we don't really *do* criminal work in this firm."

There he goes again. Humoring me, Tory thinks.

"If we can find some recourse for her, I want you to agree to handle all the paperwork." Tory feels bold and brave when she says this. Like she might be able to do something. Might offer some comfort to that poor, haunted child-woman. Might find some angle with her heart that lawyers and judges could not uncover with facts and law, that she might discover something that they, in their confidence of said, sure things, might have overlooked. When the trial was going on, Tory had not been available; now, she has nothing but time.

"Well, I doubt that we could do that—handle the paperwork, that is." John agrees. "Not our area of expertise, of course. This case has had some of the best minds from the Capital Defense Resource Center working on it for years." Sam agrees with him once again.

"So, it wasn't still Paul's case?" Tory asks.

"Well..." John waits for a moment, draws tight little circles on his legal pad. "Technically, yes. But after a capital murder case—particularly one with a public defender—is decided and the jury imposes the death penalty, well then in those cases, the CDRC usually takes over." He looks back at Tory, as though he were trying to decide whether she understood or not.

"CDRC?" Tory asks.

"The Capital Defense Resource Center. A group of lawyers from the Legal Defense Fund. They have them in every state where the death penalty is a possibility. Guys work on the appeals, take the cases from the original defense team, if there's no money."

"Oh," Tory says. "But *technically*, the case is still Paul's."

"Yes, but he hasn't fooled with it in years. The pro bono folks in Jackson have done all the appeal work. But we'll see what we can do." He and Sam nod to each other, not to Tory, closing the discussion. "Now, as I was saying, Sam and I are working on the buyout proposal. Hope to get it to you soon. Real soon." John changes the subject easily, sliding like quicksilver into present concerns.

"That's fine, John," Tory answers. "But get me the names and numbers of whoever's been involved in Jackson. I'll want to talk to them, soon." Tory is amazed at her own words—finding them startling, certain, like she has thought them out carefully and knows what she would do next.

Tory rings the office early the next morning, reaches John. He repeats his message of the day before—that he is working hard on the buyout proposal. Doesn't mention the Magnarelli case or the number of the place in Jackson that has tried to help.

"Well, that's good, John. But I want to get started today on the other item we discussed. I want to make those calls, find out if I can see Theresa. I went through the file again last night. So, I need the number of that place in Jackson that has tried to help Theresa, and the names, *now*." She comes down a little hard on "now," sounding firm and positive as if she is certain what she wants.

"Yes, well, I'll have to check the directory, see if I have a name. Seems to me a woman lawyer was involved. Can't remember just now, but I'll look into it." Tory feels herself bristle at being put off, angry that John wishes her out of the way. She hesitates, then fearing he will hang up, rushes ahead. "John, perhaps Mattie can look it up, since you are so busy."

"Yes, perhaps."

Tory hears a little sigh of resignation, as though he cannot make a strong-willed child see the foolishness of her ways. "I'll transfer you."

"I'll wait. Thank you." Again, the music fills the morning, a sentimental rendition of "Für Elise." The programmers for these systems must think that's the only piece of classical music that Americans can recognize. That and the "1812 Overture." Tory hums along in spite of herself. Then,

"Mrs. Gardiner?" Mattie interrupts.

"Yes?"

"I've found the number and a name for you."

Tory writes the information on the same card that holds her questions from the night before, thanks Mattie, and hangs up. Elise's tune rocks back and forth in her head. Tory showers, dresses, and makes her way back to the telephone.

The receptionist at the CDRC sounds like a voice from the nightly news—no accent, clipped and efficient. Tory identifies herself and asks to speak to Jane Fillmore. Again she's put on hold, but this time the music is modern, rock and roll, a song that Tory has never heard.

"Jane Fillmore here."

Tory identifies herself again. "My husband was the public defender for Theresa Marie Magnarelli."

"Yes?" Jane Fillmore's voice is noncommittal, but Tory hears what she thinks is interest.

"Well, in going through his files, I found that her case is still listed as pending, and I wondered if there is something I can do." Tory finds her voice placating, tentative, as though she were asking for another helping of dessert. "To help, if I can?" she adds.

"Help?" Ms. Fillmore asks.

"Yes, help," Tory explains.

"Well, I don't know exactly what you have in mind, Mrs. . . . ."

"Gardiner," Tory answers, "Tory Gardiner."

"Yes, Mrs. Gardiner, as I said, I'm not sure just what you're asking me. Theresa has been moved to Parchman; we're in the final stages of appeals now. Waiting for a decision from the Fifth Circuit Court. The execution date has been set, but that's subject to the court's finding."

"Already set?" Tory hears a slight quaver in her voice, wonders if Ms. Fillmore caught it.

"Yes, July 17th, as it stands now." There's a terrible finality in the words. A slamming down of life.

Both women are silent. Only the hum of the open line persists.

"Mrs. Gardiner?"

"Yes?"

"Is there something specific that you wanted to know?"

"Could I go to see her?" There, that's specific, definite, concrete. Like houses, gardens, paint on canvas.

"Go to see her? Why?" Jane Fillmore pushes Tory to think beyond her impulse.

"I don't know really. I just read her file last night. I was cleaning out my husband's office, getting ready to sell his practice to his partners, and I found the file. 'Pending,' it said. Still there, hanging somehow. I wanted to see if I could do anything to help." Tory straightens the telephone cord, pulls hard against the coils, twines them around her fingers. "You see, when the trial was going on, I couldn't do anything. My daughter, my only child—Mary Vic, we called her—she was named for me, for my mother, for my grandmother . . ." The black half-circles of the cord alternate around Tory's fingers. A silent black snake curling in and out.

"Yes?"

"Well, she was dying, in the hospital in Memphis, and there was nothing I could do at the time. I couldn't help in any way. And now, I'd like to. To help." That seems obvious enough to Tory, humane and sensible.

"Mrs. Gardiner, I don't mean to be blunt, but short of a miracle, Theresa—she calls herself Tracy now—will be executed this summer. We're trying all the legal maneuvers we can, of course, but much of what could have helped her was vitiated by the failure to file the habeas corpus." Fillmore's voice is crisp, like the ICU nurse's, filled with facts, hard and clean, no emotion.

"Oh," is all Tory can think of to say.

"I know that you mean well, Mrs. Gardiner, but there's precious little that can be done, legally." She pauses; Tory wonders if she's waiting for her words to sink in, to get through to this lawyer's wife, this woman who wasn't there. "We will pursue every avenue, naturally. And do what we can to support Tracy, emotionally, physically. But the truth is, her case was really political. She's an obvious outsider. Topless dancer from Massachusetts, unwed mother, prostitute, Roman Catholic—the child's father a black sailor—none of which brought tears to a Mississippi juror's eye." Another pause; this one makes Tory feel guilty, worse, for not having been there.

"Do you think I could go see her?"

"At Parchman?"

"Yes." Tory wonders where else Theresa might be.

"Have you ever been to Parchman, Mrs. Gardiner?"

"No." Tory thinks she drove by the gates once, when she was on the way to an art show, a McCarty exhibit in Marigold. Long before Theresa was moved there.

"It's no afternoon tea party." The edge in Jane Fillmore's voice pierces Tory, holds her silent for a moment.

"I am aware of that, Ms. Fillmore." Tory tries to match the voice, sharp edge to sharp edge. "But I still want to go."

Again, Tory hears a sigh from the other end of the phone. Lawyers seem to find her tedious.

"Suppose I drive down to see you in Jackson. You can explain everything to me. Then if you think that I could go to see her, I'll make my plans." Tory unwraps her fingers, lets the telephone cord hang free, swing against the morning air.

"Fine," Ms. Fillmore answers. "Could you come on Thursday? At ten o'clock?"

"Thursday at ten would be fine."

꒜

Tory drives carefully, ten miles over the speed limit. Paul said they'd never stop you for that. She visited with Mother Gardiner longer than she intended, and now she must hurry. Tory didn't explain the trip to Jackson, merely said that she was going on business, to clear up some unfinished matters for Paul. Mother Gardiner lifted her eyebrows, but asked nothing. Amazing, Tory thinks. I've known this woman all my adult life, deferred to her over my own mother's needs, washed her underwear, loved her son, borne his poor misshapen child—and still, we tiptoe around the edges of the truth when we talk to each other. Tory feels deceitful, somehow, not telling the whole story. This kind of evasion is something that she's learned, like walking in high heels, another little disguise that she'd adopted for Paul.

The exit ramp for Capitol Street isn't crowded by this time of the morning, and Tory quickly finds the side street where the CDRC's offices are located. A sign outside a parking garage, one suggested by Jane Fillmore, indicates that parking is still available. Tory takes a ticket from the machine, parks, and starts toward CDRC's address, grateful for the shade offered by the buildings, for the air in the city is close, humid.

Inside the office, Tory waits. There is no receptionist. The desk—a pocked metal-gray utility model, stacked with legal folders, a pencil holder, and a sad-looking English ivy plant badly in need of fertilizer and water—looks as though some overworked someone has abandoned it, overwhelmed. She picks up a magazine, thumbs through it, but sees nothing. The murmur of voices in one of the side rooms and the groan of an air conditioner fill the space. No office music here. No sleek mahogany desks, no leather chairs, no fine prints in rich Renaissance colors, no English line drawings, no Italian silk drapes. Just the bare bones of a practice, the stark outlines of an office.

"Oh, hello."

Tory looks up to see a frumpy woman, long swishy skirt and voluminous shirt, standing in the doorway. Her hair is long, pulled back at the nape of her neck, tied with a leather thong. She's wearing beads. Straight out of the '60s, Tory thinks.

"Can I help you?"

"I have an appointment."

The woman cocks her head just slightly. "With?"

"Jane Fillmore. I'm Tory Gardiner. I spoke with her on the phone last week."

"I'll tell her that you're here." The woman disappears down the hall, only to reappear a moment later. "She'll see you now." No careful waiting time imposed here to impress the client with just how busy the attorney is. "First door on the right."

Tory nods her thanks and makes her way down the hallway. The walls are covered with unframed photographs, mostly of men, unsmiling, stuck into the sheetrock with brightly colored thumbtacks. She hesitates outside the door. Wondering again what has brought her here, she taps two short taps, hears a voice say, "Come in."

"Ms. Fillmore? I'm Tory Gardiner."

"Jane." A small woman, severe in a black business suit, white blouse, no jewelry, hair sliced in a sophisticated cut around her face—all angles, this woman. She looks at Tory, extends her hand, then motions for Tory to sit.

In the brief pause that follows, Tory examines Ms. Fillmore—Jane— looking for clues as to what would bring her to such a barren place. Ms.

Fillmore opens the top file on her desk, glances over a page or two, then greets Tory's look once more.

"Mrs. Gardiner, you mentioned on the phone that you wanted to help Tracy Magnarelli?"

It's a question, not a statement, Tory notices.

"Yes, that's right."

"Do you have any particular plan, any ideas in mind?"

"No . . . well, that is, I don't know. I thought maybe you could help me with that." Tory looks away, examines her purse latch, feels foolish, stupid, as though she is a foreigner here, one who doesn't speak the language. Ms. Fillmore seems to sense her discomfort.

"Of course, we at CDRC are always glad when someone takes an interest in one of the cases we're handling. But, as I told you on the phone, the legal processes are running out for Tracy. We always are hopeful, but there are times when even our optimism is hard to come by." Jane Fillmore keeps thumbing through the file as she talks, as if she is hoping to find something vital that she must have overlooked before. "*Cert.* has been denied, rehearing denied, successor habeas corpus as well. The Fifth Circuit Court of Appeals is strongly pro—death penalty, pro-murder, these days." Jane seems to be speaking to the air, to someone else, unaware of Tory's presence. Then she closes the file slowly, with a hint of a sigh, and returns her gaze to Tory. "The only thing I might suggest is that you find a way to visit her, offer her some friendship, some human contact from outside the prison." Her voice trails away, and Tory hears no hope there.

"Is that hard to do? To get permission to visit her?"

"Not always," Jane answers, her voice lifting just a bit. "But there is a long process—writing to the warden, jumping through all the hoops. But I can make a few calls, see what I can arrange." She flips through the Rolodex, writes down a few numbers, and Tory notices that she is left-handed. Somehow she finds that comforting. Mary Vic was left-handed, like Tory's mother.

"If you have time to wait, I'll see what I can do." Ms. Fillmore dismisses Tory.

"Oh, I have plenty of time. I'll go get some lunch, then come back to see what you've discovered." Tory gathers her purse to her, hurries out so that Ms. Fillmore—Jane—can make the calls.

Tory spends the time window-shopping, seeing little, checking her watch, wondering how long she should wait. At three-thirty, she enters Jane's office once again. Jane rises, almost gives her a smile.

"Mrs. Gardiner, I have spoken with the warden and with the judge's clerk. Please, have a seat." Tory obeys, sitting only on the edge of the molded plastic chair. "Both agree that this is highly irregular—sounds like a British film, doesn't it?" Jane's laugh is brittle. "But then, her situation is 'highly irregular.' Tracy is the only woman on death row. They've built a little makeshift wall around her cell. Try to give her a little privacy." There's something so forlorn in Jane's voice that Tory feels her throat constrict. Then, "If we could declare you a 'spiritual advisor,' you could visit, and Tracy would be able to make calls to you—collect, of course."

"Oh, that would be fine," Tory agrees.

"Do you have any sort of training that would allow you to serve in that capacity?" Jane asks.

"Well…" Tory hesitates, feels inadequate again, wonders what sort of spiritual offering she might have. "After my daughter died, I did a lot of religious reading and went on a few retreats. Mainly just to work on my own grief, of course. And I've been a member of the Altar Guild, well, all my life, I guess." She hears herself laugh, and it sounds much like Jane's, brittle and dry. Perhaps this place, weighed down with the tasks tackled here, is offended by laughter, refuses it a place to flourish—like the plant on the desk.

"Have you ever taught a Bible study, Sunday School, anything like that?"

"No, not really." Tory hears herself—defensive, with a little edge of anger weaving its way into her voice. "But what difference should that make? I want to help this woman, be her friend, if I can. I was my husband's secretary when he was put on the case; then, my daughter became very ill, and I had to quit. *Now*, I'm free to do something, and I feel that this is so—well, unfinished. 'Pending,' I think you call it." Tory remembers the file hanging in the back of the drawer, swinging back and forth, just so *there*. Needing completion. Jane's face, intent, offers no sign of what she is thinking. "So, I want to be a part of what is left to do. Offer Tracy some kind of comfort, solace. What kind of credentials do you need for that, for heaven's sake?" Her sense of outrage exhausts all the available air, and Tory's chest tightens as though she is being cut off, suffocated. Jane watches her carefully, clinically perhaps, waiting for the next symptom. Wondering if there's enough anger, enough spirit here to be committed to such a project.

"Well, I'll call them back." She swivels her chair just slightly, lifts the phone. Then, "Try to inject a little spirituality into your resumé and see if they'll buy it." Jane smiles now, really smiles at Tory. And the smile chips away at the leaden air.

Finally, about four o'clock, Jane has an answer. If Tory will write and explain her reasons for coming, the prison will allow Tory to visit, if Tracy would like to see her. "At least once a week, but not more than three times in any given month," Jane finishes.

"Any given month?" Tory asks, unbelieving.

"That's what he said," Jane answers, with a faint suggestion of a shrug.

"I mean, she only has until July 17th. What does 'any given month' mean? It's May already." Tory finds the anger in her voice pinches it, makes it shrill.

"I know, Mrs. Gardiner."

"Well, of course, I'll do what they say. What's my alternative?" Tory stands now, ready to leave. And then, "But how will she know that I want to come?"

"I'll get word to her and give her your home phone number. She can call you collect, and you can set up the time with her." Jane rises, turns toward her office door, then stops. "She may not want to see you; I have to warn you of that." Jane's hand waves into the air, and again there's a hint of a shrug. "You see, Mrs. Gardiner, some of Tracy's legal problems go back to the first trial. When your husband was defending her. There were some—well, some errors, some issues that should have been raised that weren't. And I think Tracy blames him in some ways."

"What?" Tory is certain that there's some mistake. "My husband practically became a celebrity by the way he handled that case." She feels her face flush, the ends of her fingers grow cold. "Every newspaper in the whole South wrote about him, said he had done wonders—in the face of terrible odds." Tory remembers the scrapbooks of Mother Gardiner, Paul's smiling face in the *Commercial Appeal*, the *Jackson Daily News*, even the *Atlanta Constitution*, for heaven's sake. Local DA, strong law-and-order man, came across in most of the stories as the bad guy—Paul as the champion, the underdog, fighting impossible odds. David to the law's Goliath. How could Jane not know this? How could she think that Paul didn't do his best, didn't exhaust every possibility?

"Well, I'm only telling you what I perceive to be the state of her mind, Mrs. Gardiner. And I thought you should know as much as you can about Tracy. Visiting her won't be easy, I can assure you." Jane's gaze is steady—steely even, Tory thinks. Her words carry a faint trace of accusation.

"Ms. Fillmore, I am not asking for a garden party. I can assure you that I have had a gracious sufficiency of those." Tory hears her grandmother's phrase, quaint and stilted, come out of her mouth. "I want to do something that matters, something that can be counted, and I want to do it by helping Tracy Magnarelli, if I can." There's a finality, a certainty that startles Tory. She stands, giving Jane as strong and steely a look as she can muster. Jane offers her hand to Tory. "Then I hope she will agree to see you. God knows, she needs a friend. Not one person has visited her except the attorneys from here since she's been in prison. Thirteen years. No word, not a single letter or card, nothing." Tory thinks that the sorrow lying in these facts rounds out Jane Fillmore's voice, softens it, chips the edge off its hard exterior. "Keep in touch," she offers Tory. Then, "Good luck," as she closes the door to her office.

Tory heads across town toward Highland Village, parks in front of the Sundancer, checks her watch. It's after four. The bar will open soon and the luncheon menu give way to dinner. She pulls down the visor to check her makeup in the rearview mirror. What did Jane see, Tory wonders? Middle-aged do-gooder, ultimate Junior Leaguer, Altar Guild chairman, for God's sake. Tory frowns at the thought and looks more carefully. Frosted hair, expensively cut, the quiet understatement of pearls and diamonds in her earrings. Nice wide-set blue eyes (Paul thought they were her best feature), a bit of a turned-up nose, her lips a trifle thin, cheekbones accented just slightly with blush. Not a bad face—not one to turn heads, but cared for, moisturized and toned, protected from the sun, with only the beginnings of crow's feet at the edges of her eyes. But how does she *really* look? Does Jane see only tea-party possibilities? Tory desperately hopes not.

She pops the visor back in place, grabs her purse, and makes her way inside. The tables are set; crisp white napkins peep out of the stemmed water glasses.

"Dinner for one?" the hostess asks.

Tory nods.

"Smoking or non?"

"Non."

"Right this way."

As she follows the hostess, Tory looks carefully at the tables, wonders where Debbi and Paul sat before they began their last trip up the Natchez Trace, the same road she will drive shortly. What did they order?

What did they talk about? The case, the deposition, their lives, Tory? What touches were exchanged? Perhaps they sat in the back, near the exit, but more likely near the piano. Paul loved the jazz trio that often plays here. He wouldn't try to hide, would explain—gaily, with confidence—to any of their Jackson friends or acquaintances from law school who happened to see them, that this was Debbi, his court reporter, that they'd been down to take a deposition. Probably ask them to join Debbi and him for a drink, dinner maybe, then pull back the chairs, make them welcome. He would be terribly convincing. No one would think that anything was amiss. No one would call Tory to tell her they'd seen Paul in Jackson with another woman. No one would have called in any case, no matter what they thought. Tory had been part of such conspiracies herself. Keeping the silence, hoping that the husband would come to his senses before the wife found out, before somebody did something rash, foolish, irretrievable.

"Is this all right?" The hostess has stopped in front of a table near the windows. A small bouquet of daffodils and fern in a slender vase sits next to a wine menu.

"Yes, fine," Tory answers.

"Would you like a drink before you order?"

"A glass of unsweetened iced tea would be nice."

"Tea?"

"Yes, *tea*," Tory says. "I have to drive home."

ॐ

In the week that follows her trip to Jackson, Tory continues the motions of straightening her house, calling on Mother Gardiner, hurrying home to check the answering machine, trying to figure out how life is supposed to be lived. Several offers for lunch, to play some bridge, take in a movie come to her each day—kindnesses, really. But Tory declines, declares that she is doing fine, really she is, not ready to start going out just yet.

In the evenings, she forces herself to set the table, put out a clean place mat, matching napkin, knife, fork, spoon, water glass, and occasionally a wine glass. The round oak table, picked up in a junk shop the first year she was married, shines now, surfaces refinished by one of Paul's first clients. An old country man, fighting to save his farm from eminent-domain proceedings, had bartered for his legal fees. Several pieces throughout the house bear his careful work, speak of his sanding, polishing, staining in his effort to ward off what became inevitable.

———

Tonight's solitary place setting throws the table out of kilter, damages the symmetry, makes the oval table look like a Modigliani. Tory piles the silverware, the glasses, the mat and napkin on top of each other, removes them to the table in the dining room. The rectangle of the Duncan Phyfe table that was her mother's is less offensive, and placing the utensils at one end seems to anchor the table, offers her a place, not quite so obviously alone.

She brings the newspaper to the table, hoping that she can read away the meal. Her mother never allowed reading at the table, required conversation, preferably light and animated. Tory had attempted such cheerful dinner talk when she and Paul married, choosing tidbits of news from the society section, a paragraph from an art book she was reading, sometimes even an observation she'd picked up from the sports pages, trying to draw Paul into the kind of civilized talk she'd been raised on. But early on, he came to the table with law books in hand, complaining that he had too much to do to "waste time" at the table. During his boyhood, he and his mother ate Sunday dinner together, always accompanied by someone from church, he'd said. Later, when she tried to include Mary Vic in their meals, the strain of feeding her, cleaning up her spills, attempting to understand her garbled speech became too much, and Tory lost the art of conversation. In the last few years, she and Paul had seldom eaten together unless there were guests. He worked late; she ate early. He grabbed a bite at the club before coming home; she was often in her studio when he arrived. They had separated long before Paul died. So, solitary meals are not entirely new, Tory thinks. But the realization that they will remain that way, perhaps forever, makes the veal cutlet in her mouth grow cottony, take on giant proportions. She spits it into her napkin, pushes her chair back, and clears the table.

Yesterday, Mother Gardiner offered some "grief" books to Tory. They lie stacked on her bedside table. Spiritual books about dealing with loss, about building a new life, about salvaging hope. Tory thumbs through each of them, seeing nothing that pertains to her. The faces of the authors on the book jackets seem serene, confident, victorious. Or perhaps mindless. She isn't certain. Tory studies her own face in the mirror above Paul's dresser; there is no resemblance here. The worry lines have deepened, just since she went to Jackson, and Tory is certain that she can see them spreading daily now.

It's too early for bed; Tory knows that. If she goes to sleep now, she will only wake again in the dark, early hours of the morning, with fragments of unremembered dreams confusing her, hanging just outside her con-sciousness. Downstairs at her desk, she attempts to write a few more thank-you notes for the casseroles, the gifts to the bishop's discretionary fund, the United Way; to speak encouragement to those who have offered sympathy, invited her to lunch at the country club, to join them for bridge—to all those who have tried to support to her. The sharp ring of the phone interrupts her note to the secretary of the Clayton County Bar.

"Yes," she answers.

"Mrs. Gardiner, this is Jane Fillmore. Sorry to bother you so late, but I spoke with Tracy late this afternoon and told her of your interest and the possibility of your coming to see her." Jane's voice is perhaps a bit warmer than Tory remembered. Maybe she's at home, away from the sterility of her office; maybe that accounts for the difference.

"And?" Tory wonders if Jane can hear the hope in her voice.

"She said if you wanted to come, well, she wouldn't care."

"That's all?"

"Essentially, yes." Jane pauses. Then, "I think she's curious about you, about why you'd want to come at this late date, or perhaps why you'd want to come at all." The curiosity isn't hers alone, Tory thinks.

"Well, that's good, I guess. At least, for now."

"She'll try to call you in the next day or so. As I told you, it'll be collect. The prison has listed your number as one of the ones she is permitted to call." Jane seems more formal now, on more comfortable ground, lining up these facts.

"Well, I'll expect to hear from her and plan a trip as soon as I can." Tory pushes the note cards on the desk away from the Museum of Fine Arts calendar. There sit all the days of May set out in little squares below Sar-gent's portrait of the Sears children. Two little girls playing on the carpet in a Boston mansion, watched by two nannies who stand in the doorway, whispering behind their hands. The replicating of a busy, ordered house-hold, full of servants, children, life—it's always been one of Tory's favorites. Below, there's not one single entry on any day of the entire month. Phases of the moon, Mother's Day, birth and death dates of painters noted in small black print are the only notations.

As though I had a schedule to consult, Tory thinks. Any day is fine with me. I have nothing but days filled up with nothing.

Each time the phone rings the following day, Tory jumps to answer it on the second ring, not wanting the machine to pick up. Mostly, the calls are from friends, acquaintances, people trying to be kind. Tory thanks them for their concern, murmurs apologies when she declines their invitations, promises to get in touch when she needs them. The man from the monument company calls to say that the ground marker for Paul has been installed. He asks if she will go look at it, to see if it meets with her approval. Then he mentions the bill, that it will be sent as soon as he hears from her. He offers sympathy for her loss.

When she hangs up, Tory pulls the picture of Theresa from the file—a grainy newspaper photo—a young, hardened face with haunted eyes. Her dark hair curls around her face, hangs limply across her shoulders. The features are strong, perhaps a little coarse. Mother Gardiner's word. Tory remembers the description of a young woman who was confirmed the same day as Mary Vic. "Coarse features," she had said. Not mentioning Mary Vic's torturous journey to the altar rail, her awkward attempts to kneel, the leg braces clicking rhythmically against the muted flute and oboe of the organ. At the parish dinner, Mother Gardiner spoke only of the other confirmands, of coarse features, pretty dresses, who wore a hat and who didn't. Mother Gardiner did not give a fig that the Archbishop of Canterbury had said that women no longer needed to cover their heads upon entering the sanctuary, that that custom was a cultural holdover. "Ladies wear hats"—that was her final edict.

Theresa's face stares back at Tory, stony, jaw tensed, no revelations behind her hooded gaze as to who this young woman might be now, thirteen years later. This poor thing who has never had a visit, a phone call, a letter from anyone except her lawyers. There are no clues in the photograph as to what could have driven her to murder.

Finally, on Thursday afternoon, just as Tory is preparing to leave to visit Mother Gardiner, the call comes.

"I have a collect call for anyone at this number from Theresa Marie Magnarelli. Will you accept the charges?"

"Yes, I'll accept," Tory answers.

"Go ahead, and thank you for using AT&T."

"Hello, this is Tory Gardiner. Is that you, Theresa?" There is no answer, not immediately, only the open phone line's hum. "Tracy?"

"Yeah, this is Tracy."

"Well, thank you for calling me. I've been waiting to hear from you." Tory marvels at the politeness of this exchange. How can she ever get around to all that she wants to say to this young woman. How can she keep from blurting out, "You poor dear, how are you? Stuck away in that awful place, getting ready to die?"

"Yeah, Jane told me that you wanted me to call." Another silence.

"Well, I did, I really did. And I'm so glad that you found the time." What a stupid remark. Tory feels a blush rise to her cheeks at her bumbling.

"She said that you wanted to come down here to see me. Is that right?" There are metallic noises in the background; Tory wonders if it's inmates raking tin cups across the bars of their cells, like she's seen in prison movies.

"Yes, I did; I mean, I do. If that's all right with you. Would you mind if I came?"

"No, I guess not. Though I don't know why you'd want to." The noise is in the phone line, Tory decides. Maybe the prison officials monitor the calls from death row's inmates. "It's kinda boring down here," Tracy adds.

"Yes, I can just imagine," Tory answers, but knows that she and Tracy both know that she cannot imagine, has no capacity for understanding anything about Tracy's life. "Is there any day that's better than another for you? Any day you'd rather me come? I can come any time." Tory thinks that she should tell Tracy that it's boring up here as well.

"Any day suits me fine."

"Good, then suppose I come on Monday. About one in the afternoon? Does that sound all right to you?"

"Sure, I'll tell the matron."

"Is there anything I could bring you?" Tory asks.

"Yeah," Tracy says, "a pardon." Her laugh is short, high-pitched, joyless. Burdened with the weight that comes with not weeping.

⌘

On Saturday evening, at the grocery, Tory catches sight of Debbi. Down the cereal/coffee/tea aisle, walking with barely a limp, holding hands with a small boy. Tory turns her cart sharply, heads for the frozen-food section. There, she studies the fat grams in Weight Watchers entrées. The woman and the boy pass the freezer, and he whines for some Popsicles, promising that he won't drip them on his new shirt. The voice that tells him "no" is not Debbi's. It's older, weary and sharp.

Relief sweeps over Tory. She wonders when she *will* meet up with Debbi, where it will be. Will she have the grace to smile, to speak, to look her in the eye as though it didn't matter? To pretend that she knew all along, that the relationship had her blessing? That she and Paul had

66

worked things like that out, that he was allowed these little indiscretions because Tory was so busy with her own life, perhaps engaged in a few indiscretions of her own? That they had that kind of European maturity, not burdened with Calvinist guilt; that they were modern and wise, and that each little fling only reassured them of their love for each other? Or will she fling herself away, weeping at the sight of this girl who shared Paul's last dinner, last ride, last evening in bed, wailing like some banshee whose very world has been torn apart by his unfaithfulness?

Loading the cart with frozen chicken cacciatore, a bottle of good white wine—as good as the grocery store stocks—some salad greens, alfalfa sprouts, a ham hock, and some lentils, Tory waits in line for the checker. There, the magazines offer her instant cures for cancer, obesity, and failing marriages. There's a suggestion in one headline that Elvis's daughter might be a vampire.

"Unload your cart, ma'am?" the checker asks.

"Oh, yes, sorry."

"These any good?" the checker wants to know, holding up the alfalfa sprouts.

"Well, I like them. They're full of vitamins. But I never could get my husband to eat them. He said eating them was like munching your way across the front yard."

The checker laughs, runs the bar code over the scanner, hears the beep, and pushes the total. "That's $36.95," she says.

Tory rummages in her purse, finds her checkbook, borrows a pen, and fills in the blanks. Mr. or Mrs. Paul Bondurant Gardiner, JTRS—joint tenants with rights of survivorship. Maybe that was all she and Paul ever were, joint tenants—occupying the same house, eating at the same table, even sleeping in the same bed for a while, always just joint tenants. Perhaps they merely started from the wrong premise, never had a chance, four degrees off true north and thus doomed from the beginning. Maybe nobody was at fault. Perhaps they did the best they could, considering.

And what kind of rights come with such an arrangement, Tory wonders? The right to survive, that's not guaranteed in the Constitution. But, at least, if she can figure out *how* to manage it, it's something she still has. Something that Tracy is quickly losing.

"Ma'am?" The cashier holds out her hand for the check.

"Oh, sorry. Daydreaming again, I guess." Tory tries a little laugh, hoping that the girl doesn't notice that her hand is trembling.

Sunday morning, Tory wakes early, pushes back the drapes, and drinks in the richness of the garden below. Filled with late-blooming daffodils, tulips, and the last of the flowering quince, the hillside is a patchwork of deep yellow, salmon, and red. She will take a bouquet to the cemetery this morning. Maybe even go to church. Eucharist is at eight. There will only be a handful there. Maybe she can survive that.

The inside of the car smells like spring. Daffodils, the few remaining tulips, a sprig or two of the quince—stems cut on the diagonal, wrapped in a damp paper towel, encased in aluminum foil—lie on the passenger seat. Maybe Tracy would like some flowers, Tory thinks. It might make her cell a little more tolerable. The thought makes her laugh—a short little snort, cynical, not sounding like her at all. Flowers on death row. A trifle incongruous, she decides. But what could she bring to someone who is about to die? For Mary Vic there were dolls, toys, lightly salted cashews—her favorites, not on the hospital menu. She would eat them one at a time, sucking the salt away, making the handful on her tray last all morning. While she ate, Tory read *The Chronicles of Narnia*, pulled out the puzzle pages from *Highlights*, set up her little easel, handed her the colored pens as she asked for them.

"Green, now, Mama," and she would carefully color the leaves of the apples she had just drawn. When she tired, she would ask Tory to finish the picture and mail it to Daddy. Tory still has a box of drawings, awkward and unfinished, in the attic. Lettered with little messages to Paul, who was busy trying to save Tracy's life while Tory worked at saving Mary Vic's. Well, it looks as though neither of us will be successful, Tory thinks, for she has already lost her battle, and thirteen years later, it looks like Paul will lose his as well. Tory wonders if it could have been his fault. Could Tracy have been saved by someone else? Jane offered no facts, just mentioned that something wasn't filed in time. Paul could have overlooked it. After all, Mary Vic was dying.

The two marble ground markers, engraved with the beginnings and endings of Paul's and Mary Vic's lives, are smudged from the recent rains and wind. Tory wipes them clean with the damp paper towel. The granite vase at the base of the headstone has several inches of water in it, and she plunges the stems into it, arranges the flowers—moving the tulips, salmon-colored and elegant, into a more interesting shape—stands back on Paul's grave to check the symmetry, the eye appeal of her work. The distant sound of a riding lawn mower slides across the Sabbath quiet.

Whispered good mornings, nice-to-see you back, how are yous rustle through the church. Tory feels her spine stiffen at the entrance of the acolyte and Father Duncan. He has called several times since Paul's death. She has not answered the door. With her car and Paul's old truck in the carport, he must have known that she was at home, but not welcoming him, not then, not yet, not now. The green altar hangings of Trinity remind Tory that she hasn't been in church during the entire Lenten or Easter season. No period of penitence, no season of rejoicing, and now she must slog through the long green of Trinity until Advent's purple takes over. Tracy is set to die before then. Tory feels an involuntary shudder cross her shoulder. A goose walking over her grave.

Father Duncan's voice strains, not quite on key, as he sings the proper for the day. "Remember, O Lord, what you have wrought in us and not what we deserve," he intones. His homilies leave little for the imagination. Three points and a poem, every Sunday. Nothing to dazzle, to charm, or enchant; no humor, just quiet admonitions. Father Duncan stumbles briefly, as if caught off-guard by her presence. Then, hurriedly, he finds his place in his notes and moves toward the end of his sermon. Tory concentrates on looking straight at him, seeming to listen, even though her mind is filled with thoughts of tomorrow and the trip to Parchman. Parched man, dried-up man or woman waiting for her very life to be shocked away. Does Tracy go to Mass? Tory wonders. Jane had said that she was Roman Catholic, that that made her less than sympathetic to the jury. Does she know that she could ask not to get what she deserves, but what is wrought? Do the Catholics believe that? Tory isn't sure.

Tory slips by Father Duncan as he chats, holding on to Mrs. Winston's hand, leaning over to catch the old lady's words—probably a criticism of doings in the parish. She and Mother Gardiner have battled politely for years over the care of the fine linens. Mother Gardiner a strong proponent of bleach, Mrs. Winston just as adamant that salt and sun, perhaps a little lemon juice is adequate—and, she was quick to add, prolongs the life of the linens.

Just as Tory reaches her car, a little wave from Father Duncan—hesitant, as though he might catch her unawares, make her acknowledge his care of her soul—hurries her away toward the nursing home. He will bring communion to Mother Gardiner after his dinner, spend time catching her up on parish gossip; he's such a prissy man, Tory wonders that Mother Gardiner is so taken with him.

ᔓ

Tory has the car serviced late Sunday afternoon so that she can leave early on Monday. She packs a thermos of coffee, a sandwich, some flowers, in spite of her earlier thoughts to the contrary. The morning is bright and clear, the road nearly empty. A few spurts of busyness, of people going to jobs, slow her down on the outskirts of town.

The Delta stretches out before her, and Tory tries to find NPR, twisting the dial back and forth, hoping to find the reassuring voices of Nina Totenberg, Rene Montaigne, someone who speaks of efforts to discover a civilized and ordered world. All she can find is country music or fundamentalist preachers, both loud and disquieting.

A few miles below Drew, the road widens; signs warn against picking up hitchhikers, announce that the road is now patrolled by the guards of the State Penitentiary at Parchman. A second set of signs forbids stopping for the next seven miles. Tory feels another goose walk over her grave, shivers. How she will tolerate the inside of the prison itself? She slows as the speed limit drops to thirty-five miles per hour. On her right, the gates to Parchman rise against the flat Delta countryside, on the left nothing but endless fields. She signals, feeling the tick-tick of the blinker in her palm. Slowly, she pulls up to the gate. A heavy-set woman, dressed in a highway-patrol uniform—brown slacks, tan shirt, the state seal of Mississippi emblazoned on the sleeve—reluctantly puts down her book and ambles out to Tory's car.

"Yes, ma'am?" she asks.

"I'm here to make a pastoral visit." Jane has told Tory to identify herself in such a way.

"Name?"

"Mrs.—that is, Tory Gardiner."

"To see?"

"Theresa Marie Magnarelli." There's a visible reaction on the guard's face, a slight pulling back. She looks carefully at Tory, then at the books and flowers on the passenger side, turns to check the back seat.

"You got clearance?"

"Yes, my visit was arranged earlier."

"By?"

"Well, I don't know who all was involved. Jane Fillmore at the CDRC, she and I both wrote to the warden. I have a letter here somewhere from him." Tory begins to fumble in her purse, keeping her eyes on the guard, on the gun she has strapped to her waist, on the circle of bullets cinched there. Tory finds the letter by touch and hands it to the guard.

The state seal, highly embossed on the corner of the envelope, slides across Tory's fingertips as the guard takes the letter, opens it, and reads the contents, the stolid expression never changing.

"I'll have to call the front office," she says finally.

"Fine," Tory answers. "Shall I wait here?"

"Just pull over to the side. It'll take a few minutes."

Tory repositions the car in the shade. The top half of the guard's station is glass, laced through with wire, the bottom dull-gray steel. A bank of telephones, newspapers, a couple of paperback novels with garish covers lie on the shelf. A swivel desk chair squeaks as the guard makes little quarter turns while she talks. She hangs up and walks toward Tory, extending the letter—like a peace offering, Tory thinks.

"I'll have to ask you to get out, open the trunk." Tory obliges. The guard lifts the trunk mat, checks the tire tools, pulls against the strap that anchors them, shakes the extra can of oil, antifreeze, and windshield cleaner that Paul required in every vehicle he owned. She twists open the top, gives each one a sniff, twists them closed, and slams the trunk in place. Tory jumps in spite of herself.

Next, the guard examines Tory's purse. She holds the metal teasing comb with the pointed handle out to Tory, lifting her eyebrows in a question. "I'll be glad to leave that here with you," Tory offers. The guard doesn't answer, but unzips the cosmetic case, flips opens the compact, and a small shower of powder covers her hand. Brushing it away, she pulls the lipstick apart, checks the contents, running the shiny pink finger up, then down, peers into the top, and finally snaps it shut. Seeming to be satisfied, she hands the purse back. Tory wipes the exterior just slightly with her hand, notices a faint trace of powdered fingerprints on the smooth leather.

The guard now checks the rear seat. Lifting each mat, running her fingers behind the seat's cushions, up under the driver's side, then the passenger's side. She flips through the books, takes the flowers apart, stem by stem. Taking a sniff of the thermos, she looks at Tory. "Chicory?"

"What?" Tory asks. Then, "Oh, right. Café Du Monde. New Orleans brand."

"Smells good," answers the guard. She presses Tory's sandwich in the middle, and the chicken salad and alfalfa sprouts ooze out of the pita pocket.

"Open the glove compartment, please." Tory obeys. The guard sifts through the registration, proof of insurance, maintenance records; checks the names on all the documents. "Paul B. Gardiner your husband?" she asks.

"Yes—that is, he was. He died a while back."

"Oh," is all the guard says.

"OK. You'll have to leave your driver's license. And your purse. It'll be safe." Tory nods and hands it back to the guard. "Here's your pass. Hang it from the rearview mirror. Drive through the gate to the large brick building on the left. First turn. Mrs. Carol Monk will meet you there." The guard waves her hand and Tory eases through the gates; the pass, which reads Maximum Security Unit, swings back and forth under the steady motion of the car.

Several long, low white buildings with neatly kept yards are on her right. Men in white trousers, stripes running down the legs, are weeding flower beds. A uniformed guard stands on the sidewalk, casually shouldering a rifle.

Carol Monk's office is clean, tidy, with photographs of several dark-haired, neatly dressed teenagers propped against the window. A silk ficus plant stands in the corner, a live African violet on her desk. Three heliotrope blooms have opened out into the morning sun, a lovely light pinkish-purple—an old ladies' color, like ashes of roses. Tory glances around the empty office and then sits tentatively on the edge of an office chair, afraid to let her full weight down.

"Mrs. Gardiner?"

"Yes." Tory turns and is greeted by a small, trim woman, obviously the mother of the teenagers. Same dark hair, small frame, sharp features.

"I'm sorry to keep you waiting. A slew of reporters here this morning." She nods towards the other end of the building. "One of our inmates has filed a damage suit against the system. Says we are violating his rights." She shrugs slightly, shakes her head. "You know, when I first came here, there was none of that. Now, everybody here seems to know more law than is good for them." She sets her coffee cup on the desk in front of her. It says "World's Greatest Mom" on it, and has a little shower of rosebuds cascading down the side.

"Well, let's see. You have come to pay a pastoral visit to Theresa Magnarelli?" Again it's a question, and Tory feels that no one in all this proceeding is taking her seriously, even now as she sits within several hundred yards of the electric chair.

"That's right."

"She's been moved to lock-up since her..."—Mrs. Monk's voice trails a bit here, Tory notices—"appeal time is running out." Tory nods. "But we moved her back to the women's quarters this morning, since you were coming. It's much easier to visit there than in maximum." Mrs. Monk waits. "We don't feel that she's a menace," she adds.

"Thank you," is all Tory can think of to say. But she's not sure to whom or for what she's thankful.

"Of course, after you leave, we'll move her back. Have to keep a close eye on those prisoners, you know." Tory nods, even though she doesn't know.

"I'll take you to the women's camp. Matron Sprayberry will take you from there, supervise your visit."

Tory gathers up the books and flowers and follows Mrs. Monk. Outside, in the parking lot, she feels awkward hoisting herself up—a high first step into the cab. Mrs. Monk starts the engine, turns on the intercom, lifts the receiver.

"CM-89, on the way to women's. Visitor for prisoner T. M. Magnarelli. Will turn her over to Matron Sprayberry at the gate. Over and out." The radio crackles, and a deep male voice answers something that Tory cannot understand.

Along the way, Mrs. Monk points out where "free-world" people live: the chaplain's house, the clinic—then, further along, the pre-release center, the death chamber—lined along the dirt road. Silver bells and cockleshells and pretty maids all in a row, Tory thinks absurdly. How Mary Vic loved that book of nursery rhymes with its delicate watercolors of the English countryside, lush and green, with the faint pastels of foxgloves and columbines washed across the page. Here, in Parchman, the sun bakes the Delta soil into a fine gray pan, with dried angular grasses poking up in the ditches.

The truck comes to rest beside a chain-link fence, eight or so feet high, topped with rolls of razor wire.

"This is the women's camp. Used to be the sewing shop, but now the Supreme Court says that we can't make the women work, so the machines were moved to one of those colored technical schools in the southern part of the state. To teach the needle trades down there." Mrs. Monk keeps her commentary running, leaving no place for Tory to answer or to ask a question. "I've heard that those girls down there won't have a thing to do with 'em either. Say they don't want to sew on any machine that came from up here." She gives a little laugh. "Seems like we can't win either way, doesn't it?" She looks at Tory for the first time since they left the office.

"Yes—well, no, it doesn't," Tory answers.

In the sharp early-afternoon sun, a large pear-shaped woman approaches. She is dressed like the guard at the gate, her wide hips and protruding stomach straining against the masculine cut of the trousers. Her hair, tightly permed and tinted a light orange, makes no move in the light breeze. The shirt pocket has a rectangular shape just over her left breast. A large key ring glints in the sun. The three women meet at the gate.

"Matron Sprayberry, this is Tory Gardiner. She is expected." Tory nods a greeting to the matron, who searches the key ring. "She is to have an hour with Theresa Magnarelli. Then we'll move her back to maximum, before the supper count."

"They already told me." The matron has finally found the key, slides it in the lock, and swings the gate open, just wide enough for Tory to pass through. "I don't like having a red coverall in my camp, I can tell you that. But warden don't want her"—she motions to Tory—"in MSU. Might cause trouble." Mrs. Monk and the matron talk in a kind of prison shorthand, leaving Tory outside the conversation. Tory senses the matron's unease. "Sam can handle the cage," Matron Sprayberry decides.

"I think we've taken enough precautions. Tracy knows to behave—or we'll stop all visitation until her last contact. She don't want that."

"When the visit is over, call my office, and I'll come back to pick Mrs. Gardiner up." Tory understands that part.

With that, Mrs. Monk slides into the truck and raises quite a dust storm before Tory can move onto the porch of the women's camp.

Matron Sprayberry gives Tory a copy of the visitor's rule book. "If you ever come back, then you'll know what you have to do," she explains. She sounds doubtful, and there's something in her voice that makes Tory wonder if anybody ever comes back. Surely parents, children don't give up so easily, or husbands. "Have a seat on the porch while I get the cage girl." It's definitely an order. There are no niceties here. Orders only. The long concrete porch stretches across the front of the building. Several molded plastic chairs, yellowed and split, sit in a row inside the roof's shade. A twisted chinaberry tree, leaves thick with dust, offers just a hint of shadow at the end of the porch. Last year's fruit—shriveled, pale amber—the color of chardonnay—covers the ground beneath it.

It is several minutes before the matron returns, motions for Tory to follow her through the screen doors that lead into a dark, crowded foyer, crammed with a desk, a table with a coffee pot, stacks of papers, and a pervasive layer of dust. Matron Sprayberry opens a set of wide metal doors, and beyond them is a set of iron gates like huge burglar bars. Behind them, Tory can see a crowd milling about in a vast room, the length of a small gymnasium.

"When you get through with your visit, or your time is up, call the cage girl and I'll come get you."

Tory nods, feeling as though her head is not quite attached to her body. The matron turns to leave, calling out to Sam. Both doors close behind Tory. She hears their metal click-click sealing off the outside world and Mrs. Sprayberry. The matron's voice follows her inside. "Be careful, and don't let none of them ask you for nothing. They'll ask for anything." Tory tries to remember what other advice the matron had given. But the cage girl is right in front of her.

"What you want?" This must be Sam. Did Mrs. Sprayberry call her a caged girl?

"I've come to see Teresa Marie Magnarelli."

"Hey, Trace, somebody here for you." Sam shouts across the room.

"Whooooo, Trace Chain, somebody here to see you. You didn't tell nobody that you had a fucking rich white bitch coming to see you. Gonna set you free, darlin,' gonna set you free." Tory cannot tell where the voice is coming from. She feels the heat rising up her neck, the color showing in her face. Another deeper voice picks up the chant: "fucking rich white bitch, fucking rich white bitch." The sound hammers against Tory's head and she fears that she will faint. "Trace chain, trace chain, gettin' help from the main line. Fucking rich white bitch gonna set you free!"

"Shut the fuck up!" That voice is Sam's, strong and drowning out the others. At once, the sounds die into a murmur, and Tory feels herself gasp as though she had been running.

From a lower bunk, set over near one of the high windows, a small dark girl, frail-looking in this place, stands up. She has on the same thick gray duck skirt that every woman in the room is wearing. It hangs loosely at her waist, touching her hips at the widest point, and then falls just below her knees. Like a long sleeve, slid carelessly over her body, that has come to rest on the sharp angles of her hips. Her T-shirt is definitely from the outside. Most of the women wear them. Mrs. Sprayberry has told her that everybody in this camp is pretty dangerous, has to be handled with strict stuff. That's what she said: "Strict stuff." Tory wonders what that means.

"Mrs. Gardiner?" The girl is shorter than Tory, just a bit, but her thinness makes her seem tiny, child-like. Standing still, solid in front of Tory, she seems to swell like a bird against the morning cold, fluffing herself outward, filling the space, daring Tory to come any closer.

"Yes." Tory is aware of low sound refilling the room, but she concentrates on making some kind of contact with the young woman in front of her. "Theresa?"

"That'll be me." Her stance is defiant, motionless. "Only I dropped all that Theresa Marie business when I started dancing. Tracy is enough now. I spelled it with an 'i' then." There is a small jagged scar just below her earring. Like a thin dark thread had been pulled away.

"Tracy it is, then, without the 'i.'"

Tory looks around to see if there's a space to sit. "Could we go out on the porch to visit?" she asks. "Is that allowed?"

"I don't think so, but Sam said that we can use her bed. My bed and stuff is all over in"—Tracy stops, nods in the direction of the Maximum Security Unit—"over there." She picks her way through the stacked bunk beds quickly—with a dancer's grace, Tory thinks. The utility dressers next to the beds are covered with towels, pictures, cosmetics, brushes and combs. Pairs of women, watching them, are silent, strangely ghostly, still in the filtered light.

"I brought you these," Tory tells her, handing the books and flowers over, putting the guides that the guard at the gate gave her on the bed. "I didn't know what to bring, but now, next time, I'll have a better idea. And you can tell me what you need. Is that OK?" Without anything in her hands, Tory feels naked, stripped, uncovered and out-of-place in her spring suit, silk blouse, and sling-back pumps.

"Thanks," is Tracy's reply. She looks at Tory without blinking. And Tory feels more awkward than she has ever felt in her life. Only by wearing one of Mother Gardiner's enormous spring hats could she be more obvious, more alien.

"So," she begins again, with a deep breath, "how are you getting along?"

Tracy thinks for a minute, then sighs. "Well, I guess I'm OK. Glad to be out of maximum, even if it's only for part of a day. That place is fuck-

76

ing creepy." She gives a little shiver, and Tory wonders if her skirt will slide off her slender frame. "You want to sit down?"

"Sure," Tory says and checks out the bed beside her. Sam's bed, she guesses. It looks clean enough, but she wipes her hand across the gray blanket before she sits. She pats the space beside her, but Tracy stands, leaning against the iron frame, looking down at Tory. "I guess you're wondering why I'm here, aren't you?"

Tracy gives a hint of a nod.

"My husband—he just died a little while ago—was your lawyer, for the trial in Clayton City?" Tory hears her voice rise, making a question. "And during the trial, I was in Memphis, taking care of our little girl. She died about the time your trial was over. I wasn't working for him by then. He had another secretary, so I didn't know too much about it—the trial, I mean." Tory feels the wooden words clunking out, falling at Tracy's feet, wonders if there is any of this that she understands. "Anyway, after he died, I wanted to do something—and I decided that I'd like to try to help you, if I can." It sounds so lame, so unconvincing now, in this place, against the clamor that has risen again. "Do you remember him?"

"He the tall, kinda good-looking guy, came around with the older guy from the court?" Tracy asks.

"Yes, that would have been Paul." Tory smiles, feels pleased in spite of herself.

"Sure, I remember him. Real stuck-up prick!"

Tory waits, feels her face redden. "Oh, well, yes, I guess. That would be my husband."

She recrosses her legs, tries to get comfortable, tilting her head to one side underneath the wire springs of the top bunk. The noise in the background makes it hard to hear. Rhythm and blues comes from one corner, threatens to override their voices. The light from the high windows slants obliquely into the middle of the room. The walls are vacant. A television set is mounted on steel brackets in the corner, near the ceiling. Two women, arms around each other, are watching a soap opera. Somewhere in the distance, the sound of tractors humming their way over the black Delta soil. Tracy says something, more to the air around her than to Tory.

"Sorry?"

"I said I wondered why I got another lawyer when they moved my case. They said something about a new ruling." Tracy looks off towards the windows. Her profile is strong, not coarse at all. Her hair, pulled back from her face, is long, black, and curly. She picks at her skirt, then smoothes out the heavy duck over her thin thighs. "They'll be moving me back this afternoon, put me over in the little house. That's where they keep you until..." She didn't finish, but Tory knew the place. Mrs. Monk had mentioned that Tracy would be placed in solitary confinement in the little house to await her execution. Death row was a separate place. Prisoners waiting for execution stayed there for the last several days. Waiting.

"They won't test me for AIDS," Tracy says suddenly. "Said it wasn't any use. Didn't matter to them." With that quiet statement, she points to the place on her leg. "Some of them here said that I might have it. Kept them away from me, anyway." She laughed. "I wonder when they shave me if they go around this spot. None of them will want to touch it. I tried to go to the infirmary with it, but Mrs. S. said it wasn't any use."

Tory forces herself to look at the spot where Tracy pointed. It is raw and red, about three inches across. The skin around it swollen and tight. Mother Gardiner would call it "proud flesh."

"I hope they don't put the leg band over it. That would hurt." She looks at Tory, as if she is assessing what this new information will do to her visitor. Tory forces herself to return Tracy's gaze, doesn't look away, although the pit of her stomach is closing down, forcing bile into her mouth.

"I'm sure they just don't understand that it's bothering you," Tory says, finally. "Maybe I could ask Mrs. Sprayberry to get you an appointment."

"No, you better not do that," Tracy says. "It's not too good around here to have somebody on the outside trying to help you. Sometimes that just makes it worse than ever in here." She stops, looks back at the wrinkles in her skirt, and begins to push away at them again.

"A simple doctor's appointment isn't any kind of interference," Tory says. "Besides, they're supposed to look after you. It's the law."

Tracy laughs, the same laugh that Tory heard on the phone when she told her to bring her a pardon. "The law. Well, that's what got me in here in the first place. I don't look for any kind of help from them."

"Well, I'm going to say something to her anyway," Tory says, with more resolve than she's feeling. "It can't hurt."

Tracy looks at her with something like pity, Tory thinks. "Unless you really don't want me to."

"Whatever." Tracy shrugs her shoulders, and that seems to finish all that they have to say to each other. The noise from the cage fills in all the space between them.

Tory reaches down beside her to retrieve her pocketbook, only to remember that the guard still has it at the gate. "Well, I guess I'd better be going. I have a long drive back home and I don't drive after dark. Seems like I have a hard time judging distance with the headlights meeting me." She laughs a little dry laugh. "Guess I must be getting old."

"Yeah," Tracy answers, "that's something I won't be learning about." Tory feels the words hit her like so many separate accusations, and she is ashamed that she takes her life so lightly.

"Tracy," she begins again, reluctant to leave. "When I was cleaning out Paul's office, after he died, I found your file and I wanted to do something. Anything. Something that would keep me connected to him, I guess. I know it doesn't make any sense at all to you. But will you let me help you? Will it be all right, I mean? Do you see, I'm not doing it just for you—I mean, really it's for me. You see, I had a daughter who'd be just about the age you were when, when all this happened. She was all we ever had between us, Paul and me, and I lost her. In some way just like you lost Tiffany. Just gone, out of your life—here one minute, gone the next." Tory feels her face flush with such a confession, feels foolish, awkward, bumbling in the presence of this stony-faced girl.

Tracy receives the words like they were falling onto a blank page, lining themselves up in neat, orderly lines and rows, not meaning anything extra, not having any weight.

"Do you see?" Tory asks her again. "I know this doesn't make any sense, but it's important, somehow. Would it be all right if I came to see you? Got somebody to help you? Would you let me do that?" Tory feels herself begging, waiting for Tracy to nod, to indicate in some way that she has heard any of the words. The voices in the background take over the space between them, and Tracy gives just a little nod.

"I guess so. I just don't want any false hope. I don't want to think I've got a chance and then you decide that it's not worth it. After I got my hopes up. That's what your husband did—told me I had a chance, and then, when I didn't, he lost interest. Wouldn't even fucking answer my letters. Like he could just throw me away, like some piece of shit that he didn't want to think about." Tracy stops for a minute, her voice loaded with rage, her face a replica of the newspaper photo. She draws a deep breath, lets it go, and Tory is rocked by the wave of resentment that fills the space between them. After a moment, Tracy begins again, her voice quieter now. "You know, I'm set for all this now, and I don't want any hope."

Tory nods, understanding feeling thrown away, disposable, useful for a time and then cast aside. She is unable to look at Tracy, fearful that she will reveal her own desolation. The background of voices and music blend into a wave of sound. She grasps the side of the cot, feels the cold of the metal frame, the coarse sheets, the thin prison blanket, and hangs on for fear that she might drown.

"Well, I think I understand. And I know something of false hope myself; my daughter . . ." She finds the courage to look Tracy full in the face. "I know how cruel false hope can be." Another pause. "Even if I could just come and see you. That would help me. I wouldn't get you into any trouble. I promise." Tory feels the beginnings of tears. She has no handkerchief with her. Tracy leans over to the dresser beside Sam's bed to a crocheted cover that resembles a top hat and pulls out a string of toilet paper.

"Oh, thank you." Tory smiles, dabs her eyes, and blows her nose. A strange, homely sound in the midst of the music, the cursing, the sounds of so many women slapping up against the bare concrete walls. "So," Tory starts again, "is it all right if I come?"

Tracy nods, a tight little nod just barely moving her head. The black curls make a little wave down her back.

Tory wants to touch her, to brush her hair, to feel something of substance beneath this pile of prison duck and save-the-whales T-shirt.

But Tracy turns, calls, "Sam, time."

Chapter 4

Tory jerks awake, her face wet with tears, her body shaking, the recurring image of the cage in the harsh black and white of an 8mm movie playing in her head, the raucous cries of "fucking rich white bitch" crashing against her temples. She reaches for the bedside lamp, switches it on, is comforted by the soft white light, the lemon yellow and cool northern blue of a Vermeer painting, the familiar, comfortable textures and shapes of her life that come into focus. She takes a deep breath, looks around the room for reassurance.

Knowing that she will not get back to sleep easily, she grabs her bathrobe and heads downstairs. Shadows follow her, creating a *danse macabre* against the wall. Tory opens Tracy's file as she waits for some milk to heat. The execution has been set twice before, over a period of ten years, she realizes. Each time, the Resource Center was able to get a stay—she can understand that much, even though the legal jargon mystifies her. She reads the pleadings of the CDRC, sees Jane Fillmore's signature, bold and sure, at the bottom of each one. Careful arguments, reasoned pleas, case references to others who have been where Tracy is now, on death row, waiting for execution, waiting for the state to commit the same act for which they are condemned. "Murdered by the state" is how Jane phrases it.

A sign in the hall outside Jane's office in Jackson read, "Why does the state kill people to prove that it's wrong to kill people?" It was surrounded by photographs of those prisoners currently on death row. Tracy's was there, surrounded by some thirty men.

Tory pours the milk, steaming now, into a mug—a souvenir of a trip Paul took to Vail. A skier on a slalom course, turning sharply around a flag, throws a sheet of snow into the air, toward the handle, like some giant wave. Crisp black letters remind Tory that Paul competed in the ABA's

1983 ski-for-justice weekend. Tracy would still have been in the Women's Prison then. Her first set of appeals exhausted, one execution date passed.

Thumbing through the newspaper clippings, Tory finds the story of the first stay. A rehearing and a successive habeas was granted, so the article says, by the Fifth Circuit Court of Appeals. But a later date reveals that both were overruled. Denied, says the headlines. Denied. A follow-up article on the inside pages recounts the crime, the trial, the legal maneuverings. And there's a brief mention of Paul's early defense strategies, calling him "a bright, young, court-appointed attorney, dedicated, but struggling against extremely difficult odds." Tracy would beg to differ.

The deputy attorney general, Lee Stokes, has argued that Tracy needs to die, deserves to die. Must die, he says. A woman who coldly, calculatedly killed must not be allowed to think that she can get away with such a crime. "Maybe in Massachusetts, up there where the perpetrator has all the rights, the victim none—maybe up there she could have gotten away with it. But not here, not in Mississippi." Tory remembers him; he ran against his old boss in the last election. Strong law-and-order man, Lee Stokes. Won by a landslide. Even had some support in the black community, Tory recalls. He was ahead of Paul in law school. Big, loud, blustery guy, even then. The article quotes Stokes as saying that if Tracy is not executed, she'll be paroled one day. "Believe me, folks, this woman *will* go free and kill again. You mark my words. She will do it again. The next time some man does her wrong, she'll slit his throat, too. Then claim self-defense, for God's sake. Self-defense! She slit his throat while he was sleeping. After she put something in his drink." Tracy, according to Stokes, is "a vicious killer, a menace to society, a threat to the well-being of the good folk of Mississippi."

Tory tries to fashion this description around the delicate woman in the cage, as she stirs the cocoa powder into the milk. The frail child-woman who has had no visitors, who fears that the strap from the electric chair will hurt her inflamed leg. Who wonders if the prison officials will shave around the wound that festers there.

A slick skin of dark brown covers the cocoa. Tory takes a sip, and it hangs against her upper lip. Wiping it away with her tongue, she reads on. The murder was "heinous, cruel, and atrocious," the court has said. Warranting the death penalty. A second round of pleadings followed because the court had failed to define those very words. But upon appeal and a resentencing phase, the original verdict was upheld. A second execution date had been set. For early last year.

By then, Tracy's case no longer made the front pages. Tucked away in the "Around the State" section, Tory reads of the second set of denials. These went all the way to the Supreme Court. There is no mention of Paul.

One reporter, a Melinda Faye Maddox, has done a series on death-row inmates. The story featuring Tracy—complete with several pictures of her in prison, the advertisement for her dancing act, a tiny snapshot of her daughter Tiffany—makes a plea for Tracy's life. "Only 17 at the time of the murder, Theresa Marie Magnarelli was a child thrown into the darkest corners of an adult world. Abandoned by her lover, disowned by her family, a child who had borne a child, she found no way out of the hole she had dug for herself. Surely, Theresa's desperation, her fear, her utter aloneness explain her action," Melinda had suggested.

An editorial several days later quotes Lee Stokes as saying that "nowadays everybody who commits a crime is supposed to be excused because they had a bad childhood, because somebody didn't love them enough, didn't take care of them. Because they are mentally retarded. Because the state or some such institution didn't recognize their problems in time. Whatever happened to the old-fashioned idea that you're responsible for your actions?"

Stokes was quoted once again, describing how Tracy put a sleeping pill in a cup of coffee Dwayne had bought at McDonald's and then waited, "like the cold-blooded killer that she is, waited for him to fall asleep. Then she slit his throat, almost cut his head off, and stabbed him nineteen more times. Just to make sure that he would stay dead." Tory shudders, looks again at Tracy's photograph.

The picture of her child, printed at the end of the article next to the one of Tracy at the women's prison, is of a little girl, kinky-haired and dark, but with her mother's features. Below, it reads, "Tiffany Jane Magnarelli, fifteen months old, now resides with her great-grandmother in Medford, Massachusetts."

Tory switches the light in her studio on, sets down her cocoa, pulls the artist's lamp down, and illuminates the canvas. Her shadow, large and rounded, plays against the bookcase. The portrait she began of Paul soon after he died has nearly dried. She taps the sleeve of his charcoal grey suit, finds it a little tacky, wipes her finger against the rag on the shelf.

The photograph she is copying is clipped to the top corner. He had it taken when he was on the board of governors for the bar association. A proper portrait, complete with soft backlighting and airbrushing around his eyes. He is seated at a mahogany plantation desk, and the book-shelves behind him are lined with the light brown, gold, and red spines of the *Southern Reporter.* Tory has substituted the Queen Anne chair from their living room, the end of the hunt board holding a tiny snapshot of Mary Vic, a vase of tulips, and the view out their bay window.

Paul has a faint trace of a smile, but overall, the picture is somber, judicial, perfect for the *Bar Journal.* They had gone to several of the conventions when he was on the board. She to be bored by fashion shows and luncheons, he to network, glad-hand, and backslap. The old Edgewater Gulf Hotel in Biloxi, with a live oak tree sprawling all around the entrance, its roots erupting through the sidewalk, had been completely refurbished by their last trip. She attended none of the meetings designed for the wives, but drove to Ocean Springs every day, to the art museum there, to soak up the beauty of Walter Anderson's paintings, to read of his tortured life. After seeing the "Little Room" where he covered the walls with murals, Tory retreated outside to the curb under another ancient live oak and wept. Anderson's wife discovered the paintings only after his death, when she broke the door down. Another wife who found out about her husband's hidden life after he was gone. The curator from the museum had followed Tory outside after a while, asked if she was all right, offered Tory a cup of tea.

"I'm fine," Tory told her. "Just swept away by all that beauty."

"I know," the woman replied. "Me, too. Some days I can hardly work." She patted Tory softly on the shoulder, stood by her for a few minutes. "Come back inside and get cooled off, if you need to," she added before leaving.

Tory sat on the curb for nearly an hour in the fierce late-June heat. She arrived back at the hotel with a splitting headache, unable to attend the banquet that night. Paul was exasperated, wondered why she had come at all. "You haven't said 'jack-shit' to a soul since we got here."

"You don't have to resort to vulgarities, Paul."

"Well, it's true, Tory. You amaze me; you come down here and hide out like some kind of . . . ostrich or something. You might as well have stayed at home." Tying his tie in front of the expanse of mirrors in the bathroom, he shook his head, seemed disgusted, and slammed the door hard when he left, never once looked at the prints for the bedroom that she had bought.

The easel is bathed in light, the studio dark. Paul's wide shoulders and neatly crossed arms seem right to Tory. The angle of his head true to the photograph. Tory smiles as she notices that he has worn his wide gold wedding band in this picture. Gave the right image, she guesses—solid, judicious, a man with family values. In reality, he often left it at home, in the little silver cuff-link box on his dresser. He said it gave him a rash to wear it in warm weather.

She layers the vacant face to approximate his skin tones, then steps back, looks at the canvas, examines Paul's faceless body, sitting quietly in their living room in a chair he never used. There is a certain amount of strength in the pose, a definite sense of personality. She defines the cheekbones, the line of the forehead. She re-creates the features by imagining the bones beneath them. The curve of the cheek from jaw to temple, shallow as a saucer, has just the faintest indentation of his dimple. The eyes in the photograph suggest curiosity, intelligence. Often, in life, they appeared black, absent of color, especially when he was angry. Hard, like obsidian, with a terrible fire lying underneath. But there were times that the soft brown, touched with flecks of amber, revealed something else, something playful, something immensely likable.

As she paints, Tory's mind is on Tracy. She tries to balance the newspaper clippings, the vicious killer drawn in the rhetoric, against the woman she visited only yesterday. Lee Stokes's version seems a hideous cartoon, lacking substance and knowledge. Can he have ever actually talked to Tracy?

The sun has risen by the time Tory finishes the upper part of the face. She steps back, looks steadily at Paul. He seems to mock her; the hint of playfulness hasn't translated onto the canvas. Tory feels shamed by his stare, reminded of all her failures of him, of the times she was less than a wife, less than a helpmeet. With a brush dampened with thinner, she wipes broad strokes of gesso across her night's work. The eyes disappear; Paul's condemnation fades away into the pale yellow of early morning.

☙

On the morning of May tenth, Tory rings the CDRC. Jane sounds tired, distracted.

"Should I call back later?" Tory asks.

"No. I was at Parchman until about three this morning. Another execution was scheduled, but we got a last-minute stay. I'm waiting for news from the courts, to see if it's upheld. So I'm just a little tired, that's all. What can I do for you?"

Tory summarizes her visit; leaves out the shouts, the profanity, Tracy's anger rising to the surface like cream; focuses on their conversation, on Tracy's willingness for her to help. "Well, maybe willingness isn't exactly the right word," Tory laughs, "but she said that I could come back." Tory wants Jane to understand that she survived it, is glad that she went. "I've been going through her file again, Jane." Tory waits to see if Jane will respond; she doesn't. "And, well, I was wondering if there's a chance that the court would consider that Tracy didn't get a fair trial?"

"We've tried to raise that issue before, Mrs. Gardiner." Jane's weariness is palpable.

"Oh?" Tory looks at Tracy's file alongside the month of May spread out before her. The square for Monday, May 8, holds her notation: "Visit to Parchman, 1:00 p.m." Mother's Day is less than three weeks away. There is no way she will finish Paul's portrait by then.

"Yes, we tried to reopen the case because . . ." Jane seems a little tentative now. "Because the original defense failed to object to the number of preemptive strikes used by the prosecution," Jane finishes with a bit more confidence.

"Original defense?" Tory asks. "Do you mean Paul?"

"Yes"—Tory thinks she hears a sigh—"I'm afraid so. You see, the prosecution used fourteen preemptive strikes on the *voir dire*. Only twelve are permissible. And that issue wasn't raised within thirty days after verdict and sentencing. So a rehearing on that was closed to us." Jane rushes through the facts; Tory wonders if she is trying to shield her from the truth that perhaps Paul wasn't the "bright young attorney" that the media portrayed.

"So, that was Paul's fault?" she asks again.

"Well, I won't say that. But he didn't file the objection in time, nor did he ask to be removed from the case so that we could step in and enter the pleas. Perhaps it was just a matter of not knowing. Perhaps the strain of the trial, your daughter's illness . . ." Jane seems intent on giving Paul the benefit of the doubt. Tory knows that lawyers stick together, remembers Paul's defense of a fellow member of the bar who was charged with jury tampering. How irate he was over the charges—said the fellow was only protecting his client. They had argued about the lines between responsibility to a client and morality. "For God's sake, Tory," Paul had all but shouted, "leave the law practice to me. You just tend to your flowers and your do-gooding!" Tory felt blistered by his comments. She had taken

Mary Vic to Memphis to the zoo the next morning, spent the night at the Peabody, shopped before she came home.

"Mrs. Gardiner?" Jane's voice breaks into Tory's thoughts.

"Yes, but I was wondering. Could you make an argument that Tracy didn't have a jury of her peers? There wasn't a single Roman Catholic on the jury, I bet. And only one woman. What if that woman didn't have any children? Then that couldn't possibly be her 'peers,' now could it?" Can Jane hear the sense of victory that she's feeling?

Jane is quiet for a minute. "Well," her only reply.

"I mean, people have gotten new trials on shakier grounds than that, I bet." Tory's words rush out, reveal her excitement. "And another thing. I was thinking last night—I couldn't sleep, spent the whole night thinking," Tory laughs, "like I was putting together a jigsaw puzzle, but this time, I was going to get a different picture. Do you know what I mean?" She takes a sip of coffee, grimaces; it's cold and bitter.

"Yes, I think I do; I'll look into these ideas, see if there's any precedent. I'm not sure, but it's worth a try." Jane sounds a little more positive now. As though Tory's involvement might be something other than just another headache.

"And, Jane, I was wondering," Tory starts again.

"Yes?"

"Is it possible that I might get the names of the jurors? You know, the woman who was on the jury, well, she might have been pressured by all those men to vote with them. She might really have wanted to vote for a life sentence. I know I would have. Could I get in touch with her? What if she wanted to vote against the death penalty? What if she felt threatened by the men? That's possible, you know. What if she said, now, to the court, that she was against executing Tracy? Would that make a difference?" Again, Tory cannot stop the tumble of words, cannot hide her feeling of discovery.

"I'll see what I can do," Jane says. "But it will be a few days, since this other case has precedence now."

"But Tracy only has until July 17th," Tory reminds her.

"I know that, Mrs. Gardiner. I am extremely aware of the time constraints. But right now, another person is much closer to being murdered than Tracy. His case has priority." Jane's anger overrides her weariness.

"I know, and I don't mean to add any more pressure, but I feel that somewhere, somehow, there has to be some hope for Tracy." And not the false kind, Tory thinks, not the false kind. But real, tangible, legal hope.

"I realize that. I'm just tired this morning. I've taken some notes on your suggestions, and I'll try to get back to you by the end of the week."

Tory holds the receiver to her ear after Jane hangs up. She meant to ask her about contacting Melinda Maddox. And about going to see the governor. She pulls out a fresh sheet of stationery, begins a list of things to do in one column, a list of legal ideas in another, copies them on the calendar, one for each day of each week until July. She copies "go to see the governor," "contact Melinda Maddox," "find the lady juror" into each square, finding solace in the repetition. Only when she's been successful will she mark through them.

She leaves the month of July empty, stares at the little square labeled "17." A Tuesday. Jane has explained that all executions in Mississippi are scheduled for Wednesday, 12:01 a.m. "They do it in the middle of the night. Not on a Monday or a Friday—that would spoil everybody's weekend." She had laughed, the same little brittle laugh that Tory remembers from the office. "Little gallows humor," she'd said. "Middle of the night to keep down the demonstrations," she'd continued.

Tory sits back when she has finished and smiles at the days. Each one assigned a task, each week filled, May and June now ordered and purposeful.

⁊

Tory plans a special brunch for Mother Gardiner on Mother's Day. After early church, they drive to the country club, park in the shade, and make a slow procession to the dining room. Mother Gardiner, dressed entirely in black, wears the corsage of white roses that Tory had delivered the day before. "I had hoped to finish a portrait of Paul for you," she explains once they're seated, overlooking the ninth green. "But I just cannot get the face right. I'm only copying the *Bar Journal* picture," Tory hears herself apologize, "but somehow the likeness has escaped me." Mother Gardiner looks away, and Tory wonders if Mother G. could ever understand that the art is not the problem, but that Paul himself refuses to come into focus.

"That's nice, Tory," Mother Gardiner finally answers. "A portrait would be nice." They sit in silence, watching the golfers ride up to the green, plant the tee, position, then approach the ball, plant their feet with short careful stamps, then swing, one after another. As much ritual as anything done before the altar. Intent on their morning's play, they do not talk, but watch the balls lofting into long arcs over the fairway. The men are ones that Paul used to play with—for business, he'd said. He settled many a case on the golf course, he'd added when Tory complained about his Sundays spent away from church and the family.

"Ma'am?" Tory hasn't heard what Mother Gardiner has said.

"I said, this may be the hardest day of my life," Mother Gardiner repeats. "I never thought I'd see a Mother's Day without Paul." She searches her purse for a handkerchief. "You know, when he was little, he called this 'our special day,' said it was made just for us. Paul Senior would go to church with us, then go to his office for the rest of the day. Gave the whole day to Paul and me. Sometimes we took a picnic to the farm, watched the goslings, ate some of Pearlie's fried chicken, imagined cloud pictures." She watches the golfers move away, smiles a sad little remembering smile. Tory wonders when this Paul vanished, when he became the consummate pragmatist, at what time he forgot how to look at his world with that child's eyes. Was it during his father's long-coming death, or in Korea—before she ever knew him, or was it Mary Victoria's illness? Had he ever been the person that Mother Gardiner saw? Or was he faking it, even as a child?

"I know how you feel," Tory says. "The first *everything* after Mary Vic died affected me the same way." She feels a great wave of pity for this frail woman, thinks that her heart might collapse under the weight of their combined losses. Losing children is so much harder than losing husbands.

"Mother G.," Tory begins, but the waitress interrupts them. They order, simply and carefully: fruit, cottage cheese, coffee, seven-grain toast. "You certainly don't have to eat like this," Tory chides Mother G. "You and Paul could eat anything and never gain an ounce." Mother Gardiner looks at Tory, seems to be amazed that she has spoken of such pedestrian things.

"It's all a matter of discipline," she answers. "I made up my mind in high school that I could never eat all I wanted if I was to keep my figure." The morning bears heavily on both of them. The air thick even on the air-conditioned patio. Tory involuntarily sits straighter, tightens the muscles in her stomach.

They eat in silence, each picking away at the strawberries, the bits of cantaloupe shaped into little balls.

"I was going to get some Louisiana strawberries for Paul," Tory says. "On the way to the hospital. He loved them sweet and tender, when they first came in."

Mother Gardiner nods, pushes her plate away, and sighs.

"I have a busy week coming up," Tory begins again. "The partners have drawn up the agreement for the sale of the practice. I guess I'll sign that one day this week. Then I will be going back to Jackson for several days."

"On business again?" Mother Gardiner asks.

"Sort of," Tory answers, forces herself to look at her mother-in-law. "Actually, I've been meaning to tell you about it."

"About what?"

"My business in Jackson."

"I thought you said it was something of Paul's, something that was unfinished."

"Well, it is, in a way."

Mother Gardiner's gaze is steady now—no searching for a handkerchief, no reveries. "In a way?"

"Yes." Tory takes a deep breath. "Remember the case that Paul was trying when Mary Vic was in the hospital in Memphis, the last time?"

Mother Gardiner nods.

"Well, the young woman who was convicted then, Theresa Magnarelli?"

She nods again.

"Her execution date has been set. All her appeals used up."

Mother Gardiner tilts her head just slightly, raising a question.

"I'm working with some lawyers in Jackson, trying to get her execution set aside."

"You're what?" The question pulls Mother Gardiner straight up in her chair. The wide brim of her straw hat trembles. "Tory, what business is that of yours?" Her voice is strong, definite.

"Well, it's not a matter of being my business. It's just something I wanted to do. Some way to finish something for Paul." Tory wonders if the false note in her voice is audible to Mother G.

"Paul finished that, Tory. He gave that wicked young woman the very best he could. Went more than the second mile, if you ask me. What could you possibly add?" The question stands, palpable, just above the coffee cups. "Except to get yourself caught up in all that hoopla that goes on every time something like this occurs." Her judgment, emphatic and solid, rocks Tory against her chair.

"Something like this? Mother G., they are going to execute that young woman. She's going to die. Be murdered, if you will, by the state." The words surprise Tory. They come from Jane Fillmore, not her.

"Murdered? I hardly think so. She is guilty of a crime, and the justice system has done everything it could for her. Paul offered her the very best that she could have gotten. And he was only paid about four hundred dollars, as I recall. You, Tory, have no obligation at all to her. You shouldn't get mixed up in such things."

"Well, I have decided to do what I can. I have been to Parchman to see her. And I promised her that I would go to see the governor on her behalf and see if he will grant her clemency." Tory pushes her words across the table, hoping that there will be some way for Mother Gardiner to receive them.

"Clemency! That's ridiculous. She was found guilty by a jury, Tory. It was a terrible blow to Paul. Why ever in the world would you want to reopen all this? Now? It could harm his memory for some." Mother Gardiner needs no handkerchief; there is no danger of weeping. She is all defense, Tory realizes. Then, a moment later, "You've been to Parchman? Tory! What has come over you?"

The golfers glide across the carefully clipped fairway, talking now, animated, approaching the next tee. What has come over her? she wonders. Slowly, she shakes her head. This isn't how she meant to tell Mother Gardiner. She wanted her to see that it was a noble thing she was doing, a continuation of Paul's life and work. But in reality, it's more about getting back to the place where her marriage began to splinter, fracture into the civilized, quiet divisions that she and Paul created.

"Come over me?" Tory asks. "Well, I don't know exactly. Except that I need something to do. Somewhere to *be* that seems important. Do you understand that, Mother G.?"

"No, I'm afraid I don't." The answer is as immune to questioning as her declaration about hats on Sunday.

"I see," Tory answers, wishing for the kind of eloquence that Paul had, wishing that she could make a closing statement and sway this resolute woman to change her verdict. "All I can ask then is that you grant me some kind of latitude, I suppose."

"Oh, Tory"—Mother Gardiner sighs, waves her hand into the air, exasperated; the gesture, the sound so like Paul—"you have always been so melodramatic!" She searches her purse for a lipstick, and with a steady hand etches the color, ashes of roses, on her thin lips. Rolling them together, she spreads the color evenly. "Really, you have so much to be thankful for, so many things you could do. Why choose something so, so . . . distasteful?"

Tory isn't sure which accusation to answer first. Pinned to the chair by the words, she works to catch her breath. The same scalding wound that

Paul's words could inflict spreads over her. "Mother Gardiner!" is the only thing she can say. The words sound strangled, pitiful, near weeping in their weakness.

"I'm sorry to be so blunt, Tory. But you do tend toward melodrama. Why, when Mary Vic was ill, you cut off the rest of your life, Paul's as well, hovering over her day and night—and you could have had help, as much as you wanted. You could have hired nurses round the clock if you'd just asked. Paul could easily have afforded that. But no, you did it all yourself. I felt, and Paul did too, that you were playing the martyr. And in some way, you tried to make him participate in that long, sad ordeal when from the beginning everybody told you that it was hopeless." Mother Gardiner does not look away when she finishes, but continues to hold Tory motionless in her chair.

"Martyr? Mother Gardiner, she was my child. She was ill; how could I have done other than what I did? There wasn't a choice." Tory waits to see if there's any hint of understanding on Mother G.'s face.

"Well, it seemed to us—to me, for certain—that you almost enjoyed her illness. Used it to withdraw, to hide in a little world where you and Mary Vic lived all alone. You shut Paul out, Tory. And now, you think you can do the same thing all over again. Plunge headlong into another hopeless case, live some kind of high drama there—and now, you want me to cheer you on, to applaud you for it." She stops, is quiet for a moment, looks out the window at another foursome approaching the green. "Well," she adds, standing, her purse pressed against her breast bone, "I cannot. I will not sanction such behavior, and I will offer you no help. This is the most ridiculous venture I could imagine, one born of your own needs—not mine, not Paul's, certainly not that young criminal's." She pushes her chair back from the table, turns, and finishes. "I need to go back to the nursing home, Tory. I am absolutely exhausted by all this."

She walks toward the door, her back erect, her chin tilted slightly. She hesitates at several tables, nodding her good-mornings to those seated along her route.

Tory, stunned, watches her struggle with the door. A young man—a college student, Tory thinks—hurries to help and chaperones her down the stairs. Tory signals for the check, can't figure the tip, signs the chit, and hurries out, ignoring the greetings she hears along the way.

After Tory ushers Mother G. to her room, she leans against the wall in the hallway, spent, her head aching. They did not speak on the drive from the country club. Mother G. looked out the window, shoulders angled against any overture Tory might make. She nodded her thank-you as Tory helped her from the car, pulled her elbow from Tory's grasp. As they entered her room, she removed her hat, placed the long hatpin with the black jet bead on its tip into a porcelain holder. "Tory, I think it's best that you work this whole thing out before we see each other again." Mother G. delivered her final decision and moved toward the door. Tory backed away, through the opening, to hear the door slam, the lock click.

Outside the locked door, rage overcomes her. Blind and unthinking, she moves down the hall. "Damn her," she whispers, "damn her, damn, damn, damn her and her son straight to hell."

"Mrs. Gardiner, are you all right?" a nurse's aide coming out of a room toward the end of the hall stops and asks. She puts her hand on Tory's shoulder, looks right at Tory, frowning. "You look right peaked."

"Yes, I'm fine, just fine. Just a little tired is all." Tory looks into her face, flat as a dinner plate, wide-featured, heavy along the jaw line—a country face, full of pity. Tears fill Tory's eyes. The woman moves closer, puts both arms around her, pulls Tory into her cushioned body. The tears come freely now, and Tory can feel her body shaking, wracked with sobs.

"There, there, Mrs. Gardiner, it'll be all right. You been through a lot, but it'll be all right." The aide pats Tory in time with her words, as though she were a colicky baby, and motion and a soothing tone would set the world right.

Tory pulls back, searches her pocket for a handkerchief. "I don't know what came over me. I'm fine, really I am. Just tired; a little too much pressure these days. I'll be all right; I don't mean to burden you." She dabs her eyes, checks the handkerchief for mascara, tries to smile at this kind woman.

The aide shakes her head. "You don't have to explain nothing to me; it's all right to cry every once in a while. Does a body good."

"Yes, I suppose it does," Tory agrees, wondering if Mother G. has ever cried, has ever felt less than in control, has faltered for an answer, has been less than sure of her words or her actions. "You gonna be all right now?" the aide asks again.

"Yes, I'm sure I will. Thank you for offering me a shoulder." Tory tries to keep her voice light, her tone offhand.

The aide watches her for a moment. "It's all right to grieve, Mrs. Gardiner; it's as much a part of living as smiling." With that, she turns, heads into another room, and Tory hears her greet the resident, "Mrs. Ross, you looking good this morning."

A message on her answering machine from John Tolliver tells Tory that the papers for the sale of the practice are ready for her to sign. "Could you come by on Monday around 2:30 for us to finish things up? We'll talk about everything then," he promises. Short, sweet, and to the point, Tory thinks. A second recording is from Jane Fillmore: "Tory, please call me on Monday before you leave for Parchman. Thanks." Tory checks her calendar, pencils in the meeting with John and Sam, makes a note to call Jane. Her days are filling up, she thinks. She will need something to occupy her mornings now that visiting Mother G. is not among her chores. She said that she had a choice. That seems so radical to Tory. Choices involved clothes, paint colors, dinner-party menus. Caring for your child was not a choice.

In her bedroom, she tosses the books that Mother G. offered for solace in the trash can, then pulls them out, takes them to the garbage can outside, watches their weight fall against the coffee grounds and limp lettuce leaves. "There," she says to no one at all, and brushes her hands together.

Back in her studio, she examines Paul's faceless portrait. Arms folded, sitting in the chair he never used, a small watercolor of Mary Vic smiling over his shoulder, a bouquet of lemon-yellow tulips lighting up the background, he waits, expressionless. And Tory waits with him, wondering which face will appear. The dreamy child, the fearless pilot, the driven attorney, the dutiful son, or the careless husband? Will his glittering public self emerge, or his dark, private, adulterous one? She isn't sure she will recognize either of them, and cannot quite figure out where they all came from, which one she married so long ago, and what she lost in the process.

The anger of the morning begins to rise, a bilious gorge in her throat. Leaning into the bucket of paint brushes, Tory gags, brings up the remnants of the morning's brunch. She holds her head as she convulses again and again, until there is nothing left. Spent, she rests on the floor of the studio.

Later, Tory washes and dries the last of the brushes, rinses the bucket again. Then squeezes a blob of white paint onto her palette and chooses a wide, splayed sable brush. Methodically, back and forth, she presses it into the paint; traces of last week's browns dissolve, turning the white into a rich cream. In the upper-right-hand corner, she begins with long, even strokes. With each steady stroke, she eradicates Paul.

Chapter 5

Tory rings Jane Fillmore's office as soon as it opens. Her secretary answers, says that Jane is on her way to Parchman for the last visit with the man whose stay was not upheld. Tory feels a wide space open in her stomach. "Not upheld?" she asks. "What does that mean?"

"The Fifth Circuit ruled on the stay, didn't hold it to be valid." The secretary's voice is practiced, as though this kind of news comes easily for her now. Tory remembers the flower-child woman and wonders how long such numbing takes.

"So, what does that mean?" Tory says, then realizes she's just asked that.

"Means that unless the Supreme Court overrules the decision, that the execution will take place"—the voice wavers a bit now—"on Wednesday morning, 12:01 a.m." The flatness returns.

"Oh," is Tory's only answer. She reaches for the desk chair, pulls it out, and sits slowly, listening to the sound of the open phone line. "Oh," she says again.

"'Oh' is right," the secretary adds. Again, there is silence between these two, brought on by the exchange of such life-and-death information. Tory wonders if she's being melodramatic. "Mrs. Gardiner?"

"Yes?"

"Jane wanted me to tell you that Tracy is in the infirmary, and that makes it a good time to visit. No difficulty about getting you MSU clearance as long as she's in there."

"Is she sick?"

"Well, I guess so. They don't usually move death-row inmates unless there's something pretty major. They create problems for security. Most times they treat them in the cell, but they moved her over the weekend. Looks like she'll be there for about a week."

"What's wrong?"

"Jane didn't say, just said it was a good time for you to visit. That she'd clear you when she got to Parchman."

"Thank you," Tory says. "I'll leave first thing in the morning. I have a meeting this afternoon at my husband's office, then I'm free to leave."

⌇

Paul's office building, a renovated Victorian which was the childhood home of a friend of Tory's, stands apart, remote in the afternoon sun, not quite accessible somehow. Tory tries to bring it into focus, to ground it somewhere in the life that was hers only seven weeks ago. Seven, the number of completion. The seven deadly sins, the seven virtues, the seven wonders of the world, and a nice, feminine shoe size. What if she's losing her mind, jumping from thought to thought like this, everything all jumbled together, unorganized and random, like an accident?

Paul's old parking space behind the office is filled. A little red hatchback with a bumper sticker for a Jackson radio station occupies it, the sign designating it as Paul's obscured. John's Volvo and Sam's Lincoln flank it, but the space marked for Mattie Carson is empty. Tory pulls up to the sign and shuts the motor off. It is only 2:15. She wonders if she should drive around the block once more, try to collect her thoughts, to figure out how to get John and Sam to release some of her trust money to help Tracy, if she should need it.

A quick check in the rearview mirror reveals dark circles beneath Tory's eyes—the strain of her sleepless nights beginning to show. She lifts her hand to fluff her hair, notices a smudge of paint on her index finger. She dampens it with her own spit, rubs it against her thumb, but it holds, like a stain.

As she leaves the car, slings her purse over her shoulder, she notices that the curtains at the window of Paul's office move just slightly, as if a gentle wind had come up from the east. Someone moved in already? A new partner so soon?

The reception desk and front room are empty. Canned music fills the air; a hint of gardenias comes from somewhere. Tory finds a seat, flips through a magazine, sees nothing. A phone rings in the back on the private line of one of the partners. Paul had one, but Tory can't remember the number. Unlisted, and offered only to a few moneyed clients, herself,

96

and his mother, of course. She's certain that she knew it once, but it refuses to surface from the past.

"Tory." John strides across the room, extends his hand, then brushes a brief kiss against her cheek. His touch, his proximity startle her. Involuntarily, Tory pulls back. "I didn't realize you were here. Sorry to keep you waiting." John smoothes over her sudden movement.

"I just arrived," Tory assures him, regaining her equilibrium. "Where's Mattie?"

"Taking some time off. Family needs her, and we're doing some reorganizing around here. Makes her a little nervous, I think. Old dog/new tricks syndrome." John laughs, then puts his hand beneath Tory's elbow to guide her down the hall. She stops in front of Paul's office door.

"I want to go in here, John, for just a minute. For old time's sake, I guess." Tory is surprised at her ability to lie. "I'll be right out. I'll meet you in the library." John looks surprised. He puts his hand on top of Tory's as she reaches for the knob.

"Tory," he begins, holding her hand, pulling just slightly against her. "We're using Paul's office for a paralegal we've just hired. We moved his desk and files into storage after you cleared his personal things away." John has a serious hold on Tory's arm now. "We felt that we needed to get the practice moving along in a somewhat new direction—computerizing the files, things like that. We'd talked about it before Paul's accident. Realized that we needed to make the practice as efficient, as profitable as we could." He hesitates, a gentle pressure against Tory, turning her toward the library. She resists. He moves just slightly in front of the door to Paul's office. "We need to get you your money and relieve you of all this business stuff. You don't need to bother with such things." He is definitely keeping her from entering now, Tory realizes.

"Business stuff isn't a bother to me, John. I'm on my own now. It's time for me to learn how to take care of myself." The flat pronouncement, as positive as anything Mother Gardiner ever said, startles Tory by its certainty.

John shrugs, releases her arm. "Sam and I will be waiting in the library."

Tory pushes open the door as John makes his way down the hall, shaking his head. Sitting behind a new contemporary-blond desk, absorbed in a computer screen, is Debbi. She looks up, and both women grab a quick intake of air.

"Mrs. Gardiner." Debbi speaks first.

"Yes," Tory answers. Mrs. Gardiner, indeed.

"Well," Debbi begins again, then a faint flush reddens her face. The bandages are gone, her arm released from the sling. She wears a chic business suit, her hair cut stylishly short now. "How are you?"

"I'm well. Yourself?"

"Oh, I'm fine. The doctor says I've made a complete recovery." The flush deepens. Tory is aware of the office music in the silence.

"Well, that's good." Tory stares at this young woman, trying to connect her to the weeping girl beside Paul's bed. The one promising to be back; the one who shared his last meal, spent his last night with him. The girl who wore her seat belt.

"You here to sign the papers?"

"Yes. Here to finish up the last of the business. Paul's business, that is."

"Mr. Tolliver and Mr. Bench told me."

"I see," Tory says.

"I'm . . . working here now. They are training me to be a paralegal. Much easier work than court reporting."

"I see." Tory's answer is firmer now, more definite.

The music is a show tune now, Tory realizes. Something from *Guys and Dolls*, she thinks. One that Adelaide sings. About a person could be getting a cold.

Debbi tries to look back at the computer screen, but Tory holds her in place, much as Mother Gardiner had done yesterday. "You must feel right at home here, Debbi."

"Well, yes, ma'am, I do. I had done a good bit of work for the firm when . . ."

"Yes, when Paul was alive."

"Yes, ma'am."

Tory nods, keeps her focus steady. "So, now you've moved into his old office." It is not a question.

Debbi nods, looks away. "His desk and things are in storage, I think. John . . . that is, Mr. Tolliver and Mr. Bench are thinking that it'll be a while before they take in another partner, and then they might move closer to the square, find some bigger office space in a year or so."

Tory nods now. "I see." Will they sell this building, after they buy her out?

"I need to get back to this file, if you don't mind." Debbi swings her chair around, taps several keys, seems intent on the screen.

"I'm sure you do," Tory answers. "But, Debbi, just one more thing before I go." She hears her own voice outside herself float into the afternoon air, sliding atop Adelaide's lament. "I knew all about you and Paul. It was no surprise. Don't feel that you were anything new." Again, her facility for lying surfaces, and Tory is amazed at the ease with which she delivers such a hurtful statement.

Debbi looks stricken, scalded. The flush rises, then fades quickly. "Mrs. Gardiner!"

"Yes—Mrs. Gardiner, indeed," Tory says, and turns to leave.

❧

John explains the buyout to Tory—slowly, carefully, as though she is a dim-witted child. Tory sighs often and looks out the window. The hard, cruel place that she has discovered deep within herself makes it difficult to sit still, to listen, to pretend that she has any interest in what he is saying. "Tory, you do understand how this will work? How you will be paid in monthly installments for the next ten years? That it will save you taxes in the long run, allow us to pay you the full face value of Paul's half of the practice, as well as for the building?"

"John, I do understand. I have understood it the last two times you've gone over it. Just give me the papers. I will let my lawyer check them, then I'll sign them, if everything is in order, and have them back to you by the end of the week." Tory slides the stack of documents toward her, rolls them into a cylinder, and tucks them into her purse. Her lawyer? Who in the world is she talking about? Jane Fillmore? Tory wonders where this comment came from. Her comment to Debbi was sheer revenge. Giving her some kind of pleasure. But this statement, summoned up from somewhere, is as declaratory as a gospel reading. Both partners straighten in their chairs.

"Your lawyer?" John asks.

"Yes, a firm in Jackson that I've been working with. I thought it best to have a second opinion." Tory stands to signal that the meeting is over, fearful that more questions will reveal her deception.

"Well, Tory, is it a firm we've worked with? Someone Paul had associated on his cases? We could just fax everything to them if you want us to." John seems flustered, unsure of how to handle Tory now. She enjoys his discomfort, offers him no more information.

"No, it's no one you know, I'm sure. I found them on my own. It didn't seem right to use any of Paul's old friends. Might be imposing on friendship somehow." She waits, hand on the door, then repeats, "I found them on my own."

Outside, in the car, the key will not fit into the ignition. Tory's hands are shaking; the ruffle of papers in her purse spills out onto the floorboard. She glances at the office windows, all the curtains pulled shut against the afternoon sun. No one peeps to watch her leave, to watch her move out of the wake that she has created. She takes three deep breaths, wonders if she will hyperventilate. But, she thinks, that would be melodramatic.

In a moment, a calm descends upon her, and she slides the key into the ignition, hears the purr of the engine, and backs the car away from the curb. She looks at her watch. If she hurries, she can pack the car and leave for Parchman before sundown. Surely there's a motel in Drew where she can spend the night. She will pack a basket of food to take to Tracy. Some fruit and fresh flowers.

ॐ

A neon riverboat, with flashing yellow spokes on the paddle wheel, announces the Delta Queen Motel, daily and weekly rates. Underneath, a "Vacancy" sign flashes intermittently, as though it may have a short in it. Tory pulls in next to the office and goes into the little lobby. The clerk greets her, asks her if she has a reservation.

"No," she replies.

"You with the press?" he asks, not looking up from the register.

"No."

"You need the room until after the execution?" He looks at her now, his face wiped clean of any expression. The reflection of the neon from outside paints his face and hair a dull, oriental patina.

"What?" Tory isn't sure she heard him correctly.

"Execution tomorrow night—or Wednesday morning, early—down at Parchman. Motel's almost full with reporters, folks from the TV stations in Jackson, Memphis, even Atlanta. Some of the family is staying here too, I think. Registered under assumed names, of course." He looks steadily at Tory now. She returns his stare, as if to ask him if she looks like the relative of somebody on death row. Then wonders how somebody like that might look.

"No, no, I'm not here for that. Just on business."

"I've only got a single left. You by yourself?"

Tory nods.

He slaps a 4x6 preprinted card on the counter. "Fill this out, pay in advance, credit card or cash. No checks."

She finishes filling out the card, hands him her credit card; he completes the transaction and hands her the key. "Room 226, upstairs at the back. Checkout time is noon tomorrow. If you're gonna be here for another day, leave a message at the desk in the morning."

"Thank you," Tory says, picks up the key, and turns to leave.

"And have a nice day," he calls to her as she leaves.

Driving around to the back of the motel, Tory realizes that this is the first time she has ever booked a motel by herself. When she went to the Peabody in Memphis, she simply called Mattie, who arranged everything. When she traveled with Paul, she waited in the car while he organized their stay. She would watch him through the window, chatting with the attendant on duty, getting the best room in the house—usually for less money, arranging for morning coffee and a paper, finding out the best places to eat. So easy with people, so certain that he was welcome, confident that those who served him were glad to do so, were honored by the bits of himself that he offered.

Tory struggles up the stairs with her luggage, searches for the light switch once she gets the door open, and blinks as the overhead light pops on. She hates the lighting in motels, finds it merciless and tawdry. The room is furnished in standard cheap-motel style. Polyester tufted bedspread, matching curtains. Anonymous.

After hanging up her dress for tomorrow, she brushes her teeth, creams her face, and collapses on the bed. The sounds from the highway and a distant television remind her of the distance she's come.

A slow filtering of Delta morning sun awakens Tory. The last time she slept in her clothes was in the hospital in Memphis, curled beside Mary Vic, aware throughout the night of the IV tubing connecting her small daughter to a drip. She will spend today, or at least part of it, in another hospital. Next to another frail young woman.

The motel coffee shop is crowded. A hostess asks Tory if she's in a hurry. She nods. Then, "Would you mind sharing a table with someone?" Tory shakes her head and follows the woman through a sea of tables filled with people—mostly men, all white—to a spot in the corner where the lone black in the place, a young woman, is drinking coffee and reading a paper. "Is this OK?" the hostess asks them both.

"Fine with me," the woman answers, and Tory nods again.

"I'll have Tina bring you some coffee," the hostess promises, and hurries away to seat a group of men who are making loud conversation beside the counter.

"I hope you don't mind," Tory begins.

"I said it was fine," the woman answers.

"Good," Tory answers, wishing that she had bought a paper on her way in. Her coffee arrives, and she adds the sweetener and cream with elaborate care, stretching the action out in slow motion. Her tablemate refolds her paper, signals Tina for more coffee, and looks at Tory for the first time. "So, you here for the execution?"

Tory shakes her head, feeling it hard to talk with the noise of the crowd. For the most part, they seem jovial, like comrades in arms. She wonders how they could possibly be so carefree, so nonchalant, so absolutely normal if they've come for "it." The word sticks in her mind.

"Well, that's what brings most people to Drew on a Tuesday."

"Really?" is all Tory can think of to say.

"Yep, Mississippi still believes that frying 'em will work some kind of magic, I guess." The woman shakes her head, points to the headline in the *Clarion Ledger* that announces "Convicted Child Molester Will Die Tonight." The waitress brings more coffee for Tory, breakfast for the woman. "By the way, I'm Melinda Maddox, a reporter, and the execution is what brings me here. I guess I forget that there might be another reason for being in Drew. Sorry." She flips her napkin into her lap and begins to swirl maple syrup on a stack of pancakes.

"Oh," Tory says, "I know you."

The young woman looks up, startled.

"You do?"

"Yes, you wrote a series of articles about people on death row. In the paper, a little while ago. I read them all."

"You did?" Melinda smiles, fork in midair. "Well, this one is a real political football."

"How's that?" Tory asks. "I mean, a child molester. If there is a case for capital punishment, I would think this might be it." She reaches for the paper. "Do you mind?"

"Help yourself."

Tory reads the headline again, skims the article, focusing on the facts: Tommy Ray Soniat, age 32, has been convicted on two counts of murder, one out west somewhere, one in Mississippi. The first was his high-school girlfriend, the second a three-year-old girl that he raped, sodomized, strangled, and left in a dumpster. She looks at the photographs of the two victims: a pretty blond teenager, and a toddler with a head full of dark curls. The picture of Tommy Ray reveals a slim, dark-complexioned young man in a prison jumpsuit, manacled—handcuffs attached to a chain around his waist, his ankles in leg irons. He looks dazed. Tory thinks that might be how somebody high on drugs looks.

"His crimes certainly are 'cruel, heinous and . . . ' what's the other word they use?"

"Atrocious."

"He seems to qualify on all counts. After all—"

"Except," Melinda interrupts, "he's only asking for life without the possibility of parole. This guy has never been evaluated by a psychiatrist. Never. The prison in Arizona paroled him without doing any kind of testing. Tommy Ray knows he's sick. Horribly abused as a child, minimal IQ, almost no education—a real throwaway. He told me that he wouldn't take a parole, even if it were offered. Said he is afraid of what he might do. He's asked for help, time and again. Said the scenes are still so real in his mind that he can only sleep if he takes a sleeping pill." She shakes her head. "He told me that some days his despair is so great, he thinks that he will die from the memories. But our governor has his eye on Washington, on the Senate. He wouldn't even meet with the clemency board. Sent some WASP in a four-hundred-dollar suit, an old fraternity buddy, to the hearing. That jerk had about as much understanding of a guy like Tommy Ray as . . ." Melinda stops, glances away from Tory, and the silent comparison separates the women as surely as their skin color once would have.

Tory looks away, then takes another look at the paper. Is there a way to balance those two victims against Tommy Ray's agonized past? Is there a scale here, like the ones she studied in composition to create a picture that makes sense? Is it possible to create a solvable equation?

"Besides," Melinda starts again, covering the awkward silence, "it's been fourteen years since the last crime. Tommy Ray confessed, became a member of a prison congregation that a local priest formed, and the priest has tried to intervene. He made a beautiful plea for Tommy Ray's life, says the man has really repented, even despaired of his crimes, that he's changed, converted, been saved—whatever you want to call it. But"—she shakes her head—"it's all so damned political." With that, she goes back to her breakfast.

Tory looks away, troubled; takes a sip of coffee; gives Melinda time to take a bite and chew. She cannot miss this chance for help that has been dropped into her lap. "You see, I followed your articles because I have a special interest in one of those people . . . there."

"On death row?"

"Yes."

Melinda cocks her head just slightly, and a string of syrup connects her fork to her pancakes.

"Really?" she answers, and Tory can hear the disbelief in her voice.

"Yes. In fact, I have been meaning to get in touch with you. To see if I could enlist your help."

Melinda takes a bite, cuts into a sausage patty flecked with the deep red of hot peppers.

"So, who's your man?'

"My man?"

"Yeah, who are you taking a—what did you call it?—'special interest' in?"

"Oh, it's not a man. It's a woman. Theresa Marie Magnarelli. Do you remember her case?"

"Sure, only woman on death row. Really got screwed by the system. She deserves a medal, if you ask me. But the good ole boy network fucked her over but good. Incompetence in the lower court, a DA running on a strong law-and-order platform, her past a little shady, black-white couple. Another political football. She was a goner before that trial even opened."

A sweet kind of pain over the "incompetence in the lower court" part settles on Tory, and she pauses a minute to relish it. Melinda takes another bite of her pancakes. Tory's breakfast arrives, and she scrapes the cream cheese off the bagel, thinking that she told the waitress not to put anything on it.

Melinda drains her coffee. "So, how'd you get involved with Tracy?"

"It's a long story. But part of it has to do with the incompetence you spoke about. My late husband was her lawyer."

"I see. You trying to clear his memory, or reveal him for the son-of-a-bitch that you discovered him to be?"

"Did you know Paul?"

"No, I just know men." Melinda has a curious half-smile on her face, and Tory isn't sure if she's kidding or not.

"Well, I started out trying to take care of all of his unfinished business." That's not exactly true, but where does all this really begin? Sometime when Paul failed her and she pulled away? Melinda is watching her, waiting. "But the deeper I get into it, the more I believe that serious injustice has been done. Her initial counsel was inadequate. The local papers made a hero out of Paul, but his inadequacy or carelessness or . . . or something"—Tory feels herself stumbling, trying to decide what sort of blame to lay on Paul—"whatever it was, have made her appeals much more difficult. Then I got in touch with Jane Fillmore at the CDRC, read your article, then went to visit her—and now I feel compelled to do something. To undo the wrongs that have been committed. At least to get her a new trial."

"Well," is all Melinda answers.

"It's looking pretty hopeless right now. Jane is trying to find a way to get some new stuff started, but she doesn't sound too optimistic. That's why I wanted to get in touch with you. To see if you could write some more about her case, show how she really didn't get a fair trial." The excitement and hope is obvious in Tory's voice.

"Sure," Melinda answers. "I always follow these cases."

"But, I mean more than just the usual coverage. I want you to give it a lot of publicity. Mount a campaign in the press to pressure the governor into clemency." Melinda looks at her watch. "I know you have a lot to do," Tory says, "but this case really is special. You must help."

"Mrs. . . . ."

"Gardiner, Tory Gardiner."

"Yes, Mrs. Gardiner, everybody on death row is special to somebody. I assure you I plan to write about this case. I always cover capital murder." Her coat on, her briefcase in hand, Melinda turns to leave, then hesitates. "And I'd be doing it for her, not to help you clean up an old mess."

Tory feels stung, chastised, a schoolgirl again. She reaches for Melinda's arm.

"Oh, for God's sake, it's not for me. How selfish do you think I am? I want you to help for Tracy's sake. I'm not asking anything for me. I'm not the one at stake here." Tory feels the anger rise in her voice, the old accusations from Mother Gardiner restated by this young black woman. "Jane is so overworked; Tracy has no family. She hasn't gotten a single piece of mail in thirteen years. She has a daughter she hasn't seen since she was a baby."

"I know all that." Melinda picks up her check and turns to go. "Why don't we meet here for supper, about six-thirty? We can talk about it then. I have an interview with the warden this morning." Melinda extends her hand; Tory grasps it like a lifeline. They stand like a sculptured piece, watching each other intently, the clatter from the other diners falling around them, enveloping them in white noise. "I'm glad to see that you really mean business, Mrs. Gardiner. See you tonight." She slides her hand away, slipping her slender brown fingers free.

෩

The guard at the gate gives her car a thorough search, "Sorry about this, ma'am," he says, "but things is tighter than a drum around here. Warden told us to double-check everybody."

"Oh, that's fine; I understand," Tory assures him as he pokes a slender metal rod in between the seats. He empties her parcel, fans the books, shakes the bath oil and the box of candy, drives a thin nail into the soaps, takes the basket of fruit apart, squeezes with thick hairy fingers the produce she chose so carefully, then runs everything through a scanner. He calls the office, finds that Tory has clearance for the infirmary, waves her through, telling her to park at the administration building and that someone will take her from there.

Tory waits outside Carol Monk's office, holding her parcel on her lap—like the ten-o'clock scholar outside the principal's office, she thinks. The guard has handled the contents unmercifully, and Tory thinks that she can feel the bruises on everything in the sack.

The books on meditation and finding inner peace, the little luxuries neatly wrapped and tied suddenly condemn her. Whatever was she thinking? What difference could a few niceties make to Tracy? She could have assembled this parcel for a friend in the hospital, someone who had just had a hysterectomy, or to welcome home a neighbor from a trip to Europe.

Carol Monk introduces Tory to a trusty (Zack, for Zacharias) who will take her to the infirmary, asks Tory to check out with her office when she's ready to leave. Tory agrees, follows Zack to the parking lot, is surprised when he opens the truck's door for her. Such manners in this place seem pitiful, somehow, and cause a catch right above her heart.

Dust boils up in little tornadoes behind the prison truck. Tory holds on to the door handle to keep her balance as they drive along a bumpy dirt road to the infirmary. A black stripe running down the outside of Zack's prison trousers indicates that he is trustworthy. Tory can think of nothing to say.

Men on horseback, carrying rifles, line the road, and the gangs of field hands dot the landscape as far as she can see. Zack adjusts the dial on the radio, tunes in a rock-and-roll station, and keeps time with his right index finger. He slues the truck into a driveway and stops under a dust-covered oak tree. "Here we are," he announces.

Tory scrambles to get her things gathered up, thanks him as he sweeps open the truck's door, like the doorman at the Peabody. She wonders if she should tip him as she steps into the gritty Delta afternoon.

The acrid smell of cotton poison from the morning's crop-dusters weighs the air down around her. Her nose burns and her eyes water. That smell is enough to kill somebody. Two guards lean against the infirmary door, armed and smoking. They ask to see her pass. Tory shows it, and they open the door for her.

Inside, the smell is the same as every hospital. Disinfected and sterile. A nurse comes from behind the desk to ask if she may be of help.

"Yes, I've come to see Tracy Magnarelli," Tory tells her. The nurse, too, asks for her pass. She takes it from Tory and examines it carefully, eyes her package, waits for a minute, then says, "Right this way."

Tory follows her down the hall into a long ward with barred windows which extend across the back of the building. The cubicles are separated by curtains, just like the intensive care unit in Kosciusko.

"She's right here." The nurse points to an area, again guarded by two men with guns. "She's a bit weak today and has been sleeping quite a bit. They've given her some pain killers, so she may not stay awake for a long visit."

Tory flashes her pass to the guards without their asking; they nod, and she pulls back the curtain. Tracy is sleeping. Tory is startled by how thin she is, how drawn and pale she looks against the white hospital sheets. Her hair spreads out like a fan against the pillow. An IV drips slowly in rhythm with the hum of farm machinery outside.

Tory sets her bag down, unfolds a chair, and pulls it up to Tracy's bedside. The scrape of the metal legs against the concrete floor disturbs Tracy, and a frown crosses her face. She makes a little cry, then settles back into sleep. Quietly, Tory pulls one of the books from the bag, thumbs through it, dog-earing the pages that deal with hope and confidence. She reads until Tracy stirs.

"Good morning, Tracy," she says.

"Oh, it's you. Hi."

"How are you feeling?"

"All right, I guess. The antibiotic must be working. My fever's just about gone." Her smile is weak, like Mary Vic's when she'd battled an infection. Tory reaches toward Tracy, wants to touch her, wants to brush her hair against the pillow. But the same invisible barrier that she felt on her first trip stops her hand in mid-stroke.

"The nurse says you've been sleeping a lot. Fever makes you do that."

Tracy nods, struggles to keep her eyes open. "Yeah, the infection on my leg." She lifts her hand, points.

"I know. Would you like me to get you something to eat? I brought some fruit, some cheese and crackers. And . . ." Tory lifts the flowers out of the sack. Some of them have wilted a bit. "I'll see if I can get a vase or a jar from the nurse." Tracy nods and closes her eyes.

Tory flashes her pass, gets a plastic urinal from the nurse, and fills it with water from the bathroom. As she arranges the bouquet, she notices that Tracy naps in fitful starts, jerking awake, then fading again.

"I didn't think you'd come back," she says.

Tory looks up from her reading. "I said I would."

"I know, but lots of people say something and then don't do it."

"That's true," Tory agrees. "I hope you don't mind."

"No, I don't mind. But I don't get it—why you're doing this. There's nothing in it for you." A hint of the belligerence, the old Tracy, the one in the newspaper photograph, appears.

"Well, there is something in it for me. I told you that, but even so, I suppose that people can do something even when there's nothing in it for them, don't you?"

"I guess." Tracy closes her eyes, then jerks wide awake with a shake that rattles the entire bed. "That happens all the time now. I get just about asleep, then my head starts playing tricks on me." It's not an apology, but a flat statement, like how many days in the year, how many cups in a pint. And there is no hint of self-pity. "I see him and my daughter. He was standing over her, her diaper was off. She should have been potty-trained by then." That's the apology, Tory realizes. "But with turning tricks and dancing every night, I never could be with her long enough." Tracy lets out a long sigh. "Dwayne agreed to take care of her, until I could find a day-care or night-care, whatever . . . But there he was, dick stretched out like some soldier at attention, looking ten feet long next to my little baby. Well, you know what I thought."

"Oh, Tracy, oh, my God!" Tory drops her book, reaches to stroke her hand, but Tracy turns toward the window, closes her eyes, grimaces, then fades back into sleep.

Tory retrieves her book, opens it, but the words blur into a single string of black. I know I've read everything about this trial, Tory assures herself. There is no mention anywhere in the transcripts or notes of suspected child abuse. That would have been a mitigating circumstance, she's certain of that. And what must Tracy have felt, thinking that Dwayne was... was doing such things? Tory shudders, remembers Tommy Ray's crime, the horror of all this information rushing over her like a black wave. Any mother would have done what Tracy did, any mother. Tory is certain of that.

Tory leans back in her chair, exhausted, tries to erase what Tracy has told her. The smell of freshly poured disinfectant and the hiss of a mop brushing the floor bring memories of other hospitals. St. Jude's in Memphis, Montfort-Jones in Kosciusko, the Dana Farber in Boston with her hairless mother, the cardiac unit in Jackson with her difficult father. I'm always the healthy one. Always the caretaker. But what kind of care can she offer to this woman? Where can she find words of comfort that don't feel like a sentimental Hallmark card?

"So, you think they'll do it?" Tracy wakes, startles Tory, who has been reading a meditation on eternal security.

"Do what?"

"Kill Tommy Ray tonight?"

"Well, I don't know, but the motel was full of reporters. I met one who had an interview with the warden this morning. Jane Fillmore's working hard on his case, too." Her words sound hollow and echo in Tory's head.

"They say all the lights dim when they do it," Tracy says. Another statement of fact, a lesson in electricity, in voltage, in resistance overload.

"Tracy, don't spend your energy thinking about such things," Tory answers, aware that she sounds prim and prissy, like a schoolmarm.

"What do you suggest that I think about?" Tracy's voice is stronger now, bitter. She stares at Tory, her mouth drawn into a tight little line.

"You're right. I'm sorry." Tory slides a silver bookmark, monogrammed with her mother's initials, into the crease of the book; takes a deep breath; and begins. "Look, Tracy, there is no way on God's green earth that I can understand what you are going through." She hesitates, wavers—then, "But I am committed to doing everything I can to keep you from being..."

"Murdered by the state." Tracy finishes the sentence for Tory.

Tory nods.

"That's what Jane Fillmore calls it. Murdered by the state."

"That's what I call it too, Tracy." Tory's voice is quiet, and she realizes that she means it, in spite of Tommy Ray Soniat, in spite of "cruel, heinous, atrocious," in spite of Mother's Gardiner's righteous stance. Murdered by the state does not solve the equation, does not bring the composition into balance.

Later, the nurse offers to bathe Tracy. "No, I don't want you touching me." She struggles to sit up, to protect herself from this woman. "You fucking almost killed me when you changed the bed this morning. Jerking around on me like I wasn't even human."

"Well, excuse me, miss." The nurse turns on her heel. "I was only trying to be helpful."

"Get out of here," Tracy calls to her as the nurse pulls the curtains back in place.

"Anything you say, missy," slides in over the afternoon air. The guards laugh, and one of them says to the nurse, "She's got a lotta damn gall, don't she? She'll be singing a different tune come July." Tracy jams her hand into the space above her bed, lifts her middle finger into the air, gives it three fierce jabs; the opaque IV line swings below her elbow. Embarrassed, Tory looks down at her book. Slowly the stillness settles back around them.

Tory waits for a moment. Then asks, "Tracy, would you like for me to give you a bath? I'm pretty good at it. Took care of everybody in my family when they were in the hospital, one time or another."

"Aren't you afraid you'll catch something?"

"No, I'm not." She keeps her gaze steady, not allowing Tracy to brush her away. "Besides, I brought some nice soap and bath oil, too. Mary Vic—that was my daughter—used to get so tired lying in bed. Often, a nice bath and a massage would help her rest, let her get some sleep." Tory pulls the lavender soap and the cruet filled with herbs, spices, and oil from the sack, holds them up for Tracy to see.

"OK, I guess," she agrees. "But, if I change my mind, you have to stop. Right fucking then, OK?"

"OK," Tory agrees. "Right then."

The prison pajamas are pinned at the waist, the sleeves and trousers rolled up. Tory quickly unpins, unbuttons, and slides Tracy onto the towels. She pulls the sheet over her, fills the basin with warm water, mixing in the bath oil. The smell of lilacs and lavender fill the curtained area. "If you'll roll over, I'll do your back first." Tracy holds the headboard, rotates her body, and Tory washes her shoulders. A tiny yellow butterfly tattooed just outside the shoulder blade startles her.

"I've never known anybody with a tattoo before," she comments. "It's really quite attractive."

"I got it done in Boston. Tiffany's father and I—his name was Raheem—had identical ones. But his didn't show up very well. He was black, you know."

"Yes, I'd read that."

"So, you read everything about me?"

"Everything I could find."

"Why's that? You just nosy?"

"Maybe, but maybe not." Tory washes Tracy's lower back, her hips, thighs, then the calves, notices the goose bumps on her hips. "If you're too chilly, I can get another sheet to put over you, up top." Mary Vic would be covered with bumps, nervous and cold. Poor circulation, the doctors said. The catheters made it hard for her to turn over. The sensitive area where the spine had been closed made her back difficult to clean. Angry red scars raised on her thin, child's back.

"Naw, I'm OK."

Tory rinses Tracy's back, squirts a dollop of body lotion into her hand, and finishes with a massage. "Now, turn over, and we'll do the front."

Tracy works to turn, to stay centered on the towel. Tory looks away. "You don't have to be like that. Everybody and his brother seen every fucking thing I got." Tracy smiles, seems to enjoy Tory's discomfort.

"Seems to me you could stand a little privacy then."

"Privacy! Here? You got to be kidding!" Tracy's bitterness knifes through her laugh. "Body searches, dykes fucking each other while the rest of those cunts cheer them on. Shit, lady, privacy is something I don't know about any more." The look she throws at Tory is a challenge, to see if she will back away. Neither woman moves. Neither takes her eyes from the other.

"Then let's finish this bath." Tory breaks the silence.

The water in the basin has grown cool. Tory refills it, makes orderly, efficient work of the rest of Tracy's body. She makes a clear circle around the wound on her leg as she washes, then finds a dry towel. Careful, she pats the whole area dry, looking up after each touch to be sure that Tracy is not in pain. Next, she rubs her legs until the skin is pink.

"Now, let's use some of this lotion; helps the circulation, so you don't get bedsores." The voice from her mother's hospice room surprises Tory.

"I won't be here long enough for bedsores, Tory."

Tory catches her breath, hesitates, then pulls the lotion down Tracy's thin arms, rubs it across her collar bone, is careful to avoid the nipples. Tracy says nothing. Tory adds more lotion, moves her hands down slowly to the rib cage, feeling each rib against her palms. On Tracy's concave stomach, with her hands moving in small, oily circles, Tory notices a faint stretch mark. Without meaning to, she follows the slender white mark from hip bone to navel.

Tracy starts—a little convulsion, like she's been shocked. Tory glances up quickly. "Sorry," she murmurs. "Did I hurt you?"

"No, I'm okay."

Tory looks back at the faint white thread across Tracy's abdomen. Tracy's body is quivering, and Tory forces herself to look at her. She's weeping, and the bed shakes in sympathetic rhythm. Tory lifts the small, thin girl-legs to oil behind the knees, around the heels, between the toes. The quivering, like some kind of ecstasy, continues. Tory massages the soles of Tracy's feet and anoints her with oil, adding her own tears.

༄

The motel's dining room is crowded. Tory scans the crowd, locates Melinda—sitting near the window with a man wearing a priest's collar. She hurries through the tables, filled again with gesturing, laughing diners. Amazing! she thinks to herself. Tommy Ray Soniat is set to die at one minute after midnight tonight. Some of these people will be the witnesses. Tory shudders at the thought. "Sorry I'm late, but I stayed at the infirmary so I could feed Tracy her supper. She's very weak, you know."

"Actually, we just got here," Melinda assures her. "Tory Gardiner, this is Henry Lee Addams, rector of the Church of Our Savior in Meadville."

Tory extends her hand, looks at the rector, smiles, and takes her seat. Henry Lee Addams is young, with the kind of quiet good looks of a certain kind of southern Episcopalian. Sewanee, Tory thinks. She flips her napkin in her lap, glances at the menu, then asks, "How did it go, Melinda? With the warden?"

"Same old shit," Melinda says, and makes no apology to the rector. "Warden says he's 'just doing his job, carrying out the wishes of the state'—same bullshit he gives me every time it comes to this. Henry Lee came to spend the day with Tommy Ray, be with his family afterwards."

"I'll be headed back as soon as I have a meal and a shower." Henry Lee speaks for the first time, and his voice is a lovely, melodious tenor. "I can stay with Tommy Ray until eleven o'clock. I've brought him communion," he says, and pats a small leather case sitting beside him, identical to the one Father Duncan brings to Golden Years, to Mother Gardiner.

"How did your day with Tracy go?" Melinda asks.

Tory shrugs, fears that she will weep if she tells them. "OK," is all she can manage. Recovering, she tries to smile, asks Henry Lee how Tommy Ray is holding up.

"Pretty good, I'd say." He squeezes a lemon into his tea, rattles the ice just a bit. "We've been through this before. Got all the way up through the last contact visit when he got a stay." He takes a sip, shakes his head. "Now *that* whole thing was cruel, heinous, and atrocious, if you ask me. He'd been shaved, everything, then the stay came about 11:30, and he went back to his cell, all by himself. Horrible on him, his family."

"Could that happen again tonight?" Tory asks, looking at the menu, not trusting herself to face this conversation. "Do you think that's possible?"

"Not really; the governor wouldn't meet with us today. I had the moderator of the synod and the head of the Presbyterian Church send him a letter urging clemency, reminding him of his church's stand on capital punishment." Henry Lee's voice is strained; Tory thinks he might cry.

"What a bunch of crap!" Melinda's voice is sharp, staccato against the noise of the dining room. "The guy is about as interested in his church's stand as he is in the black vote. He's looking at the Beltway, and no preacher is going to get in his way."

"Melinda, he is a man of real moral conviction, I believe, and I think the pressure from his church might sway him. If I could only get in to talk with him." Henry Lee's quiet urging balances Melinda's anger.

"Well, I'll bet you next month's salary that you don't get inside the governor's door tonight. He might send that bubba out to meet with you, but you can be assured that he ain't about to look like he's wavering one bit." Melinda signals the waitress, tells her that they're ready to order.

Tory scans the menu quickly. "I'll have the fried shrimp, garlic bread, and rice pilaf," she says, realizing that she hasn't eaten since breakfast. Melinda and Henry Lee order, and the waitress gathers up the menus. The table is quiet for a moment.

"Tommy Ray ordered two chili dogs, coleslaw, sliced tomatoes, and pecan pie," Henry Lee tells them.

"Oh, my God." Tory chokes on a sip of water. And again, "Oh, my God!" She can no longer hold back the tears, and buries her face in her napkin. Melinda says nothing. Henry Lee stands, puts his arm around her, and comforts her with long, even strokes across her back.

"There, there," he croons. "It's all right; it's all right."

"The hell it is." Melinda's voice, sharp and angular against Henry Lee's comfortable words, draws Tory up straight.

"No, it's not all right," Tory agrees, "but thank you, Henry Lee. Nothing about this is all right. And if I'm going to be there for Tracy, I guess I'd better learn to be a big girl." She dabs at her eyes, leaves streaks of mascara on the napkin, tries to smile at them both.

When their food arrives, all three pick at their dinners, chasing the food around the plates with idle gestures. "I wish I'd ordered what Tommy Ray is having," Henry Lee says finally. "After the Bishop of Tanganyika was exiled, he would only eat what was available to his people. Wraith-like, he was." He pushes back his still-full plate, stands, mentioning again his need to get back to Parchman.

"Henry Lee, good luck tonight," Tory says, and feels foolish immediately. The look he gives Tory belongs to an old, world-weary man.

"He'll need more than luck," Melinda says.

"A generous helping of grace, I should think." But he smiles, and Tory doesn't feel scolded.

"This probably isn't the time to ask, but whatever happens tonight, would you help me with Tracy's case?" Tory feels presumptuous.

"I can't see past midnight tonight, Tory," Henry Lee answers, "but keep in touch. I'll have to see." His eyes begin to tear and he turns quickly to leave, weaving his way through the tables, slowing down once when he hears his name called by a heavy-set, red-faced man holding a wine glass in the air. He does not speak, but quickens his pace toward the door.

"Good man," Melinda says, "but this ministry at Parchman is sapping his soul." She pushes back her plate, rests her arms on the table. "So, what are you going to do, Tory?"

"I don't know. All I can think of is her lying there, desperately sick, and the state treating her with antibiotics so that they can electrocute her." Tory is near tears again. "Is that the most absurd thing you've ever heard?"

"Not as absurd as the whole idea of capital punishment, but it ranks right up there as backassward stupidity," Melinda says.

"I've decided to go to the governor later this week, while the Tommy Ray case is still headlines. I hate to think like this, but if they kill—murder—him, maybe Tracy's death won't seem so necessary. I know that's an awful way to think, but I have to admit, I am grasping at anything that might help her."

Melinda is silent.

"She told me today that she suspected that Dwayne was molesting her little girl." Tory waits to see Melinda's reaction. "She had evidence, had seen things that made her believe that. But it was never introduced into the trial. I couldn't believe it."

Melinda sighs. "Yes, she told me that, but in order for that to have been introduced into evidence, she would have had to take the stand, and her defense didn't want to put her on. Felt like she would have hurt her case more than helped it." Melinda waits, then adds, "There's always the chance that it wasn't true and that the jury would have seen through it."

"Oh," Tory says, "it never occurred to me that she would make up such a story." A silence falls over the table. Then, "Paul would have had to have her testify?"

"Right."

"And he chose not to?"

"Yes, it was his call. Maybe he didn't believe her. Who knows? And, of course, she didn't know the ramifications—had to trust him on it. And since she didn't testify then, she couldn't in a later trial."

"I see. Did anybody ever examine the baby, Tiffany? Was she given a physical exam? Seems that would have been the thing to do. If there was physical evidence, then couldn't the doctor have testified?" Tory asks.

"The baby was sent to the grandmother in Massachusetts the day after Tracy was arrested. Getting an examination would have meant flying the grandmother and the baby down here, finding a doctor to do the examination. That adds up to too fucking much money. It all comes down to that." Melinda rubs her fingers against her thumb. "Money, and how Tracy didn't have any."

"Oh." Tory feels the despair mounting right on top of the solid core inside her. "I promised Tracy that I'd come again in the morning. If they go through with Tommy Ray's execution tonight, she's going to need me."

"She's gonna need more than you, Tory." Melinda's voice and angry stare take Tory's breath away. "But I'm glad she's got you. God knows, she's got fucking little else to fall back on."

"So, I'm better than nothing?" Tory asks.

"Yeah," Melinda answers, and smiles.

"Thanks." Tory returns her smile.

"Tory. Tory Gardiner," someone calls. Tory turns, sees Glenn Perry, the DA from Clayton City, coming to her table. He holds out his hand, beaming with too much wine. "Tory, so sorry about Paul. I've been meaning to give you a call, see if there was anything I could do." He shakes her hand vigorously, and Tory has to work to keep up. He glances at Melinda, doesn't acknowledge her. "What brings you to Drew?"

"I'm here on business," Tory answers. "This is my friend, Melinda Maddox. Melinda, Glenn Perry, the DA from my hometown." Melinda nods hello, does not offer her hand.

"Business? Well, me, too. On my way to Parchman. Have to have three DA's present tonight." He stops, as if he's waiting to see how much Tory and Melinda know.

"Yes," Tory answers. "I thought you might be here for the execution."

"Yes, nasty business. But this guy is really an animal," Perry answers, shaking his head.

"Perhaps," Tory says, "but are we still in the eye-for-an-eye stage, Glenn?" Tory looks solidly at the DA, notices the broken vessels splayed across the end of his reddened nose.

"That's a little strong, Tory." The smile hardens.

"Well, call it what you will, it's barbarism."

Glenn steps back, fixes his politician's smile in place, waves his hand. "Good to see you, Tory, and again, I'm so sorry for your loss." Quickly, he takes his place at a table to Tory's left with three other men.

"Goddamn him," Tory murmurs.

"Right," Melinda answers.

"He was the DA when Tracy was tried."

"I know," Melinda nods. "I tried to interview him for the article on Tracy. Wouldn't give me the time of day. Fucking bastard."

"Right," Tory agrees.

"I'm headed over to Parchman to meet with Henry Lee before he goes in for the contact visit," Melinda says. "Breakfast in the morning, about 7:00?"

"Sure," Tory says.

The news at 10:00 covers the pending execution, has a brief comment from Henry Lee urging the governor to commute the sentence to life without possibility of parole, makes a plea for Tommy Ray's life. Tory marvels at Henry Lee's composure.

The cameras record the crowd of protesters, candles alight, holding hands, singing "Amazing Grace." The floodlights swing back and forth, catching the glistening razor wire atop the fence around the Maximum Security Unit. White towels hang from several windows; a roll of flaming toilet paper tumbles down from the second floor, making a brilliant wave of yellow and red against the night sky. Next, the reporter speaks with the warden, who recounts all the things that he told Melinda this morning. "Bullshit," Tory says, and surprises herself.

The final frame of the footage is of the death chamber, lights glowing from every window. The reporter reminds his audience that unless the governor intervenes, the execution is set. The segment finishes and the screen fades to black. At midnight, Tory is certain that the lights dim.

Chapter 6

꒢

The morning paper is full of news of the stay of execution for Tommy Ray Soniat. The Supreme Court, in some legal jargon that Tory doesn't understand, found reversible error in an earlier decision, something very technical, based on a ruling just rendered in a case in Alaska. It came at 11:51, the paper says; Tommy Ray was already strapped in the chair. The old grainy photograph of him is reprinted, along with a new one of Henry Lee speaking to the crowd outside the prison. Tory tucks the paper under her arm, settles at a table near the window to wait for Melinda. An editorial mentions that this should do it for Tommy Ray. Two stays, another post-conviction hearing should seal things, allow the governor to commute the sentence to life without parole. Tory sighs, wonders if this could possibly be a trend. Maybe the court is trying to stem the tide of executions in the "death belt."

"Guess you saw the headlines?" Melinda looks tired this morning.

"Yes, good news for our side," Tory responds.

"I guess. You ordered?"

"Just coffee."

"Henry Lee was marvelous. Turned the crowd into church! I'm not into that, but he was great."

"What does this do for Tracy?" Tory pushes aside the paper, tries to pull Melinda into the morning.

"Well, it could be good. But then again . . . Thanks"—Melinda holds her cup out for the waitress—"I don't know how to read it." She glances at the headlines. "Did you see my piece?"

Tory shakes her head. "Not yet." She waits. Then, "What about Tracy? Should she be encouraged?" Tory asks.

"Depends on how the governor handles it. He can commute, say that he doesn't want to spend any more of Mississippi's tax money on another trial, just to have the court overrule. Make it sound like he was backed into doing it. If the polls show that this action doesn't hurt his ratings, then he might grant Tracy clemency. But, on the other hand, if he takes a dive, seems soft on crime, it hurts her." Melinda might as well be giving the stock-market quotes.

"Oh, I see," Tory answers, but she doesn't really. She creams and sugars her coffee, glances at the menu, decides to forego breakfast, her spirits wavering in the face of Melinda's caution.

"Tonight, I think I'll drive to Jackson," she tells Melinda. "Spend tomorrow at the CDRC, see if I can get a hearing with the governor." Melinda makes no comment. "I need Henry Lee's phone number. I'll try to meet with him, see if he's willing to get involved in this one." In the midst of her plans, Tory hears the weariness in her own voice.

Melinda scribbles her home phone number on the back of a business card, checks her address book, adds Henry Lee's home address, the numbers for his office and home, and hands it to Tory. "Thanks." Tory picks up her check, stands. "I'll see you in Jackson?"

"Sure. Call me when you hear from the governor." She extends her hand; Tory ignores it, leans over, grasps Melinda's shoulders, and embraces her. Melinda's hair smells of citrus, lemon and orange, and feels like slubbed silk against Tory's cheek.

"Thank you," she whispers.

At the prison, Tory follows the routine from yesterday: security check, scanner, a wait in Carol Monk's office, a ride with a trusty to the infirmary, her pass examined at several checkpoints, a brief nod to the nurse, then to the guards; finally, the sight of Tracy, framed in hospital white. "Morning," she smiles.

"I guess you saw that they didn't kill Tommy Ray."

"Yes, that's good news, isn't it?"

"For him," Tracy answers.

"Yes, for him, if the stay is upheld." Tory unpacks her bag, offers to fix Tracy some fresh oranges. "You need the vitamin C," she says, poking her fingernail into the thick skin, pulling away the rind.

"Why? So I'll fry in good health?"

"Oh, Tracy."

"Well, it's true, isn't it? They're getting me well so that they can kill me."

"Maybe we'll fool them. Get you able to stand a new trial, be granted clemency, have your sentence commuted. I've been reading some books on . . . on capital punishment. If your sentence were commuted, all the time you've already served would count toward parole." The orange juice stings Tory's index finger, a faint paper cut along the knuckle. She sucks it, waiting for Tracy to answer.

"Sure, fat fucking chance!"

"Tracy—" Tory reaches for Tracy's hand, but she jerks it away, pulling the IV needle against her skin.

"Shit," she cries, "that motherfucking nurse taped it too tight. She does everything she can to make it bad on me." Tracy carefully realigns the needle with her other hand.

The sight of the ragged cuticles, nails bitten to the quick, weakens Tory so that she feels that she cannot bear it. Her own fingers, sticky with juice, rest against the rough, sun-dried sheets. "Listen to me," she says, "and listen good. I am not about to give up without the damnedest fight you've ever seen. Do you hear me?" The phrase, one of her mother's, rings in Tory's ears. Do you hear me, Mary Victoria, do you hear me?

"Right, that's what they all say. But when push comes to shove, all you do-gooders fade away," Tracy answers, her face hard, closed as a drawn curtain. "Your husband did. Said he'd help, hang in there with me, but when your little girl got sick, he sorta wasn't there anymore. I mean, his body was there, but he wasn't. You know what I mean?"

Tory nods. "You think it was Mary Vic being so sick that made him not do everything he should have?"

"I don't know. Maybe." Tracy straightens her legs, arches her back. "Could've been anything. Maybe he just got tired of me and all my troubles. He wouldn't be the first one to give up on me. How long do you think you'll last?" She stretches again, then blinks slowly as if she might drift away into sleep. Tory does not look away, though she finds the silence, the accusations stinging. The voices of the guards and the nurse ride in over the morning air.

"I would like an orange," Tracy says, softening, and offers Tory a bit of a smile.

"You are beautiful when you smile, Tracy."

"Raheem thought so," Tracy says. Tory waits to see if she will offer more, but Tracy draws her smile into a thin, grim line.

"Here." Tory offers the orange crescent to her, and Tracy opens her mouth like a fledgling.

Later, toward sundown, Tory sponges her with an alcohol rub to fight the afternoon's rise in fever. "Tracy, I'm going to Jackson tonight, spend some time with Jane and a reporter I've met. I want to see the governor, if I can. Then I'll be back, as soon as I know something."

Tracy nods.

"And I want to get in touch with your family. If I can get the governor to agree to a clemency hearing, I think it would help if somebody, some family were there." Tory doesn't look at Tracy, continues to rub her arms, the smell of alcohol diffusing into the afternoon quiet.

"No." Tracy's voice is cool and distant; she pulls her arm away from Tory.

"But it might help if your grandmother spoke in your behalf." Tory works to keep her voice calm, reasonable.

"No fucking way." Tracy's response is solid, unwavering. "She threw me out of the house, disowned me—said fornication was a venial sin, but with a nigger it was an abomination. She tried to have me excommunicated, for God's sake!"

"I'm not sure that excommunication is ever for God's sake," Tory says. "I'm no theologian, but I can't believe that he'd be in favor of that."

"Probably not," Tracy answers, smiles.

The two sit in the fading afternoon light; Tory reaches for Tracy's hand again, holds it as the day gives way to darkness.

ॐ

Tory decides against the Heidelburg or any of the downtown hotels, chooses instead a new motel just off the interstate. Checking in is more comfortable here; she feels adequate, even remembers her license-plate number.

"How long will you be staying with us, Mrs. Gardiner?" the night clerk asks.

"Several days, maybe. I'll let you know."

Her room is a repeat of the one in Drew—a bit more tasteful, but offering the same anonymity. Tory picks up the complimentary newspaper on the bed, sees Melinda's byline, and reads her responses to the events of the night before at Parchman. The piece is good—succinct, unsentimental, and moving. It includes a statement from Henry Lee, rejoicing in the stay. "A victory for justice," he is quoted as saying, "a victory for humanity." Tory wonders. If it is excusable, justifiable for Tracy to kill Dwayne, could the state then kill Tommy Ray? The law makes distinctions about mitigating circumstances. Tracy's belief that Dwayne has molested her child—does it mitigate? Tory knows that she could have killed anyone who hurt Mary Vic, remembers the deep, rending anger she felt against doctors, nurses, LPNs who handled her daughter roughly, without caring. And Tommy Ray's atrocious acts—they were against a child, helpless and innocent—does that give the state the right? Tory holds her head in her hands, sighs, and a shiver runs through her. The puzzle loops back upon itself, a Mobius strip that threatens to dislodge her reason. Riding along that strip, Tracy's words that Paul faded away after Mary Vic got so sick. Is it possible that he felt the same things she did? How could she have missed it? Tory cannot picture him from that time. How did he look? Sound? All that she can conjure is his bruised, bandaged face, his voice low in his throat.

In the shower, she hums "Amazing Grace," picturing the protesters from the night before with their candles, holding hands and swaying in their absolute certainty that no one deserves to die. Tory wishes that she could be so sure about anything.

The secretary at the CDRC says that Jane will be in later, by early afternoon—tells Tory to come by then, if she can. Tory hangs up the phone and wonders what she will do alone in Jackson for a whole morning. Clothes, antiques, an art show—all her previous reasons for coming to the city seem to belong to someone else. A someone who needed to fill up her days, who was searching for excuses to justify her existence. She flips through the address book inside her wallet, runs down the names, marks with a faint check the names and addresses of six sorority sisters who live here. Alice Andrews is first, married to a doctor—one of the people Tory planned to call from the hospital in Kosciusko. She and Alice had college algebra together under Dr. Simpson, had to hire a tutor from the math department to get through it. Tory borrowed money from her clothes allowance to pay for the sessions. Alice majored in elementary ed, shrieked down the halls of Bishop Dorm when she lost her notes for a kiddie-lit test.

A long series of rings, the whirr of an answering machine, and Alice's voice announces that they are away from the phone right now, offers the children's separate number as consolation to teenaged callers, gives Andy's page and beeper service, and finally, with a little laugh, mentions that if, miracle of miracles, the caller wants to talk to Alice, then leave all the pertinent information and she'll call back. A series of sharp beeps, and Tory hears the tape click on, then spin and spin. She has no message for this bright-voiced woman, and quietly, carefully, returns the receiver to its place.

Jane Fillmore's desk is stacked with law books, folders, express-mail envelopes, and the slick curled-up paper of faxes. She apologizes, and with a sweep of her hand creates a clean space in front of her. She wears jeans, penny loafers, a sweat shirt from UConn, and no makeup. "Sorry about keeping you waiting, Tory. I tried to sleep in this morning, but gave up and came to work. The letdown hasn't started yet. I keep waiting for the phone or the fax to tell me that the stay has been overruled." A quick swipe through her hair places it behind her ears, and she looks as young as Tracy. Perhaps she is, Tory thinks. They could easily be the same age.

"So." With that one word, Jane is in control again, at least as old as Tory. "What can I do for you?" Her question feels dismissive.

"Nothing for me, Jane; everything for Tracy." The two women watch each other carefully.

"Right. What can I do for Tracy?"

"Did you look into any of the ideas that I gave you over the phone? The name of the juror? The possibility of a meeting with the governor?"

Jane offers a little bit of a sigh. "The truth is, no. I haven't done a thing about any of those possibilities." She looks down, moves a file to one side, begins to thumb through a stack of correspondence. "I haven't even had the courage to file Tommy Ray's documents yet."

"But time is running out for Tracy, Jane."

"I know that, Tory." Her two statements, flat and spiritless, hang between them with no contradictions, no excuses.

"I have made contact with Melinda Maddox, and she's agreed to help. I have Henry Lee Addams's phone number, and I plan to call him today. I met him at the motel in Drew. I think he'll help. But I want to see the governor. Can you arrange that?" Tory watches Jane, then the jerking minute-hand on the clock behind Jane's head. "Can you, Jane? Or do I need to find another route?"

Jane is quiet for a minute. "The governor is going to feel a lot of pressure about the capital punishment issue . . . He was very vocal about Tommy Ray and had the rug pulled out from under him by the court. He's bound to be a little edgy right now. He'll wait to see how things go down with the media, with his ratings. Same old political shit as always." The weariness in her voice, in her tomboy's body, is palpable.

"I know all that, but I think I need to see him as soon as possible, while he's feeling unsure about things, about how he's looking in the media.

And I want to see him soon, so that I can get back to Parchman to see Tracy." Only the sharp metallic clicks of the clock's minute-hand are audible. Then a phone rings in the outer office, and finally, the muffled voice of the flower-child secretary.

"She's very ill, you know."

Jane nods.

"What does she have, Jane? Has she ever told you?"

Jane shakes her head. "Probably something left over from her days on the street, something she caught from a john. Maybe even AIDS. I don't know. I was able to get a specialist from the med school here to agree to see her. But the red tape involved because she was on death row slowed everything down, and the first appointment I could arrange was the sixth of August." The terrible irony of making a doctor's appointment nearly three weeks after the execution releases a strangled cry in Tory, something primitive, garbled.

The door to the office opens to admit the frumpy secretary, beads a-jangle, her eyes wide open.

"It's okay, Sarah, we're okay." Jane gives her a sweeping motion with her hand, and she disappears, pulling the door shut once again.

Then there is a great stillness; even the click of the wall clock is hushed against the wail that seems to hover just beyond the outskirts of sound, waiting to be released again and again in anguished protest. Both women sit in the silence, and Tory is stunned that she feels no shame or embarrassment.

"I'm sorry, Jane," she begins, "I don't know what came over me."

"All of us who work with people like Tracy reach that point, this level of frustration, eventually, Tory," Jane says. "You got there sooner than most, but it was just a matter of time." Jane's words wash over Tory as balm, a quiet benediction.

"Yes," Tory answers, "and this whole thing is about time. The governor, Jane, how do I get to see him?"

꒳

Jane's list of prominent Mississippians with ties to the governor or with statewide influence reads like the roll call at the bar convention. Tory puts check marks by all those she knows, a little circle by the ones that Paul knew—the ones he had played golf or poker with, exchanged stories with or about—every one that she feels might offer her some kind of entrée to the governor. From her motel room, she begins to call. Paul would be amazed to see her polling the old-boy network, she thinks, and smiles at the unlikelihood of it herself—definitely not part of her original script!

Many tell her that they are no longer involved in state politics, didn't actively support the current governor in this last election, or are undecided as to what they will do if he should run for senator. All of them express sympathy for Tory's loss. A lawyer from the coast gives her the name of one of the governor's aides and the number of an inside line. Says he might be able to get her in for a quick, informal visit.

"Governor's Mansion, Richard Allman speaking."

"This is Mrs. Paul Gardiner," Tory begins. "I got your name from a dear friend of my late husband's on the coast. Hewett Gaston?"

"Yes, how is Hewett?" The tone is familiar, warm, political.

"Doing well, enjoying private practice, keeping things hopping on the coast." Tory offers Richard a little, conspiratorial laugh. Hewett hadn't really given much information or conversation, just a few condolences, and he seemed anxious to get off the phone, Tory thinks, but he turned out to be her only connection, so she embroiders their conversation just a bit. "He suggested that I call you since I'm interested in setting up an appointment with Governor Steadman—this week if possible."

"Governor Steadman has a trade delegation from Japan visiting this week. His calendar is really rather full." The aide's voice fades to neutral. "Can I tell him what this is in reference to?"

"Well, I'd rather speak with him, if possible. But"—Tory wonders how much she should tell this man, how many cards she'll have to play—"my late husband, a classmate of Governor Steadman's in law school, was the public defender in the original trial of Tracy Magnarelli, a woman on death row. I want to talk to him about her."

There is a long pause on the other end of the phone. Tory rubs her thumb along the paper cut on her index finger, remembers Tracy's nails bitten to the quick. "Well, the Governor is certainly concerned about the issue of capital punishment, as I am sure you are aware." Another neutral statement and a pause; Tory wonders if Richard is trying to decide which script he should use. "Is there something specific that you wanted the Governor to do?" He's laying out the bait.

"Mainly just talk to me, listen to what I have to say. For Paul's sake, for the governor to hear another side of the argument." Tory hears the unwillingness in her voice to read the rest of her script. Can Richard hear it as well? she wonders. "I am in the process of selling my husband's partnership, and this matter seems a bit unfinished." There, that should be enough to get him interested, she thinks.

"I'll check with his appointment secretary. See if I can arrange something, Mrs. Gardiner. And then I'll call you back. Are you in town?"

"Yes," Tory answers, "and I'll *be* here until the governor can see me. You can leave any message with the desk clerk, if I'm out."

Another call, this one to Melinda, sets up a dinner meeting. Tory has all afternoon to wait. In the lobby, she picks up a *Glamour* magazine which offers an article on power-dressing. Shoulder pads, heels, no-nonsense accessories—absolute necessities if a woman is to be taken seriously in corporate America, the article declares. In a nearby shop, Tory finds all the requirements: her first shopping trip with an honest-to-goodness purpose—the thought amuses her. Back in her room, she tries on all her purchases, takes a lesson from the article about the body language of power: shoulders back, chin tilted up just slightly, ankles crossed, no dithering or fidgeting with hair or purse strap, good eye contact. She moves a chair in front of the full-length mirror on the bathroom door, practices looking calm, confident, casual-but-serious—just as the article recommends.

Richard Allman returns her call at 5:30, when she had just about given up, was getting ready to call him back. He says the governor will see her at 9:00 the following morning. "But only for about fifteen minutes," he cautions. "The Japanese breakfast begins at 9:30."

Tory thanks him, catches sight of herself in the mirror, looking less than powerful. She straightens her shoulders, large with the bulk of the shoulder pads, lifts her chin, and asks Mr. Allman about the procedure for getting into the Governor's Mansion. I sound casual but serious, she thinks.

Dinner with Melinda is taken up with questions about how she should handle her time with the governor. Melinda says that the death-penalty advocates are pushing him hard, telling him that the people won't put up with a senator who's soft on crime, sympathetic to criminals.

"So, it looks bad for Tracy?" Tory asks.

"Yep."

"How should I talk to him, then?"

"I'd push the woman's angle—how young she was, how dislocated she had become—play on his sympathy, all his macho leanings." Melinda pushes the bow-tie noodles around her plate. "The overriding issue for him is his race for senator, not Tracy's life. You have to remember that."

She spears a noodle, then a slice of red bell pepper, drags it through the white wine sauce, then puts her fork down. "Steadman doesn't score very well with women—no pun intended; they find him too macho, too old-boy, if they think about politics at all. You might mention that women's attitudes toward the death penalty are much less defined than men's. They tend to look at the specifics of a case, decide each one on individual merits. No sweeping sense of right and wrong"—now she takes a bite, chews slowly, looks at Tory—"in keeping with old Freud's idea that women are amoral." Melinda's laugh seems to come from some place ancient and bitter. "You might remind him that women did get the vote; some even vote their own minds!" she finishes. Tory feels her face flush. She recalls looking over her shoulder in the voting booth, feeling subversive as she pulled the lever for Hubert Humphrey. Paul had served as the state Republican chairman to elect Richard Nixon.

"But, if the state can kill Tommy Ray for horribly abusing a child, why can't Tracy kill Dwayne if she thinks he's doing the same thing?" Simplistic reasoning, Tory knows.

"Well, at least Tommy Ray got a trial."

"I know that, but at the bottom of it all, isn't the question really who has the right to kill?"

"I don't know many people who would argue that anybody has that right. Definitely not a guarantee in the Constitution!"

"Okay, so I don't argue her case based on rights. What do I plead?"

"How about just plain humanity?"

"Since when did that get any good press?"

Both women are silent, concentrating on the now-cold pasta, the tablecloth, their still-full wine glasses.

"If he could only talk to Tracy, see her, he might feel differently." Tory's voice is low, almost a whisper.

"Right. But he won't. He can't afford to. No governor since Bilbo has looked a condemned prisoner in the face," Melinda answers, "and that man was black. Hardly human to Bilbo."

Again, the women are silent.

"Well, I'll just hope for the best in the morning, hope I can come up with something persuasive in the middle of the night." Tory stands to leave, reaches for the check. "I think I'll call Henry Lee, get some pointers from him as well."

"Good idea. But I wouldn't give him any credits in the interview with Steadman. Henry Lee is Steadman's prototype for a bleeding-heart liberal.

Reminds him of all those preachers in the civil-rights movement. Steadman has a long memory."

"Okay, I won't. I'll call you after the interview, tell you what happened."

"Oh, you won't have to do that; I'll be there, covering you."

"Covering me?"

"Yeah, I plan to let it leak to all my media friends that the influential widow of one of the state's leading attorneys has taken up the cause of Theresa Magnarelli. Has come to plead for her life, as a memorial to her late husband's strong desire to see justice done in Mississippi."

"Melinda!"

"Well, you said you wanted me to get involved, put on a campaign for Tracy. This is how it begins. Besides, you are much more interesting than the Japanese delegation." Melinda smiles, pats Tory's hand, and slides the check from it.

Tory leaves a wake-up call for six, flips on the nightly news, sees the secretary of commerce directing a tour of the Ingalls ship-building plant to a group of Japanese businessmen scurrying along in hard hats, catches the weather forecast—it may be too warm tomorrow for the suit she's just bought—rotates her head from side to side trying to loosen the tightness in her neck. A check of her messages at home includes one from Golden Years Nursing Home in Clayton City, asking her please to call.

The morning sun glistens against the dome of the Capitol; the traffic is dizzying. Tory re-reads Richard Allman's directions at a stoplight, follows the line of traffic around the circle, stops, speaks to the guard standing in the shade of the portico at the edge of the driveway leading to the Governor's Mansion. He checks his clipboard for her name, waves her through, pointing to a visitor's parking place under a line of huge oak trees. Gathering her purse and a legal-sized folder that she has stuffed with blank pages—hoping to look ready, official—Tory steps out into the warmth of the Mississippi morning. She checks her watch: 8:55. The article said that to appear too early was interpreted as unprofessional eagerness—late was read as careless or arrogant—so she slows her pace, trying to set her steps so that she will reach the door at 8:57. Three minutes can't look too eager.

The grounds around the Capitol are dotted with gardeners, raking, pulling weeds, spreading pine-bark mulch, giving the air a resinous smell. One man kneels in a bed of tulips, snipping off the dead blossoms, tossing them into a heavy cloth cotton sack. The blooms eliminated, he braids the slender green leaves, pulls them together, fastening the plaits—now long, tapered cocoons—with a green metallic tie. He stands to move to the next bed, and Tory is startled to see that he wears prison garb. A long black stripe running down his leg, black prison boots. She looks at the other men in the yard. They are all inmates.

Richard Allman meets Tory at the side door, just as he promised. He is warm, personable, a little distant, as if he is sizing her up. He offers coffee; she refuses. Then he shows her into a small, elegant sitting room. There she waits, hearing the hum of voices in the hall outside, watching the gardeners, dressed in their white prison garb, move about the yard slowly, like mimes in a tuneless dance. At 9:05, Allman returns, says that the governor is coming down. Five minutes of her interview time lost, Tory thinks. Careless, arrogant? She wonders, do the same rules apply to governors, to men in general?

Lacy Steadman is a tall, silver-haired man in his late fifties. Slender still, with just the vague beginnings of dewlaps on a ruddy face—definitely senatorial. Tory stands when he enters, offers her hand. Richard Allman makes the introductions.

"Yes, Tory"—Steadman breaks into a broad smile, steps forward to shake her hand—"I remember you from law school. So sorry about Paul. The state lost a good man, good lawyer, fine citizen." He rattles off Paul's virtues like a recipe, then motions Tory toward the sofa as he sits in a high-backed Queen Anne chair. "So, what can I do for you?"

"I'm here to talk about Theresa Magnarelli." Direct, to-the-point—the article said that was good strategy when dealing with a busy person. "About her upcoming execution," Tory adds.

"Oh, yes," Steadman replies. "Paul was involved in her case?"

"Yes, court-appointed public defender," Tory explains. "Not long after you both graduated."

"I remember. Did a fine job; really worked hard to get her a fair trial. Papers in Meridian—that's where I practiced before I ran for the House—carried the story."

"Yes, well, that was a long time ago. Tracy—that's what she's called—has been on death row for about thirteen years, her appeals are nearly exhausted, and I am here this morning to ask you to convene the clemency board on her behalf, for you to look at the possibilities of commuting her sentence from death to life without parole." The speech, practiced before the mirror in the motel room, sounds hollow, lifeless to Tory, invested with none of the urgency she feels.

"Well, now, Tory"—Steadman is not smiling now; he rubs his fingers, thumb along his jaw line, pushing the flesh up towards his ears like a face-lift—"her crime was serious, premeditated, vicious, as I recall. Stabbed that fellow again and again, nearly decapitated him."

"Governor Steadman," Tory interrupts, "the original trial and the hearings that followed never revealed that she had reason to believe that the victim, Dwayne Dewey, had molested her infant daughter. The child was never examined. That would have been a mitigating circumstance, certainly; any mother would have been desperate in such a situation. She drugged him because she is only five feet tall, weighs less than a hundred pounds. He was six feet four, over two hundred pounds. She would never have survived a fight with him. She was homeless—destitute, really." Tory's words fall one upon the other, sounding as desperate as she imagines Tracy to have been. "She was only sixteen when that child was born; disowned by her family, she came to Mississippi to find the father of her child, to marry him, to be a good mother, a good wife, to live as a family with her husband and child. But he had already shipped out when she got here; the Navy refused to give her his address—she wasn't legally listed as his dependent. She was thrown into despair; what could she do?" Tory fears her voice will break. She sighs, "Governor Steadman, don't you see that some of the most important facts in this case were never brought to the trial? Some of the issues that should have been raised were not?"

Steadman turns away, looks out the window, his face troubled. "Tory, your husband defended her. Doesn't that matter to you?"

"Of course it matters. That's what got me involved in the first place. But, Governor, justice was not served. Theresa Magnarelli is as much a victim as Dwayne Dewey. She does not deserve to die; she..." Tory voice shakes and she cannot finish her plea.

"Have you thought about what your involvement here does to Paul's memory?" The governor's voice is quiet, not accusing.

"Well, I think I have. I think I've thought it all through. But this I do know. Paul is dead; his life is over. Tracy Magnarelli's is not. She did a terrible thing, but killing her is not the answer."

Richard Allman appears, on schedule. "Governor, it's 9:30."

Steadman waves him away. "I'll be there shortly. Give those Japs some orange juice and make yourself personable, Richard."

"But the trade delegation from the coast is here, sir. They'd like a word with you as well," Allman persists.

"Damn it, Richard, I said I'd be there. Give me five more minutes."

Tory relaxes just a bit, wishes she knew what this meant.

"Tory, get the CDRC to send me the files. I can't promise anything. But I will look into it. For Paul's sake, if nothing else." Tory hears just a slight shift in his voice. He is silent for a minute. They both catch sight of Richard Allman, motioning from the hallway. The governor stands, looks out the window, then turns to Tory. "Spring in Mississippi is beautiful, isn't it?"

Tory nods, follows his gaze, sees only the inmates, shuffling from one flower bed to the next.

✌

The governor and Richard Allman move into the large reception room across the hall, into the maze of voices—slow Southern ones punctuated by the uneven staccato of Japanese. Tory is left to show herself out the small side entrance. She wonders how it went, as she gathers her purse, her fake file folder under her arm. Now she can head back to Parchman, be there in time to feed Tracy her lunch, maybe give her a bath, read to her for a while. Bring her some good news.

The brilliance of the morning sun shocks Tory, causes her to squint against it—pulling the inmates, lined against a ligustrum hedge at the edge of the garden, into focus.

"Mrs. Gardiner, Mrs. Gardiner." Voices come at her from every side of the Mansion's steps. "What did the governor say? Did he agree to review the case? What does he feel about capital punishment? Is he going to convene the clemency board?" The questions ricochet back and forth, and Tory sees a camera balanced on the shoulder of a small, wiry man standing next to Melinda. She smiles at her, but there is nothing in return, no nod of recognition. A woman with a thick mane of hair pushes to the front of the crowd. Tory thinks she's seen her before, maybe on the Channel 5 nightly news. "Mrs. Gardiner, what did the governor say about clemency for Theresa Magnarelli?" Tory throws a look at Melinda, asking with her eyes what she should do. Melinda nods to the cameraman, and the flash erupts just as Tory opens her mouth.

"Mrs. Gardiner, will you give us a statement?" a young reporter shouts from the back of the crowd. Another flash bulb goes off. The whirr of a video camera begins.

"Well," she says, and the crowd grows quiet. "First, I am most appreciative to the governor for meeting with me." She pauses, then adds, "It was a very good meeting—productive, I'd say."

In the pause that follows, several reporters shout new questions. Tory finally catches Melinda's glance; still, there is no encouragement.

"The clemency board, will it meet on Magnarelli's case?" The woman from Channel 5 moves closer to Tory, pushes a microphone in front of her face.

"I think that it is too early to say," Tory says, aware that she is being recorded.

"Is there reason to believe that he might push the courts for a new trial?" Melinda's voice drowns out the others.

"Sorry?" Tory asks.

"I said is there *any* reason to believe that Magnarelli might be granted a new trial? Some new light on the evidence, some mitigating circumstance that has not been brought before the court?" Melinda knows there is, Tory thinks. They talked about it just last night, at dinner. She knows, she knows.

"Well, Tracy Magnarelli believed that Dwayne Dewey was molesting her infant daughter. That information was never introduced into the record, nor was the child ever examined."

"So"—Melinda has the attention of all the other reporters now; they are scribbling on yellow legal pads, pushing their tape recorders into a semicircle before her face—"there might have been less-than-adequate investigation, or perhaps inferior representation of Magnarelli's rights in the original trial?"

Tory grabs a quick breath. Does Melinda expect her to reveal Paul's inadequacy in front of all these people?

"Mrs. Gardiner," Melinda insists, "is that the reason for your getting involved in this case? That you feel that the original trial did not grant Theresa Magnarelli the fullest protection under the law?"

Tory cannot bring Melinda's face into focus; only the sting of her questions has any substance in the morning air.

"Mrs. Gardiner," Melinda shouts, "is that what you're saying?"

In the moment that follows, several other reporters pick up on Melinda's line of interrogation, shouting similar questions, pushing their microphones closer to Tory's face. Tory is reminded of a program she saw on PBS on sharks and feeding frenzy.

"Well, as Ms. Maddox is aware"—the crowd stills under Tory's voice—"there are issues that, according to some experts, should have been raised that were not raised." Silent, the crowd seems to lean forward as one person. "It would certainly not be my place as an ordinary citizen to question how the trial was conducted. That's for the court to decide. But . . ." Tory feels her energy drain away. "But I do feel that there are things that warrant looking into—certainly before the state moves to execution."

Melinda offers Tory a slight smile—of victory? Tory wonders.

"Could you tell how the governor is leaning, how he really feels about the death penalty, Mrs. Gardiner?" Channel 5's anchorwoman takes over again.

"I cannot believe that he could possibly be for it," Tory answers.

"Why not?" Another voice, this time from the middle of the crowd. "What did he say?"

"Well, not so much *what* he said. But I think he's definitely leaning toward clemency." Melinda, now in the back of the crowd, allows a frown to cross her face. "Of course, it is hard for me to believe that *anyone* could really be in favor of the death penalty." Tory feels her face flush.

"What makes you think that the governor might feel the same way?"

"Just his way, really." Tory feels herself stumble now, wondering if she has ventured into treacherous waters.

"So, he didn't promise you anything?"

"No, not really," Tory answers, and the cameras drop away from the faces of the men, the flash attachments illuminated only by the sunlight; the reporters shove yellow legal pads into overstuffed carryalls, stick pencils behind their ears, and begin to move away.

Tory is left standing in the shimmering morning, alone. Behind her, inside the palatial reception rooms of the Governor's Mansion, Lacy Steadman is moving among the Japanese delegation, hoping to lure more yen into the state's economy; in front of her, at the end of the driveway, the reporters and cameramen drive away, content with a sound bite for the evening news. None of the actors in the morning's drama remains to play the next scene. Tory has never felt so alone in her whole life. Slowly, the inmates move out of the shade of the ligustrum and return to their gardening.

∽

Tory checks out of the motel after leaving a message for Henry Lee, decides to take Highway 61—path of the blues—up through the Delta to Parchman.

The routine at the prison hasn't changed. News of her visit with the governor still unknown here. The nurse on duty nods, checks Tory's pass, says that Tracy is responding to the antibiotics and will be moved back to her cell tomorrow, if she remains free of fever. Tory's heart sinks. There will be no contact visits there, only one hour allowed and conversations through Plexiglas.

"Do you think she can manage? In her cell, I mean?" Tory asks. "After all, she can hardly sit up long enough to eat."

"Well, it won't be for long, any way you slice it," the nurse replies, studying the chart she's pulled. "Temp's been normal for about eight hours; soon as it's twenty-four, she's outta here."

Tory feels the anger rising. "How can you say that?"

"How? Easy; she's a pain in the ass, and I'm sick of her bitching and complaining every time I try to do what the doctor tells me to. She's not one to make things easy, that's for sure."

"Pain and fear make anybody cross," Tory says. Mary Vic had taught her that.

"Lady, this little bitch is more than cross." The nurse flips the clipboard's aluminum cover back in place, hangs the chart under a hook labeled "Bed 3," and begins to fill out some kind of report at her desk.

Bed three, Tory thinks. Tracy can't even have a name here. In the unit, she's a number; in the infirmary, bed three.

"Can I go back now?" Tory asks, trying to recapture the nurse's attention, get a fix on this hard woman.

"Sure."

The hallway has been mopped recently, and faint swirls from the mop's head remain, silvery and slippery. Tracy's guards sit propped against the wall, chairs tilted on back legs. One covers the magazine he's reading with a beefy hand, but not before Tory catches sight of a nude in thigh-high boots, sliding her hand up her leg.

Tracy is sleeping; the IV drips slowly, her hair fanned against the pillow. She might be any young woman wasted by an infection. Tory pulls her chair to the bedside, and Tracy stirs.

"Hi," Tory smiles.

"Hi," Tracy responds, but with no smile. "How'd it go?"

"Well, I got to see the governor, and he agreed to look at the files. That's a good first step, I think."

Tracy nods.

"How are you feeling?"

"Pretty good, I guess. The nurse says my fever's gone." Tracy doesn't sound so sure about this.

"She told me."

"You know what that means?"

"She told me that, too."

"She hates me." Tracy is definite now.

"Maybe not. Maybe she just hates her job."

"Whatever," Tracy shrugs.

"And you don't make things easy for her, do you?"

"Why the fuck should I?"

"Oh, I don't know. My mama used to say that you can catch more flies with honey than with vinegar." Tory can hear her mother's voice, urging Tory, time and again, to be a good girl, not cause anybody any trouble.

"Who'd want to catch them either way?" Tracy laughs.

"I never thought about that," Tory admits. "But, a little cooperation might earn you a few more days here in the infirmary." Tory hates how that came out—earning a few more days. Poor choice of words, she thinks. And that might be all Tory is gaining for her—just a few days. Please, she thinks—almost a prayer—no false hope. Not even a few days.

"Right, sure, I'll cooperate with a fucking system that's curing me so it can kill me. Nice!" The bitterness in Tracy's voice reminds Tory of Melinda's: full of ancient transgressions, world-weary. "I bet you always cooperated, didn't you, Tory? Never gave nobody any trouble. There were lots like you at St. Mary's in Medford. The nuns loved them. Hail Mary, full of grace. They were full of grace; I was full of hell." Tracy gives a little chuckle over her joke. "They cooperated, got little prayer cards from the sisters on their birthdays. Me, I got the ruler across my palm, detention hall, where I had to memorize lists of mortal sins versus venial ones. Cooperate, sure." The speech seems to leave Tracy spent. Finally, she shakes her head. The murmur of a tractor moving down the long cotton rows outside the window ebbs. Then, "What did cooperation ever get you, Tory? I bet the system screwed you just like it did me."

Tory strains to hear the tractor's distinct hum, clear and distant against the afternoon. "Did it? Oh, I don't know, Tracy. But you're right; I cooperated. All the way." She feels the cost of it seep into her bones: the compromises, the diminishing. "I remember once wanting to take a water-color course, for a week, down on the coast, near where you were, Tracy." Tory still has the fifteen-year-old brochure in her filing cabinet. "I had arranged for somebody to take care of Mary Vic; Paul was going to a meeting for the bar association. He wanted me to go with him, entertain some judges' wives, dress up fit-to-kill . . ." What a terrible thing to say, Tory thinks. "And smile," she adds quickly, trying to cover up her insensitivity. "In the end, I didn't go to the class, and before we got to the meeting, Paul had me convinced I didn't even *want* to." Tory remembers the sense of relief she felt dismantling her plans. As though giving them up made her better somehow, that not wanting anything for herself was some kind of badge of honor, some sign that she was a good person. She sighs, shaking her head. "You want some fruit? A bath? Anything?" Tory asks, finally.

Tracy shakes her head, turns toward the window, is still, watching the slight movement of the tree limbs outside. The quiet surrounds them, and Tory wishes that she could stop the minute-hand on the prison clock.

"Tory, do you miss sex?"

"What?"

Tracy laughs, a big round sound this time. Tory feels the blood rush to her face. Wonders if Tracy notices that she's blushing. "I said, do you miss sex? Your husband's been dead for a while. Do you miss it or him?" Tracy looks straight at Tory, not allowing her to look away.

"Well, I really haven't thought about it."

"Haven't thought about it! Shit, that's unbelievable. How can you not think about it?" Tracy's look is full of disbelief. "You must have thought about it. Everybody thinks about it. After I got to Biloxi, couldn't find Raheem, I thought I would go crazy. I thought about it all the time. Don't you ever feel that way?"

"I can't say that I do—" Tory begins, but Tracy lets out a hoot that causes the guards to shout back, tell her to pipe down.

"Man, you're something!" Tracy says, shaking her head.

Tory doesn't trust herself to respond. She feels diminished, the schoolgirl again. Does she ever think about it? No, she decides, she doesn't. Somehow, it was never a priority in her marriage. Something she has failed to notice until now?

Tracy rubs her hand back and forth along her jawbone, as if she might be deciding how it felt to her lover. She closes her eyes, rubs the faint edge of her collarbone underneath the hospital johnny. "Raheem would rub all my bones, make me shiver all over. Touch me till I thought I would die. When I couldn't find him, I thought I *would* die. Really. He was a chocolate color, down to his dick. Creamy chocolate. All over." Tracy's voice is just above a whisper; she might be telling secrets girl-to-girl at a slumber party. "Tiffany had that same chocolate skin, just like his."

"I saw her picture in the paper; she is beautiful," Tory answers, grateful to speak of Tiffany, of something she's sure about.

"When I thought of Dwayne putting his hands on her, touching her with those big ole hairy, freckled hands of his, doing god-knows-what, I just went crazy." It's the closest thing to an explanation, a confession, that Tracy has ever granted. "Goddamn redneck cocksucker," Tracy finishes.

Tory feels a blush begin again, reaches down, retrieves an orange from the bag of fruit, begins to pull away the rind.

"So, you telling me you never miss sex? Man, that's unbelievable!" Tracy says again.

"No, I guess I don't. Wasn't ever much a part of my marriage." Tory feels apologetic, somehow, as if she has just discovered a character flaw.

"Sex don't have to be part of marriage, you know," Tracy explains, like Tory is a slow learner.

"I know. Paul took advantage of that. But, for me, somehow an affair wasn't an option." Tory's voice is flat; she might be reading the weather forecast.

"See, I told you the system fucked you over, just like it did me." There's a sense of triumph in Tracy's voice.

Again, the room falls silent. Both women stare into middle distance, thoughtful. There seems to be nothing left to say.

The nurse sets Tracy's supper tray on the hospital table—rice, white gravy, a slab of square unidentifiable meat, two rolls, and a glass of milk—monochromatic except for the slab of green melting Jell-O, sitting atop the mound of rice. Tracy shoves it to one side, spilling the milk into the plate. "Get that shit outta here." Tracy throws a glance at Tory, then adds, "Please."

"Look, missy, I don't care if you eat it or not. Starve to death or fry, it don't matter to me." The nurse grabs the tray; the spoon clanks against the glass, a little bell sound in the evening air. She turns quickly on her heel, the rubber sole of her shoe adding a squeak to the silence.

"So much for cooperating," Tracy smiles.

"Right," Tory answers, and they both laugh, the strain of what they know growing, erupting into silly giggles.

"Hey, keep it down in there," one of the guards calls. Both women cover their mouths with their hands, but the laughter rolls on, filling the white enclosure. Tory is certain that she sees the curtains sway, moved by the power of their delight.

～

The guard at the gate calls Tory by name, wishes her good-morning as he checks her pass. He pencils in 7:30 a.m. beside her name. Tracy is to be moved today, back to Maximum Security. Last night, the nurse told her that she could have a fifteen-minute visit if she got here early enough. The routine searches, the calls for clearance to the administration office, the checking of her identification, so familiar now, make Tory fret. Her time with Tracy is slipping by; she fears that they will move her just out of spite, before she gets there.

Carol Monk offers a cup of coffee from the lounge in the administration building; Tory refuses, saying she'd like to get to the infirmary as soon as possible, before Tracy is moved.

"Sure." Carol Monk seems cautious this morning, standoffish. "We'll see what we can do about that." She looks back at the collection of statewide newspapers scattered across her desk, puts check marks beside some of the stories, drops them into an "out" basket. The clock clicks loudly; the minute-hand moves to twelve, the hour-hand jerks to eight.

"Mrs. Monk, I do hate to bother you, but I am certain that the nurse said that they would be moving Tracy this morning by eight-thirty. I got here at seven to be sure that I could have a visit. Is there some problem?" Tory finds herself fidgeting with her purse strap, grateful that she was allowed to bring in some fresh fruit this morning. Tracy hasn't eaten a bite of the infirmary's food for several days. "She hasn't got worse in the night, has she?"

"Not that I've heard about." Carol does not look up from her task.

"She's really quite ill, you know. Hardly able to feed herself. Extremely weak." Tory hears herself cataloging the medical data much as she did to Mary Vic's doctors in Memphis. Mrs. Monk shows no interest. "I can't see that she's ready to be moved, myself," Tory continues. "I have had some experience with . . ."

"Mrs. Gardiner"—Carol Monk places the newspaper flatly on her desk—"I'm sure your intentions are the best in the world, but Theresa

Magnarelli's care is the duty and responsibility of the state of Mississippi, not yours or anyone's else's, for that matter." The authority in her voice, the rebuff, stings Tory, reminds her of Mother Gardiner.

"I'm aware of that, Mrs. Monk," Tory says, careful to use the formal address as well. "I certainly appreciate the latitude that the system has allowed in letting me visit her while she's been in the infirmary. I have been most grateful for your assistance in that."

Carol Monk nods, accepting Tory's thanks, checks her watch. "Morning countdown should be finished now. I'll see if Zack is here." She takes her #1 Mom mug with her as she leaves. Tory walks to the window, sees the trucks loaded with inmates heading for the fields.

"Mrs. Gardiner." Mrs. Monk speaks from the doorway.

"Yes?"

"Zack is waiting for you at the front door."

"Thank you." Tory smiles at her, receives nothing in return. As she stoops to gather her purse, the cloth bag filled with fruit, she sees the front page of the *Clarion-Ledger.* Her own face stares back at her. She's standing on the steps of the Governor's Mansion; there is no smile there either—she marvels at how earnest she looks. Tory glances at the headlines: "Attorney's wife pleads for life of murderer." Then, in smaller letters, "Thinks the governor is leaning toward clemency in the Magnarelli case."

"Oh, my." Tory fumbles for the straps to her parcels, looks up at Carol Monk standing in the doorway, her coffee mug steaming.

"'Oh, my' indeed," she replies.

A blue state van is pulled up beside the infirmary. Two guards stand at the door, two at the back of the van. They have come for Tracy, Tory is sure of that; they are trying to spirit her away before she can see her. She thanks Zack, hurries to gather up her things, and runs toward the entrance, the bag of fruit bouncing against her leg. Flashing her pass to the nurse, she makes her way quickly down the hallway.

"Tracy," she calls. "Tracy."

"Yeah, I'm still here."

Relief washes over Tory. "Oh, thank God. I was sure they would move you before I could get back."

Tracy is sitting in a wheelchair beside her bed, the IV pole anchored through the rings at the chair's side. In her red prison jumpsuit, she looks like a child playing dress-up in her father's work clothes. "I didn't think you'd make it." She motions for Tory to close the curtains, move in closer.

"They are fucking mad as hell about the article in the paper. I could hear them ranting and raving this morning. Called you a nosy, prying cunt." She waits to see if Tory will answer. Then laughs, "Bet you've never been called that before, huh, Tory?"

Tory doesn't trust her voice, shakes her head, then manages, "Who knows?"

"Must be the company you're keeping these days." Tracy winks at her and laughs again.

A fragment of laughter from the day before wells up inside Tory. She shakes her head.

"Well, here is what I think of them," Tracy continues, and thrusts her fist into the space above her wheelchair, moves it with the slow pulse of a royal wave, middle finger extended. The IV tube swings back and forth in the morning air.

"I couldn't agree with you more," Tory says, and lifting her own hand, imitates Tracy's gesture, feeling both self-conscious and daring at the same time.

They are still laughing when the nurse arrives with her chart, asking Tracy to sign the release paper.

"And what if I don't?" Tracy asks.

"Then I'll jerk out that IV, forge your name, girlie, and send you back to MSU in a New York second. Just because you think you got friends in high places"—she throws a look at Tory—"doesn't mean you scare me one bit; you remember that."

"You fucking—" Tracy begins.

"Miss Rawson, I am sure that we can get the paperwork done as soon as I have my morning visit," Tory interrupts. "I think you told me that I could have fifteen minutes this morning, if I got here early enough. Could you step outside and let us finish our business?"

"Yes, ma'am," the nurse answers, bows with exaggerated politeness.

Nurse Rawson steps outside, leaving an opening in the curtain. Tory pushes her head through it, taps the nurse on the shoulder. "Miss Rawson, could we have some privacy?" Tory watches as she moves down the hall, tapping the chart against her leg.

"Look, Tracy, we've got to get a plan going here. Once they move you, I won't be able to see you but once a week. I can spend the rest of the time working on the clemency hearing, but I need your help." Tory unloads the fruit on the bedside table, offers a bunch of yellow-green seedless grapes to Tracy. She picks one from the bunch, pops it into her mouth, and pushes it into her cheek. Then she puts another one in the other side.

"Chipmunk?" she asks.

"What?"

"Don't I look like a chipmunk?"

"Get serious, Tracy." Tory immediately wishes that she didn't sound so priggish.

"I *am* serious, Tory, most of the time. As serious as a heart attack. So you want a plan? How about a file in a cake? Now, that's a plan!" She pauses, wrinkles her brow. "But I think that one's been used before."

"Oh, Tracy, listen to me."

Tracy repeats the grape routine. "Maybe a gerbil, or a hamster," she suggests. "That's more like it. I run around in little circles just like them. Always moving: lockup, lockdown, exercise time, shower twice a week—with my bracelets on. That's it, a hamster." She moves her arms and hands like a robot, swift, jerky motions that bring her to laughter again.

"Tracy, listen to me."

"I am listening to you, but I don't hear you saying anything. Except to be serious. So, now, I'm serious. What's new?" Tracy sucks both grapes into her mouth, chews slowly.

"Tracy, if you won't let me call your grandmother, which I still think is a good idea—"

"No, no, no," Tracy interrupts. "I told you, no fucking way. She is not gonna come and gloat about how she was always right about me. How she knew how I'd turn out. No way, José."

"OK, then." Tory holds up her hand to stop the flood of words. "Suppose I try to find Raheem." Tory waits. Tracy is silent, stops her chewing.

"Time's about up." The guard pokes his head through the curtain. Tracy seems startled by his voice, and a look of uncertainty, maybe even fear, flickers across her face.

"Raheem? Tracy, for the hearing?"

"I don't know about that."

"It might help."

"We need somebody there besides me and Jane Fillmore. Somebody who will make the board see you as a person, not a . . ."

"Monster? Hooker? Nigger-lover?" Tracy finishes the line for Tory, using the words of the prosecution. Tory wills herself to look at Tracy, refuses to flinch in the face of such a harsh assessment.

"Yes," is Tory's only response.

Chapter 7

❧

On the trip home, Tory squints into the sun—the stack of newspapers she's purchased on the seat beside her. Three of the major papers carried the story on the front page, along with a picture of her looking so terminally earnest, like such a do-gooder. In the Tupelo paper, her mouth is open, drawn up in a most unflattering little "o." Mary Vic's favorite poem was about Jonathan Jo, "who had a mouth like an o, and a wheelbarrow full of surprises." Tory can only hope for a few surprises, just enough to gain a clemency hearing. A shiver runs down her back in spite of the heat. She pushes the seek button on the radio, hoping to find some music or news or anything to fill the car with sound. She would sing, if she only knew a song.

The house smells stale, week-old air recycled through the air conditioner. Tory throws open the windows, props the kitchen door ajar, feels the wind begin to move through the house. She realizes that she has never been gone from home this long since Mary Vic was sick. Never has she come home to a completely empty house. Tracy is back in the MSU by now, no windows and doors thrown open. Tory winces as she remembers the nurse removing the IV this morning. Jerking it out—viciously, really—just before the guard locked the waist chain to the handcuffs, then attached the leg irons. Tracy can hardly stand on her own, for God's sake; she couldn't run ten feet unencumbered. Why they had to do that, Tory cannot fathom. She tried to hug Tracy good-bye, but the guards stepped in the way. The one with the girlie magazine pushed Tory back, said, "No physical contact." Tory's eyes had filled with tears. They do again, upon the memory. She slumps into the chair by the bay window in the living room and crumples with exhaustion.

The 7:00–3:00 supervisor at Golden Years offers Tory another cup of coffee; she again refuses. Must be the way institutions put you off, delay giving you the news, she decides. Katie Lou Littlejohn, who owns the nursing home, greets Tory in the sunroom. "Tory, so nice to see you." She flashes a smile, then changes it into concern. "How are you doing, my dear? You've been through so much." The look deepens, her brow wrinkles. Tory is certain that she practices.

Tory smiles, nods, and realizes that the word "gush" could have been coined to describe Katie Lou. Her hair, frosted as Tory's is, has been set on large rollers, teased underneath, and then sprayed into a smooth helmet that a gale-force wind couldn't shake. Tory knows the procedure; she and Katie Lou once used the same beautician. She pulls her fingers through her own hair and realizes that she feels a great sense of relief that she has learned to fix her own, now—a short shingle cut requiring no permanent, no backcombing.

Katie Lou's afternoon dress, a maroon-and-blue silk stripe, is the right mixture of chic and understatement; her jewelry, genuine and expensive. Years ago, they had been friends, played bridge together.

"There were several messages on my answering machine, about Mother Gardiner," Tory begins.

"Yes, yes," Katie Lou says, offering Tory the quick, practiced smile. "We wondered where you were. Been missing seeing you around here."

Tory doesn't explain her absence. The breach between her and Mother G. is nobody's business but theirs; Katie Lou would never understand her friendship with Tracy.

"Then, of course, we all saw you on the news."

Tory nods.

"Why then, we realized you'd been out of town."

Tory nods again.

"Well," Katie Lou sighs, "that is mighty exciting, your business in Jackson." She pauses, offers Tory another chance at explanation. Tory does not oblige her.

"About Mother Gardiner. The messages were that she was not doing well."

"Well, she's not, really. In infants, we'd call it 'failure to thrive.'" She hesitates. Tory remembers that term; they used it early on about Mary

Vic. Katie Lou, however, would never have heard it from a pediatrician. She has four big strapping sons: the two youngest have joined her in the nursing-home business; the two eldest bought the local funeral home. Paul said that any way you sliced it, you'd have to deal with the Little-johns on your way out.

"Has Dr. Bolton been by?"

"We've called him, kept him up-to-date on her, but there's not really anything specific. Just a kind of listlessness."

"Is she eating?"

"She's never been much of an eater, you know." Katie Lou flashes the look of concern once again.

Tory remembers the bird-size portions that Mother Gardiner chose at family dinners, and nods. "Always kept her eye on her schoolgirl figure," Tory says, and Katie Lou smiles.

"You know what I think, Tory?" Katie Lou lowers her voice. "I think she's depressed." Then, almost in a whisper, "Lonely, really. I don't think it's medical at all."

"Oh," Tory answers.

"Well, when you think about it, she's lost her son, her only child; she has no family left." Katie Lou offers a sympathetic shake of her head. "Except you, of course," she corrects herself.

"Mother Gardiner does not consider me her family." Tory offers this not as explanation, but as fact, definite and certifiable, based on nearly thirty years of observation.

"Oh, Tory, you know that's not so. Why, you've been like a daughter to her." Katie Lou sounds shocked, sits back quickly in her chair as though she has never heard of such a thing. "You've been so faithful to come by, see to her laundry—always remembered her special days. Now, Tory, you mustn't say such things. You mustn't blame yourself." Katie Lou reaches out to pat Tory's hand. Her nails are manicured, varnished with a touch of pink, a mother's ring with four colored stones on her right hand, a huge diamond solitaire and wedding band on her left. She touches Tory just slightly, and Tory pulls her hand away, embarrassed by the implications.

"Whatever I was to her, I was never a daughter," Tory says, and reaches into her purse for a handkerchief. "I may end up being her caretaker, but she will never look upon me as her child." I was simply married to her son, Tory thinks; whether that made me co-conspirator, rival, or high-priced prostitute, I have never known. "I will certainly check in on her and see if I can help."

"We'd really appreciate that, Tory." Katie Lou stands—anxious, it seems, to finish this conversation. "I'll tell the nurse that you'll be in shortly."

"Thank you, Katie Lou."

"And, Tory, we really must get together sometime soon. I miss our bridge games and the luncheons at the club. Nobody's seen hide nor hair of you in far too long. I'll call, and we'll make some plans." Katie Lou heads off down the hall, calling for a nurse.

"It's time for Mrs. Gardiner's afternoon meds; I'll tell her that you're here." The nurse, round as a dumpling, freckles across her nose, appears in the doorway to fetch Tory.

"She may not want to see me, and that's all right. If not, just tell her I came by to check on her."

"Oh, now, I'm certain that she'll want to see you. You know she dresses up every morning, just in case she has callers. That's what she calls them—callers. The preacher comes by every week, and another lady from the church drops in regularly, and she's always dolled up for them. She likes company, that Mrs. Gardiner does."

"In any case, ask her if she wants to see me—her son's wife. Another Mrs. Gardiner."

"Oh, I know who you are. I've seen you here before, and I saw you on the television. We bring the patients that's up to it into the TV room to watch the news every night. And there you was on the Jackson station just a few nights ago. In front of the governor's house. We all saw you. Mrs. Gardiner couldn't hardly believe that it was you. She said so to all of us. Kept saying over and over, 'I can't believe that's the Tory I knew.' Said it over and over." The nurse stops in front of Mother Gardiner's door, puts her hand on the knob. "You just wait a sec and I'll check," she says, and slides through the opening. "Hello, there, sweetie."

Tory knows Mother Gardiner will stiffen at the forced familiarity, the unearned endearment.

"Guess what? You got company. Yes, ma'am, you got a visitor. Let's get this pill down and then you can have some company." A small silence—then, "There's a good girl, take that right down." Another break—then, "Yes, ma'am, your daughter's here."

Tory stiffens at this one. "Only her daughter-in-law," she whispers.

"I'll tell her to come right in." With that, the nurse reappears and opens the door wide for Tory to enter. "I'll just leave you two to have a good little chat," she says, smiling at them both.

The afternoon sun pours in the window, casting the room in a buttery light. "Hello, Mother Gardiner," Tory begins.

"Tory," Mother Gardiner nods.

"Katie Lou says you've not been doing too well."

"Is that so?"

"Yes, ma'am."

"Well, I suppose she's right."

"I'm sorry to hear that."

"Are you?"

"Yes, ma'am." Tory marvels at the power this woman still has to reduce her to monosyllables. Like I've never had one single adult thought in my life. "I've been away."

"Yes, I know."

"I thought you did." Tory fears that she will suffocate under the unsaid condemnation. "I know you don't approve of what I'm doing. I know how you feel, and I think I understand. But I feel this is a good thing to do. The right thing, the moral thing." Tory wonders at the language she hears coming from her own mouth. "I am committed to doing everything I can to save Theresa Magnarelli's life." She finishes, amazed by her own declaration.

"I see."

"No, Mother G., I don't think you do." Tory faces her mother-in-law squarely, watches to see if any hint of understanding might be hidden behind that closed face. "If there's anything that I can do for you, you know I will be glad to do it. Otherwise, I will be spending the next three weeks in Jackson and at Parchman." Tory pulls her cotton sweater tightly across her chest.

"Tory, you always were a silly fool. Giddy and emotional. I warned Paul when he told me he was going to marry you."

Tory feels the force of Mother Gardiner's words slapping her cheeks. "I'm sure you did. I only wish he had heeded your advice."

Tory opens a bottle of wine when she gets home, fills a glass, noting that it is only three o'clock. On vacation, Paul used to say that it must be five o'clock somewhere. She swirls the deep red liquid around, samples the bouquet, and heads out to the back porch. Her daffodils are in need of dead-heading; the irises look spent, the pansies leggy. The neglect of her garden tears at her heart. Giddy, emotional, a crybaby, she thinks. Whatever else is she becoming?

⁓

The secretary of the Navy does not return her call; neither does Senator Potts nor Representative Cowan. Frustrated, Tory calls Jane Fillmore, hoping to get some help in locating Raheem. Jane suggests that she start with the officer of the day at the Navy base in Biloxi, work from the bottom up. "Sometimes those kind of people are a lot more helpful than the big guys," she tells Tory, and there is a hint of accusation in her voice.

"Right," Tory says.

"How was she?"

"Tracy?"

"Yes, when you left her?"

"She's really weak. I think she was still running a fever, but that witch of a nurse wouldn't let me see the chart, wouldn't take her temperature while I was in there. She wanted to send her back to MSU." The memory of Tracy in irons, struggling to stand, weakens Tory at the knees. "How's the legal stuff coming?"

"We're filing everything we can, but most of it comes down to the last week."

"I see," Tory answers, looking at the calendar; only three weeks to go, she thinks, and shudders. "When will we hear about the clemency hearing?"

"Probably not for another ten days or so. I called the governor's office this morning, but he was 'unavailable'—waiting for the polls, I guess."

"Did I ruin her chances, Jane?" Tory asks. There is a silence on the other end of the line. "Did I?"

"Well, of course, I can't say." Jane's answer is hesitant, thoughtful, as if she's weighing her words.

"I didn't mean to jeopardize anything. It just came out. I did feel that he was leaning our way, I really did. But the press made it sound so different, like I had a definite response from him." Mother Gardiner's accusations—"giddy, emotional"—rise up in Tory's mind.

"You mustn't worry about it now, Tory," Jane says. I did hurt her chances, Tory thinks, and her despair threatens to take her breath away. "Governor Steadman will have to do something now. It's gotten too much play. He can grant the hearing, look as though he's wrestling with the problem, and get some good press out of that, perhaps . . ." Jane's voice trails off a bit here. "Or he can deny it, still get lots of front-page stuff, but run the risk of being denounced by church leaders and the rest of the traditional liberals in the state." Jane runs through the possibilities like a shopping list.

"Oh, Jane, I'm so frightened." Tory is shaky, weak with fear.

"I know; so am I."

"If I've hurt her chances, I will never forgive myself." Tory's voice is only a whisper.

"Wait just a minute, Tory." Jane's voice is firm, collected. "Her chances were zero to nothing when we started. We've raised awareness, gotten her case publicized, and we stand a chance at a clemency hearing, if not a new trial. Buck up; we've just begun this fight. Now, try to get in touch with Raheem, check on the juror you mentioned, and watch it if the press comes calling. OK?"

⌇

The Navy base in Biloxi has records of Raheem's being shipped out on a carrier in the fall of 1974, three weeks before Tracy arrived on the coast, then being stationed in San Diego after that. Tory asks if there is something more recent, something that will give her a current address. The officer of the day agrees to search the files, and promises to call her back. She's told him that it is in regard to a child-custody matter.

The records of the trial at the courthouse list the jurors by last name and first initial. Tory cannot tell which one is the woman. She photocopies the names, addresses. At home, she checks the phone book. One listing—Jeanette Calvert, on old Highway 6—might be the J. Calvert of the jury. She writes down the number, hesitates, then enters the numbers and holds her breath.

"Hello."

"Mrs. Calvert?"

"Uh-huh."

"My name is Tory Gardiner, and I'm wondering if you might be the J. Calvert who served on the jury when Theresa Magnarelli was tried in Clayton County, oh, about thirteen years ago?" Get right to the heart of the matter, Tory thinks.

"Why do you want to know?"

"My husband was her defense lawyer, and I'm working on her case now."

"I see." Mrs. Calvert's voice is wary.

"I wondered if I could talk to you about the case. Nothing official, just ask you to think about some questions."

"Well, I don't know. It's been a long time, and I don't remember much about it."

"Anything you remembered might be helpful. I could drive out some time that was convenient and we could just talk about it. Would that be all right?"

"I guess so, but you need to know ahead of time that I don't remember much, not much a-tall."

"I'm sure that anything you can remember will be fine, Mrs. Calvert—anything. I could come this afternoon, if you're going to be at home."

Mrs. Calvert agrees, reluctantly, and gives Tory directions.

The house sits right on the edge of the road—a little FHA job, brick and tidy. Prince's feathers and cannas are wilting in the flower beds across the front. Concrete steps lead up to a small, square front porch and a white front door. Just as Tory is about to knock, it opens. A sturdy farm woman peers around the door jamb. "Mrs. Calvert?" Tory asks.

"Miss Calvert," the woman corrects her.

"Good afternoon. I'm Tory Gardiner; we spoke earlier on the phone?" The woman's face shows no recognition. "About the Magnarelli trial?"

The woman nods, doesn't move.

"May I come in?"

The woman nods and opens the door just a bit wider. "Hot as blue blazes in here, I'm afraid," she apologizes. "My fan broke, and I won't turn on the air conditioner until July first. A rule I got. Besides, it just eats up electricity."

"Doesn't it just?" Tory agrees.

"You want a glass of tea?" Miss Calvert offers, and Tory thinks she may see a little softening in the scowl that greeted her.

"If it wouldn't be too much trouble."

"Not a-tall." Miss Calvert disappears into the kitchen, then calls out, "It's already sweetened, is that OK?"

"That's fine," Tory answers.

They sit in the suffocating heat of the living room, surrounded by a variety of school pictures framed in dime-store gilt, a sampler that says

"Jesus Saves," and talk about the weather. "Are those your nieces and nephews?" Tory asks.

"My brother's kids," Miss Calvert acknowledges.

"Nice," Tory nods. "Do they live close by?"

"On the back side of the place." Miss Calvert inclines her head toward the kitchen. "On the farm my mama and daddy left us."

"Oh, I see," Tory answers. "You know, I told you on the phone that I wanted to talk to you about the Magnarelli case?" Miss Calvert nods. "Well, she is due to be executed"—the word hangs in Tory's throat—"in about three weeks." Miss Calvert nods again. "And since my husband— my late husband—defended her, I have been working on her case, along with some people in Jackson, trying to be sure that justice is being served."

Miss Calvert nods yet again. Tory takes a deep breath. "There were some—well, some irregularities in the trial, and we're hoping to get some evidence that will gain her another trial. I thought you might be able to help."

Miss Calvert doesn't take her eyes off Tory, reaches for her glass and takes a little sip. "Seems to me we settled that thing once and for all, as I recall," Miss Calvert says. "She said she did it; what else was there to know?"

"Well, for one thing, she thought the man she murdered, Dwayne Dewey, was molesting her little girl. Would that have made a difference to you"—Tory hesitates—"if you'd known that?"

Miss Calvert pushes her toe against the linoleum floor, starts the rocker moving, and slowly shakes her head. "Well, I can't say about that. Seems like she got herself into all that mess on her own. Don't know what she expected, being a whore like she was, dancing in them bars on the coast, living with some old pimp. Seems to me it was the wages of sin, sooner for him and later for her."

"But she was only a girl, just seventeen when all this happened; she hardly had a chance."

"Bible says to flee youthful lusts; seems to me she made her first mistake when she didn't heed that one. Wasn't she looking for some nigger sailor when she came down here, trying to find the father of her little girl? Leastways, that's what I remember." Miss Calvert is looking out over Tory's head, moving the rocker against the stillness of the afternoon.

"Yes, that's right." Tory feels the defeat settling around her like a thick wool blanket.

"Has she been saved?" Miss Calvert wants to know.

"Saved?" Tory asks.

"You know, made a profession of faith, repented, and accepted the Lord Jesus as her personal savior?"

"Well, she was raised a Catholic, went to Catholic schools; she was baptized, I know that. But I don't think she'd use those words—exactly."

"Those are the words of the Bible, Mrs. Gardiner; why wouldn't she use them?" Tory feels the flutter of hope die within her. "Reckon she's just paying for her sins, like everybody's gonna do one day. Have you witnessed to her?"

"Witnessed?"

"Yes, offered her the plan of salvation? Seems to me that's what she needs more than a new trial." Miss Calvert gives a determined little nod, as though she has solved Tracy's problem once and for all.

"Well, we do talk of spiritual things," Tory says, finally. "And she is repentant, I believe."

"Has she said so?"

"Well, not in so many words . . ."

"My brother's boy, the eldest one there"—Miss Calvert nods toward a picture of a lanky boy in a basketball uniform—"he's doing time for stealing a car. Serves him right. Didn't listen to his daddy or his mama, or me for that matter. Lord knows, I tried to witness to him, but he was too smart, too cocky, and now he's working for the county. He's sorry enough—sorry that he got caught—but that's not repentance, Mrs. Gardiner, that's remorse." Another grim little nod from Miss Calvert. "Young folks these days don't fear the law nor God nor the Devil." Tory feels the steel in Miss Calvert's voice, the unyielding voice of the puritan.

"I'm sorry to hear about that, Miss Calvert. Young people do get off on the wrong foot sometimes, but it seems to me that they're in need of a great deal of mercy, not condemnation." Tory stands to leave. "Thank you for the tea."

Miss Calvert nods, pushes the rocker back into motion. "You need to get that girl saved, Mrs. Gardiner," she calls after Tory. "That's a better way to spend your time. That counts for eternity."

Better way, indeed, Tory fumes as she turns the car around, pressing the accelerator and sending a spray of gravel into Miss Calvert's yard, showering the deep maroon heads of the prince's feathers, bending them in the blast from the car's exhaust.

The officer at the base in Biloxi has information about Raheem and a last-known address. Tory thanks him, puts in a call to the only R. DeJanes listed in Roxbury, Massachusetts. No answer. She will try again tonight, she decides, after her fury over Miss Calvert has subsided.

Jane Fillmore's secretary reports that the governor hasn't set a hearing yet, and that Henry Lee will come if there is a hearing, and if they think he can help. Tory thanks her, then phones the nursing home to check on Mother Gardiner, finds out from the nurse that she's "doing right well today." She asks Tory if there's a message. "No," Tory answers, "no message."

In the diminishing light of a long, late June afternoon, Tory moves through her house, touching the familiar: a Caithness paperweight on the desk in the study—a memento of Mother Gardiner's trip to Scotland to research the Gardiner clan, a leather-bound copy of *The Prophet*—a gift to Paul when they got engaged. A sentimental book from a romantic girl, so young and so naive. Tory doubts he ever read it.

Where am I in all this? she wonders. If I were swept away this instant, what would be left of me? Who could read this house and find the me I have become? Discover more than an envelope of carpet samples, swatches of upholstery fabric, snippets of wallpapers, all stapled to 4x6 cards, organized room by room? No more substance than a second-rate interior decorator would have brought to this place.

In her bedroom, Tory folds back the bedspread, slips off her shoes, stretches crosswise on the sheets, and drifts into an uneasy sleep. She dreams of disappearing down a long hall, dimly lit and strangely silent. She wakes with a start. It has grown full dark. For a moment, Tory cannot remember where she is. The lighted dial on the clock on the bedside table reads just past seven. Her stomach growls, and she wonders if there is any food in this house, in this now-alien space that defined her entire world for so very long.

Downstairs, she scrambles an egg, makes a piece of toast from frozen bread, and stares at Raheem's number as she eats. Dishes rinsed and stacked in the dishwasher, she makes a cup of instant decaf, turns it a gray-brown with a dash of skim milk, and sits before the phone.

After six rings, the call goes through, and a man answers.

"Hello, I am trying to reach Raheem DeJanes." Tory's voice is formal, strained—to her ears.

"Just a minute," the man says, then shouts away from the phone, "Raheem, hey, Raheem. Phone for you." In the background, there is music. And noise. Lots of noise. Tory hopes that he can hear her over this din.

"Yeah?"

"Is this Raheem DeJanes?"

"Yeah, who is this?"

Tory is taken slightly by surprise; he has a thick accent, one she doesn't recognize. "Well, my name is Tory Gardiner from Clayton City, Mississippi. You don't know me, but I'm calling about a young woman you once knew." Why didn't she plan out what she was going to say? Tory wonders. How does she begin to tell him that he has a daughter, that his former lover is about to be executed for the murder of a man she believed was molesting his child?

"Who?" Raheem answers, then shouts to the noise in the background, "Hey, knock it off. I can't hear a fucking goddamn thing."

"I'm Tory Gardiner," Tory repeats. "I live in Mississippi, and I'm calling to ask you about a young woman you used to know."

"Yeah, I heard that." Raheem seems impatient. "Who is the woman? I don't know any women in Mississippi, except a few from around the base in Biloxi." Tory thinks he laughs just slightly. The noise makes it hard for her to tell.

"Her name is Theresa Marie Magnarelli. Do you remember her?"

"Theresa?" Tory is certain that she can tell a difference in his voice, an interest, a caring there.

"Yes. You do remember her, then?"

"Yeah." Raheem's voice settles back into indifference, Tory thinks.

"Well, Mr. DeJanes, I don't know quite where to start," Tory begins, "but a lot has happened to her since you knew her. Do you have any idea about where she is or what's been going on with her?"

Raheem shouts again to the background noise, then, "Well, I knew her when she was in high school, back before I joined the Navy. We were pretty good . . . friends," is the word he decides upon. "Then, when I left for Biloxi, I kinda lost track of her. I moved around a lot, after basic training and all; I never heard from her after that. What's this about, anyway?"

"It's a long story. But if you can hear me, I'd like to ask you to help me and her, if you could."

"Well . . ." Raheem is wary now; Tory can hear it in his voice.

"After you left, Mr. DeJanes, Theresa—she calls herself Tracy now—found out she was pregnant." Tory waits for this to sink in. "Her grandmother threw her out, disowned her . . ."

"Pregnant? Are you sure?"

"Yes, absolutely," Tory answers. "Your child. And her grandmother—"

"Damn old bitch," Raheem interrupts again, his voice hard-edged with anger. "She never cared one fucking thing about Theresa. Stayed on her case all the time. Told her over and over again about how she was no damn good, and how her mother just dumped Theresa on her and split."

"Yes, well, as you might imagine, she had no place to turn. So she followed you to Biloxi."

"Oh, man." It's almost a groan.

"Yes, but you'd shipped out, and the Navy wouldn't tell her where you were. So she had the baby down there. A beautiful little girl, named Tiffany."

"Oh, shit; you're not shitting me, are you?"

"No, Mr. DeJanes, I'm not . . . shitting you. She had no one to help her, no money, and she . . . well, she got into a lot of trouble. Dancing in bars, working for a pimp, doing all the things she had to do to survive," Tory continues. "But, the worst part was that she thought that the pimp was abusing her—your—daughter."

"Oh, fuck."

"Yes, so she murdered him." The words fall, one on top of the other, hard as crystals, just as clear.

"Shit, shit, shit!"

"And now, Mr. DeJanes, Theresa is about to be executed by the state of Mississippi for this crime."

This time there is no response. The music in the background reminds Tory of the music in the cage—driving, pulsing rhythms.

"Mr. DeJanes?"

"Yeah?"

"I know this is a lot to take in one telephone call. But do you understand what I am telling you?" Tory gentles her voice, tries to cushion the blow of her words.

"I think so. Yeah, I know so." Raheem's voice quiets, softens, then sinks under the knowledge.

"So, I'm asking you if you would come to Mississippi, to a clemency hearing. We are trying to get her sentence commuted, or a new trial, or anything that will keep her from being . . . murdered." Tory chooses the word carefully, hoping that the enormity of it will convince Raheem to come.

"Theresa murdering somebody. That's crazy. She couldn't do that. Why, she wouldn't even let me use a rubber. Said it was a fucking sin. For Christ's sake! This is fucking crazy!"

"I know that, Mr. DeJanes, but it is also very true. She is to be executed in July—unless something changes. Will you help her?"

"What the fuck could I do? Tell them I knocked her up? Then shipped out? What good would that do? Isn't that what those sons-of-bitches in Mississippi expect from a nigger?" Tory recognizes the bitterness she's heard before, the same age-old weariness that she's heard from Melinda.

"I can't say what they'd expect. But if you told them about the Theresa you knew, the one who worried about sin, about her home life, about how her grandmother treated her, it might help."

"Oh, man." Raheem's voice is shaking. "It's her grandmother's fault. That's for fucking sure. She made Theresa's life hell. Theresa's mom was a slut, so she decided that Theresa was too. Told her so every fucking chance she got."

"She has your daughter, Raheem, right now. Tiffany is living with her. You don't want her to suffer that way, do you? Tracy might be able to get her back, if the hearing were successful. Won't you help her?" Tory pushes the words, the plea toward him. "I think she'd be a fine mother, if she only had the chance." The recounting of just the essential facts leaves Tory spent.

"Man, I don't know."

"I'll buy your ticket."

"Shit, man, I couldn't get out of Mississippi fast enough to suit me. You sure they won't string me up, too? Isn't that what they do to niggers who mess with white girls?" His laugh is a million years old.

"We would do everything we could to guarantee your safety, Raheem. We would be meeting with the governor. You'd be safe there, I promise you. You wouldn't even have to spend the night, if you didn't want to. You could fly into Jackson, come to the hearing, and leave. Think about doing it—for Tracy, for your little girl, and just because it's the right thing to do." Tory knows she's pushing him, but desperation overtakes her. "You think about it. Call me back. Collect, after you've had some time." Raheem takes down the number, then hangs up.

The buzz from the open line throbs against Tory's eardrum. She puts the receiver down, rests her head against the desk top, and breathes deeply, steadies herself against the oncoming night.

Chapter 8

☙

Tory sleeps in her studio now, surrounded by her own things: photographs of Mary Vic, her mother's engagement picture, a snapshot of her father hunting in Texas, a little silver heart-shaped dish—a Valentine's gift from her first boyfriend. A bud vase from a sorority sister holds two early-blooming roses.

The dishes from last night's supper are stacked helter-skelter in a pile on a tray covered in delft tiles. A blouse and skirt hang on the back of the desk chair; underwear, stockings pulled inside out lie strewn across the filing cabinet. Her robe has fallen to the floor in a silky heap on top of her bedroom slippers. A wine glass, with a sip of merlot remaining, sits next to Mary Victoria's Jenny Lind bed. Files and folders, newspaper clippings, drafts of letters cover the floor around it. Tory stretches awake, conscious of the sun illuminating every corner of her room. Just camping out, she thinks, right on the edges of that other life.

On the easel hangs a charcoal sketch of Tracy. She's smiling, the little half-smile that flickered across her face when she spoke of Raheem, of his lovely chocolate self. But she hasn't captured Tracy's eyes; there's no sense of the young woman behind them that Tory has come to love. It startles her when she thinks that. Loving her parents and Mary Vic was biological, obligatory—a requirement, not a choice. And Paul, perhaps that was as well. She doubts that she could have married anyone very different from him. Her world had space only for a husband such as Paul. Professional man, good family background, handsome—she had written him in early. All those were givens, she realizes. Never could she have chosen, as Tracy did, someone so opposite of herself. No, she decides, Paul was—if not biological, obligatory—required as well. The responsibility of the choice hers alone.

Time ran its course for her parents; the endless cycle of pain made Mary Vic's life intolerable, her death a release. And Paul, well, he simply played the odds one time too many; his luck ran out. Long before they both expected, long before the final act that she had imagined.

All that dying did not crush her; but Tracy's death could, might, will. Launching into love that is not required, not pressed upon her, Tory fears that she will crumble under it. Mary Vic's life was as good as it could have been; her parents' full and long and blessed. Paul knew success, and as much love as he could accept. But Tracy—Tracy never had a shot at anything good. It's not fair, Tory thinks, resorting to a child's playground response to harsh reality.

She works on the sketch until noon, finally capturing just a hint of the strength, self-reliance, the suggestion of impishness that lies behind Tracy's eyes. Spraying the piece with fixative, she hangs it to dry and packs the car for the trip to Parchman. The heat shimmers off the pavement, and Tory turns the air conditioner up full-blast. Late June, and the earth is parched already. MSU will be like an oven, she realizes. The sketch, rolled and packed in a cylinder on the back seat, pleases her. She hopes that Tracy will like it, will find it flattering. Perhaps the guard will let the prison workshop frame it for her. The news from Raheem is promising, Tory thinks—another bright spot for Tracy. It should be a good visit.

The routine at the gate is slower than usual today. Unless they hurry her through, Tory will not get in before the afternoon head-count, and she won't see Tracy until tomorrow. She frets under the wait and the stifling heat.

"Mrs. Gardiner"—the guard comes back from the phone—"Mrs. Monk asks you to come in and find her, if you would."

Tory nods, takes the pass from him, and hurries to the parking lot. Inside the administration building, Tory speaks to the girl at the information desk and asks for Carol Monk. "She's in a meeting right now, but if you want to wait, she'll be out in about an hour."

"Could you tell her that I'm here? She wanted to see me before I went to Maximum Security this afternoon. If I don't hurry, I'll be too late to visit today."

"She said she was not to be disturbed." The secretary's face is impassive, wide and flat as a dinner plate. She chews her gum, masticating evenly up and down, like some contented cow.

"But she told the guard to have me find her when I got here."

"And she told *me* not to disturb this meeting, Mrs. Gardiner." A flicker of the enjoyment of power plays around the edges of the woman's mouth. Quickly, she stifles it and returns to her gum.

"Surely, she wouldn't mind just a brief message that I'm here." Tory's voice is tight, rising.

"I'll see what I can do," she says, slides from behind the desk, and makes her way ever so slowly down the long hall, carrying her coffee cup with her. Tory watches to see which door she enters. The last one on the right. Tory thrums her fingers impatiently on the cylinder in her lap. The secretary returns with the message that Mrs. Monk cannot be disturbed.

"Did you explain to her about the time?" Tory asks.

"Yes, ma'am, I did, and she said that she would see you when she finished meeting with the warden."

"And how long might that be?" Tory can hear the anger in her voice, wonders if this secretary is aware of it.

"She didn't say," the secretary says and flips on the computer screen, dismissing Tory.

After several minutes, Tory asks about the restroom, and the young woman points down the hall without looking up. Tucking her bag under her arm, she makes her way down the hall; at the ladies' room sign, she glances back at the woman at the desk. She is still reading the screen, working away at her gum. Tory hurries on, stops at the last door on the right, and knocks.

"Yes?"

She opens the door, apologizing as she enters. Carol Monk sits up in surprise; the five men around the table turn as one, watch Tory's entrance. "I am so sorry to bother you, Mrs. Monk, but I have only about forty-five minutes before afternoon lockdown, and I wanted to get a visit with Tracy this afternoon." There is no response from any one. Tory's words hang in the silence of the room.

"Mrs. Gardiner"—it's Carol Monk's voice, startled and quavery— "you will have to wait until I'm finished here."

"But, I will miss my visit." Not one of the men has moved; all stare at her as though she were an apparition.

"Mrs. Gardiner." Carol has left her chair now, taken Tory by the elbow, escorted her into the hall. She pulls the door closed behind her. "Really, Mrs. Gardiner," she begins, "this is most inappropriate."

"I'm sure it seems that way to you, Mrs. Monk, but I really must see Tracy, *this* afternoon." Tory feels the pressure on her elbow to move down the hall, away from the conference-room door.

"Visiting with inmates, particularly those in Maximum Security, is not a constitutional right, Mrs. Gardiner. The prison administration reserves the right to monitor all such visits. You cannot barge into meetings and demand to see someone. Your status as a pastoral visitor is valid only so long as you abide by our rules." There is nothing shaky about her voice now, Tory notes. "Besides, when I saw that you were coming, I checked on your status. It seems that you have exhausted all your allotted visits for June. While Theresa was in the infirmary."

Tory is stunned. All her allotted visits? There's a rationing on pastoral care? "I will be happy to discuss a future visit with you later." She has ushered Tory down the hall, back into the lobby. She removes her hand from Tory's arm. "And, Mrs. Gardiner, as you might remember, when Ms. Fillmore called about your concern, we—that is the prison administration—agreed to three visits a month. You do recall that, don't you, Mrs. Gardiner?"

"I can't say that I do. Maybe Jane mentioned it; I can't remember."

"Well, that was our agreement." Carol Monk turns to head back to the conference room, then adds, "Whether you remember it or not."

That bitch, Tory thinks. That goddamn bitch.

At the information desk, Tory asks the girl if she might leave a package for an inmate.

"No, ma'am. Nothing hand-delivered into the units. Has to come through the good old U.S. post office. There's one right down the road in Drew." The smile is broad this time, and triumphant, Tory thinks. "And, Mrs. Gardiner, you'll have to leave your pass with me." Tory fumbles in the bag, jerks the MSU pass out, and slaps it on the desk.

"I'll be back," she promises. "Tomorrow."

In the parking lot, Tory fumbles for her keys, grinds the starter, and backs over the curb. A squeal of tires follows her as she turns onto the main road to the gate. She does not return the guard's wave as she leaves.

Down the highway, a few miles from Drew, she pulls over on the shoulder and bangs her head against the steering wheel. The combination of sweat and makeup leaves a greasy mark on the leather, and Tory shouts "Damn, damn, damn" to the broad Delta landscape.

Tory calls Jane from the motel. Her words, recounting the events and Carol Monk's message, weaken her, and she stumbles against the bed, breaking into angry tears.

"Now, Tory, calm down. That was the arrangement. Remember, I told you that at the beginning. So, get ahold of yourself."

"Jane, I can't believe this! Three visits a month. She has less than three weeks, for God's sake." Tory's hand shakes as she pushes in the air-conditioner button. The blast of cold air hits her squarely in the face, shocking her, causing her to gasp.

"Tory? Are you all right?"

"No, I am *not* all right. I am, am—furious. That's what I am—furious." Tory hears herself sputtering, shivers against the artificial cold.

"Tory, you've got to calm down. Now. We can only work within the system. Those people, like Carol Monk, they have all the power. We cannot jeopardize Tracy by a fit of pique." Jane's words are harsh, cold, and Tory blushes beneath their accuracy.

"What can we do?" Tory asks.

"I'll call Carol. Explain that you were frustrated, anxious, emotional because of the shortness of time. That you didn't understand that the infirmary visits were being counted, didn't realize that you had used up your allotment. Something that will give her a chance to be forgiving." Jane pauses; Tory is stunned.

Emotional? Is that all anyone sees in me—a collection of wriggling, raw emotion? Hysterical female? Helpless, hysterical female.

"Tory?" Jane's voice is softer now. "I have some good news. The governor has set a clemency hearing. For Thursday, July 12th."

"July 12th?"

"Yes. We have to direct our energy toward that. OK?"

♂

The days drag by, and Tory finds solace in her garden. Each morning, she rings the nursing home to ask about Mother Gardiner. The answer is always the same. She is "failing," as the supervisor puts it—"seems to have lost her old spunk."

"She didn't even dress this morning," an aide tells her. "You know that ain't like Miss Annie." No, Tory thinks, it's not—at least not until now, not until everything had fallen down around her. How much of that is my fault? How much blame lies at my feet? Tory wonders if the hint of judgment in the aide's voice is imagined.

"Would you tell her that I called?" she asks. "If she needs anything, get in touch with me." As she hangs up the phone, Tory notices a smudge of dirt marking her hand print on the receiver. A swipe with her other hand widens it into a dark, earthen comma. The silence in the house, in her life here, overwhelms her. Mother Gardiner will not issue any such request, Tory is certain of that. Both will remain isolated, solitary: Mother Gardiner waiting for the repentance, the apology, the offer of truce that Tory is unable—or is it unwilling?—to grant.

Outside, the wind chimes move slightly in the mid-morning breeze; the smell of freshly turned earth fills Tory's nose with a rich, fecund odor, full of promise. She mixes peat moss and desiccated cow manure in the hole she has dug, adds a cupful of water; then, careful with the lacy hair-like roots of the beef-steak begonias, she tamps the dirt around each plant. Finishing with the flat of begonias, Tory stands back to look at the line of forest green leaves shot through with silver and coral blooms, edging the border of the garden. The effect pleases her; "lust of the eye," she thinks, remembering one of Protestantism's deadly sins. Only three, as she recalls. The RCs have to deal with seven. Tracy knows them all.

Tory works around the edge of the yard, pushing her wheelbarrow, loaded with tools, along the perimeter. Her body, damp with perspiration, feels long and lithe in the shade beneath the pin oaks at the edge of the yard. She kneels there, stretches, and pulls against the tangle of winter weeds. When they break free, the aroma of woods' dirt is strong, and the muscles in her neck and upper arms throb with a pleasant ache, like the tiredness that comes after sex, the swollen fatigue of seldom-pleasure that sex with Paul had brought. Tory rocks back on her heels, startled at her feelings, uncomfortable and embarrassed. Tracy would laugh at her.

Quickly, she gathers up the dead debris with a rake, dumps it into the compost, gathers her tools into the wheelbarrow, and hurries into the house. In the shower, Tory washes herself again and again, scrubbing heels, knees, and elbows with a loofah sponge until her skin stings pink. Under the pulse of the water, she caresses her body, pleased over the firmness of her skin, the sense of her muscles growing stronger from the work in the garden. Then, cautiously, she places her hand between her legs, and slowly, gently, under the warmth of the water, she moves against it until release comes. Then, naked, without drying herself off, she stretches across the bed and sleeps.

Waking to the slant of the afternoon sun, Tory is startled, disoriented for a moment. She sits and pulls at the sheet to cover herself. A damp shadow outlines her sleeping self behind her. The curtains stand wide open, and the branches of a dogwood tree dance outside the window, touching the panes with an occasional click like castanets. Amazingly rested, she wonders at the morning. Sex doesn't have to be a part of marriage, Tracy told her. Well, Tory thinks, it doesn't even have to have a partner. She blushes at her thoughts, hurries to dress.

She spends the late afternoon at her desk, writing her daily letter to Tracy. Each day, she looks for cartoons in the paper, a funny story, a picture—anything that might cause her to smile. Today, she gathers a stack of photographs from the bottom drawer of the desk. She chooses one of her house, the back garden, a shot of herself—sitting on the patio in late-afternoon sun. "Thought you might like to see where I spend my time these days," she writes. "Since the prison officials say that I can't come back until July 1, I'm keeping busy, working in the garden, painting, and writing to you. What an exciting life I have!" She draws a little smiley face, then quickly she crosses out the last line. Searching for the white-out, she uncovers a picture of Mary Vic when she was about four. Her heavy leg braces had caught the camera flash, and a jagged edge of white covers the bottom of the photograph. Mary Vic smiles as she holds up her Easter basket. A hint of chocolate brushes down her cheek. She found the Golden Egg that year at the church Easter-egg hunt, Tory remembers. They had saved the gold foil-covered egg until the summer, and the smell was terrible. Tory smiles at the memory, wonders if Tiffany has had her share of Easter baskets and egg hunts.

〜

The first week in July is hot and dry; Tory spends the afternoons moving the hose from place to place to try to salvage her dying garden. She buys more soaker hoses, more sprinklers, vows that she will have a sprinkler system installed before next summer. I am a veritable prisoner of my yard, she thinks, as she drags the hose to the edge of the garden, pulling against it to straighten out the kinks and get a few more inches of length. Fretful in the heat, she rests on the bench at the back of the yard, deciding where to add a perennial bed. Suddenly, the overwhelming grace that comes with being able to plan for the future consumes her. The possibility of another Labor Day, Thanksgiving, Christmas, New Year's, Lent, Easter, another season. Unexpected tears sting against the sunburn on her cheeks. She hastens inside for the air-conditioned comfort of her bedroom.

The next morning, Tory prepares for the trip to Parchman, packing clothes that will withstand the heat and the humidity. Jane has phoned to say that Tory is again on the pastoral visitation list, and that her visits will be extended to six during the month of July, since the execution date is only two-and-a-half weeks away. She has asked that Tory go to Parchman for a visit, then come to Jackson so that they may plan for the clemency hearing. "Expect to be away about ten days," she suggested, "this time." Tory ponders the "this time," wondering if there will be another. Jane has offered no real encouragement beyond the clemency hearing, indicating that they will have several strategy sessions in the evening after the office closes for the day. "Do you have a place to stay in Jackson?" she asked.

Tory mentioned that the same motel was fine with her, and Jane offered to make the reservation. "No," Tory told her, "I can do it myself."

Now, driving across the parched Delta, Tory notices tractors in the fields kicking up whirlwinds of dust, obscuring the drivers in thick brown clouds. There is no other movement in the air except the pair of buzzards making wide, lazy arcs across the unrelenting blue of the sky. At the edges of fields, rows of trees, their leaves filmed with dust, border an occasional sluggish creek—the bed dried, mud cracked open in the heat. The slow dying of a moist spring under the fierce blast of summer.

The guard at the gate moves slowly against the heat as well. Almost careless in his search, the dark, sweaty patches beneath his armpits stick to his doughy body. "Everything's seems A-OK, Miz Gardiner," he says, and waves her through the gate with a half-hearted swing of his arm. Inside the administration building, Tory is given a new pass. July 1989 is stamped on the bottom, "pastoral visitation rights" written in a schoolgirl hand that dots the i's with little circles. Carol Monk's writing? she wonders. The secretary at the information desk asks for her purse, her driver's license, the keys to her car. Tory hands them over as the woman—a different one this time—calls for the prison truck to take Tory to Maximum Security. This will be her first visit there.

"You know you can't take anything into Maximum, don't you?" the woman asks. Tory nods. "Stay toward the outside of the railing, don't walk near the cell doors, and walk with the guard at all times." It sounds like a set speech to Tory, but it causes goose bumps to rise on her arms. She nods again. "The guard there is"—the woman looks at a computer printout—"Harold Short. He'll meet you at the gate. Wear your pass on your collar." She seems to be finished. "Here's your ride."

Tory nods her thanks and follows the trusty to the prison truck, left idling at the curb. The trip across to Maximum Security is quick. Dust billows behind them, the ruts and potholes jangling Tory's nerves. At the gate, a small, wiry man in a khaki shirt and dark brown pants, carrying a rifle and wearing a pistol, opens the door for Tory. "Miz Gardiner?"

"Yes?"

"Harold Short." He extends his hand. Tory shakes it, is aware that the flesh is dry and brittle.

"Tory Gardiner," she answers.

"Yes, ma'am. Here to see Magnarelli?"

"Yes."

"Right this way." He motions her through the gate, under the rolled razor wire, through a second gate, then across the yard to the door of the three-story red-brick building. The windows, mere slits really, are covered in bars, with only two, maybe two-and-a-half inches between them. You could barely get your hand through there, Tory realizes. Just inside, the hall is long, shadowy, topped with double rows of unlit fluorescent bulbs. Refracted and oblique outside light filters into this place through a barred window at the end. Harold Short's shadow follows him along one wall. When he motions to Tory to turn left, the shadow responds in a faint gray arc. He opens a door on the ground floor. The lights are on in here. Harsh artificial white bouncing against a Formica-topped counter, divided by a Plexiglas shield that has been pierced with about two dozen holes. A molded plastic chair sits on either side of the divider. A door matching the one where Tory entered completes the other half of the room.

"You can sit here and wait for the prisoner," Harold Short tells her. "It'll take us a while to get her."

"Thank you," Tory answers.

"And you'll only have an hour."

"Oh," Tory says, "I thought..."

"That's the rules, one hour."

"All right," Tory agrees, remembering Jane's comment about where the power lies in this world. Harold Short pulls the door closed behind him, and Tory hears the tumblers in the lock fall into place. She wishes for a handkerchief to pat the sweat off her face. Leaning down, she uses the wrong side of the hem of her dress to touch her cheeks, her forehead, beneath her chin. A makeup smudge strings across the hemline.

After a quarter of an hour, Tory hears a rattle at the other door, keys in a lock, and the murmur of voices. The door swings open, and another guard—this one big, burly, and black—ushers Tracy inside. She is dressed in her red prison jumpsuit, her hands cuffed, chained to her waist, her ankles in irons which are attached to the waist chain as well. Tory is amazed that she can stand, much less walk, under all this weight. The guard releases her elbow, and Tracy shuffles in mincing steps to the chair. Once she is seated, the guard turns to leave, locking the door behind him. Only then does Tracy look at Tory. Neither woman speaks. Tracy's face is drawn; she's pale as ash, her hair matted against her head. Tory cannot bear to look at her. She glances away, trying to find somewhere to turn her eyes so that Tracy does not see her anguish.

"Well," Tracy speaks finally, "here we are."

"Yes," Tory answers, "here we are, indeed."

Again, the silence is palpable. Tory realizes that there are no farming sounds here. No sense of life outside the walls, the bars, the locks, the chains.

"How are you, Tracy?" Tory finally finds her voice, but it is strained, cracked, dry as cotton.

"Oh, just great, Tory," she answers, the layer of sarcasm strong in hers. "Peachy keen."

"Yeah," Tory says, "ask a stupid question, get a stupid answer." Tracy nods. "I have thought about you every single day. Did you get my letters? The picture? Did they tell you I had come and they wouldn't let me in?" Tory raises her voice so that the words will slide through the little holes there and reach Tracy complete and whole, and convey her love somehow.

"Yeah, I got them. But only after some son-of-a-bitch or other had opened them and gone through every fucking thing." She shakes her head, her eyes fierce and hard, as though this is the final indignity. "Once or twice, they put something on the envelope about removing 'an item.' That's what it said: 'One item removed,' I don't know what. They didn't say."

"Oh," Tory says. "I can't imagine what I would have put in them that you couldn't have." She shakes her head slowly, trying to remember what could be wrong with anything she had sent. "Whatever it was, it doesn't matter now, does it?" She smiles at Tracy, hoping to get a smile in return, to recreate how she looked in the sketch she had drawn.

"I guess not."

"Did you like your sketch?"

"Yeah"—now she smiles—"you made me look pretty good." She curves her back in an attempt to reach her hair. "Not a bit like I look today." She tries to fluff her hair away from her head, but the chain is too short. There is a throaty rattle as it strikes the cuffs, then the waist chain.

"Shit," Tracy says. "I only get two showers a week, and I have to shower with the irons on, so I can't wash my hair. Can't really get myself clean; just cools me off a bit."

"Oh, Tracy, how awful!"

"Yeah," Tracy agrees.

"Maybe I could ask Jane to get that changed? Do you think?"

"You could ask, but I doubt that it will do any good."

"Well, I'm on my way to Jackson tonight; I'll see what I can do. Can't hurt to ask."

"Can't hurt to ask," Tracy mimics her. "You think you got all the right answers. Breeze in and out of here when it suits you. When you need to get a little feel-good motherly buzz. Then you'll just drive on down and see ole Tracy. Is that it?"

"Of course not, Tracy. That's not it at all."

"Well, let me tell you, if you're waiting for me to be grateful, you got a long wait coming." Tracy's voice is flat, unemotional.

She's thought this all through, practiced it, Tory realizes.

"You said you needed to do this to help yourself, remember? That first day, you said so yourself. Like you needed to clean up some old mess— and here's Tracy. Let's help her and make me feel good."

"Yes, I did say that, and it was true, *then*."

"And what about *now?*"

Tory hesitates. "I'm not sure about now. Now, I care about you. And I want to do what's right. I think that means helping you." She rubs her forehead, feel the perspiration that has blossomed there. "Somehow, I feel that I've not been very good at helping people I love . . ."

"I am not your dead daughter, Tory, come back to life, at least for a little while, to give you some kind of second go at it."

"I know that. I think I did try to replace her with you. Some way. I'm sorry. I was a daughterless mother—you, a motherless daughter. It seemed like a good idea . . . That wasn't fair to you, to her, to either of us."

"Yeah, there's a lot that's not fair. Like being on death row." Tracy's voice drops to a whisper. This part feels unrehearsed. She rests her head on the counter, over her crossed arms, like a kindergartner.

Tory waits in the heat for the waves of bitter words to work their way through the narrow window, out into the still, hot air.

"And I don't think it would hurt to ask if you could shower without your manacles." Tory leans into the barrier, quietly pushing the suggestion to Tracy.

"Yeah, it can." Tracy lifts her head. "Guards in Maximum don't like any favors. They figure you get here, you aren't fucking human. And that's how they treat us." Tracy waits for a minute—far away, Tory thinks. "You know they're gonna put me on a suicide watch?"

"No!" Tory leans back, shocked. "Why?"

"Shit, I don't know. Regulations, the guard told me. How in hell could I commit suicide? I can't even go to the bathroom without help. Suicide, huh. Like I'm gonna save the goddamn state of Mississippi the cost of killing me? Not on their fat fucking asses!" Tracy slumps against the back of the chair, the movement of the chains muffled by her body; she seems exhausted by the speech.

The time drags by; Tory tries to make conversation, but it sticks in her throat. Tracy glances regularly at the door, seeming to will the guard's return.

"What do you think about Raheem coming to the hearing?" Tory asks. Tracy shrugs.

"I think it will help. I really do. He seemed so nice on the phone, Tracy. I think it would be good if he came. What do you think?"

Tracy shrugs again.

"Jane and I will do a lot a planning for the hearing. That's where I'm going as soon as I leave here."

"You said that already."

"Oh, I did, didn't I." Tory feels the correction sharply, in her stomach. The room is stifling; she can feel that sweat dripping down her legs, into her shoes. The windows open only a crack, and there is no breeze.

"Look, Tracy"—Tory tries to get her attention—"look at me." She's surprised at the severity of her voice. "We can't let them get us down. We've got to have faith, courage, whatever it takes to get through this. And don't give up. Promise me that, that you won't give up. We've still got a fighting chance. I know we have."

Tracy doesn't look up. She is examining her hands, picking at the cuticles. Finding a loose bit of skin at the base of her thumbnail, she leans against the chain, pinches the flesh in her teeth, pulls it away from the nail bed and spits it on the counter. A tiny drop of blood oozes to the surface; she watches it pool, then licks it away. "I saw a program on vampires once, on Sally Jesse Raphael, I think. She said that licking your own blood proved that everybody loved the taste of it, that we were all like hidden vampires." She shakes her head slowly. "You promised me no false hope, Tory. Right at the beginning, you promised, and here you go, preaching faith, courage, and all that other bullshit to me." The deathly quiet of her voice cuts Tory to the bone.

"I'm sorry, Tracy. I did promise, and the speech was for me, and it was all full of . . . bullshit. Forgive me." Tory voice breaks; she touches the hem of her skirt to her forehead, dabs her eyes again. "They won't even let me bring a handkerchief in this place!" The anger and the absurdity washes over her, bent over her knees, as though she is manacled as well. When Tory looks up, Tracy is staring at her, and she seems to have retreated somewhere within herself, trying to find a space where she can rest. A chill comes over Tory, as though she is staring into the very face of death.

"I'm scared, Tory, real scared." Tracy's face is drawn, eerily white, as though her bones have leached through the skin.

Tory can find no words. Nothing from the books of meditation on peace, eternal security, God's love and redemption comes to mind to relieve the horror of this truth. Tracy's bottom lip trembles; she bites hard against it, and the last bit of faint color drains away.

"I don't want to die. I'm guilty, but I'm not sorry, and more than any fucking thing, I don't want to die."

"No"—Tory's voice is barely a whisper—"I know you don't."

"The nuns won't be surprised; neither will my granny. They all thought I'd come to something like this." Tracy licks away a second spot of blood; another surfaces. She brushes her finger against her coverall. The stain, dark, red-on-red, spreads slightly, eating up the coarse fabric. The chains jangle in the air between the two women. "Guess I just proved them right."

"Maybe you just did what you had to do. You loved your child, and you had to protect her. That's an act of courage, Tracy." The words leave Tory breathless.

"Yeah, maybe. Anyway, here I am, getting ready to fry. And everybody saying we told you so." The tremble of her lip is gone. Her eyes and face have hardened once again.

"I'm not saying that, Tracy. Not at all. I don't think anything of the kind. I feel very fortunate, even blessed to have known you. You have a great capacity to love, and I admire that."

"God Almighty, Tory. Don't get all snotty-nosed on me. You sound like those queers in the cage." She leans over, tries to push her hair out of her eyes, and watches the shadow of the wrist chain swing on the floor.

168

"Maybe so. But I know you loved Tiffany. You couldn't have done what you did if you hadn't loved her—even more than you loved yourself." Tory realizes that she is crying, tears running down her face, puddling on her chin, her nose beginning to drip. "Damn," she whispers, wipes her eyes, nose, and chin on her hem again, leaving another wider smear. "And remember, the clemency hearing is only a week or so away. That *could* change everything. That's not false hope. That's a real hope. It may be the last one, but it's still out there, and until we exhaust it, we can hang on to it. Can't we?" Tory is pleading now. Hoping that somehow the words are sifting through the holes and making a dent in the shell that Tracy has constructed since her return to Maximum.

"Yeah, I guess so. But it's not much. They say this governor is not much on clemency. So, don't get my hopes up. OK?"

Before Tory can answer, the guard returns, bringing the faint smell of body odor. "Time's up," he announces. Harold Short comes in on Tory's side. The men escort them out their prescribed exits. Tory calls to Tracy as she leaves, "Tracy, Tracy?" She has no idea what words she would fling down the long hall should Tracy answer, but she doesn't turn around, her steps shuffling in double-time alongside the guard. Her shoulders shaking.

Chapter 9

The road from Parchman to Jackson is four-lane, stretching across the edges of the Delta, then easing into rolling hills, and finally into an urban landscape. Tory sees nothing along the way; instead, she replays the past few hours: the click of the tumblers in the lock, the foul smell of the guard, the other smell—that of deep, abiding, no-safe-haven fear. She shivers again, caught in the terror of it herself, wonders how Tracy manages the long days and fierce hot nights, waiting for her death. It's one thing to know in the abstract that you're going to die, another entirely to know the date and time. Perhaps that was the knowledge that she had seen on Tracy's face. The certainty, the time, the place, the method. Tory remembers hearing, in her young married days, people saying how they would choose to die. In my sleep, in bed, after a good screw, Paul had told her once.

The groan of the single air conditioner, located outside Jane's office, is intermittent—like alternating current, Tory thinks. She is working her way through the files yet again, re-reading the newspaper articles, checking a list of questions that Jane has provided. Henry Lee is here. He and Jane are sorting through another stack of folders. The stale smell of coffee, long-brewed, moves listlessly on the night air.

Tory jots down the date of one article in a Meridian paper which questions a tactic of the defense. Paul's name is omitted; a quote from the DA calls the claim absurd. She takes Raheem's letter from her purse, reads it again, feels the weight of his words fall against her heart. He won't be coming, he says—too much for him. But he has included a letter to be read at the hearing. Tory includes it in the folder.

Down the hall, on her way to the bathroom, Tory stops to look at the pictures of those on death row. Twenty-eight in all—twenty-seven men and Tracy. The photographs are black and white, both in finish and race. More blacks than white, overwhelmingly more male than female. The lavatory's slow drip and the rust line in the toilet speak to the poverty here, in this place. No tasteful prints here, no Kitty Hawk soaring over Kill Devil Hill, no monogrammed towels. This place is pared down to the essentials: single-sheet toilet paper, brown paper towels, and an air freshener that has eroded away, leaving only its slender plastic stick jutting up into the night—its shadow, against the wall, giving the finger to all comers.

By midnight, they have completed the strategy. It is simple. Jane will cite all things legal, then add Raheem's letter—one that lists the long string of abuses and deprivations that Tracy suffered as a girl. Then they will appeal to the governor's sense of pity for a poor young girl, cast-off and desperate; remind him that women voters will tend to see the case differently than men; imply that this could greatly enhance his chances in the Senate race. Tory understands that Jane will present cases which deal with "inadequacy of counsel," indicate the numerous trial errors that could have had the case overturned, had they been filed in time.

"Can you bear that, Tory?" Jane asks.

"I think so." Henry Lee reaches over to touch her shoulder. "I'm OK. Really. I know what has to be done to save her, and I can do it." Tory is surprised at the confidence her voice offers them. Wonders how it will sound when she criticizes Paul publicly, in front of such an audience.

⟡

They drive to the Capitol in silence the next morning, as if the heat and the humidity has sucked away their voices. Inside the Capitol, a uniformed trooper directs them to the hearing room. Tory notices a large oil painting of Lacy Steadman hanging in the rotunda. A good likeness. The background of flags—both Mississippi's and the United States'—offers a splash of color in contrast to the dark seriousness of his clothes and his demeanor. Silver-haired, tall, and definitely senatorial, Lacy Steadman would be a presence wherever he went. Tory wonders who the artist was. Whoever it was has artfully removed the beginnings of the dewlaps. Instant face-lift, Tory thinks, and smiles. Henry Lee notices and gives her a nod of encouragement.

The hearing room is floored with marble, and every footstep falls definite against the cool surface. The walls are paneled in a heavy oak, the windows draped with velvet, the state seal embroidered in gold in the center of a deep swag. The same crossed flags from the governor's portrait stand to one side of the windows, and in front, a long mahogany table is surrounded by seven maroon leather chairs. Henry Lee, Jane, and Tory are the first to arrive. "Does this mean that only four people will come? Besides us, I mean?" Tory asks. Jane and Henry Lee both shrug "I don't know." They take chairs on the window side of the table and busily unload their files. Tory has nothing to unpack, nothing to place on the table in front of her chair except her purse. She places it in front of her as she sits. With a Kleenex, she wipes a dust streak from the front, a little trace of Parchman in this fine, ornate place. How far removed are these who will make the decision from that wretched place, she thinks—Tracy's thin, manacled frame appearing in her mind.

At 10:02, the first of the clemency board appears—a lawyer from the coast, where the crime was committed. He introduces himself, shakes hands, and slings a slender leather file case on the table. From it, he takes a yellow legal pad and begins jotting down notes. Tory strains to see what he writes. He notices her glance and curves his left arm across the top of the paper, shielding it from her view. Tory feels the flush rise to her cheeks, quickly turns to face the bank of windows. Henry Lee and Jane are whispering, pointing to a notation in the margin of a brief that Tory had seen the night before.

The second member arrives, a woman who serves on the state's correction board. She does not smile as she introduces herself. Her handshake is firm, Tory notices, and her nails are cut very short. No nonsense, this woman, Tory decides.

Finally, in a flurry of activity, Richard Allman swings open the door, all but shouting over his shoulder to the press who have gathered in the hall. "I have no comment, gentlemen, and neither does the Governor." Tory catches sight of Melinda among the gentlemen, and is relieved when she gives a quick thumbs-up before the door is closed.

Richard Allman takes his seat at the head of the table, hitches his chair up, and crosses his arms and leans on them. "Well," he says, "it looks like we are all here." Tory throws a look of panic to Jane, then to Henry Lee. "I suppose that you have met each other and we can begin." Then, seeming unsure, he continues, "I'm Richard Allman, special administrative assistant to the Governor. This is Ms. Rachel McQueen, chair of the corrections board, and Harvey Ginn, district attorney for Stone County." He waves toward the side of the table where they sit. "And this is Jane Fillmore, director and chief counsel for the CDRC; Henry Lee Addams, rector of the Church of the Redeemer, Meadville; and Ms. Tory Gardiner, spiritual advisor for the defendant." Another wave of his hand includes the three of them. "Governor Steadman requests that he be excused from this session since pressing matters in his family require that he be away this morning." Tory does not risk a look at Jane or Henry Lee. "However, I do have his notes, and if the circumstances require, I can offer those as testimony—should we need it." That bastard, Tory thinks. That cowardly bastard. Family matters, indeed. Saving his own skin— Tracy would say saving his white fucking ass: neither comes under the rubric of family matters. A short sigh catches her off-guard, and she quickly looks around the table to see if the others have noticed.

"First, I'll give a recap of the facts, as they appear of record." With that, Richard Allman opens his file and begins recounting the crime, the trial, the appeals, the overturned stays, all the machinations of the court for the last thirteen years. At the end, he closes the file, looks to Harvey Ginn, and asks if he has any further comments. Ginn clears his throat, takes out his legal pad, and begins. "You've done an excellent job, Mr. Allman, reviewing what appears in the record about this vicious crime. I only bring the sentiments of the good folk of Stone County who wish to see justice done, the law served, and the decision of the original jury, twelve good and honest men, put into effect—finally, after thirteen years. Theresa Magnarelli has had benefit of counsel, access to the courts, and thirteen years of life that was denied to the victim. We say that her time is up. We trust that the state will proceed with what has been mandated."

Tory feels that she will smother under his pomposity. Ginn has confiscated all the air in the room, and she fears that she will faint.

Rachel McQueen nods in agreement. "I have nothing more to add, Mr. Allman. The prison board, for whom I speak, feels that if justice is to be served, then the sentence must be carried out."

Allman looks at Jane. "Ms. Fillmore?"

Jane straightens her shoulders, opens her file, and begins. Point by point, she counters Ginn's statement, citing case law and precedent. Her voice is strained, nearly breaking as she reads the statement from Raheem. She pauses, giving his plea for the life of the mother of his child time to register on the members of the commission. Then, she begins again. "Finally, Mr. Allman, we feel that under other circumstances, this defendant might have been convicted of man one, not capital murder. The . . ."—her voice breaks; she does not glance at Tory, but continues, pushing her words into the morning—"shoddy defense in the first trial, the failure to file for new evidence in time, the numerous errors that were committed speak to the probability that with different counsel, Theresa Magnarelli would be out of prison now, taking care of her daughter, and leading a life that would benefit society. She was not, and is not, a hardened criminal; she was a poor young woman, caught in the maze of a no-opportunity life. We cannot believe that executing her will deter crime or benefit the state." Jane closes the file, and her shoulders fall just a bit under the weight of her speech.

Henry Lee speaks next. He mentions that Tracy is a child of God—guilty, perhaps, "but of what?" he asks. "Of being poor, friendless, an outsider?" He waits, giving the words time to carry around the room. Like his best point in a sermon. "She is not the same woman who was incarcerated, tried, and convicted thirteen years ago. She realizes that what she did was a terrible deed. Never has she tried to pretend that what she did was right. But in a moment of panic and desperation, she took the only road that she thought was open to her. What she did was wrong. There is no argument about that. But killing her will not give Dwayne Dewey back his life. Commuting her sentence to life, even life without parole, will allow her the chance to atone in some way for her act. Certainly that is a better option. She has not asked to be set free; she has simply asked that you not continue this sordid mess by murdering her to prove that her murdering someone was wrong. In the name of God, don't perpetuate this horror by killing this young woman." When he finishes, Henry Lee is visibly moved. And he hardly knows her, Tory thinks.

"Mrs. Gardiner?" Richard Allman turns to Tory.

"Yes?"

"Would you like to add anything?"

Tory takes a deep breath. "Yes, I would." She pulls at the purse's strap, then drops it, remembering the article on power dressing. She begins the speech that she has rehearsed in the motel bathroom less than two hours ago. "As some of you may know, my late husband, Paul Gardiner, defended Ms. Magnarelli when the trial was moved to Clayton City. At the time of the trial, our only child, a daughter, was critically ill. She died just as the trial ended. For that reason, and for the ones cited by Ms. Fillmore, I feel that Paul's defense was colored by his personal . . ." What word can she use that will not be an outright lie? Anguish won't work, for he never felt that wrenching despair as far as Tory could tell. Everyone at the table is watching, waiting for Tory to continue. "By the distraction of her condition. Mary Vic died on December tenth. The trial was over on the seventh. During the next thirty days, during the time that he should have filed whatever he should have filed, we buried our only child, tried to console his aging, grieving mother"—Tory wonders if, like Pinocchio, her nose is growing—"tried to figure out a way to get through Christmas and begin a new life." She pauses, wondering if this is true. "As a result, I think that inadequate counsel is something that must be considered in this case." Harvey Ginn looks shocked. Ms. McQueen and Richard Allman do not change expressions. All three watch her as though she were a rare albino species, exhibited in the Jackson Zoo. "Furthermore, in my conversations with Tracy, I know that she killed Dwayne Dewey because she thought he was molesting her daughter. That evidence, mitigating the circumstance of the murder, was never introduced. The child was sent to live with its great-grandmother . . . the same woman, I must add, who severely abused Tracy as a child. Never was little Tiffany examined for signs of molestation which would have corroborated Tracy's claim."

Again, the room remains silent as Tory gathers her courage. "Surely, anyone in this room who has ever been a parent can understand—not condone, but understand—Tracy's actions. I, for one, know the anger I felt in my heart for those who hurt my daughter while caring for her in the hospitals. The nurses who moved her carelessly, the doctors who ran tests that made her cry out in pain. I know that I could have done murder if my child had been viciously treated." Tory is out of breath, the burden of the words more than she can carry. She looks at Ms. McQueen, Mr. Ginn, and Allman. "And I trust that you would do the same." There is no response. No one moves. Tory sits back from the edge of her chair, grateful to lean against its sturdy leather cushion.

৵

Outside, Tory squints into the morning sun. Henry Lee and Jane hurry ahead of her, down the steps, into a flurry of reporters. Jane fields the questions, smiling, looking hopeful. Tory hangs back, stepping behind a thick stone column.

"Tory?"

She jumps, pulling her purse to her chest, steps further back into the shadow.

"I didn't mean to frighten you." It's Melinda.

"Oh, no. I'm just jumpy, that's all."

"How did it go?"

"That bastard, Steadman, didn't show up. Said he had 'pressing family matters.'"

"No show. That figures. Doesn't want to 'get involved.'"

"I guess. I couldn't tell a thing about how the board felt. They looked like stone. Just about as interested as this column here." Tory taps her hand against the shadowed coolness, and her wedding ring clicks against the surface.

"Would you give me a statement to that effect?"

"A statement?"

"Yeah. I'll hold it until we hear the board's decision, but if it goes against her, I plan to blast Steadman to hell and back."

"I don't know, Melinda. Could it help? At that point, what can we do?"

"Keep that son-of-a-bitch from getting to the Senate."

"How can that help Tracy? She'll be . . . gone by then." The tears that have been threatening all morning rise to Tory's eyes, and she feels the convulsion of a sob shake her chest. Melinda touches Tory's shoulder, draws her into an embrace just as a flashbulb brightens the space around them.

"Bastard!" Melinda shouts. The photographer, still hidden behind the camera, backs down the steps, snapping two more shots as he flees. "We may make the front page tomorrow, Tory." She offers Tory a tissue.

Over coffee at the CDRC, they rehash the meeting, trying to read into the silence some hint of the outcome. Jane is not optimistic; Henry Lee has more confidence in the human heart.

Tory is exhausted. "When will we hear?" she asks.

"We only have six days to go. If they are not going to recommend clemency, then they must let us know soon so that the final appeals can go forward," Jane says. "I think we'll know something by tomorrow. Thursday, at the latest." She shakes her head. "We're beginning the last counts," she adds.

"Last counts?" Tory asks.

"Yes, the last Thursday, then the last Friday, last Saturday . . . you know. The last of everything."

"Oh, Jane." Tory's voice is strangled. "What can we do? How will we stand it?"

"We'll stand it for Tracy. The stakes are much higher for her." Tory doesn't hear condemnation in her voice, only fatigue. "Why don't you go back to Parchman; I'll call you as soon as we get the news. I'd rather Tracy hear it from you than from the TV." She closes the file, shoves it to the center of the desk. "If it's a no, then I'll come up and spend some time with her. But I think you should be there, whatever the news."

Tory nods and gathers up her purse. "I'll talk to you soon," she calls to Jane and Henry Lee as she leaves.

The Maximum Security Unit is stifling. Tory asks the guard for a fan for the office as she waits for Tracy. "Sorry, ma'am, can't do it. Security risk." Tory wonders if he thinks she will rip the fan apart and offer a blade to Tracy so that she can cut her way out. She laughs in spite of herself. "I know, ma'am, seems silly, but you never can tell about these folks."

"These folks up here are hot, just like folks anywhere," Tory says. "You all might think about that for a change."

"Yes, ma'am, we might. But we don't." He steps outside the door, closes it behind him, and leans against the frame, the butt of his gun visible through the window. The guard ushers Tracy into the room, seats her in the chair opposite Tory. Her face is drawn, the dark circles beneath her eyes heavier than before. "How are you holding up, Trace?"

"Pretty good. They've offered me a pill to help me sleep, but I haven't taken one yet. I keep thinking things may get worse and I'll need one more, later. You know." She spreads her hands in a gesture that is so futile, so helpless, that Tory thinks that she may crumble in the face of it. She looks away, bites the inside of her cheek, hoping that the pain will keep her from crying.

"The clemency board met this morning."

"I know."

"I think it went pretty well. They seemed to listen to our statements. We had a long letter from Raheem to show them. He has asked for clemency. It was very beautiful. I brought it for you to read." Tory presses the letter, written on lined notebook paper, against the plastic barrier for Tracy to see. The handwriting cramped, words crossed out, a plea for mercy. Tracy spreads her hand on the other side, flat against the writing. The manacle's rattle startles them both. "I'll give it to the guard for you."

Tory taps her nail against the door, pulls it open, and hands the letter to the guard. Whispering, she asks him to take it to Tracy.

"Have to clear it through the warden first." He scans the page, and Tory feels the anger rise in her throat. She takes the letter from him, folds it in upon itself, slides it into the envelope.

"Fine. You check with the warden and let me know."

"I'll have to take it with me. Let him look at it."

"OK. But it should only be read by him. It's personal."

"Sure, miss. I got no reason to read it in the first place."

"Exactly." Tory turns to reenter the room. Seated, she feels the silence press against her. Tracy is looking out the window. "Tracy?"

"Yeah?" She turns, eyes wide and vacant.

"What can I do to help? Anything?"

"I don't know."

"Jane said she would call as soon as she gets the clemency board's decision."

"Yeah."

"We have to keep our hopes up."

"Yeah."

"It could go our way, you know."

"Yeah. And it might not."

"I know."

The whirr of the clock as it marks off the minutes is loud as thunder.

ᴣ〜

The man at the front desk of the Delta Queen buzzes Tory's room. She has a message. Jane's voice is tight, restrained. The board has not recommended clemency. She promises to be at Parchman by eight the next morning. Will Tory get to the prison before then and break the news to Tracy?

Tory sinks into the bed. Holds the phone against her ear long after the connection is broken.

"May I help you?" The desk clerk asks.

"What?"

"Would you like to make a call?"

"No, no. Thank you, no."

"Well?"

"No, nothing."

"Do you need help, Mrs. Gardner?"

"No, I'm fine."

"Would you like to hang up the phone then?"

"Oh, certainly." Tory puts the receiver down quickly, feeling foolish. She runs her fingers through her hair, feels her nails against her scalp, is aware of a long, guttural cry that rings its way around her room. No clemency—how can they do this? Despair wraps around her like a glove, and for the first time, she looks clearly into the next few days and realizes that last counts are truly upon them. Sleep is a long time coming. Tory faces the unblinking night, knowing that she must gather her strength, her courage, find words of comfort. Only comfort, maybe, not hope.

For the third time in her adult life, Tory wakes, fully clothed, to the early slant of sunlight. The neon "Delta Queen" has faded overnight, seems pallid against the strong rays of early-morning sun. Tory washes her face, runs a comb through her hair, and heads for her car. She picks up a cup of coffee at a drive-through, pushes the accelerator toward the floor. She must get to Parchman before Tracy hears the news. At the gate, the guard seems sleepy, lackadaisical, bothered by her early-morning arrival. His check of the car is cursory, his wave offhand as he ushers Tory into the prison parking lot. There is no one at the front desk; Tory taps on Carol Monk's door. No answer. A guard from the end of the hall asks if there's something she needs.

Tory explains her reason for being there. He hesitates, wonders aloud if she can be admitted to Maximum this early.

"But, don't you see, I have to go tell her myself. She can't hear it on TV. That would be terrible." The guard is not moved. He offers to call the warden's office, to see what he can do. Tory nods as he directs her to a seat, says he'll be back in a few minutes.

The inside of the reception area, cool and tidy, is strangely quiet this morning. No sounds of telephones ringing, computers and printers starting up; no sharp report of troopers' heels against the linoleum. A deadly quiet; only the occasional metallic click of the clock, above the double doors leading out into the prison yard, breaks the spell.

Tory wonders what has happened to the hope and courage that she originally brought here. Who or what drained it away, sucked it out? When she first arrived—was it only six weeks ago?—she had so little at stake; but now, now everything is different. She can't explain it, certainly not to Mother Gardiner (not that she'd want to hear it), but everything *is* different, totally different, and Tory cannot change that. Why didn't someone warn her that this might happen? Why didn't someone tell her that she might discover the urgency of life—not only Tracy's, but her own? What has happened to the scripts she wrote for her life? The good-girl/good-wife/good-mother script that promised everything. How has Tory ended up just a bit player in her own life? At least Tracy has had the starring role in her bad-girl drama, played center stage, played it for all it was worth.

The guard reappears and says that the warden would prefer that Tory wait until morning count and breakfast are over.

"I can't do that," Tory says.

"But, ma'am—" the guard begins.

"Don't you see? She'll see the television report by then. Or somebody will have heard and told her. I cannot wait. It would be too cruel. Cruel, atrocious and heinous . . . you must ask him again."

The guard shrugs, walks away, and Tory feels a wash of defeat threaten to undo her. Suddenly, in the distance, she hears a phone ring, then the startup sounds of a tractor. The last Friday of her last week has begun at Parchman.

Only after Jane arrives does the truck appear to take them to MSU. They sit thigh-to-thigh in the dusty truck, bumping over the rutted road. Tory braces herself against the dashboard, fighting to keep herself from being slung against Jane's erect little body.

"Sorry," the trusty murmurs as he hits a pothole dead center. "We're fine," Jane answers, looking straight ahead.

Not really, Tory thinks.

It takes just over half an hour for Jane and Tory to pass through the checkpoints, get settled in the "office" at MSU. The room set aside for attorney-client meetings has no perforated dividers. There's a metal desk, a phone, and three plastic chairs. The windows are barred, and the morning light is superseded by a row of fluorescent lights.

Tracy arrives, disheveled, looking hung-over. She lifts a hand to shake Jane's outstretched one. The wrist chain swings slightly. "I already heard," she announces. "Cocksucker."

"Yes," Jane answers. Tory nods.

Jane removes a file from her briefcase. "Here's the next set of proceedings, Tracy. The Mississippi Supreme Court will get these this morning. They should rule by tonight; then we'll start over at the Fifth Circuit." Her voice is weary; the telling of last things is getting to her, Tory thinks. "There's a possibility that even if all this fails, we can ask for a successor habeas corpus from the U.S. Supreme Court, if I can figure out some new legal issues to raise." She flips through the papers, and Tory wonders if there's any hope lodged in there, something that they have all overlooked. "Anyway, Tracy, remember I have just begun to fight." Jane's laugh is worn, tired, devoid of any humor. Silence falls back into the room.

"Tracy?" Tory asks.

"Yeah?"

"I'm sorry."

"Yeah, me too."

The three women sit, facing each other, staring at the floor or out the window. There are no words. The morning slides away from them into silence.

ॐ

On Saturday, there is a follow-up story in the Jackson papers about the clemency hearing. Steadman has refused to intervene, he says, because "I don't have the authority to do so except in the case of an obvious miscarriage of justice." Besides, he adds, "the case is still under review by the courts, so it would be improvident for me to insert myself into the legal process." Tory throws the paper down on the breakfast-room table with such force that her coffee sloshes over, dampening Steadman's senatorial pose on the front steps of the Capitol.

Jane told her that she would best serve Tracy if she went home and gathered her strength for the last Monday and Tuesday. Then, she needs to be at Parchman, full-time. Tory wonders how she will spend the time between now and then. How will she pass these hours? How does one gather strength? For Mary Vic, it was easy, she thinks. She slept when the child slept, ate when the tray of hospital food was delivered by a woman with a thick hairnet over a helmet of sprayed-stiff hair, picked at the edges of her food, felt it turn to dust in her mouth. But the certainty of death was never there, never inhabiting the room as it had in the office at Parchman. Never so palpable, so definite. Of course, the doctors had said that Mary Vic wouldn't live to adulthood, but they could have been wrong. Tory had heard of hundreds of cases where people lived long beyond the time when the doctors said they would. It happened all the time. Miracles, some said. Missed diagnoses, according to others. But now, this feels so definite. Jane has mentioned that the last-minute appeals that she is filing may serve only to keep the death clerks at the various courts busy. She has said that they refer to these filings as "gang-plank appeals." Tory mentioned that she has never found gallows humor very funny. Jane agreed. They ended their conversation with a promise to see each other on Monday. And Tory is left with two days to fill. She wanders around her house, marveling that it seems so foreign, a place belonging to a woman she once knew only vaguely. The house needs only a quick brush of the floors, a swipe of the dust rag around the edges of tables; no one has disturbed a thing. There has been no life here for a long time, Tory realizes. The overall effect is appealing to the eye, but anyone could live here. The house is anonymous, she thinks—a stage set for a rather dull domestic piece of business; whether it would come across as comedy or tragedy would be anybody's guess.

In her studio, Tory is greeted by the clutter of art books, turpentine, and brushes; a coffee cup with the skim of mold clinging to the side; her pajamas, pants legs inside out, slung over the back of a chair. Leaning in the corner, paintings from that time before Paul died, dried, waiting for the juried show in the fall at the local gallery. Tory puts a large oil landscape on the easel. Steps back to look, appraise. The view, a farm pond and barn, near the spot where Paul and Mother Gardiner spent their Mother's Day picnics. The evening sun hangs just above the horizon, throwing golden arrows of light across the water. A russet blanket holding an open picnic basket, a blue pitcher, and a baseball and bat is in the foreground. At the last moment, she had added a lady's summer hat, complete with tulle band and streamers. Tory had thought it would be a nice Christmas gift for Mother G. Now, she sees it for the sentimental, tawdry thing that it is. One by one, she puts her work on the stand; one by one, they hold out some idealized view that promises and promises, then disappoints and fails her.

In the garden shed, Tory saws each painting in half with her pruning saw, breaks the stretchers into kindling, slits the canvas, and stuffs the remnants into the garbage can reserved for grass clippings. The sweetly putrid smell of rotting grass fills her nose as she packs the contents in and snaps the lid in place. Dragging the can to the curbside, she retrieves the day's mail, tosses it on the kitchen table, and puts the kettle on to boil, feeling finished somehow, finished with this house, this hobby of art.

Tory sifts through advertisements for sales in Memphis, flyers, the electric bill, and a letter from Jeanette Calvert. She tosses the stack into the garbage can, then fishes out the bill and the letter. She's past due on paying Mississippi Power and Light, she notices; how ironic, she thinks, as she slides her thumb under the flap on Ms. Calvert's letter. The shriek of the kettle fills the air. She fills the cup, unfolds a single sheet of note-book paper, written in pencil:

Dear Mrs. Gardiner:

I notice in the paper that you are still trying to save that murdering whore from the electric chair. Why are you spending the Lord's good time and everybody's money when your real job ought to be saving her soul? Have you done that? Like all sinners, her time is running out. I hope you think about this and get her right with God. You better do the same thing for yourself.

Yours sincerely,
Jeanette Calvert

Tory reads the letter once, twice, then a third time. The anger she felt upon the first read dissolves upon the second, and by the third time, she is laughing—her sides shaking, her head thrown back, and the sound of her voice rollicking, careening around the kitchen. "Oh, my dear Miss Calvert. Would that it were so easy!" She sinks onto the floor, leans against the refrigerator, spent. "Save her soul!" she hoots. "Yes, indeedy, save her soul! Would that I could. And save my own, while I'm at it. Oh, if you only knew, Miss Calvert. I'm capable of all that she has done and more, I assure you. I just lacked her courage." With her confession, Tory's laughter ceases, and she faces the clear, blazing light of truth.

The phone's sharp ring brings her to her feet. It's Katie Lou Little-john, with a message from Mother Gardiner. She would like to see Tory—this afternoon, if possible. "Fine," Tory answers. "What time?"

"She usually wakes from her nap about two-thirty. So, anytime after three."

"I'll be there," Tory promises.

Tory sinks into a long, hot bubble bath, shaves her legs, under her arms. The long, dark hairs on the razor indicate how long it has been since she's been aware of her grooming. Mother Gardiner would be shocked. Tory smiles. But she takes extra time pressing a linen blouse, choosing a navy skirt, sandals, the string of pearls that were her wedding gift from Paul. She puts on her makeup carefully, fluffs her new no-nonsense hair-cut, even uses the curling iron on her bangs. Still deferring to her, she thinks. Dressing for the part she expected me to play: sweet little wife who overlooks all her son's indiscretions, Paul's little cheerleader. Tory feels the hairs on her neck rise, a sour taste fill her mouth. But in spite of everything, she marvels, here I am answering her call as though it were a royal summons.

Mother Gardiner is sitting in bed, propped against her pillows, carefully coiffed, the mauve bed jacket tied in a neat bow at her neck. "Tory," she says.

"Mother Gardiner."

"How have you been?"

"Well, thank you."

"That's good."

"Yes, ma'am, it is. And yourself?"

"I am fine."

"I'm glad."

"I asked Katie Lou to call you."

"Yes, ma'am."

"I wanted to talk to you."

"Yes, ma'am?"

"About this business you're involved in, down in Jackson."

"Yes, ma'am. This business of trying to save Tracy Magnarelli from the electric chair?" There's a sharp edge in Tory's voice.

Mother Gardiner doesn't seem to notice. "Yes, that business."

"And what did you want to tell me?"

"Well, that I find it, at best, distasteful. At worst, disloyal to Paul."

"I thought you might."

"Have you had no second thoughts about it?"

"No, ma'am." Tory is struck by the realization that this is not a lie.

"Not at all?"

"No, ma'am. Not at all. My second thoughts all have to do with not getting involved sooner. So that we might stand a better chance *now*." Tory feels the weight of time running out lodge against her heart.

"I saw this in the paper on Friday." Mother Gardiner holds the front page of the Jackson *Daily News* out to Tory. There, in a photograph, she stands, in front of the Capitol, Melinda embracing her. "Really, Tory, this has gotten out of hand." Mother Gardiner sighs something that sounds a little like a tsk-tsk, a scolding for a naughty child.

"Out of hand?"

"Yes. Definitely. Out of hand."

"How so?"

"Oh, Tory, don't be obtuse." Again, Mother Gardiner sighs.

"Obtuse?"

"Yes, and dramatic. Your picture hugging a colored girl on the front of the Jackson paper! Really, Tory." She shakes her head, just slightly.

"That 'colored girl' is a fine journalist, Mother Gardiner, and she is doing everything she can to save Tracy's life."

"Well, I'm always pleased when they make something of themselves. You know that, Tory. When Annie's daughter went to nursing school, I was one of her chief benefactors. I have nothing against any of them, when they try to better themselves. I'm all for it, in fact." With that pronouncement, she places the paper across her lap, begins again. "But, your involvement in this sordid mess, Tory, is more than I can stand."

Tory rises from her chair, smoothes the front of her skirt, tucks her blouse into the waistband, and gathers her purse to her chest. "Mother Gardiner, I respect your feelings. I did not get involved in 'this sordid mess' to upset you. But I must tell you that I will be involved to the end. Even entering the witness room to watch Tracy die, if it comes to that and she wants me there." Tory takes a deep breath. "I plan to arrange Tracy's funeral, bury her next to Mary Vic, if none of her family comes to claim the body, and then go to Boston to find her little girl." This speech startles Tory, yet she realizes that all along, in the back of her mind, she's been making her own last-count plans.

Mother Gardiner looks stricken. "Bury that criminal in our plot? Oh, Tory, you *have* lost your mind. I won't have it."

"As I recall, one of the plots is designated for me. The one next to Mary Vic. You can have the one next to Paul. Tracy can have mine."

Mother Gardiner pushes the call button lying on the bed next to her. "Get out of here, Tory. Before I have a heart attack. You are, without doubt, the most impossible woman I have ever encountered. Whatever in the world would your dear sweet mother think if she could hear you?" She pushes the button again, with such force that her thumbnail turns white.

"I should hope that she would think that I have finally found my backbone, Mother G." With that, Tory opens the door, collides with the aide—who falters, then steps back into the hall, apologizing for interrupting.

"You're not interrupting anything," Tory tells her. "Mrs. Gardiner and I are finished."

185

Chapter 10

ॐ

On Sunday, Tory cleans her house top to bottom, vacuuming, dusting, scrubbing bathrooms, scouring sink and oven, the refrigerator. By noon, the smell of disinfectant, soap, and furniture polish fills the air, and dust motes move lazily in the sunshine that pours through the double French doors. Tory rests on the steps leading to the patio. She cleaned with the same fury the week after Mary Vic died. Determined to find every stray sock, every crayon, every doll dress so that they would not be waiting to shock her back into numbing grief. Paul left for a week to ski in Colorado, asked her to come along, but didn't make a second request after her refusal. That was probably the beginning of the end, Tory decides. No way to reconnect after that. While they were unraveling, Tracy's chances for a new trial were sliding away as well.

First, she swept the house clean of her child; next, she exorcised her husband. Today, she erases her mother-in-law. There's no one else to remove from her former life. The sudden understanding of her losses threatens to fling her away to some place where there is no safety net, no comfort. The only place she can go is into the arms of a "colored girl" who has "made something of herself." The bittersweet irony of this pushes Tory to the phone. She rings Melinda, leaves a message: can she meet Tory for dinner tonight in Drew?

Tory stops at St. Peter's Cemetery on the way out of town. Mary Vic's grave has settled, the earth hollowed into a cup like the palm of a hand, the Easter tulips dead and drooping in the vase at the base of her head-stone. Tory removes them, folds them into her palm, counts the dry pop-ping sounds as they break. Paul's marker, with its freshly cut death date, glistens in the morning sun. The earth, still mounded over him, is sprigged with St. Augustine grass. She tosses tulips into the shrubs sur-rounding the plot, hurries to her car.

The clerk at the Delta Queen Motel calls her by name, tells her that he's saved her a ground-level room on the back, away from the traffic. She thanks him, asks if there are any messages for her. He ruffles through a stack of pink "while-you-were-out" memos, hands her one from Melinda, agreeing to meet at seven for dinner. The relief that she feels is obvious; she smiles at the clerk, feels strangely buoyed by this good news. The room, with its cheap polyester comforter, matching curtains, and thin mahogany veneer furniture feels more like home to Tory than the carefully planned, polished showpiece on Canney Farms Road.

Waiting for Melinda, Tory checks the list that Jane has given her as the strategy for the next forty-eight hours. They have until one minute past midnight on Tuesday to work a miracle. Tory's faith is flagging, she realizes. She flips through a book she has brought with her. The memoir of a priest who makes death row inmates his congregation outlines what to expect on the last day. She turns away from the page, unable to read. The afternoon drags along, the late afternoon sun moving lazily down the arc of the Delta sky.

Melinda's on time, waiting in the dining room when Tory scans the supper crowd. They embrace quickly, settle into pleasantries, and read the menu. Tory thinks that she will not be able to eat, to talk, to breathe.

Both women pick at their food, converse in flat tones about nothing. Over coffee, Tory asks Melinda if she will come to her room to talk. Melinda checks her watch, nods, and follows Tory to the cash register.

Settled against the headboard, Tory wonders what it is that she wants to say to this woman. "Melinda, how do you manage?"

"Manage?"

"Yes, manage to keep your distance, write objectively, to do this over and over?"

"Well, I don't, really. I'm not objective, even if my columns might seem so. Well, maybe I'm even-handed, but not dispassionate. Guess I learned that at Ole Miss, learned not to let race, gender, old rage, new angers cloud my writing."

"Ole Miss? You went to Ole Miss?"

"Yeah. Does that surprise you?"

"I guess it does. I know it shouldn't, but yes, it does."

"You still see it as that white country club in the Grove?"

"I guess I do." The air thickens between them. Tory fears that Melinda will leave. She feels as out of touch as Mother Gardiner, a holdover from some ancient culture that died slowly, strangled by its own hand.

"Well, you're not alone, you know."

"Yes, I fear I do know that. But I didn't ask you here to talk about how hard old ways die. Though, God knows, they *do* take their own sweet time. I really don't know why I asked you to come. You seem to be the only one left for me to talk to."

"So, what is it that you want to say? Ask?"

"That's just the trouble. I don't know."

"I don't think I can help you there."

"I know that. Really. I discovered just yesterday that I have no past. Every vestige of my old life is now erased. My child dead, my husband unfaithful and killed in a wreck with his mistress in the car. Yesterday I cut the final tie with my mother-in-law. And here I sit in the Delta Queen Motel in Drew, Mississippi, fighting to save the life of a woman who I didn't even know three months ago . . ." Tory's voice falters.

"And that's a problem?" Melinda asks.

"Yes and no. And for some reason, I feel that you can understand. Crazy, isn't it?" Tory moves the pillow behind her head, tries to find some comfort there.

"Death row makes strange bedfellows, I guess."

"You know, Melinda, I could be on death row, myself."

Melinda looks startled. "You?"

"Yes, me."

"How do you figure that?"

Tory takes a deep breath, rearranges the pillows again. Suddenly wishes she had a drink. "When Paul was in ICU—that's my husband, Paul—"

"I remember."

"When he was hooked up to all those machines, I was there. One of the monitors went off." The staccato sound resurfaces in Tory's mind. "I didn't call the nurse. I just sat there, so angry. I *wanted* him to die. Wished him dead, wished that I had jerked that respirator cord right out of the wall. Wanted to watch him gasping for breath, wanted him to know that I, his wife of all those years, had pulled the plug." The sharpness of her voice penetrates the closed space between the two women. "When I had tried to comfort him earlier that morning, he hit me. Maybe it was a reflex action, maybe it was from the pain. But he hit me. Hard. Like he wanted to lash out at me, like it was something he had wanted to do for years. That's how it felt. Like long-withheld anger." Tory no longer sees

Melinda, but the image of Paul, his bandaged arm swinging at her in the stark light of the ICU. "And I wished him dead. And I didn't call the nurse." Her voice is quiet now. "I could have murdered him. Maybe I did. Who knows? Certainly I hated him enough to commit murder. And at times, after he died, I was so angry at him for dying. Because I didn't have the chance to kill him." The quiet of the room remains unbroken. Melinda comes back into Tory's vision.

"But you didn't," Melinda says. "You didn't, and Tracy did."

"I lacked her courage."

"Maybe."

"Tracy and I have a lot more in common than meets the eye. She had no mother; I had no daughter. Both of us were playing out scripts that somebody else wrote for us. The nuns, her grandmother wrote her bad-girl role for her. She decided to play it, be the star. I opted for only a bit part in my own life."

Melinda doesn't speak. She moves to the edge of the bed, gathers Tory into her arms, and absorbs the cup of trembling Tory offers.

Melinda finally speaks, her breath ruffling Tory's hair. "Seems to me that you've been moving to center stage ever since I met you." She sighs; Tory feels the hair above her ear move. "I better go. Long drive to Jackson." Melinda releases Tory, stands to leave.

"You can't drive this late at night. Stay here."

"You're sure?"

Tory nods.

Melinda slips into the bathroom. Tory hears the splash of water, the flush of the toilet, uses the time to put on her nightgown. Melinda reenters, dressed only in her slip. Awkwardly, Tory folds back the covers, fluffs the pillows, gestures to the bed.

In the darkness that follows, neither woman speaks. Melinda's slow, measured breathing soon fills the room. A kind of spiraling happiness fills Tory. The promise of knowing and being known. And hidden within that knowledge lies the possibility of love. Tory listens deep into the night, comforted.

☙

Monday morning brings the threat of Delta thunderstorms. Tory bids Melinda good-bye over tepid room-service coffee. They agree to meet at

Parchman, later in the day. "Thanks" is as much as Tory can manage, while Melinda stuffs her cellular phone, note pad, tape recorder into her purse.

Last Monday. The morning news reports that the Mississippi Supreme Court has turned down the appeal. The appeal now rests in the Fifth Circuit Court of Appeals in New Orleans. The no-accent voice of the newscaster says that "conventional wisdom has it that the Fifth Circuit will rule that the technicalities of law were not raised in a timely fashion, and will give the justices reason to reject this appeal, as it has in the past." Then Jane Fillmore's face fills the screen as she announces that the petition for a successor habeas corpus will be filed with the U.S. Supreme Court should the Fifth Circuit turn them down. She looks haggard. "We have personnel in New Orleans, waiting for the judges' decision. Time is running out, and we want to file in Washington before the day's over. If we have to." There's a resignation in her voice that sweeps across Tory as despair.

The road to Parchman is crowded this morning—farm trucks and tractors scattered among the state-trooper cruisers, the television vans, and passenger cars. Security is tight, and the checkpoints closely monitored. Tory frets in the heat, waiting her turn. The yellow MSU pass must be visible at all times, the guard reminds her. She nods, clips it to her collar, waits for the truck to drive her across the flat Delta morning.

Today, the guard mentions that her visit will be just an hour. "Lots of stuff to do before tomorrow night," he adds. Tory feels the bile rise in her throat. She does not challenge him, but follows him down the hall, waits for him to unlock the visitors' room. The guard relents a bit, tells her that she can be with Tracy all day tomorrow. "Just as soon as we clean out her cell." The enormity of his words leaves Tory speechless. She feels the contortion in her face, fights against the tears, swallows hard, and bitter gall slides down her throat. "That is, unless she gets a stay," the guard finishes.

"Yes, a stay." Tory finds her voice.

"It's always possible," he adds.

"Yes, possible," Tory whispers.

Tracy's hair is still wet when she enters from the other side. Her face drawn and taut. She nods slightly to the guard, who pulls the chair out and seats her, as if she were in a fine restaurant.

"An hour," he reminds them. They both nod.

"So?" Tracy begins.

"So," Tory answers. The hum of the fluorescent lights reminds Tory of a time in her childhood when she visited a farm, saw a beehive, and sucked honey from a comb. "Are you able to sleep at all?"

"Not without the pill."

"Oh."

"I asked for one last night. Too fucking noisy on the row."

"Oh," Tory says again.

"Jane says that the Supreme Court in Washington won't rule until sometime tomorrow. Won't know till then, really." Tracy sounds as though she is talking about someone else, someone in whom she has only slight interest.

"Oh."

"The waiting's the hardest fucking part." Tracy shakes her head just slightly. "The others on the row have started talking to me."

"Really?"

"Yeah. Saying things like, Remember Tommy Ray. Went right up to the lick-log, they say. Then got a stay."

"That *is* good to remember. Isn't it?" Tory's voice rings false, and she regrets it immediately.

"I guess. Mainly, I just want to know what's going to happen. I think I'm ready for whatever. I just don't know how to get from here to there. You know what I mean?"

"I think I do."

"I want you to do some things for me, Tory. After all this is over." Tracy looks at Tory straight on, something she has not done in several visits. "Will you promise me?"

"You know I will."

"Even if it's hard stuff?"

"Even if it's hard stuff."

"Okay. Here's the list." She moves awkwardly, pulling a much-folded sheet of paper from her coverall pocket. "I want you to find me some clothes to be buried in. And I don't want to be buried here, at Parchman. I want a real grave, somewhere that maybe, some time, Tiffany can visit. I don't want her to have to come here to see her mama's grave. I want you to mail a letter to Raheem, after . . . after everything's done. You know?

"Yes, I know. I've already made arrangements for you to be buried next to my Mary Vic, if you want to be. If it comes to that."

Tracy is quiet; Tory waits, wondering if she has heard her. Slowly, Tracy nods. "That would be real nice, I think. Is it pretty there?"

"I think so. I've planted lots of flowers around the plot, mostly tulips and daffodils."

"We never had a garden in Medford." Tracy seems to regret that. She sighs, just slightly, looks toward the window and the morning sun.

"And I want Tiffany to have the picture you drew of me." She looks back down at the list, folds it with one hand, and slides it back into her pocket. "I guess that's about it." Then she laughs. "Doesn't take long to get my affairs in order, as they say."

"And it may be that we don't have to do any of this." Tory works to find some hope to put in her voice.

"And it may be that we do."

"I plan to go to see Tiffany and Raheem, whatever happens, Tracy. Maybe get them to come see you, some time."

"Don't do that to me, Tory. Don't hold out any fucking hope. You promised, remember?"

"Yes, I remember. I'm sorry."

"Right."

"So, what would you have me tell Tiffany? When I see her?"

"Tell her that her mama loved her, I guess. I know she won't believe it. My granny's poisoned her against me, I'm sure of that."

"Tell me about when she was born." Tory leans back just a bit in her chair, like a child waiting for a story.

"She was born in the hospital in Biloxi. I don't remember the name of it. But it was in the middle of the night when I went. I took the last bus along the coast, and had to walk for a mile or so. I remember it was cold for down there. And I had sand in my shoes, rubbed a big old blister on my heel. Hurt like hell. When I got to the hospital, the woman on duty was asking all kinds of questions, like how the fuck I was going to pay for this, where was the daddy, did I have any insurance. Then my water broke all over the floor, and she just hollered out for somebody to bring a mop." Tracy laughs and Tory joins her, glad to find another sound against the morning. "She came quick, they said, for a first baby. Must have been all that dancing!" Tracy laughs. "And when I saw her, I thought I would die. She was so beautiful." Tracy smiles, remembering. "I guess everybody thinks that. But she was, really she was."

"I know. I've seen her picture."

"Right then, I promised that I'd do better. Be a good mama to her. Find Raheem. Do what I was supposed to." Tracy is looking past Tory now. Her voice is soft. "But when I left the hospital, Dwayne was waiting for me. Telling me to get over this, fast. Get back to dancing. He gave me a hundred-dollar bill to live on until I could go back to work." She shakes her head. "All my promises to Tiffany went right out the window. Shit, I didn't last two hours." The hard edge has come back into her voice. "I was dancing again while I was still on the rag. Dwayne keeping Tiffany in the motel room. I was back on the corner when she was only seven weeks old."

"You did what you had to do, Tracy."

"That's bullshit and you know it, Tory. I did what I wanted to—always have. Look where it got me." She spreads her arms as far as the manacles will allow. "Shit, shit, shit." Tracy shakes her head, stands, knocks for the guard.

"Tracy?"

She doesn't turn around, but is ushered out, shuffling, weighed down by her manacles.

"I'll be here in the morning, Tracy," Tory calls after her; but there is no answer.

ॐ

Tory meets Jane, Henry Lee, and Melinda at the cafeteria for free-world workers. The conversation floats above her as they discuss the next thirty-six hours. Jane is certain that the Fifth Circuit will deny, and she has already faxed the final appeal to the death clerk at the Supreme Court in Washington. She has rented a cellular phone for the next two days—a big expense for the CDRC, she says. Henry Lee has agreed to meet with the delegation from Amnesty International, has a call in to the bishop of Mississippi, and has arranged for an all-night vigil outside the gates. Melinda has an interview with the warden and the governor. Only Tory seems to have nothing to do. They talk around her, pumping up their courage with busyness.

"She doesn't want to be buried at Parchman," Tory interrupts them. "I am going to call her grandmother and see if she plans to claim the body. If not, I'm going to bury her in my plot, at St. Peter's, in Clayton City." The words slide across the table like oil on water, covering, stilling the others' plans. "And I'll need to get her some clothes. She asked for something other than her prison coverall." The three others look at Tory, as if they just realized that she was there. "Henry Lee, would you perform the service?"

"If it comes to that." His voice is low, filled with resignation.

"Thank you. I want to be able to tell Tracy." Tory looks down at her hands, pushes back the cuticle on her thumbnail. "If it comes to that."

They all nod, slowly, as one. Jane moves first, citing a need to call her office. Henry Lee moves back from the table, and Tory thinks that he is the oldest man she has ever seen. Melinda covers Tory's hand with her own, says she'll meet her at the motel for dinner. "That won't be necessary, Melinda. I'll be fine."

"I know you will. But I may need you tonight."

A small dress shop in Drew has a simple white dress that Tory likes: a gently scooped neckline, fitted bodice, and loosely gathered skirt in a fine pima cotton. The smallest size they have is a six. She figures that will have to do. She wonders about shoes, realizes she doesn't know what size to buy. She adds a pair of lace panties and bra, a slip, and a pair of white textured hose to her purchases at the cash register.

"Summer school graduation?" the clerk asks. "Perfect for that, I think," she adds, as she holds the dress up by the shoulders and folds it in upon itself in a quick, precise motion. "Shall I put everything in a gift box?" She offers a smile as she rings up the last item.

"No, that won't be necessary." Tory cannot return the smile, fumbles for her credit card, looks beyond the clerk to the curtained dressing rooms in the rear of the store, thinks of the trips to Memphis with her mother, of cubicles such as these where her mother tried on beautiful clothes and smelled of gardenias. The clerk, a fiftyish matronly sort, examines the card and says, "Oh, you're Mrs. Gardiner."

"Yes," Tory answers, looking hard into the woman's face, "Tory Gardiner." The woman struggles to get the bar to slide across the face of the sales slip and checks twice to see if the imprint is legible.

"Sign here, please." The clerk does not look at her.

Tory signs the slip quickly, not checking the amount of purchase—something Paul would have chastised her for. Outside, in the afternoon sun, the car is stifling. Tory presses all four window buttons with as much strength as she can muster, tosses the package on the seat beside her, and rests her head for a moment against the sticky, hot leather covering the steering wheel. The clerk in the shop is on the phone, gesturing toward Parchman.

Back at the motel, Tory calls the funeral home in Clayton City and speaks with the eldest of the Littlejohn sons. He seems reluctant to pick up a body at Parchman. "The state won't pay for a funeral outside the prison grounds," he tells Tory.

"I realize that."

"Well, as you know, Mrs. Gardiner, we require payment before we begin our services." His voice is unctuous, patronizing. Tory feels the anger rising in her throat.

"I understand, Mr. Littlejohn. Since I have been good for my last two funerals, I think you can trust me on this one." Tory takes a deep breath. "I cannot get a check to you, as I am in Drew, but I will have it for you when you arrive at Parchman. Surely, that will be sufficient, given my credit rating." The finality in her voice seems to convince him that he can bend the rules just a bit. "I will call you on Tuesday night, if the situation arises that I will be needing your services in the early hours of Wednesday morning. And you might get in touch with the caretaker at St. Peter's, have him ready to open the plot next to Mary Vic's." Tory is certain that the cough he offers is a covering for his disbelief. She allows him a moment to recover. "Will you handle that for me, Mr. Littlejohn?"

"Oh, yes, ma'am, I will." He stumbles a bit in his answer, but he's too much businessman, too much Katie Lou's son to miss the sale. Disgust fills Tory as she hangs up the phone.

Melinda meets Tory in the motel dining room and recounts the interview with the warden and with the governor. "Steadman is still hanging onto his earlier statement that he cannot intervene until the issue is no longer in the courts. That could be as late at 11:30 tomorrow night." Melinda tears the top of two packets of sugar off in one motion, dumps them into her iced tea. "Bastard! He could intervene any time he wanted to, save the courts all this last-minute mess, and commute her sentence." She stirs the tea with a fierce swirl, mashes the lemon slice tightly against the side of the glass. "But he's waiting to see the latest poll. Goddamned politician."

Tory can't think of a thing to say.

"The warden, well, he is just making sure that everything is 'on schedule.'" Melinda stirs, continues, not looking at Tory. "Says he is just a servant of the state, and it's his job to carry out the will of the people and the rulings of the court." She stops, shakes her head. "Didn't they rule out that defense at Nuremberg?" Tory is certain that they did.

"So, what will happen tonight, Melinda?"

"Well, security will be really tight. No time out of the cells for anybody on the row. This is a tough time for the rest of them. Lots of crazies there, and this countdown makes them all a little nuts. And then . . ."

Tory nods. "What?"

"Well, tonight, they do the dress rehearsal."

"What?" Tory fears that she has screamed, looks around quickly to see if the others in the restaurant have noticed.

"The dress rehearsal. They find a guard or prison employee about the size of Tracy and they go through the whole thing. See how long it takes to get from one place to the next, adjust the straps on the chair, read the death warrant aloud, approximate the time for Tracy's last words—everything, so that they have a timetable for tomorrow night."

"Oh, my God!"

"Justice may not be swift, but it is efficient—at least at this point."

Tory pushes her chair back from the table, hurries to the door and out into the thick Delta night. At the end of the motel's porch, she vomits. The gagging lasts long past the time her stomach is emptied. Melinda's hand feels warm against her back. "Tory?" she asks.

"What?"

"You need some rest."

Tory nods, and they walk to the room together.

⟋

Tuesday morning's sky is overcast, and the air is thick with moisture. Tory feels her clothes wilt as she steps into the heat. The guard nods, gives her car a quick check, and asks her to wait inside the reception center. There, the air is cool, and Tory is grateful for the relief from the heat. Carol Monk has left a packet of things for Tory. Opening the manila envelope with her name printed on the front, Tory reads the message:

Mrs. Gardiner:

Here is your pass for Tuesday. I have included several booklets to inform you as to the procedures. You must wear your pass at all times. Should you determine that you do not wish to be a witness—the prisoner has asked that you be included—please inform my secretary and we will offer the pass to someone else.

Sincerely yours,
Carol Monk

Tory turns the pass over and over in her hand. A black rectangle, the number 26 emblazoned there. In smaller letters: MSU, Tuesday, July 17,

1989. Made up especially for today, Tory thinks; use it or lose it. Who could possibly be waiting for this? Who in God's name could want it? She wonders if she can attach it to her collar, if she can lift number 26 to her throat. Tory is aware of voices, feet hurrying along the linoleum floors, telephones' muffled ringing in offices behind closed doors. Inside one booklet is a list of visiting times for Theresa Marie Magnarelli, July 17, 1989. Her name is listed for 10:00 a.m., Henry Lee's after hers. Then Jane. Then a long blank fills the afternoon. Carol Monk has penciled in *family?* for the long afternoon.

From her purse, Tory retrieves the telephone number that she has gotten from directory assistance. Grace Mary Magnarelli, Medford, Mass. She must make the call before she visits Tracy. She asks the receptionist if she might use one of the offices to make a credit-card call, and is ushered into Carol Monk's office. The silk ficus is still in perfect health. The blooms have dropped from the African violet. One of the leaves touching the edge of the terra-cotta pot has withered and died.

"Miz Monk won't be in till noon, so you can call from in here. Dial 9 to get outside."

"To get outside," Tory echoes.

She sits behind the desk, watches the phone for several moments. Several notes are lined up in military precision on the desk. All have Re: TMM, 7/17/89 printed across the top. Tory takes a deep breath and lifts the receiver.

The phone rings twice, three times. Then, a muffled hello. Tory asks to speak to Grace Mary Magnarelli.

"Speaking."

For a few seconds, Tory fears that she cannot support the weight of the receiver and will be forced to hang up.

"Hello?" The voice is old, harsh, questioning.

"Mrs. Magnarelli?"

"Yes?"

"My name is Tory Gardiner. I'm a friend of your granddaughter's. Of Theresa's?"

"She got a friend?"

"Yes, ma'am. She has me, at least."

There's a quick snort on the other end of the line. "Well, that's good, I guess."

"Yes, ma'am. It's good. She doesn't know that I'm calling you, but I felt like I should." Tory waits to see if this woman will offer her anything to make this conversation any easier. There's nothing. "Well, I'm certain that you know what today is?" Again, nothing. Tory plunges ahead. "There are still some matters before the court, but things don't look very . . . promising at this point."

"Yeah."

"And, if the appeals are rejected by the Supreme Court and the governor doesn't intervene, Theresa will be executed tonight." The words seem to come from somewhere else, some other planet, some space that is unfit for human habitation.

"Yeah, I know that."

"You know that?"

"Sure. The people at the prison called me."

"They did?"

"Yeah. One day last week. Asked me if I wanted to make plans to come down there."

"Oh."

"Yeah, I told them, and I'll tell you. I don't have a reason in the world to come to Mississippi. Not a one. I didn't before Theresa got into trouble, not when she was first in trouble, and not now."

"I see." Tory doesn't see, doesn't see at all. "Well, I have a visit with her this morning. I wondered if there was anything you wanted to tell her. Any message you wanted me to give her."

"No. None."

"None?"

"None."

"Would you like to talk to her?"

"No."

Again, there's silence. Tory feels the dampness under her arms despite the air conditioning.

"Well, I don't mean to pry or offend you, but there are some questions I need answered. First, does Tiffany know? Would she like to send her a message?"

"Tiffany isn't home."

"Will she be home later on? I think Tracy might want to call her."

"I don't know where she is."

"But she does still live with you?"

"When she's not out whoring around, just like her mama, just like her grandmama. All of them no-good."

"So, do you have a number where I might reach her and talk to her?"

"Nope."

"I see."

"Anything else?"

"Yes, there are a few other things." Tory pulls herself erect in the desk chair, rolls her head from side to side. "Tracy has asked that she not be buried in the prison cemetery."

"So?"

"Yes, and I wondered if you or any of your family will be claiming the body?" The words fall into the receiver, and Tory fears that they will refuse to go through the line, come crashing back to wound her.

"Nope. We won't be claiming anything. Except good riddance." The line hums between the two women.

"I think that's all, Mrs. Magnarelli. I think that's all."

"Yes, I believe it is. Theresa got herself into this and now it's caught up with her. The priest here said he would say a novena for her, but I told him it wasn't worth his breath. He'll do it anyway, I guess. But I won't be joining him. So, you can tell Theresa that or not. I don't care." The only sound left is the dial tone.

Chapter 11

❧

At 9:55, the prison truck appears, and right on schedule, Tory is ushered into the office for her visit. Tracy enters at 10:01. Tory marvels at the efficiency. The guard quickly steps out into the hall. There are no barriers here, nothing but space and time to separate them.

"How're you holding up?"

"Pretty good."

"That's good."

"Yeah, I guess."

"Are you able to eat anything?"

"A little."

"That's good."

"Yeah, I guess."

The words are batted back and forth, a quick volley—like a tennis match, Tory thinks. Tracy sits, pushes her legs out full length, slides down in the chair. Tory notices that her feet are small, slender. "So, what can we talk about that will help, Tracy?"

"Nothing I can think of."

"Would you like some paper, a pen to write to Tiffany? To Raheem? I think I can get some from the guard."

"I done that already."

"Oh."

"Tory, do you think it will hurt?" Tory feels as if she will choke, cannot answer, only shakes her head. "I'm all set, really. I *am* scared about how much it will hurt. That's all."

Tory can offer Tracy nothing, feels that she may not survive the honesty of the moment. She merely nods. Then, "Tracy, the fear of the thing is always worse than the thing itself. At least, that's been true for me."

Tracy nods. "You know, if I'd killed Dwayne three months later, I'd be in the gas chamber. Rule says you die by the method that was law at the time of the crime. I just killed him a little too soon, I guess." She looks out the window, and Tory thinks that the little smile on her face will be the way she will remember her.

"Tracy?"

"Yeah?"

"I hope we don't have to use any of these, but I've made plans for you, just in case."

"Just in case?"

"In case the appeals are rejected." Tracy forces Tory to say it. "I have bought you some clothes. I'll bring them tonight. And I'll go see Tiffany and offer her a chance to come and spend some time with me, if she wants to. I need a daughter. She could visit your . . ."

"Grave." Tracy finishes the sentence.

"Yes."

"Thank you."

"The woman at the store about died when she realized who I was and what I was buying. You'd have thought I had leprosy or something."

Tracy laughs at this. "You think she knew you?"

"I guess, from the pictures in the paper."

Tracy laughs again. "You're getting famous, huh?"

It's Tory's turn to laugh. "Or *in*famous, maybe?"

They both are left smiling—for a second.

Tracy drops hers first, glances around the room, wonders aloud when the guard is coming.

"At eleven," Tory answers.

"There's nobody scheduled for the afternoon."

Tory nods.

"Henry Lee said that the bishop might come, but then I heard he was busy."

Tory nods again. She has seen the news story as well. The bishop had "pressing plans"; the president of the Southern Baptist Convention didn't feel that he had the right to contact the governor on a situation that "was clearly secular." He mentioned the bit about "rendering unto Caesar the things that are Caesar's." Henry Lee had been devastated by his fellow clergymen's refusal. "Ass-saving" is what Melinda called it.

"I'm sorry. What did you say?" Tory asks.

"Nothing. The noise is outside."

"Oh."

The rest of the hour passes in silence. When the guard comes to the door, Tory reaches for Tracy—only to have him step between them. "This is not a contact visit, Miz Gardiner. That comes tonight."

ᴣ

Jane is able to rearrange the afternoon so that Tracy is allowed out of her cell. "Highly irregular," the warden's secretary tells them, "but since she has no family to visit, he's bending the rules a bit." Jane thanks her; Tory hears Grace Magnarelli's voice and judgment in her head. Tracy rejects an offer from a parish priest in Leland to come and give her extreme unction. Henry Lee is given a second visit; Jane's is extended to two hours. Tory is to be included in the last meal, the matron tells her. Sitting in the holding room with several officials from the prison, someone remembers that Tommy Ray asked the warden to join him for chili dogs and coleslaw with lots of onions and iced tea. The matron tells them that Tracy has asked for clam chowder, fried dough, and a Molson beer. "I bet they get the goddamned chowder out of a can," Tracy had said.

As the afternoon passes, Tory fidgets inside the reception area, rewrites Grace Magnarelli's phone number on a clean sheet of paper, in case Tracy wants to call Tiffany. Finally, at 3:30, Jane returns, mentions that it's 4:30 in D.C. Both women offer a little sigh to the afternoon noise and busy themselves with watching. "They're cleaning out her cell now," Jane says.

"What does that mean?" Tory asks.

"They bring her a box, ask that she indicate who gets what, put that stuff in the box, then they strip the cell of everything else."

"My God!" Tory shakes her head. "Kind of like having the Jews dig their own graves. How barbaric can this get?"

"Well, they can kill her," Jane answers. "That's pretty barbaric."

Tory nods, and they fall silent again.

At 5:30, the guard tells them that the warden has okayed them for the last contact visit—three hours ahead of schedule. "He's bending a lot of rules," the guard mentions again.

The prison chaplain, a pasty middle-aged man who sweats along his receding hairline, joins them in the van. "The prisoner has never asked to see me," he confesses. "All along maintained that she was Catholic." It sounds like an apology; Tory and Jane nod. "I would have gone to see her—before now, I mean—but she never asked for me." He looks from one to the other, as if he needs absolution. Neither woman offers it. He sighs and ruffles the pages of his Bible. Tory notices that it's the *Good News for Modern Man* version.

The van stops at the first checkpoint outside the chain-link fence. The razor wire shimmers in the late-afternoon sun. The gate, some two hundred yards from the death chamber, is manned by two guards standing at attention, armed with rifles. They wave the van through. At the second checkpoint, the guards are mounted on a matched pair of bays, their chunky upper bodies thickened by bullet-proof vests, heat-streaked with sweat. Jane, Tory, and the chaplain leave the van slowly and are met by a guard, dressed in camouflage. His counterpart awaits, at parade rest, by the door. They are escorted through the heavily barred door, down the hallway, to the two-tiered section of Maximum Security, into cellblock 3. There in the stripped cell is Tracy. One guard steps back to allow his partner to open the door. Tracy has to be helped to stand. Her feet are covered in paper slippers, like those provided by a hospital. She is manacled. Tory is stunned by the silence on the row. There are men in the other cells, moving as shadows against the afternoon sun that slides in between the bars. But none of them makes a sound.

The chaplain speaks first. "Tracy?"

She nods.

"Is there anything I can do for you?"

She offers him a hard stare, then a small, ironic laugh. "You mean, *now?*"

The chaplain is embarrassed. He nods slightly, and Tory notices that he has reddened into his thin hairline.

"No, I don't think so."

The chaplain looks relieved, throws a glance at the guard, who steps back to let him pass down the hall. Tory hears the metal finality of the door as he leaves the cellblock.

"Ready?" the guard asks Tracy. She nods.

Tracy, a guard on either side, leads the way down the hall to the "office." As they enter, one of the guards seats Tracy, with a kind of gentlemanliness that threatens to consume Tory. His wide wrists, so adolescent, clamp the back of the chair like an unsure boy at a first formal dance. "You can have your supper here," he tells them. "Then, Miz Fillmore, you'll have to leave at 9:00." Jane nods. "Miz Gardiner, you can stay until . . ." Tory nods. "The warden will come about 11:30, if nothing don't happen before then." Tory, Jane, and Tracy nod, in unison. "I can't take the cuffs off before supper, but then you can leave 'em off until . . ." They all nod again.

The room, hot and airless, shrinks with the exit of the guards. Tory doesn't know whether she should sit or stand. Jane seems confused as well. The hum of the lights accompanies their breathing.

"Tracy, we still haven't had a decision from the Supreme Court," Jane begins. "I'm afraid they'll keep us in suspense until . . ."

Tracy nods.

My God! Is there nobody left on this planet who can finish a sentence with "until" in it? Tory wonders. Jane should be better at this; somewhere deep within her, Tory feels her anger rise, born of utter helplessness.

"Well," she begins, and both women jerk around to look at her, as if she may have some hidden news, some magic to offer the moment that will change everything. Tory falls silent again, unable to find her voice. She is conscious of the big institutional clock on the wall, the hands inching around the white, white face.

"I've asked them to bring the dress to show you, Tracy." The words fall into the silence, flat and weighted. "And to give us a Bible, in case you want me to read something to you." These offerings seem so paltry that Tory thinks she may bang on the door, begging the guard to open it, to let her out into the wide Delta landscape.

"That'd be nice," Tracy answers; her voice seems dreamy, far away. The utter defeat there makes the room spin. Tory fears that she will be sucked into it. She puts her hands on either side of the chair to steady herself.

"You okay?" Tracy asks.

"As good as I can be."

Tracy gives Tory a little smile. Tory looks away; Jane is staring out the window.

A tap on the door catches Tory off-guard. How much time has passed, she can't tell. Two guards—two women dressed in white, with smudged aprons and hairnets—bustle through the door, carrying trays. A small Styrofoam cooler hangs from a plastic rope on the arm of one. The guards stand to one side as the women unload the trays; one unloops the cooler, frees her arm. The white plates are topped with aluminum covers. The smell of fried fat, fish, onion fills the air. Tory cannot breathe. The homely smells are all too human for such a time, such a place. The guard steps into the hall, brings the box from the shop in Drew, a Bible, and places them on the desk by the phone. Then he reaches for the key ring that is chained to his waist.

"Tracy?"

She stands, holds her hands out to him. His thick fingers fumble with the cuffs. When he removes them, Tracy massages her thin wrists. He kneels before her, lifts the legs of the coverall just slightly, and works the locks around her ankles. Finally, he removes the waist chain, and Tracy stands free. Tory thinks that she might float away, unfettered.

Jane removes the covers from the three plates, and steam escapes into the air. "Chowdah?" she asks, trying to sound like a New Englander.

"Su-ah," Tracy answers, making it two syllables. They laugh, and Tory searches for her place in their joking. She tosses the salad with two plastic forks that have had the points clipped off. She arranges the napkins and spoons around the table. Jane asks the guard for a beer opener. He steps in and pops the caps off, slides them in his pocket, and sidles back into the hall.

The three sit around the table, looking carefully at the bowls in front of them. Jane lifts her bottle. "Here's to good news."

"Good news," Tory echoes.

Tracy touches her bottle to each of theirs, but cannot find the words. Finally, she speaks: "If it's not good news, then let it be quick, fucking quick," and takes a big swallow. Tory brings the bottle to her lips, but is unable to tilt it. The yeasty smell of beer fills her nostrils.

"Fucking quick," Jane whispers. This time it's Tory who cannot answer the toast.

"When I was little, before my mom left, we used to go to Canobie Lake in the summer and I'd eat fried dough until my stomach hurt. I always puked on the way home." Tracy smiles at this memory.

"I used to get sick on watermelon," Tory remembers.

"For me, it was ice cream," Jane adds. "Now I think they call me lactose-intolerant." The conversation comes full stop.

"What's Canobie Lake?" Tory asks, hoping that Tracy can remember enough to overcome the silence.

"An amusement park, just over the line in New Hampshire. Lots of rides and junk."

"Oh," Tory says. "Did you go there a lot?"

"Once or twice a summer. When my mom was home, sober or between men." She shakes her head. "That wasn't too often, though."

"Do you know where your mother is?" Tory asks.

"Nah, she just dropped out of sight when I was about thirteen, I guess. She's probably dead by now. Maybe I'll see her soon," she whispers. Tory feels the sharp intake of air in her throat; her eyes fill with tears. Tracy watches Tory, carefully. "In hell, I guess," she finishes, with the same hard edge to her voice that Tory remembers from other times.

After supper, when the dishes are removed, they pass the time in small talk. Tracy fingers the box of letters she has saved, finds the clipping Tory has sent her about the man who found the alligator in his back room. Tory smiles, remembering. "Guess my alligator is ready to bite my ass," she remarks.

"You know, Trace, I've decided there's a 'gator in everybody's back room."

They smile together, nod, and then the room falls back into silence.

"Suppose you try on the clothes I brought?" Tory suggests.

Tracy shrugs, then turns her back to Tory and Jane and drops the prison coverall, her prison underwear; her back is thin, the tattoo bright yellow against her skin. She slides the silk and lace pants over her hips, fastens the bra, then turns it around and pulls it over her breasts. A little shimmy and the slip eases down her body. She's careful with the dress, holding it above her head, then letting it fall gently over her head. She turns to face them, sits, and guides the lacy texture of the stockings over her legs. Carefully, she feeds the stocking up each calf, taking time to cover the sore that has begun to heal. Finally, she zips the zipper, buttons the neck, and stands in the center of the room. Tory and Jane smile at the sight. Tracy is pleased, it seems, and twirls around like a ballerina in a music box. The soft folds of the skirt wave in the air, then settle around her thin hips.

"You look beautiful, Tracy," Tory tells her. "Just beautiful."

"I never had such a fancy outfit before," she remarks. "Too bad I won't be able to enjoy wearing it." Her voice wavers, and Tory wonders if she will finally cry. "I wish I had a picture of me, looking like this."

"I never thought to bring a camera," Tory confesses.

"That's OK. Who'd want to see it?" Tracy answers.

At nine o'clock, the guard comes for Jane. She embraces Tracy and reminds her that she will be in the office of the warden, in case there's a call from the Supreme Court.

"I know," Tracy says, "but if there isn't, tell everybody I said thank you."

Jane agrees. The guard clears his throat, and she picks up her briefcase and hurries out the door. Tory is certain that she is weeping.

"Just you and me, Tory, and that alligator." Tracy announces this to the empty spaces in the office. She undresses quickly, folds the clothes neatly in the box, and replaces the lid. The reverence in her movements threatens Tory's balance.

"Henry Lee is coming at ten, you know. We'll have some time with him. He's agreed to stay, if you want him to."

Tracy shakes her head. "I don't think so. He's nice enough, but after he reads the Bible to me and says a prayer, he can go. I don't think we need a fucking crowd, do you?"

Tory nods, notices the "we."

At 9:15, the guard arrives to take Tracy back to her cell. "I thought I could stay with her from now on," she says.

The guard seems uncomfortable, looks toward the door, anxious, looking for help from the hall. He points to his head, a frown on his face. Tory is puzzled. "I was told I could be with her . . . all the time."

"Miz Gardiner, we have to get her ready." Again the guard looks out in the hall.

"For Christ's sake, Tory"—Tracy's voice is just above a whisper—"they've got to fucking shave my head!"

Tory sinks into the chair; the words fly around the room and echo in her head. "Oh," is all she manages to say. Tracy and the guard leave, and Tory wonders how she will bear the next few hours.

ॐ

Henry Lee arrives promptly at ten. He looks worn, weary. He offers Tory a quick hug, asks how she's holding up, then sinks into the chair. "The vigil has been moved across the road; some fundamentalists have set up out there, too. Lots of shouting and carrying-on." His head in his hands, he takes a deep breath, continues. "Amnesty has set up a phone bank to try to get calls through to the governor. I hear he's out of town."

Tory stands behind his chair, massages his shoulders, feels the knot of muscles there, and wonders how many more of these nights Henry Lee can stand.

"Where will you go tonight, Tory?"

"Back home, I guess."

"Would you ever do this again?"

"I don't know. Right now I'm feeling that once in any lifetime is a gracious sufficiency."

Henry Lee nods, agreeing.

The sound of footsteps outside the door causes both of them to look. The khaki shirt of the guard blocks the view. Then, the door opens and Tracy enters. She has been recuffed, and her head is bare, shaved to the skull. She looks smaller than ever—a little plucked bird, defenseless, forlorn.

"Hey," she says, "I may start a fucking trend." She laughs, and the sound is hollow as a grave.

"You just might be able to pull it off, Tracy." Henry Lee's voice is warm, encouraging, and Tory marvels that his weariness seems to slip away as he embraces Tracy. She allows it, even sinks into it, the shiny ridges of her skull catching the light. Holding her carefully, Henry Lee begins, "Tracy?"

Her answer is muffled in his chest.

"We've got to face this thing."

She nods, bumping his chin with her head.

Slowly, he releases her; they sit, and Tory joins them. Henry Lee pulls a small Bible from his pocket. "I thought you might want me to read some passages for you." Tracy nods. Henry Lee begins; his voice, warm, runs over them like balm, the encouragement coming from some distance.

Henry Lee finishes. "St. Paul was in prison when he wrote that," he mentions, then closes the book and his eyes. Tory believes that he is praying. A tap on the door signals the entrance of the guard. He motions to Henry Lee. They confer in the hall. Tory feels lost in the space without him, without the sound of his voice. Tracy hums a little; her head bent, she picks at her fingernails. Tory notices a spot where the razor has nicked her scalp. A little drop of blood has solidified there, just beginning to brown against the flesh.

Henry Lee returns, opens his arms to Tracy. "Jane just called," he whispers. "The Supreme Court denied." She looks at him for a long moment, as if the sound isn't carrying too well in here, then glances at Tory. Stepping back, straightening her shoulders, she sighs and nods. "Well, that's it," she says.

"There's always the governor," Henry Lee remembers, but the three of them know that he has left town. Speaking to a group of supporters on the coast, the morning paper reported.

"No false hope, Henry Lee. That's what I promised Tracy." Tory finds her voice.

Henry Lee nods, looks away, and Tory moves to embrace Tracy, but she steps away.

"I think I'm ready," Tracy says, her voice strong. "I know what I did and why I did it. I'd probably do it again, if everything was the same." Tory moves toward her. Tracy raises her hand, stopping her. "What I'm sorry for is the whole fucking way I screwed up my life. That I won't be able to see Tiffany grow up, scared shitless that she'll turn out just like me, that my granny was right. That's what I'm regretting. Not killing Dwayne."

"Tracy," Henry Lee begins.

"No," she interrupts, "there's no excuse for that. It was just the final thing. The final screwup. It's where I was headed from the beginning. Nobody's surprised that I'm here."

It is nearly 11:00 when the guard reappears to take Tracy back to her cell. He allows Henry Lee and Tory to follow. Outside her cell, a phalanx of guards surround a short, sweaty balding man. Henry Lee nods to the guards, speaks to the gentleman in the center.

"Warden Carrouthers." The warden acknowledges Henry Lee with a handshake, nods to Tory, then to Tracy.

Tracy stands in front of the door to her cell. Warden Carrouthers holds a sheaf of papers in one hand, dons his reading glasses with the other. "Theresa Marie Magnarelli, hear the sentence of the State of Mississippi." He then reads in full the judgment imposing sentence. "The prisoner, Theresa Marie Magnarelli, having been convicted of murder in the first degree by an unanimous verdict of the jury and duly returned at the December 10, 1976, session of the Criminal Court of Clayton County, Mississippi, and the jury having unanimously recommended the penalty of death . . ." Tory hears no more. The words echo throughout the cell-block. She steels herself against falling, tries to focus on Tracy so that she might send her protection against the force and power of the warden's words. "And may God have mercy on her soul. Signed Homer J. Fox, Presiding Judge." The silence that follows is deafening.

Henry Lee hands a small booklet to Tracy, patting her hand as she reaches for it, then he turns, offers one to each guard, the warden, and finally to Tory. He asks that all of them follow along and join him in the final prayers. "Remember not, Lord, our iniquities, nor the iniquities of our forefathers; neither take thou vengeance of our sins: Spare us, good Lord, spare thy people."

Tory alone finds her voice to answer, "Spare us, good Lord."

Henry Lee recites the familiar "Lord, have mercy."

Tory answers, again, "Christ have mercy."

Henry Lee responds with "Lord have mercy."

During the Lord's Prayer, several of the guards join in.

Henry Lee's voice is strained as he continues. "Oh, God, whose nature and property is ever to have mercy and to forgive . . ." A trio of voices answer, "Amen." Tory realizes that Tracy has spoken for the first time. During the prayer for those under the sentence of death, Tory is aware only of the language: lovely, majestic, pure King James. It rings hollow in this strange place.

He offers Tracy a time of confession, leaning near to her lips, nodding as she whispers. He makes the sign of the cross upon her forehead; she responds slowly, touching her forehead, her chest, then each shoulder. When he steps away, he looks at each man there and begins again. "The Almighty God, who is a most strong tower, be now and evermore thy defense; in the Name of our Lord Jesus Christ."

A quiet circle of amens rings the group. Tory is certain that she can see him wince as he lays his hand upon Tracy's head. "Unto God's gracious mercy and protection we commit thee."

The amens are louder this time. Tracy is staring at the ceiling, oddly removed from this place, as if she has already left them. Henry Lee gathers up his booklets, and one of the guards puts his hand on Henry Lee's elbow, ushering him quietly to the door at the end of the hall. Tory jumps as the door bangs shut with a metallic clang.

"Miz Gardiner?"

It is the warden speaking.

"Yes?"

"We need to get the prisoner dressed. Would you step into the office again? We'll come get you when it's time."

The roar in Tory's ears makes it impossible for her to answer.

A hand on her elbow moves her along the corridor. "It'll just be a minute," the guard promises. Just a minute, Tory thinks, when there are so few.

"I can help her dress, you know," she tells the guard.

"No, ma'am, that's not allowed. One of the matrons will do it."

While she waits, Tory attempts to remember the "comfortable words" of the old prayer book, but nothing surfaces, and she focuses on the crack in the ceiling, looking for an omen, a reading of bird bones, anything that will drive the night away.

When the guard returns, he asks that she not touch the prisoner now. "The last contact is over." Tory feels that she will crumble under this news.

Tracy is dressed in the red coverall that she has worn for most of her stay in Maximum Security. Her manacles are in place, and she staggers as she begins the walk down the cellblock hallway. Tory wonders if it is because of the diaper she's required to wear. The guards quickly steady her. Several of the prisoners lift their hands; some make the sign of the cross; others turn away and stare out the narrow, barred windows. There is only the sound of feet moving along the concrete floor.

At the door to the death chamber, the guard guides Tory towards the witness room. She stops. The entire procession comes to a halt. The men between her and Tracy step slightly to the side so that she has Tracy in full view.

"Tracy?"

She nods, her eyes wide and unblinking.

"You are a good woman. It's true. You need to know that. And to know that I love you and I am going to miss you."

Tracy nods again.

The buzz of the lights, the muffled sounds from the witness room fill Tory's ears.

"Tory," Tracy sounds as though she will strangle, "I'll miss you, too."

A man in a prison uniform takes Tory to the witness room. The buzz of voices stills as she sinks into her chair, drained. The door to the chamber is opened by a small wiry man, dressed in black. He ushers Tracy, the guards, and the warden into the chamber. The warden lifts the phone off the hook, speaks into it, waits for a moment, then turns to the group. "There is no word from the governor commuting this sentence. We will proceed. Does the prisoner have any last words?"

All the men in the chamber turn to face Tracy. The witnesses lean forward, in strained concert, as though they fear the microphone will not catch the sounds.

Tracy straightens as the guard removes her leg irons, the wrist bracelets. "Just this. Tory" — she looks into the one-way glass, searches for a second — "thank everybody for me." She pauses, leans forward a bit, squints. "And I know you didn't do it just for you." Then she closes her eyes, sits back. Tory can just make out the rise and fall of a sigh.

The guards fasten Tracy's arms and legs to the wooden chair, fit the band around her head. She glances again at the window. Tory lifts her hand to wave just as the hood is dropped around Tracy's head. The warden notes the time, jots it down on a clipboard, and all the men step outside the chamber. Tory refuses to blink, holding Tracy in her sights, willing the moment to be swift. Tracy's fingers thrum against the arms of the chair, then her feet arch, lifting her heels away from the concrete floor. The hands of the clock jerk around to one minute past twelve.

The sound of the electrical surge fills the entire room, and Tory forces herself to look. Tracy convulses once, twice; the muscles in her arms and legs constrict, pulling her hands and feet into a grotesque contortion. A secondary shudder pulls her arms and legs against the straps. Tory looks to see if the leg strap is pulling against the nearly healed sore, is certain that she can smell the sear of burning flesh. For the third time, Tracy jerks against the restraints, then she is still. It is finished, Tory thinks, as a thin curl of smoke rises from beneath the hood. The small wiry man reenters the chamber and draws the curtain. Tory watches, unblinking, straining to keep Tracy in view. The air smells like the end of a brutal summer thunderstorm, when lightning has cracked the sky and left the ozone fractured.

Tory moves along, carried with the crowd toward the door. Outside in the heavy midsummer air, she draws her first full breath in hours. There are several prison vehicles waiting to take the witnesses back to their cars, back to the free world. A guard, standing in the doorway to Maximum Security, is waving a white flag. He announces to all, "At 12:13, on July 18, 1989, Theresa Marie Magnarelli was pronounced dead by the prison doctor and the state medical examiner." Stumbling toward the van, Tory feels the gorge rise in her throat. The clam chowder, fried dough, and ale resurface; she swallows hard, determined to keep it down. The other witnesses skirt around her, silently move into the van, never look at her as she enters. She can smell her own breath, feel the acid against her teeth, and the tears, warm and salty, on her cheeks.

In the parking lot, near the reception area, Jane and Henry Lee are waiting. Both will make a statement to the media before the sun rises. They gather around Tory's car, offer each other small smiles and simple encouragements. Tory catches sight of the hearse from Littlejohn's Funeral Home, gathers the box of clothes from Henry Lee, and crosses the lot to begin the final preparations.

By 2:00 a.m., she is on the road, following the sleek, black hearse, just as Paul followed her and Mary Vic when they left Memphis for the last time. A hearse looks like any other car from the back, she realizes.

Chapter 12

⁂

Just at sunrise on Thursday morning, clustered around the newly dug grave, Jane, Henry Lee, and Melinda join Tory for the funeral. Tory has chosen the time carefully and asked the local police to send away any gawkers. Funeral grass covers the graves of Mary Vic and Paul. The sod covering Mother Gardiner's unused plot has withered and turned brown in the relentless summer heat. The service is straight out of the prayer book. Jane, Melinda, and Tory join in unsteady responses. Hearing Henry Lee's voice, Tory tries to erase the sounds, giving only minimal attention to his words. The flowers are from the CDRC and from Tory's garden. A riding lawn mower sputters in the background. A man is using a weed-eater along the edge of a walled plot. The sweat is running down Tory's calves, into the tops of her shoes.

With the final prayer, the coffin is lowered, and Henry Lee sprinkles a handful of soil into the grave. The hollow sound of dirt against wood joins the morning sounds. Jane and Melinda move to the edge and drop their handful.

"Tory?"

"Yes?"

"Your turn."

"Oh, yes." She stoops, scoops some of the dry, loamy soil, holds it over the cavity, hears it fall. Sprinkling — like the sifting of gentle rain, she thinks.

Leaning against the hearse, in the shade, two of the Littlejohn sons wait, holding coffee mugs that steam into the early-morning air. Tory waves to them; they nod, signal to the maintenance men that the grave can be closed now. Tory has settled her account with them the day before.

Lunch at Tory's is quiet, subdued; moments of conversation fall away, as though they all knew something important once, but none of them can remember quite what it was, cannot quite sort out just how their lives, carefully knitted together for a while, will look after today.

Tory stands at the doorway into the kitchen, French bread buttered and filled with garlic and cheese; the trio at the table watches her. "I leave for Boston tomorrow, try to find Tiffany, give her the few things her mother left her, invite her to come and spend some time with me, if she wants to." Tory's throat tightens, "I'll deliver the letter to Raheem for sure. I know where he lives."

All of them nod, seem to find her plan acceptable. They return to their bowls, ladle the cold summer soup into silent mouths.

After they finish, Tory clears the table, and Jane and Henry Lee leave soon after dessert. Both promise to keep in touch, thank Tory for all she did, wish her well, all the while inching toward the door.

The afternoon's quiet wraps around the table again. Tory and Melinda pour another cup of coffee and watch the shadows lengthen.